By Lisa Black

DEFENSIVE WOUNDS
TRAIL OF BLOOD
EVIDENCE OF MURDER
TAKEOVER

LISA BLACK

DEFENSIVE WOUNDS

HARPER

An Imprint of HarperCollinsPublishers

HARPER

An Imprint of HarperCollins*Publishers*
10 East 53rd Street
New York, New York 10022-5299

First Harper mass market printing: September 2012
First William Morrow hardcover printing: October 2011

HarperCollins ® and Harper ® are registered trademarks of Harper-Collins Publishers.

Printed in the United States of America

Visit Harper paperbacks on the World Wide Web at
www.harpercollins.com

10 9 8 7 6 5 4 3 2 1

For Elaine

PART I

MARIE

CHAPTER 1

WEDNESDAY

The first volley came in the form of a text message.

CM QUIK. SUM1 DED HERE.

Standing on the twenty-third floor of the Justice Center with her cousin, Theresa MacLean translated slowly and aloud. " 'Come quick. Someone dead here.' "

"That from the lab?" Frank asked. He had met up with her after her testimony in an officer-involved shooting case, ostensibly to take her to lunch but more likely to get an update on the trial's progress.

"No," she told him. "It's from my daughter."

Now she and Frank pushed past the worn glass-and-brass doors into the vast lobby of the Terminal Tower, passing a microcosm of society on the way: panhandlers in ragged clothes with plastic cups, repeating "Got any spare change?" until the sound blended into the backdrop of bus engines and cooing pigeons; teenagers freed from home and school, dressed like gangsters-in-training regardless of socioeconomic background; sharp young men with crisply knotted ties and ladies arriving for lunch, armed with credit cards and fashionable scarves. Their voices bounced off the marble walls and echoed down the hallway before plunging into the cacophony of the Tower City Mall.

The Terminal Tower had been built in 1928 by the odd but quite brilliant Van Sweringen brothers. It remained the tallest building in the world for twenty-five years. Its 708 feet of height reached from the rapid-transit station in the basement to a glitzy shopping mall, two hotels, and floors and floors of offices topped off by an indoor/outdoor observation deck. This deck had been closed since the September 11 attacks, a policy considered extremely silly by locals—as if terrorists would target Cleveland. Clevelanders love their city but have no illusions as to its status per the rest of the planet.

Theresa entered the lobby of the Ritz-Carlton, the heavy glass door closing on its own. Any sound from the streets, the mall, the rest of the city was sliced off and left behind.

"How long has Rachael been working here?" Frank asked. He had called his partner in the homicide unit to learn that a person had indeed been found murdered at the hotel. Two other detectives had been assigned, but that would not dissuade him. From the body he kept in shape to the neatly trimmed mustache, Frank lived for his job; besides, with no children of his own, he took on the role of papa grizzly when it came to his "niece." Rachael's own father checked in only between girlfriends.

"About two weeks. Front desk. She likes it, likes being downtown, says her boss is decent." The lobby spread out around them in tasteful shades of cream and beige. A man with bulky leather bags waited without apparent patience to check in, and a lean young waiter served a Bloody Mary to an older woman in a pink twinset as she lounged in an overstuffed cream armchair. "I—"

"Mom!" Rachael appeared, long blond hair flying, torso encased in a tidy uniform that didn't quite disguise her curves. At eighteen she had her mother's height and lean build but her father's excitability. "Hi, Uncle Frank. What took you so long? You look nice," she added, taking in Theresa's black skirt and somewhat styled hair.

"Court." That allowed her to explain both. "What's going on?"

Showing a new sense of discretion along with her uniform, Theresa's daughter looked around and lowered her voice before speaking. "A guy called from the Presidential Suite and said there's a woman murdered there and that it's really gross and bizarre. She's all tied up, and there's blood everywhere—"

"Did you see this body?" Theresa asked, dreading the answer. Dead bodies were her job, not her daughter's. Never her daughter's.

"No. I was going to go up, but Shawna was on break and I couldn't leave the desk—"

Theresa felt herself making one of those "mother" faces. "Rachael—"

"I just thought I'd check it out! You know how you always say Dispatch calls you and tells you there's blood all over the place and then you get there and there's, like, three drops? So I wanted to go make sure it was really worth getting Karla out of the Housekeeping meeting, but like I said, I couldn't leave the desk alone, so I did get Karla—she's the GM, general manager—and she went up. Then I guess she called you guys, because she didn't call us back." Rachael didn't seem upset or even shaken, only stirred by this great drama, her hands fluttering as she spoke. The guest had taken his bag and departed, while the other young woman at the front desk studied Rachel's mother with great intensity, no doubt having heard about her line of work. Rachael went on. "Karla said there's a ton of blood, and William says that they can't figure out how she got in there. And get this—"

"Theresa!" A Homicide detective she recognized crossed the heavy carpet toward them. John Powell had thinning black hair and a layer of doughy fat under the skin on his face, but his body looked tough enough. He carried a small camera and a notebook, which left no hands for shaking. He glanced at Frank without much welcome and at Rachael with more, taking her in from toe to chest so skillfully that Theresa might have missed the absently sweeping look. She didn't. "Thanks for coming," he said to her. "We have a woman in the luxury suite. She—" Another glance at Rachael. "I'll fill you in on the way."

"This is my daughter," Theresa said.

He nodded without interest—apparently, scanning the teenager was simple male reflex—and then spoke to Frank, "What are you doing here, Patrick? Doesn't she go anywhere without you?"

"Good morning to you too, Powell. I'm just tagging along," Frank said, controlling the bristle. He and Theresa had worked a lot of cases together, and those cases always seemed to be the insane ones; it had become a stereotype. Each detective in the homicide unit had a theory about this: that they were unlucky, or lucky, cursed, or somehow cheating. "Anything to get out of court," he told Powell now.

"Well, you need to stay outside the tape unless you're assigned. No sense cluttering up the contamination checklist with rubberneckers—and there's going to be a lot of them," Powell added with a sigh. The mild belligerence leaked out of him, deflating his shoulders. "This is going to be a cluster."

"Stay here," Theresa told Rachael, eliciting a groan of protest, and followed Powell to the elevators. But two hotel guests got into the car with them, precluding conversation during the trip. Instead Theresa's introduction came about in the form of an array of bright halogen lights set up outside the double doors to the tastefully marked Presidential Suite and a small army of policemen, hotel managers, and two EMS responders. They were not needed but lingered anyway, and no one wanted to create the bad blood that would surely result from kicking them out. Frank remained with them, firmly on the civilian side of the crime-scene tape, no doubt gnashing his teeth.

Theresa stepped into the Presidential Suite behind Detective Powell.

The trail began inside the double doors, only a few scattered stains across the fawn carpet. They could have been mistaken for dirt by someone not so familiar as she was with the black-red color of dried blood. Powell stopped to talk to another man, but she ignored them and continued past a small kitchen with granite countertops and a conversation area furnished with heavy armchairs, watching for any tiny scattered bits of evidence before she placed each foot. Thick drapes had been pulled back, and privacy sheers let the room fill with softened light. All seemed tidy. But through another set of double doors she could see the blood trail pick up.

A bedroom, large enough for a king-size four-poster, a desk and more armchairs. The requisite fluffy comforter was turned down, the exposed sheets smooth and snow white. The room was crisp and perfect, but with enough touches of old money, enough sconces and carved details and deep wood to make it seem worth the price. Theresa wondered what the room had smelled like before it took on the scent of raw meat that had been left in the refrigerator a little too long.

Against the opposite wall sat an end table and two

armchairs; one cushion had been shoved out of place, and a drinking glass and a magazine lay on the floor. Blood drops increased now, accompanied by splotches, smears, and vague suggestions of footprints. A man with a detective's badge stood to her left, jotting notes to himself.

Theresa stared, as the sounds of activity and voices around her faded to a vague hum. She saw death every day, and murder many days, but this—this was the sort of thing one should see only on television, and really not even then.

Thank God it wasn't Rachael who found this.

The victim was stretched across the middle of the carpet, almost equidistant from the foot of the bed, the armchairs and end table, and the bathroom. She lay on her stomach, head turned, right cheek resting on the floor with her hands stretched back to her ankles and tied there. She wore no clothes, and her bare skin had been spattered with blood. Long black hair obscured part of her face, and blood obscured the rest, soaking her hair and spilling onto the carpeting. Except for two red slashes across the right shoulder blade, all of the killer's fury had been visited on the victim's head, the scalp split by at least three heavy blows. Theresa crouched down— something that would have been a lot easier in her usual working uniform of khakis and Reeboks—to get a look at the face, with its pale skin and already clouding brown eyes. And then she looked again. "She . . . I . . ."

"We think it's Marie Corrigan," the detective explained—his name could be Nelson, but Theresa couldn't quite remember—stood next to the bed. Closer to her age than Powell's and taller than both of them, he had receding brown hair, dark lashes, and a smile that made you want to keep an eye on him. "No ID, but it looks an awful lot like her, and her office said she's supposed to be here."

"It's her. I testified in front of her a few months ago." Theresa shook her head, trying to reconcile the dead person with the live Cleveland defense attorney she'd known. "Why would she be staying at the Ritz?"

"She wasn't staying here. She was attending the convention." At Theresa's raised eyebrows, he explained. "The hotel's full of lawyers. They're having a convention for criminal defense attorneys, can you believe that?"

"Everyone has conventions," Theresa said. "Who rented—"

"That's just it. No one was registered to be in this room. I guess they can't make enough off their dirtbag clients to afford the Presidential Suite. Almost makes me feel a little better."

"Almost," Powell added, coming in behind her.

Theresa said nothing about their evident bigotry. She respected attorneys but often didn't like them, and she had no doubt they felt the same about her. It simply went with the territory of the adversarial system of law. Nothing personal. At least not usually.

"So she wasn't staying in this room." It made sense, since there seemed to be nothing there save for the victim, her scattered clothing, and the hotel-provided magazines. Theresa could see into the thoroughly mirrored bathroom; it contained enough towels to stock a locker room, but no toiletries broke up the white-on-white accoutrements of the sink area.

"No, it was vacant. Except somebody got a key," Nelson or maybe-Nelson said. "They decided to ditch the latest legal scoop for a little luxury-suite whoopee with no room tax. He and Corrigan get their kink on, but then lover boy gets out of hand."

"Any suspects? A boyfriend?"

"Don't know yet, but suspects? A hotel full of them,"

Powell said. "And I can't wait to question them. How are they going to lawyer up?"

"They'll all represent themselves and say nothing," his partner guessed. "This is going to be oh so much fun."

"Marie Corrigan," she said, still trying to take it in.

"Yeah. The bitch finally got what was coming to her."

"Finally," Theresa breathed.

CHAPTER 2

Many aspects of forensic science, Theresa knew, were not designed for the faint of heart. Among them: Zipping on a Tyvek suit that made her sweat in the dead of winter so she could move around an efficiency apartment with a four-week-old corpse oozing across the kitchen floor. Or asking a pedophile to open his mouth so she could rub two large Q-tips on the insides of his cheeks to collect his DNA. Or searching through a series of kitchen drawers looking for a murder weapon while cockroaches the size of ore carriers scuttled out from under every item touched.

But the worst, the absolute worst, was having to put on a conservative black skirt and a pair of sensible heels and take a seat in a hushed, paneled room. A hot seat.

The last time she'd seen Marie Corrigan alive, the seat had grown warm enough to sear flesh.

Can you tell us what's in that envelope, Ms. MacLean?

Three months previously: In the witness box, Theresa opened a manila envelope, the red seal already torn from the attorneys' examinations, and shook out a smaller envelope. From that she pulled a piece of glassine paper folded to about one inch square.

"These are the fibers I removed from the suspect's shirt."

"Which you say came from the victim's sweater? This sweater?" Marie Corrigan held up an opened paper bag, helpfully giving the jury another peek at the blood-stained scarlet cardigan.

"They all have characteristics in common with that sweater," Theresa corrected. "I can't say they positively came from that sweater. I have no idea how much of this thread has been produced or how many sweaters are in circulation."

"You said they are"—Marie made a show of picking up Theresa's report from the defense table and quoting it directly—"'alike in all discernible factors'?"

"Yes."

"Can you show the jury those fibers?"

"They're very small," Theresa warned. Even the closest jury members wouldn't be able to see them, and, if passed around, they would surely be lost. Static electricity, a sneeze, or clumsy fingers would see to that.

Marie said to do it anyway. As usual, the prosecutor did nothing, did not wish to be seen as coaching or protecting the state's witness. No sense handing the defense grounds for an appeal.

Theresa unfolded the paper, then held up three fibers of neon pink. The jury could see them, all right. The last row of spectators could see them, and a child could see that they bore no resemblance to the bloodlike color of the victim's sweater.

"These aren't the right fibers," Theresa said.

"I beg your pardon?"

"These are not the fibers that were in this envelope," Theresa said, unable to conceal the quaver in her voice.

She'd never had her evidence stolen before, much less while in front of a jury.

"My chambers!" the judge snapped. "You, too."

Theresa unhappily repeated her assertion in the cramped, white-walled office while the judge glared at her, the prosecutor, and Marie Corrigan. The fibers had been switched. Both offices had had access to the envelope, and both attorneys insisted they had no recollection of even looking at the fibers, just at the signatures and dates on both envelopes.

The prosecutor reluctantly accused Marie. "She's the only other person who could have—"

"Along with a dozen interns, paralegals, and bailiffs," she countered. "And you."

"And why would I torpedo my own case? The fibers are all we have, since your client strangled this poor girl with his bare hands. No blood, no murder weapon, her nails too short to get his DNA. The cellmate he confessed to is in the wind—no one can locate him."

"Exactly. Fibers aren't conclusive. You knew you'd never get a jury to convict on them only. This stunt buys you time to find your mystery witness."

The judge turned to Theresa. "Are you sure those fibers have been switched?"

"Positive."

"Do you have any photographs of the original fibers?"

"Um," Theresa had to say. "No." Due to budget constraints in the suffering county, she still used an ancient Zeiss comparison scope. It had an inconvenient and balky camera attachment, which required more talent with 35-millimeter film than she possessed. She could have asked the photographers for help, but . . . "No. However, it's obvious I wouldn't have said that the colors were identical when these are so radically different, Your Honor."

The judge pondered, seeming to tune out the protestations of the attorneys. Theresa pondered as well, wondering how this could adversely affect her career, how it could affect the trial, and what might resolve it. No solution presented itself.

Finally the judge declared a mistrial, and Theresa paused in the hallway to give her heartbeat a chance to return to normal.

The Justice Center in Cleveland loomed twenty-six stories into the sky, and Theresa pretty much despised each one. Not the court system—she had great respect for that—but the design of the building itself. Built to be chock-full of people who had committed crimes and yet shockingly unconcerned with security. Some stairwell doors locked, and others didn't. Hallways turned and twisted, taking one quickly out of the sight of others. Worst of all, courtrooms were clustered four to a floor, with offices and judges' chambers placed around the outside of the building. The hallway to the courtrooms ran from the elevator bank to the east wall, where wide windows opened onto a stunning view of the city and the lake—even more stunning on a summer's day when the window tint only deepened the blue in the sky. But mere mortals could not visit this calm oasis, because the judges' chambers opened onto the space. People waiting to appear in any one of the four courtrooms, people under stress, worried, upset, traumatized, with small, needing-to-be-entertained children—people who could have benefited from the panoramic scene outside the glass—had to stay corralled in the 1970s modular seating next to the elevator bank, under the weak fluorescent lights.

Theresa loathed the Justice Center.

Two weeks later, with no other evidence and the mystery witness still missing, the prosecutor dropped the charges. Marie Corrigan's client was free to kill again.

And he did.

Three weeks later another strangled girl turned up in the same alley. When the police went to pick up the suspect, they found nothing but ants and candy wrappers in his rented room. He had not been seen in Cleveland since, and nationwide BOLOs failed to locate him.

And now Theresa loathed nothing so much as Marie Corrigan.

Theresa gently shooed the two detectives out of the rooms, pulled off the keys hanging around her neck, and slipped them into a pocket, then switched on her twelve-megapixel digital camera. She began to photograph the two double doors leading into the hall and progressed inward, remembering to turn and shoot behind her. The second detective, maybe-Nelson, followed, either curious or just wanting to make sure she didn't move or discover any item he didn't already know about. Though he seemed to be most fascinated by the curve of her calves, he proved handy when she continued to ask questions as they occurred to her. "Who was the last person to occupy this room?"

"The CEO of some aluminum company, but he checked out five days ago. Didn't know there was that much money in aluminum."

Far too long for Marie to have been here all that time. "And the last time someone saw her?"

"Yesterday's luncheon. Apparently she stuck in the conference coordinator's mind, and not in a good way.

We haven't had a chance to talk to anyone else yet, and I'm not willing to turn them over to patrol. I want to do it myself."

Theresa took a snapshot of the magazine on the end table, arrested in the process of sliding off after its compatriots. The lamp, however, stood perfectly within its faint circle of non-dust. "Are they going to call off the conference or cut it short?"

"No reason to. These people's firms ponied up big bucks so they can party at the Ritz and learn how to keep even more scumbags on the street. They're lunching at the Muse while John and I scarf down Mickey D's and pound out reports on ten-year-old computers. I am definitely on the wrong side of the law."

Theresa stopped in the process of placing an L-shaped ABFO ruler on the floor next to a footprint-size smudge of blood to glance at him. He flushed, reluctantly, as if his fair skin couldn't help itself.

"I'll bet you think I'm a right bastard for thinking that."

"No. I think I'm a right bastard for agreeing."

He laughed. "Anyway, the organizers sure as hell don't want to hand out refunds, and we don't want anyone to leave. You might say we saw eye to eye on that. So the conference goes on as planned, and we'll look for the boyfriend among the attendees," he added more briskly, with the tiniest hint of a lilt to his voice. Plenty of Irish had immigrated to Cleveland, but the accents had long since faded.

Theresa had moved into the bathroom. The sink and the bathtub were completely dry and without any visible water spots. No one had used them to clean up after the bloody attack—unless he (or she) had dried both his hands and the porcelain when he was done. She counted the apparently untouched bath towels, hand towels, and washcloths—five of each. Nothing missing.

"Who found the body?" she asked, without raising her voice. The rooms were so well insulated that she and the detective might as well have been in a cocoon.

"Well, okay. That takes us back to this damn conference."

She waited. Was the water in the toilet less than crystal clear?

"A lawyer from Des Moines. Says he came here to meet a friend. Swears he doesn't know Marie Corrigan from the devil and has never been to Cleveland before this."

Theresa turned, brushed past the detective and over the body of the victim to retrieve a bottle of Hemastix strips from her crime-scene kit. A quick dip in the toilet and the yellow pad on the end of the strip turned a medium blue color.

"What does that mean?" maybe-Nelson asked.

"It means the killer washed his hands in the toilet."

He made a face.

"That way he didn't have to turn on any faucets, risk leaving fingerprints he might not wipe off. He didn't take a towel to dry them, though. Maybe he wiped them on his pants or used Marie's clothes. Why *not* just take a towel, though?"

Not to mention that she had just trodden all over any latent footprints. She tiptoed back to the door, walking on the periphery. She'd keep everyone off the ceramic tiles until she could get to them with a fingerprint brush.

Time to move on to the body.

The body: Marie Corrigan. A woman who had pranced in front of the jury box, berating Theresa for a scratched-out digit on an evidence label. A woman with an enviable figure and even more enviable cheekbones, and the glossy hair and fashion sense to go with both. A woman who seemed composed of sheer energy, so brutal and rapacious it should have rendered her incapable of dying at all, much less being murdered. At least not without a stake through her heart.

Powell appeared at the other end of the bedroom. "Neil!"

That's it, Theresa thought. First name or last name?

"We got Des Moines back."

"He talking?"

"Won't stop."

Neil followed Powell, and Theresa followed Neil. Sensing her on their heels, they both turned.

"I want to see him," she explained. "Has he had any time to clean up between reporting the body and now?"

"Let's find out."

In the corridor she gave the contamination officer—the uniformed guy guarding the door—strict instructions not to let anyone in until she returned. Frank had disappeared.

"We've got no place to talk to him," Powell explained as he led them up the hallway toward a slouching, youngish man. "The other suite is occupied, and the rest of the floor is the Club Lounge. They have snacks and shoeshines and other stuff for the high-dollar room people, and apparently the Ritz doesn't feel like kicking them out so we can use it. We get the hallway."

They cornered the man at the end of it. He wore an indie-band T-shirt and khakis a bit too small for him. Theresa supposed he got enough of suits and ties at the office.

"Detective Neil Kelly," the cop said by way of introduction. "What were you doing in that room?"

"I shouldn't speak to you without an attorney present," the man said, biting one nail.

"You *are* an attorney."

"I know, but—" He sighed. "I just feel so dumb, doing what I always tell my clients *not* to do, but . . . I really don't know that woman or how she got . . . in there."

"Start from the beginning," Neil said in a kindly tone, which didn't fool Theresa for a second, and she doubted it would have any more effect on the lawyer. "Why did *you* go there?"

Another sigh, as if a decision had been made. "Okay. This morning I had a small hangover, so I missed my first session on recent Supreme Court decisions. I walked in at the very end, and this guy in the last row said he'd make me a copy of his handouts. My firm is paying for this trip, so I wanted to make good, you know?"

"Admirable," Powell said.

Theresa watched from behind the cops. The man's hands were clean, and no spatters of blood appeared on the bare arms or the light-colored pants. Of course he'd had plenty of time to change. She believed him about the hangover, picking up the scent of alcohol excreted along with the nervous sweat.

"He said come to the Presidential Suite during the next break and he'd give me the copies. So as soon as I got out of my 'Defending Child-Pornography Cases' seminar, about ten to ten, I came directly here."

Both detectives paused at that, but Neil said only, "In the elevator?"

"You think I'm going to *walk* fourteen floors? I come to the door, I knock. No Bob."

"How'd you get in?"

"It was open. Not standing open, but ajar, you know? So I push it open and go in—no Bob. I glance in the bedroom, I see her, I pick up the phone and call the hotel."

"Which phone?" Theresa asked.

"Who did you call?" Neil asked.

"The phone next to the sofa."

"In the outer room?"

"I sure as hell wasn't going into that bedroom. And I guess I called the front desk, that's what the little bimbo said when she answered."

Theresa bristled.

"Took a minute to get her to figure out what I was saying, but she did. I waited by the door until about three people showed up. I don't even know who they were. Managers, I guess."

"Where'd you go then?"

"The lobby bar. I needed a drink." The lawyer ran a hand over his forehead, flipping one lock of hair out at an angle. "I needed a drink *bad*."

"And you never saw the victim before?"

"No. I don't think so. How can I tell? All I saw was blood and black hair."

"Her name's Marie Corrigan. She's a lawyer, too. You know her?"

"No," the man insisted, and kept insisting. He didn't know a soul in this city except two civil-defense chicks from Michigan he'd been up drinking with the night before—and Bob.

"You hadn't arranged to meet Marie here? She was pretty hot. Maybe you guys decided to ditch the child-porn lesson together?"

"Absolutely not. Didn't know the woman."

As if on cue, the elevator bank gave a *ding* and a tall, bespectacled man with a skinny tie and skinny lips stepped off to blink in surprise at the cops and the lights. "What's going on here?"

"Bob!" the young attorney breathed in relief.

The fresh arrival confirmed the story, but not the agreed-upon location.

"You said Presidential Suite," the attorney from Des Moines insisted.

"Junior Presidential Suite." Bob pointed to the door next to them. "Junior."

"I never heard 'Junior.' You were all 'I got the best room in the hotel' this morning. You said you had a presidential expense account to go with the suite!"

"*Junior* suite," Bob said, rapping on the discreetly labeled door for emphasis.

Neil broke into their bickering to establish that Bob had never seen the door of the senior Presidential Suite open or ajar and had heard nothing from inside it in the two days he'd been at the hotel. He insisted he did not know Marie Corrigan and volunteered that he had not said "Presidential Suite" simply to make himself sound more prestigious. Neil and his partner finally got the appropriate information from both of them and left them to it. Theresa asked the attorney from Des Moines if he had returned to his room between the suite and the lobby bar, but he said he had not, and as they walked away, the two detectives doubted they could get a warrant to search his room.

All three of them returned to the crime scene, the contamination officer dutifully noting same in his log. Powell and Neil traded theories while Theresa continued to examine the body of Marie Corrigan.

"I don't believe him," Powell said. "I think Corrigan decided to mix business with pleasure. All these out-of-town guys, they can't come back to haunt her. Locals would use any history to stab her in the back when she poached one of their clients."

"True."

"They're power junkies, lawyers."

"Then why is *she* the one tied up?" Neil asked.

Theresa took a close-up photo of the dead woman's

wrists. She'd been bound with a pair of nylons, probably her own.

"Because she's tired of being the powerful one, wants to be dominated for a change."

Because women can't handle power? Theresa's mind asked, forming one possible conclusion for Powell's line of thought. She felt, had been feeling, a twinge of gender guilt for letting them disparage the victim. Marie Corrigan had climbed into the arena with a cabal of aggressive, ruthless men and beaten them at their own game. She'd faced belligerence and opposition and the dreaded accusation of not being "feminine" on a daily basis and persevered, something Theresa would never choose to do. Theresa should stick up for Marie Corrigan.

But she didn't. Because Marie Corrigan had won not by besting the legal system but by manipulating it for her own ends. Theresa knew that for a fact and would save her championing for a more deserving recipient.

"That's a big deal in this S&M crap," Powell had continued. "This guy from Des Moines shows up for his appointment—maybe he and Bobby were going to do it together—but then dominating isn't enough. He has to go further. Power junkies."

Theresa moved to the heap of clothing located partially under the end table between an armchair and the overturned desk chair. She removed each item, holding it up and snapping a picture—difficult to do with only two hands—and then placed each item in a separate paper bag from her kit. Marie had worn a black pencil skirt, a red satin blouse of exquisite cut, a set of black lace underwear from Victoria's Secret, and a pair of glossy black pumps by some designer Theresa had never heard of but which probably cost more than the entire contents of Theresa's dresser drawers. A mirror, or perhaps the antithesis, of Theresa's courtroom costume: a straight black skirt, ivory blouse, black pumps that were not glossy or towering but had extra cushioning for the instep, nylons from the drugstore, and underwear by Hanes. Sisters they were not, neither under the skin nor over it.

Only the blouse had a few smears of blood on it. The other items were clean. No purse.

"Maybe," Neil said about Powell's theory. He slumped as if to sit on the edge of the bed, thought better of it, and surprised Theresa by asking her, "What do you think? Is Des Moines lying?"

"No."

Both detectives raised their eyebrows.

"This room isn't rented," she explained. "He could have killed her, shut the door, and left. Her body might not have been discovered for days or weeks. Why alert us?"

They thought on that. Powell said, "Guilty conscience. Some guys call in the body because they can't take the stress of waiting for it to be found."

"True," she agreed. "And he could have gone to his room, cleaned up, and changed clothes before he made the call, or afterward when he was supposedly in the bar. But I don't think so."

"Maybe he wanted to be in on the action," Powell went on, "see the results of his handiwork. Power again. It fits with the . . . with the way she's trussed up. Maybe it was his idea in the first place."

Neil snorted. "Can you see that dorky little weasel out there talking Marie Corrigan into anything? For that matter, can you see Marie Corrigan wasting one flip of her hair on him? I can't picture those two people together unless *he* was the one chained to the wall getting whipped."

"There's that, too," Theresa said. "I don't see any bruises or red marks on her wrists."

"So she was tied up voluntarily," Powell said. "Just

what I've been saying. Besides, you want to hurt someone, you use rope. Nylons are soft and sexy."

Neil said, "You know a little too much about this
dominatrix stuff, partner."

"We worked that case last year, remember?"

"But," Theresa told them, "a few things bother me.
That bed is pristine, not a hair or a fiber in the sheets, so
far as I can see without moving the linens."

"Maybe they started on the bed, moved to the floor."

"Possibly." She'd have to use the ALS—alternate light
source—on both the bed and the floor to check for semen. A hotel room—no telling what a rainbow of results *that* might produce. "She has a smudge of blood on
her blouse, but nothing else, and obviously the clothes
would have to have been removed before she was tied.
There's also a spray of blood spatter on the bindings."

"Oh," Neil said, getting it. "You think someone
clocked her with the chair, then removed her clothes and
tied her up, then finished the job on her skull."

"I think it's a possibility."

"So the whole sex angle is to throw us off? Can you
tell if she actually *had* sex?"

"We'll take swabs at autopsy."

Theresa focused her camera on Marie Corrigan's
battered scalp. She could see at least four distinct tears
where some blunt object had split the skin—obviously
the wooden, straight-back chair meant for use with the
cherry desk near the doorway. Red stained the rear left
leg, and dots appeared on the other legs. The top of the
back remained clean. The killer's hands had not been
bloody when he swung it up and over, onto the head of
his victim. "Then again, he used a weapon of opportunity, not one he'd brought with him, so maybe it wasn't
planned and you're right, it was a sex act that got out of
control. Maybe the clothes were already off but he got

blood on the blouse when he picked it up and moved it. Except I found it partially under the skirt, and the clothes appear to have been tossed, not piled or folded in any particular way. If the tying-up was voluntary, it would explain why there's no bruising, why she wasn't straining against the bounds. Heck"—she took another look—"the knots aren't even that tight, and nylons are stretchy. She probably could have slipped out of them but cooperated up until the first blow. Then she didn't struggle because she wasn't conscious. But it still doesn't answer how either of them got into this room."

"Bribed a maid," Powell said. "Place like this has a huge staff, and half of them make minimum wage. How hard could it be?"

"Harder than it used to be," Theresa said. "Hotels use electronic swipe cards now."

"Those can be faked. You can get blank cards or really use any card with a magnetic strip and write them yourself. I learned that during a stint in white-collar."

Neil said, "But the killer would still need the codes from the hotel here—and the right code. Those cards can be programmed to let staff in only where they need to be. The hotel might limit staff access to these expensive suites."

Powell sighed. "I'll go track down their IT guy."

"Cheer up. Maybe they're so sophisticated that they can tell you exactly whose card—or whose card clone—last opened that door."

" 'Scuse me if I don't hold my breath."

CHAPTER 4

Theresa had photographed every part of Marie Corrigan's body, her clothing, and the bloodied wooden chair. Now came the nerve-racking part. She would have to start moving stuff. Cut off the bindings, roll over the victim, have the body snatchers come in and take it away. And, as always, risk the possibility that she might miss something, that some tiny fragment of significant clue lay just under her hands, waiting to be lost in translation.

But it couldn't be helped.

She got out a magnifying glass.

Neil breathed out a *phuff* of air. He'd been watching carefully, which she didn't enjoy—who ever likes to have someone else watching over her shoulder?—but she didn't particularly mind it either. "You're thorough."

"This is a hotel. Strangers go in and out of this room almost every day, shedding their hairs, their fibers, their skin cells. Even if I find a thread or a drop of saliva that matches our suspect, he might have a dozen reasonable excuses for how it got here. But finding something right on the body, that's a lot harder to explain."

She started at one set of pedicured toes and moved upward. Two long black hairs, almost certainly Marie's, two short whitish hairs, a brown hair, and something that looked like a hazel-colored fiber.

She turned her attention to the nylons. They had been looped around each wrist and then tied in a double square knot. Something, a fiber or a hair not dark enough to be Marie's, had been caught in the knot. Theresa diagrammed, marked each end with a colored twist tie— red for toward the victim's left side, green for toward the right, like lights on a ship—and cut it. The victim's limbs relaxed slightly, pulling a few inches out from each other. Theresa tugged on one arm, then pushed the body away from her, just enough to glance at the stomach. No injuries, just a deep cherry lividity that did not change when she pressed her index finger against the stomach. The blood pooled at the body's lowest points and then coagulated. "Lividity is completely fixed, and so is rigor. It's nice and cool in here, so that would keep the process slow."

"How long, then?"

"The pathologist can be a lot more specific, but I'm guessing she's been here all night."

Theresa moved some of the black locks, stiffened with blood, off the victim's face. Her eyes were open, the irises a deep brown, already clouding. Marie Corrigan had an elfin chin and perfectly groomed eyebrows. Glossy mauve lipstick had smeared over the edge of one full lip and onto the fawn carpet. Her front tooth had chipped, the loose piece of enamel caught in the rug fibers below.

Neil looked thoughtful. "So maybe it *was* a date. Conference is over for the day, let's have a few drinks—"

"Except they didn't. No glasses, not even wet spots on the nightstand."

"He was smart enough to clean up, take all that stuff with him."

"Maybe. And be smart enough to take a complete set of towels—bath towel, hand towel, and washcloth—so that it would seem that all sets are present."

"What about the bath mat? Is that there?"

"Good thought. But yes, it's there." The pristine bed still bugged her. She'd made enough beds in her life to tell the difference between one with the covers turned back and one that had been occupied, with its tiny crumpled wrinkles. And as a female, she firmly believed that she could tell the difference between clean and spotless. The room wasn't merely clean—it was *spotless*. As if Marie and her killer had walked in, the murder had taken place, and the killer had walked out. But why? If there hadn't been some wild sex romp, why did he kill her? And if he planned to kill her, why had Marie gone so easily to her own slaughter? She must have walked in under her own steam—no killer would trot around an expensive hotel with a fully grown dead weight.

Maybe she had trusted him.

Theresa reined her mind in from running down endless alleys of what-if and took a closer look at the carpeting. What had first appeared to be footprints were only smudges, about a half inch by a quarter inch, randomly distributed. By lowering her face to the floor as far as she could without actually laying her cheek on the carpet, she could tell that the two smudges between Marie and the bathroom door coincided with indentations in the plush fawn surface. The killer had gotten a drop of blood on his foot and walked around with it. But the indentations didn't have the smooth, firm edges of a shoe print. Perhaps the killer had been barefoot? He'd shed his clothes as Marie did the same, preparing to take the edge off after a day of lectures? Theresa used a sterile, disposable scalpel to saw off the stained carpet fibers and drop them into a manila envelope.

The hotel around her seemed to press in like a force against her skin, and she finally figured out what oppressed her: the silence. The only sound in the room came from the faint creak of Neil Kelly's shoes as he shifted his weight. The scalpel droned against each twisted strand of carpeting. The building's walls had been insulated and soundproofed until she could crouch in one room in the middle of the day and not hear the slightest evidence of another human being above, around, or below, as if the room had been hermetically sealed. Marie Corrigan could have screamed, and no one would have heard her.

"So how do you know Marie Corrigan?" Neil asked, probably bored with all the watching and no doing.

Theresa sealed the envelope with red tape, aware of the detective's observation. "The first case I had with her was before we got our SEM—our scanning electron microscope—so we were still doing gunshot residue with atomic absorption. Of course, that only indicates gunshot residue, doesn't prove it, and gunshot residue only indicates that someone was in the vicinity when a gun was fired."

In her peripheral vision, Neil nodded.

"She'd obviously been watching too much *CSI* and expected me to say that the GSR proved that her client had pulled the trigger. I didn't, but she already had her line of questioning prepared, so she spent ten minutes having me read texts aloud to establish how I couldn't say what I hadn't said. It confused the jury and irritated the judge. She was never real fond of me after that."

"That explains why she wasn't fond of you. But why weren't you fond of her?"

Ms. MacLean, do you recognize the envelope I just handed you?

"Long story. What's yours?"

"She wanted a partner of mine back in organized crime prosecuted for police brutality because her client had a bruise on his forehead in the booking photo. His girlfriend had given it to him, not my partner, but Corrigan talked it all the way to an IA investigation. I don't know who I wanted to kill more—her or the idiots in our chain of command that opened the file."

Now Theresa observed him. Not tall, not bulked up, but when he moved, a layer of muscle like steel glimmered under his skin.

"It was four years ago. I'm over it."

"Okay." Theresa took her fingerprint kit to the bathroom floor.

"Maid's not going to be happy about that," Neil observed as she brushed the fine black powder over the tiles.

"The hotel should count their blessings. If she hadn't been found until she started to decompose, they'd have to replace all the carpeting and maybe any other upholstery in the bedroom. This way they can do a steam cleaning with a little bleach and their wealthy patrons will never know." Two distinct patterns appeared on the cream-colored tiles, superimposed on the swirling marks of the maid's cleaning rag. The faint set of smooth-soled triangular shapes belonged to Theresa. The other—"Let me see your shoes."

Neil picked one up, balancing on the other foot.

"Not yours."

"Shouldn't be, I never went in there. Just poked my head. I'll bet it belongs to John."

Theresa collected it anyway before proceeding to the other side of the room, her knees protesting a bit at having to crawl over the hard tile. No other patterns revealed themselves.

Powell returned and confirmed that they were his prints—he'd wanted to make sure the place was properly "cleared," that the killer wasn't hiding in the shower—and his shoe had a piece of old gum stuck in the left tread that matched the pattern.

"Odd," Theresa said. "He didn't fly over to the toilet, but he didn't leave any shoe prints or footprints. I suppose he could have had freshly washed feet, or very dry skin, or new shoes without a rubber tread."

"Or he wiped up the floor after himself," Neil supposed.

"Without using the towels or leaving water marks in the sink or tub," Theresa said. "Toilet again, I suppose."

"What's the deal with the toilet?"

"You don't have to touch anything to turn the water on. It's already there."

"Come on," Powell said to his partner. "I've got the hotel security chief out here. And he used to be one of ours."

"What's his name?" Neil asked quietly.

"Marcus Dean. Tall black guy. Narcotics, a few years in Persons. I didn't know him. You?"

"Hell yeah," Neil said, obviously surprised. "When I was in Vice. We were partners for a while. He's good people. What's he doing *here*?"

They went into the next room, their voices clearly audible. Theresa had never heard of Marcus Dean, but his voice rolled past the others', deep and firm. After the two ex-partners spent a few minutes catching up, Powell asked him if they would have any record of who had last entered the Presidential Suite.

"No such luck."

"A place like this, you don't have that kind of technology?"

"Door keys are there to restrict access. They aren't

some kind of a Big Brother, always-knowing-who's-where—slash—payroll system," the unseen Marcus Dean explained.

"So who had access?"

"To this room? More than— Look, a regular guest room, no one needs to get in there except the guests and the maids, and the maids can only get into rooms on the floors that they're supposed to be working on. And then, for cases of emergency, me and the manager on duty. Then there's places like the Club Lounge, restricted to only the people who work in there. The guests can leave jewelry and cash lying around all the time, never gets touched, but the liquor supply, that's a whole 'nother stretch of road in some staff members' minds. That ain't really stealin' to them. So access to most places is limited by that little magnetic strip on the back of their ID card.

"But the suites," he went on, "these people pay for some serious pampering. They want facials and massages in the privacy of their own home-away-from-home. People send them flowers. They go out shopping and have the stores deliver their packages here so they don't have to be bothered carryin' those big bags along the sidewalk. They have guests and clients, to be ushered up. They want room service and chilled anniversary-day champagne waiting for them when they get back from the theater. Then all this stuff has to be taken away afterward, and we don't want them putting their dirty dishes out in the hall. Looks tacky. Busboys, waitstaff, spa staff, porters. Practically everybody needs to get into these rooms."

"Our suspect pool is the entire staff, then?"

"Minus only the maids who don't work on this floor. But everybody else, yeah."

"Got any cards missing?"

"Checking now. Nothing's turned up so far. Staff are

pretty careful with those cards, let me tell you. They get in huge trouble if they lose one, and even huger if they don't tell us about it right away. I put the fear of God into them on their first day about that. We don't have lapses in security here. This is the Ritz, not a Super 8."

The conversation lapsed for a moment. Theresa finished dusting the bathroom floor, then heard Powell ask something about Narcotics.

"Yeah, seven years, two with Neil here," Dean said. "A few years in Persons before that, and five on the street before that."

"You left before you had twenty in?"

"My wife couldn't take those hours anymore. That and she wanted to start a family, kept nagging how she'd be raising these theoretical children all by herself if I took a bullet. Gotta make choices, you know what I mean?"

"Yeah."

The body snatchers arrived with their white plastic bag. Theresa supervised the removal of Marie Corrigan's body, then pressed adhesive tape to where she'd lain to collect any trace evidence trapped there.

The bloodstain hadn't spread out too far from underneath the head, but it had soaked the carpet pretty good. Perhaps Theresa had been wrong about the steam cleaning.

Neil Kelly and Powell apparently finished with Marcus Dean and reentered the bedroom. "Whoa," Neil said, looking at her squat, square-shaped machine with a flexible cable protruding from its front. "What's that?"

"ALS. Alternate light source."

"Like a black light?"

"Like a black light."

"Whoa," he said again, grimly. "This is going to be interesting."

Using a black light in a hotel room, along with reading the health department's report on your favorite restaurant, fell into the category of Things You'd Rather Not Know. The detectives drew the curtains, and Theresa switched off the bathroom light. She passed out orange goggles and turned the machine on. After churning through a few different wavelengths, she settled on one around four hundred nanometers. This would excite certain enzymes and proteins in bodily fluids—particularly semen—and cause them to emit a bluish fluorescence. Then she picked up the small machine, warning the detectives not to trip over the cord. The room was dim, certainly, but wearing the goggles made it even darker.

She passed the light, slowly, over the open bed, weaving from side to side, trying to cover every inch of the exposed white sheets.

Powell let out a breath he must have been holding. "I don't see anything."

"Me either," she agreed. Nothing. Not a fiber, not a spot, and certainly not the glowing blob of semen she'd expected to see.

"So wherever they did it—if they did it—it wasn't in the bed," Neil surmised.

Theresa threw the covers back into place so she could see the surface of the comforter. A splotch burst into a faintly yellowish glow as the light passed over it. And another. And another.

"Yuck," Neil Kelly said.

Powell, at her elbow: "What did they say about that expensive suite Mike Tyson was in? They found how many different semen samples?"

"You would think it would show up better on these white comforters and they'd have to wash them more often," Theresa said. "Only five here. Not as bad as the Tyson suite."

"You going to collect them all?" Neil asked.

"Have to. Don's not going to be happy," she added, referring to the lab's DNA analyst. She moved the light to the floor.

"Yuck," Neil said again.

"Eww," Powell added. "Look, it goes up the *wall*. I don't know whether to be disgusted or jealous."

"The *bed*, people," Neil instructed the phantom guests. "That's what the *bed* is for."

"Most of this is probably urine," Theresa assured them. "Someone may have been incontinent or have some very odd habits. Most likely they smuggled a pet into the room. They may even *allow* pets in this room."

Neil said, "Probably. The Paris Hiltons of the world have to be indulged."

Theresa followed the glowing splashes around the bed, to the bathroom, to the desk, and out the door, debating on what to collect and what not to. She didn't want to overload Don or rip up more of the Ritz's property than she had to, but at the same time there was never a good way to explain why she *hadn't* collected a piece of potential evidence. She decided to gather a swab or two from the wall between the bed and bath, take the entire comforter, and clip a few carpet fibers around the body's resting place. Trying to find the swabs, break open the package, locate the tiny disposable plastic vial of sterile water (were those things a godsend or what?) to wet the swab, rub it on the wall, get out the swab boxes and fold them into the correct shape without setting the swabs down, and then label the boxes, all in the near dark, severely tested her dexterity. But she didn't want to mark up the walls with a Sharpie marker, or the hotel would have to repaint for sure and then think about billing her for the cost. She began to clip carpet fibers, the ALS head propped on her shoulder and held in place with her chin, cutting only a few here and there so the damage wouldn't show before the huge bloodstain reminded her that they'd have to replace the carpeting anyway. She took a scalpel and began to cut three-inch-square pieces of carpet to test, along with one clean piece as a control sample. Who knew what kind of cleaners or stain blockers they might have used on the carpet? On rare occasions these could affect the DNA sample.

The detectives offered to help, but there was little they could do beyond Neil Kelly's holding the manila envelopes open for her as she dropped in carpet samples. Finally she could wrap up the cords and open the curtains with the sense of relief a minorly claustrophobic person feels to see daylight again.

Neil and Powell searched the room as she gathered her envelopes. They found nothing save for a paper clip and the corner of an ancient Twinkie wrapper wedged behind the nightstand, next to a dead cockroach and half of a Len Barker baseball card.

"Engorged with Twinkie crumbs is not a bad way to go," Neil pointed out, "but who rips up a perfectly good baseball card?"

Len Barker had pitched a perfect game for the Indians in 1981, only the eighteenth no-hitter in major-league history. "Would that be worth a lot?" Theresa asked.

Powell said, "No, they're not that rare. But I'll bet it's got a story behind it. Just not one involving Marie Corrigan."

The two detectives kept up a running vaudeville act on the various possible explanations for all the stains they'd seen, like the overgrown boys they were. Theresa escaped to process the door to the hallway for fingerprints, as well as the hallway door to the stairwell, and then she could finally strip off the gloves and gather up her envelopes and equipment from the plush carpeting. "I think that's about it."

Powell moved to the outer room to make a phone call. Neil Kelly took one more look around, then said to her, "I want to ask your daughter a few questions. Do you want to be there?"

Theresa got to her feet immediately. "You better believe it."

CHAPTER 5

The lobby bustled with human activity. Dinner hour approached with check-in time, and new guests queued up at Rachael's desk. The conference sessions were breaking up, and small groups of people with identical name badges gathered, discussing the murder and also where to get a decent steak.

Theresa made Neil wait until Rachael had checked in a group of tourists from Norway and could turn her counter over to another girl, feeling that tiny frisson of anxiety one does when introducing one's child to another adult, especially this man—a peer, sort of. Would he have the good sense to discern the obvious superiority of her offspring? Or would he remain clueless, uninterested in the child's intelligence and wit? Not that it mattered to Theresa, of course.

Rachael joined them next to a statue of three running horses, realistically captured in bronze. "We'll have to talk fast, 'cause I'm not supposed to hang around the lobby. So who did it? Do we have some psycho killer running loose in this place?"

So much for wowing Mom's new acquaintance. "Rachael! This isn't a TV show."

"Sorry," she said. "I guess I can afford to be flip—I don't have to go into some empty room off a silent hallway all the time like the maids. They're totally freaked out. I think they may revolt."

"That's not funny."

"It wasn't meant to be. They're talking about walking out unless the hotel provides armed security guards on each floor."

"I don't blame them," Theresa said.

Rachael's line of sight swung to a young man in a cook's white shirt who was leaving the lounge. He toted a white cardboard box labeled POTATOES and headed for the restaurant but paused to give her a nod and a grin. Rachael burst into a smile of such wattage that for a second or two Theresa forgot about the dead lawyer. "Let me guess—that's the William I've been hearing so much about."

"The very same," Rachael happily confirmed, her gaze lingering on the kid until he disappeared behind the frosted-glass doors of Muse. The Ritz-Carlton's well-known restaurant served both foie gras and macaroni and cheese, which happened to be an excellent culinary representation of the city at large and its distinct and varied populace.

Neil Kelly leaned an elbow on the stallion's rump and cleared his throat, so Theresa got back to business—which happened to be the safety of her only child. "So you're here in the lobby for your entire shift, then."

"Yeah, unless Karla sends me off on an errand. But usually—oh, come on, Mom. I know what you're going to say."

"Yes, you do. You're confined to this lobby until we wrap this up. No going anywhere in this building alone, got it? I don't care if Elvis Presley checks in and wants a mint julep."

"Isn't Elvis dead?"

Neil cleared his throat again, loudly enough to be heard even over the growing hubbub of conversations around them.

"Rachael, this is Detective Kelly. He needs to ask you a few questions."

He gave Rachael a grown-up handshake and asked, "Neil Kelly. As exactly as you can remember, what time did you get that call from the Presidential Suite?"

Rachael squared her shoulders, which were reflected in the marble wall behind her. "One thirty-one. I remember because I was staring at the phone display. When anyone calls from one of the suite rooms, we're supposed to address them by name. Like, I'm supposed to answer the phone 'Yes, Mr. Jones, how can I help you?' But the display was blank, and I couldn't figure out why—I get it now, because no one was staying in that room, but at the time it made me totally stuck."

"So when you answered, what did the man say?"

Rachael went over the conversation, telling them nothing they didn't already know. Finally Neil thanked Theresa's daughter with what seemed like genuine warmth and left to find his partner. Rachael said that her shift had ended, but she volunteered to wait and go home with Theresa, avoiding a long bus ride.

"I'm done here. We'll just run by the lab so I can hang up her clothing and make sure the blood dries, and we can go. What happened to your uncle?"

"The Ambassador Room, seventh floor." Rachael's hair swung toward the elevator bank. "They're talking to all the lawyers. Who's that guy, the one who just talked to me? Do you know him?"

"Vaguely."

"He knows you."

"Here, grab this ALS—and what does that mean?"

"He likes you. I can tell."

Theresa shook her head as she shuffled her load. Despite firm biceps, an ability to ride a skateboard, terrific mathematics skills, and a local Halo championship under her belt, Rachael was all girl. A born people manager, and there was nothing she enjoyed managing more than her mother's love life. "How nice. Just wait for me here, okay? And try not to get murdered."

"Not allowed."

"To get murdered?"

"To sit around in the public areas. It's a no-no for staff. I'll wait in the office behind the desk. Come and get me there."

Rachael passed the ALS back. Theresa first stored her equipment and evidence in the county station wagon and then went in search of the other family member present.

Every available Homicide detective had been assigned to assist, which was how Frank Patrick came to be sitting in the Ritz-Carlton's Ambassador Room. The Ambassador Room had been designed for seminars given by very well-to-do corporations or perhaps for the elegantly understated second wedding with a limited guest list. Walls the color of a pale burnt sienna contrasted with rich bronze draperies. Sheers underneath blocked the harsh world outside, creating a quiet haven of good taste. Apparently the conference hadn't needed this room; tables were set up with matching but unblemished tablecloths, each chair in place. The ten or so people in the room hovered at one end of it, around uncovered tables with mismatched folding chairs. The hotel would give the police a room to work in so long as they didn't mess up the place settings, like Frank's mother protecting the dining room on a bridge-club day.

Normally, witnesses would not be questioned in the same room, but with a pool this size, speed and efficiency were of the essence. Cops kept their voices low, and the attorneys were doing the same. His partner, Angela Sanchez, had arrived as well, and now the olive-skinned woman with shoulder-length raven hair sat across from a young attorney, leaning away as he zoomed in on her pert nose and scoop-necked T-shirt. *Good luck there, pal,* Frank thought. Half the force had already tried, with no more success than that turn-of-last-century's baseball team, the Cleveland Spiders.

His cousin appeared in front of him, with a weary look and a smudge of black powder on both her chin and the ivory blouse. "Getting anywhere?" she asked.

"These are defense attorneys."

"Refusing to talk without, what, an attorney?"

"No," he sighed. "Obviously trying to confuse me, they've all been pretty forthcoming. At least half of them are from out of town, so maybe they're more willing to let their guard down and set a dangerous precedent of cooperation. Except for the last guy, and him only because he doesn't want his wife or his boss finding out where he spent his expense account last night. Otherwise they've been surprisingly open. The last sighting of Marie Corrigan, so far, seems to be five-thirty last night, in the bar. A group of them, all from different cities and all men—no surprise there—bought her drinks and planned to go over to East Fourth, hit Michael Symon's place for dinner, and then do the bars. Marie left to powder her nose and never came back. They drank for another hour, then figured she'd ditched them and staggered off to East Fourth on their own, but, being from out of town, they headed west instead and wound up at Brasa's."

"Which is just as good, assuming their expense accounts can keep up. And they never saw Marie again," Theresa said, as if to clarify.

"According to them. I've gotten five other statements from people who recognized her photo, having been in the same audience at this or that lecture. They have quite the agenda. Today they had 'How to Make Not-Guilty Happen,' 'Criminal Defense in a Down Economy,' and 'Defending Child-Pornography Cases.'"

"Sounds a lot racier than forensic conventions. We have things like 'The Life Cycle of the *Cochliomyia*.'"

"What?"

"Blowfly."

"Oh. There's also 'Forensic Science in the Courtroom,'" he added, reaching over to rub the powder off her face with one thumb. "Maybe you should sit in on that."

"Maybe I should. What did the five other people say about Marie?"

"Never saw her after the sessions were over."

"So she died, approximately, between five-thirty and"—Theresa thought about the condition of the body—"say, midnight. That doesn't narrow it down much. These people were all coming, going—"

"Looking forward to relaxing after a busy day of learning how to keep their clients on the street, free to commit more crimes."

"Not much of a loss, is she?" someone said from behind Theresa.

Frank groaned inwardly. Sonia Battle.

Never had a woman been more appropriately named—the Battle part, not Sonia. She'd been Theresa's college roommate and gone on to become a criminal defense attorney. He knew that Sonia had gone into law because of some incident with her brother, and her passion to help the little guy oppressed by an uncaring, big-oted state had not abated, only grown stronger. Frank and Theresa, of course, were considered agents of this uncaring state.

Theresa hugged the woman. "Sonia! You were at this thing, too?"

"Of course. You know how dedicated I am to getting my scumbag clients back on the streets." She glared at Frank.

"Please sit down." Theresa retrieved one of the nicely cushioned chairs from the set tables and placed it across from Frank. The hotel would have to adapt.

Sonia sat. She continued to glare—at him only. She cut his cousin slack, everywhere but in the courtroom.

Marie Corrigan had, when alive, looked exactly like the kind of person she was—sexy, glitzy, driven, ready to eat men and even other women for breakfast to get what she wanted, without much concern for people's feel-ings, the rules of law, or justice. Sonia Battle's life could also be read from her appearance—weary-faced, with straight hair she didn't bother to style, round glasses to ease the eyestrain from reading briefs all night instead of going on dates, and a body she didn't have time to tone underneath the ill-fitting clothes she bought because she couldn't afford anything more on an Office of the Public Defender salary. Sonia had great concern for people's feelings (people other than cops and prosecutors, that was), the rules of law, and justice. So much concern that it seemed to eat her alive.

Theresa asked, "How are you? Did you know Marie?"

Sonia pressed fleshy lips together. "I knew her. And I know how the cops felt about her. Hell, I know how *you* felt about her."

"Last year she practically accused me of planting paint chips from the suspect's car on the victim's jeans,"

Theresa pointed out. Frank knew that there were more recent—and more virulent—experiences with Marie Corrigan, but if his cousin wasn't going to mention that to her old buddy, neither would he.

"She asked if it was a possibility there'd been cross-contamination at the lab, that's all."

"No, she asked, 'Did you take paint chips from my client's front bumper and put them in an envelope to indicate you'd found them on a pair of jeans?' And how did you know about that anyway?"

"I keep up on who's trying what case and its outcome. We all do. Cleveland's a small town in a lot of ways, and like any profession, ours can get a bit incestuous. You disliked Marie because she was good at her job—you just won't admit it."

"I disliked her because she flat-out lied to juries. She told one that two hundred years of fingerprint analysis should be considered junk science."

"Well, you can't prove that there *couldn't* be two people with the same fingerprint!"

"No, and by golly, I can't understand why we would think that when there's approximately *six hundred billion* comparisons done every *day* across the globe and we *still* haven't found two the same—"

"Ladies," Frank interrupted. "Can we talk about Marie Corrigan?"

Sonia turned to him. "That's exactly who we're talking about, Detective Patrick. The woman you all despise because she beat you at your own games. Tell me you haven't done a fist bump over her cooling body. Reporters are already prepping sound bites wondering if Marie's own handiwork came back to haunt her in the form of some psycho she kept on the streets. Some sensible-looking lady in the bar asked me if the bitch was really

DEFENSIVE WOUNDS 47

dead. Why should I believe you're going to properly investigate this murder?"

"Let me get this straight," he said. "*You're* worried about someone getting *off*?"

Sonia threw up her hands. "See what I mean? We're below some Quincy Avenue gangbangers in your estimation. You're waiting to pin a medal on whoever killed her."

"Yeah, a big shiny one. But I'll still have to catch him first. Are you going to help or not?"

"Sonia," Theresa said, probably figuring she'd better get a lid on her friend before the attorney could work up a really good fury of righteous indignation, "when did you last see Marie?"

The woman sighed. "At the luncheon yesterday."

Frank stopped her to ask if she would sign a statement, and she agreed, but then he let Theresa ask the questions.

Sonia told them, "I grabbed a spot at her table, for the same reason she had—because the 'Recent Supreme Court Decisions' speaker was sitting there, and I wanted to ask him about *Melendez-Diaz v. Massachusetts*."

"And what did Marie want?"

"To sit with a speaker and not just a bunch of schlubs. Marie had the art of career networking down pat." Sonia shook her head, but with a small, admiring smile. "Anyway, before you ask, we just talked about the seminar and what to do in Cleveland and the high price of parking. Marie seemed fine, glowing, the life of the party, just like always."

"No arguments, complaints?" Theresa asked.

"None."

"Did she flirt with this speaker?"

"Yeah, but he didn't seem to be going for it. He had a wedding ring on."

48 **LISA BLACK**

Frank stifled a chuckle at the idea that a ring would stop a man at an out-of-town function. Theresa went on. "Anyone else seem especially taken with Marie?"

"Only the usual—every guy at the table checking out her rack."

"Someone mentioned that Marie had raised some sort of a fuss at the luncheon?"

Sonia rubbed her eyes, devoid of makeup. "No. She sent her veal piccata back, said it tasted old, and refused another one. She got pretty curt with the waiter. I felt sorry for him, but with Marie—she either wanted more attention from the speaker guy or just an excuse not to eat her lunch. I've seen her at a lot of functions, and she never eats much. I've always suspected bulimia there. Did you know that surgeons and trial lawyers have the highest rate of alcoholism, drug addiction, and eating disorders? And she's got to keep her figure to keep her image. No one's afraid of an attorney who looks like me," she added, prodding her own rolling waistline.

"How long have you known Marie?" Theresa asked. Frank cleared his throat, to let her know she had veered off topic. She ignored him, of course.

"Since law school. She's our age."

Theresa goggled. "Then how does she look like she's twenty-five?"

"By not eating, I guess." Sonia shrugged. "Maybe a tuck here or there. I told you, she took care of her image."

"Can we get to more recent history?" Frank asked, before they could start exchanging diet tips. "Was she planning to hook up with anyone in between seminars?"

"I wouldn't know. Marie was nice to me— Don't raise your eyebrows, she really was. Even though I obviously have the social status of a half-dead rat, she has always been nice to me. Steered me toward a civil-rights statute once that proved a lifesaver. But still, we were acquaintances, not BFFs."

"It's a conference. They're like a high school where everybody is the new kid. Word gets around."

"Sorry to disappoint you, Detective, but I don't have any intelligence to share on hookups."

"Does she have a boyfriend?" Theresa asked. "Husband? Fiancé?"

"Never a husband, so far as I know. But I can't believe that you don't know who she's dating."

"Why would I?"

Sonia smiled, not very pleasantly. "Because he's a particular favorite of yours."

Oh, boy.

Theresa thought a moment, then exploded. "Britton? The one that rakes me over the coals about ASCLD certification and whether I can prove I used sterile tweezers to pick up a fiber? The one who exclusively defends murderers and rapists? The only attorney in Cleveland even sleazier than Marie Corrigan?"

The attorney talking to Angela turned to stare. Detective Powell, guiding another interviewee into the room, started to laugh. Sonia threw up her hands again. "And you tell me you're going to be objective."

"*Britton?* Well, I see where Marie got the fingerprint-analysis line of questioning. But Britton can't be at this conference, too. I just testified in front of him this morning, about the East Sixth shooting." Cops and carjackers had gotten into a shoot-out, which ended with two bleeding officers and one deceased carjacker. Now the suspect's family had brought a civil suit against the police department *and* the dead suspect's partner. "I *thought* he seemed in a hurry, though he still found time to spend twenty minutes questioning me about crime-scene procedures. Not questioning anything I actually did or actually found or actually analyzed, of course, just talking long enough to irritate me and put the jury to sleep so that they won't remember what I *did* find or *did* analyze. Does he ever have a real point to make, or is that considered old-fashioned?"

Sonia ignored this tirade. "Of course he's here, in between court appearances. *He* ate lunch at the keynote speaker's table."

"Without Marie?" Theresa calmed slightly. "She couldn't have been happy about that."

"I'm sure she wasn't, but it's par for the course. I've seen them together at 1890. She's running at full wattage, but he spends half the time on his cell phone. He's the king of the hill, and she's hot, and that's all that's keeping that relationship together. Kept."

Frank spoke up. "So where was he last night?"

"That's the question I'd *like* you to ask. Because if you have a suspect list, I suggest you put him at the top. You want a scumbag off the street, make it him."

"Why?" Frank and Theresa asked in unison.

"I got assigned a kid picked up with some other guys for possession. Less than felony weight, so I should have been able to get him out with time served. As I arrive for the pretrial hearing, Britton is just leaving, and my client wants to plead guilty to dealing, says all the drugs in the group were his."

"What happened?" Frank asked.

"The kid's outfit offered the kid something to take the fall. Take care of his family, give him a lump sum when he got out, or else he'll be killed in his cell before the trial can even begin. That's the standard deal."

"And Britton brokered it."

"Had to. He conspired to coerce my client to commit perjury and obstruct justice. And yet I'm sure that in his mind he only delivered a message for his client. Period."

"Yeah."

"Yeah, except my client didn't make his full term. A fight broke out in the cafeteria one day, and he never saw his nineteenth birthday."

Theresa said, "I'm sorry." Something in the lawyer's expression made Frank feel sorry as well. Sonia Battle might be a pain in the ass, but she was a sincere pain in the ass.

Sonia shook it off. "I filed a complaint with the Office of the Disciplinary Counsel, for all the good it will do me. He'll win in the end. There's too many routes for jailhouse communication. I can't prove it was him. I can't even prove that a deal was made."

Nor could she implicate Britton in Marie Corrigan's death. Sonia, unlike her partying compatriots, had gone back to the PD office immediately after Tuesday's final session to work on what had piled up on her desk during the day. She hadn't seen either Britton or Marie and had no idea where they'd been during the evening.

"So you don't have a particular reason to think Britton did it," Theresa clarified. "Any other suspects?"

"Who knows?" Sonia sighed again. "We've all got enemies. It comes with the job."

"Even you?" Frank asked.

"Well, let's see. One of my clients' ex-wives sent me a Barbie doll that had had an unfortunate encounter with a blender because I couldn't keep her ex-with-benefits out of jail. Then there's the surfer girl who met me in the parking lot one day and gave me a fat lip and a chipped tooth before the attendant pulled her off. I represented the driver who'd totaled her brother's car. Strong little thing. I think she spent some time in the Roller Derby."

"Sonia!" Theresa grasped her friend's arm.

"Hey, being a lawyer is like being a cop—if you're not willing to get your ass beat once in a while, you'd better find another line of work. There's also a Peeping Tom who graces me with an obscene phone call every couple of months—*after* I got him a reduced sentence, the ingrate. And the saintly-looking grandmother of my client's alleged victim once sent me a box of oatmeal cookies with a razor blade lovingly baked into each one."

"Wow."

"Yeah," Sonia said. "A tragic waste. They had chocolate chips in them, too."

Frank said, "I thought families considered you the good guys."

"Most of my clients *do* end up in jail, Detective. Families think *I'm* the one who needs to be punished."

This exhausted the conversation, so Theresa bade adieu to her cousin and went to collect her daughter. Sonia came along, stepped carefully over the elevator threshold, and kept talking about Dennis Britton. "I filed my complaint with the bar last year. But he just keeps schmoozing the board and having it postponed."

"It's the same way he tries his cases," Theresa said. "He just delays and delays until he gets the best deal he can, and then suddenly the guy he'd been insisting was as pure as the driven snow pleads guilty. Do you know anything else about Marie's relationship with him? Anything at all?"

"Like, were they into S&M?"

Theresa rolled her eyes. "I take it the crime scene isn't much of a secret anymore?"

"You want something kept secret, don't let that squirrelly little guy from Des Moines in the room. He'll eat lunch on that story for the next three months. I don't know what they did for sex—except that they probably met at the Hyatt to get together. I told you I saw them at 1890 more than once."

"Why a hotel? They live on opposite sides of town or something?"

Sonia gave her that pitying look again. "You don't know that, either? Britton's married."

"Married."

"To one of the Vaughn girls. You know, Vaughn Aircraft?"

Theresa formed an O with her mouth. "Big bucks."

"If your forehead were a neon sign, 'Hello, Motive!' would be flashing across it. You are so transparent, Theresa. That's why I love having you on the stand."

"Am *not*."

"Are you going to report everything I tell you back to your cousin?"

"Of course I am. We're trying to solve a murder here. How long have they been—"

The lobby had quieted some. Theresa came to a halt near the front desk and waited until the harried young woman there arranged for Housekeeping to deliver yet more towels to Mr. Trask in room 1402. "I don't know what he's doing with them, and I don't want to know. Just don't lose count." Then a new call erupted from a Mr. McManus who wanted his regular suite, but it currently contained an aging actress with the *Wicked* tour, and surely he would understand that they couldn't uproot such an esteemed and fragile lady. But apparently Mr. McManus did not feel quite so understanding, and so the girl put both calls on hold and rubbed her forehead, then handed a white envelope to the young man Theresa had seen earlier in the day.

"Hi," he said to her. Brown eyes, good skin, clean-shaven. "Are you looking for Rachael?"

She confirmed this.

He jerked his head toward the elevator bank with a pleasant-enough smile. "Come with me. I'll show you our hideout."

"Lead on," she told him, grasping Sonia Battle's elbow.

CHAPTER 6

Sonia dragged her feet, both literally and figuratively. "I really should get back to work. I've been gone all day, and my desk—"

"Not. I've been listening to you vent about how we're all nasty agents of the prosecution and egging on the killer. The least you can do is ooh and aah over my kid for a minute or two. You haven't seen Rachael since she was, what, ten?"

Sonia stepped into the elevator, eyes on the floor, and mumbled a reluctant assent.

William pushed button number thirty-three, then turned to face them.

"Your hideout is in a penthouse?" Theresa asked.

He merely smiled. "You'll see."

William's name had been popping up in conversation, steadily and increasingly for the past two weeks, so Theresa used the ride time to observe. About five-eleven, dark brown hair in a conservative but not-too-short cut, no visible piercings, looked her straight in the eye. So far so good, even if the straight look held a bit more defiance than affability. She stuck out her hand. "It's nice to meet you, William."

He gave a perfunctory smile, using decent teeth. Theresa introduced Sonia, who still fidgeted, and he repeated the process. Smile, shake.

Sonia's pasty complexion turned a bit green. Perhaps she was claustrophobic. Or had a problem with heights. Even Theresa felt a bit dizzy when they stepped off onto the thirty-third floor, though it could have been from the slight stripe in the carpeting. It complemented the walls and the framed black-and-white photographs of the Terminal Tower at various stages: in the thirties, the fifties. Theresa barely had time to glance at them or at the office doors they passed as William led them around to a second elevator bank. There the carpeting and the decor stopped. The fancy wood paneling and glossy floor of the car were covered with huge panes of steel or aluminum. It didn't look like something you wanted to step into and be suspended thirty-three floors above the ground.

"Where are we going?" Theresa asked.

William held the door open. "It's a surprise."

"I hate surprises," she muttered, and kept a firm grip on Sonia's elbow. The lawyer looked ready to bolt.

As the doors closed, William pushed button number forty-two, and Theresa could guess their destination.

"The observation deck is closed," she said.

"Yes, it is," the young man agreed.

Theresa felt a worried thrill. In her forty years in the city, she had never been up to the observation deck—or if she had, she'd been too young to remember. It had been officially closed since 9/11, but it had been closed off and on before that. The firms on the thirty-third floor got tired of the tourists trooping past their doors and lobbied to restrict access to weekends only. Providing guides and guards for the deck eventually cost more than it brought in.

The doors opened to a room in no better shape than the elevator—a bare, dusty floor, peeling paint, exposed ceiling pipes, a few scattered cigarette butts and empty fast-food wrappers. Under construction, obviously. Empty, and growing dark.

Everything about the situation felt wrong, and neither woman moved.

"Where's Rachael?" Theresa demanded, surprised by the quaver in her voice.

"Here," William said without inflection. He walked off, leaving her no choice but to follow. Sonia trailed behind her.

He led them into a hallway. To the left sat a small room with three large windows, overlooking the Cuyahoga River. Theresa's bout of nervousness melted into delight to see the Flats, the Hope Memorial Bridge, part of Steel Valley—even more of it when she turned to her right and the larger room, with sweeping views of Lake Erie.

But still no Rachael.

"This way," William said, and plunged into the dim inner core of the deck, again without waiting for a response. Theresa turned to be sure that Sonia would follow and then went behind him up a circling metal stairway. Her feet complained about the prolonged use of leather pumps on hard surfaces, and she promised them it wouldn't be much longer. The air grew darker with each ringing step as the natural light from the observation room remained below.

William's shadowy form approached a door, rimmed with sunlight and, giving a small grunt of exertion, pushed it open and freed them into the upper observation deck, an outside ring that formed the highest point in the city of Cleveland—at least on this side of Ontario Street.

She could immediately hear her daughter's voice. Now she followed William without hesitation, sucking in the water-scented breeze. The outside deck couldn't have been more than four feet wide and made of shingles layered, plastered, and painted over through the years until the surface beneath one's feet had an uncomfortable give to it. This surface and the chest-high outer wall had been freshly painted in brilliant white.

About a third of the way around, this channel had been plugged by a small scaffold for men working on the tower's brickwork. Rachael sat on the platform, arms resting on a wire railing while her legs dangled seven hundred feet above the city of Cleveland. Another girl rested next to her, with a boy on the steps leading up to the platform.

"Get down from there!" Theresa burst out before she could help herself.

Rachael just grinned. "Come up here. Are you ready to go now? It's three hours past the end of my shift, and I am so over the drama."

"Who you kidding?" William protested. "You're all *about* the drama."

"That thing looks like an Erector Set, and you're trusting it—"

"Come up here," Rachael demanded again, because she knew her mother. And Theresa slipped off the pumps and did so, slowly, gingerly, but ultimately unable to resist the delicious freedom that comes with perching high atop the rest of the world, tempting both fate and gravity.

The wind was hearty but not cold. She sat in the middle of the small platform and then scooched to the edge, destroying her nylons and working hard not to flash the innocent youth around her. The "railing" made of three cables would reach only her hip while she was standing, and she had grave doubts that it would stop someone from tumbling over, though it felt rigid enough to the touch.

William tucked himself into the foot of space between the steps and the outer wall, gripping the railing post, his fingers an inch from Rachael's thigh. Sonia stayed on the deck, leaning on the outer wall. Theresa reintroduced her, and the attorney dutifully produced a *My how she's grown* beam at Rachael. "But are you supposed to be up here?"

"No," the girl admitted. "But we're not hurting anything. The guys working on this are never here. They've got some contract dispute going."

William pulled off the white chef's smock, revealing a taut torso in a plain black T-shirt. His stare, while not hostile in any way, felt piercing enough to make Theresa think about squirming with discomfort. But then, she thought as she looked at her daughter, didn't all excitement begin with discomfort? "You're investigating the murder?" he asked Theresa.

Rachael answered for her. "She's been picking up hairs and fibers and using a black light on our signature light-as-air comforters."

"But it's a hotel room," the other girl pointed out. "All sorts of stuff in there."

"Exactly. So give it up, Mom. If you want to know what really goes on in this hotel, you need to talk to us." Rachael obviously enjoyed the role reversal, with herself as the dispenser of information.

William had gotten that right. Rachael *was* all about the drama.

Interviewing witnesses had never been part of Theresa's job. Usually she avoided witnesses, victims, and suspects as much as possible, to keep from becoming biased by their opinions and because people under stress could be problematic and unpredictable— not to mention a pain in the ass. And prickly detectives didn't take kindly to what they saw as interference. Too soon to tell whether Kelly and Powell fell into that category. But age had taught her that the fruit of vital information could tumble out of any tree. "Okay, tell me."

Rachael introduced the black girl and a pudgy boy as Lorraine and Ray. Both gave their location when they'd heard about the murder and a detailed theory as to what had occurred. Theresa nodded until her neck began to hurt. Sonia, uncharacteristically, said nothing.

Lorraine reported, "So Bobbi said that our maintenance guy is always hanging around the Club Level floor when he's not supposed to be, and no one's seen him since this morning—"

"He's in the machine room with the electrician," William corrected. The wind picked up a lock of Rachael's hair, and he reached out to slide it back over her shoulder in a gesture that expressed way too much familiarity between them. "I keep telling you that. The A/C in storage is out, and the soap's getting soggy."

"Yeah, but have you *seen* him?"

William argued further. "Who's going to be stupid enough to kill a shorty in the place where you work? You'd know they're going to look at us first thing. It's got to be a guest. The chick hooked up with the wrong player. That's all a hotel is about, really—hooking up."

"That's all *you're* about," the dark girl teased, making Theresa wonder if that was true.

He had the sense to shake his head in the presence of the mother whose daughter he was flirting with, ever so subtly. "In this place nobody knows who you are, and nobody cares. She thought she'd have some fun, but then he couldn't pull out—know what I mean?"

"What about other people?" the rounded boy on the steps suggested. "There's delivery people here all the time."

"But they don't leave sixth," Lorraine said. "No reason for them to be up by the Presidential."

"Could be taking liquor to the Club Lounge."

"They drop it on six, Ray. Flunkies—'scuse me, *porters*—tote it the rest of the way."

"Wish they could drop a case on the way," Ray said, then added to Theresa, "They're renovating this for the eightieth anniversary of the Terminal Tower thing. Even though it will be like the eighty-third anniversary. So there's construction guys, guys who fix the elevators, guys still patching the floor on eleven after a leak."

Just as their adult counterparts would have, the kids obviously saw the advantages of blaming the death on an outsider, someone they didn't know and couldn't be responsible for, someone who had moved on, no longer a threat. A very comforting scenario, practiced in every small town, school, business—any finite area in which a murder had taken place. And usually wrong.

She glanced over at Sonia to see if her friend had caught this. At that moment she finally noticed that the loquacious Sonia had completely shut up. The height didn't seem to bother her—she leaned against the outer wall without hesitation—and the woman would hardly be intimidated by teenagers after years at the PD.

Theresa abandoned that line of thought and steered the kids toward more useful information. "How could someone get into a room without having a key?"

She expected a few knowing looks and sly allusions to different methods, but all four stared at her blankly.

Then, one by one, they shook their heads.

"Nope."

"Can't be done."

"Those doors don't open without a key card."

"You'd have to break it down."

Ray tried to help. "If you could go earlier and stuff the little hole that the bolt goes into, then when the door closed, it wouldn't lock."

"But you'd still have to get the door open at some point, you moron," William said.

The appellation did not bother the kid. He grinned, scratched his ear with the stub of a partially amputated index finger, and suggested that the killer could have gotten hotel management to open the door earlier, for a delivery or repair. He beamed when William agreed.

Theresa asked, "Have any recent guests stood out to you, their behavior or appearance or requests? Seen anything . . . unusual in a room?"

"Like whips and chains?" Rachael asked, clearly delighting in Theresa's reticence.

"Sure. Or more blood than what would result from a shaving cut. Or any arguments you might have seen or overheard."

"Are you allowed to ask us that?" Lorraine wondered.

"I don't see why not. I'm not asking you to search their belongings. We're just talking about what you might have already observed in the normal course of your duties. Just as *you* were before I walked in."

The kids visibly racked their brains to produce tales of the weird and strange, telling of a guest who wore a long black cape and of things found in rooms, ranging from bizarre pornography to inch-deep confetti ("clogged three vacuum cleaners in a row").

Rachael confessed that on her second day on the job, a well-kept older man had approached the front desk and asked where he could find a prostitute. "And he

was very matter-of-fact about it, as if he were looking for the ice machine. I'm thinking, 'Buddy, I'm an
eighteen-year-old girl. Do I *look* like I'd know how to
hire a prostitute?'"

Don't scream, Theresa told herself, *at the thought of
this dirty old man approaching your teenage daughter.
Please don't scream.* "So what did you do?"

"I told him that while the Ritz offers its guests many
fine amenities, that isn't one of them. He stood there for
a minute or two, like he thought I was being a smart al-
eck. Then I guess it dawned on him that he could hardly
complain to my manager that I'd refused to find him a
hooker, and he went away."

Theresa stole another glance at Sonia, who appeared
to listen, and yet the attorney's face had lost its ruddiness
and the kaleidoscope of emotions that usually churned
there had smoothed out into a carefully still mask. Sonia's eyes flickered from Rachael to the boy William,
once, twice. Then she interrupted Lorraine midsentence
to say, "I have to go. Nice to see you again." She nodded
to the group in general, turned, and disappeared around
the curve of the outer observation deck.

"Can you—" Theresa called after her.

"Yeah, fine."

Okay, not afraid of heights or of elevators. So what
was up with the assertive public defender?

Lorraine went on. "I had a guy say he found a . . .
um, sex toy in a room that he checked in to, like it was
left by a previous guest. Thing is, the room hadn't been
rented for a few days before he checked in, and he said
he found it right beside the bed on the floor, where no
way I wouldn't have seen it. He wanted us to comp the
room because he was so *offended,* but the GM said not
happening. That was the GM before Karla. Karla would
have caved. You'd be amazed what they pull to try to get

you to comp the room. Problem is, they do it by trying to get *me* in trouble."

Kind of like defense attorneys, Theresa thought.

"Might want to rethink your career choice," William said.

"People always sayin' that to me," the girl admitted. "'How can you be cleaning up after rich white folks, scrubbing their toilets all the time?' But it ain't that bad of a job." She shifted on the platform, rubbing her lower back, and turned her face to the setting sun. "It keeps me moving, and it gives me plenty of time to think. And it's quiet. I don't have a supervisor breathing down my neck all day. And the shit . . . well, once you've changed diapers, you can touch anything. At least here I got rubber gloves. I'd rather be a maid than a waitress, scrambling around with people yelling at you all night."

"Waitresses get tips," Rachael pointed out.

Solemnly, Lorraine agreed. "There is that. Nobody tips maids. They don't see us, so we're out of mind. I think she was fighting with somebody," she suddenly added. "That woman who died."

Everyone listened.

"If it's the same one," she amended with a shrug. "I dunno. But if she had long black hair and fu—um . . . high heels—then I might have seen her coming out of the Diplomat. Seventh floor," she clarified for Theresa's benefit. "The meeting rooms. She was with some suit, and she was ripping him a new one. Something about a baby."

"What did she look like?" Theresa asked.

"Tight skirt. Red top—I think. Karla loaned me to Catering, so I had to clear the water glasses from the Plaza Room. I was wheeling my little cart up the hallway, and they came out of Diplomat. She opened the door and stood there, and I heard 'Blah, blah, blah, BABY!'

Then she shoved the door like Godzilla or something and stalked out. I remember thinking she would put holes in the carpet, stomping around in those spikes."

"What did the man look like?" Theresa asked, nearly holding her breath.

"White, brown hair, suit and tie. Dunno. Nothing special." Requests for further details elicited only further shrugs. Apparently the man hadn't been half as interesting as Marie's shoes.

"Where did they go after that?"

"I think she went to the elevator. The guy just stood there. I pushed my tinkling little cart away and left."

"She was knocked up," William said, but grimly. "That's what they were arguing about. That's why he killed her."

"Or he called her 'baby' and she didn't like it," Rachael suggested.

Lorraine giggled. "Yeah, he tried that—'Baby, you know I didn't mean it'—and she told him what he could do with *that*."

A breeze wafted around the curve of the deck. Theresa had not heard the heavy outer door or a single footstep, but suddenly the woman from the front desk stood there. She did not speak but swept each kid with an evil eye worthy of an old-country grandmother. Then she walked away, and one by one the now-silent kids carefully removed themselves from the scaffold and went back to work, or home, or at least they stopped discussing the internal workings of the Ritz-Carlton hotel.

"That's Karla," Rachael hissed to her mother.

"Oh, I see. She's had a hard day."

"No," Rachael said as they crowded into the elevator. "She's always like that."

Theresa left Rachael in the lobby of the medical examiner's office to be cooed over by the night receptionist and hung Marie Corrigan's clothing in the drying room. Only the blood on the shirt needed such treatment, and the light smears had already dried, but procedure had to be followed—and besides, it allowed her to get in and out in five minutes. Then she hustled Rachael back into the car so they could finally call it a day.

"So that's what it's like when a body turns up, huh?" Rachael mused as they drove up Cedar.

"That's what it's like."

"It's so . . . I don't know, disruptive. Everyone's life goes on hold. Like when there's a tornado and you have to stop what you're doing and go down in the basement."

"Yes. And also that sometimes the damage isn't immediately visible."

"At least it was a defense attorney."

There are things you won't admit, Theresa thought, *not even to yourself. And definitely not to your children.* "Don't say that."

"Mom, you hate defense attorneys."

"No I don't. Not really. Defense attorneys can some-times seem like the bane of my existence, yes. But I un-derstand them, too. I get that a lot of people—most of the people—in the criminal-justice system are not hardened, soulless monsters. They're just Joe Schmo who drove too fast because he was mad at his boss, who took too many drugs and got addicted to them, who just couldn't resist dipping his hand into the till. Do they deserve to answer for their crimes, yes, but are they a permanent danger to society, no. They need someone to advise them and walk them through the system. Serial rapists, child molesters, drug kingpins with eight executions under their belts—*they're* a permanent danger to society. Attacking *me* to get *those* people off easy, that's what I object to."

Rachael stared out the window, watching a plane land at Cleveland Hopkins as they took the narrow curve over I-480. "What do you mean, you understand them?"

Theresa braked for a slowdown at the Bagley exit. "People think I'm a ghoul because I can walk up to a brutally murdered body and not blink an eye. But I do that because I'm thinking, 'Okay, I have to photograph, then sketch, and then get out the markers, and I can't forget to take that cigarette butt and that drop of blood.' I don't want to make a mistake, because other people's lives are involved."

"Uh-huh," Rachael prompted.

"I figure it's the same way with attorneys. When they're assigned to someone who committed some awful crime, they don't have time to sit there and think about the poor victim and what sort of human being would do something like that. They think about what they have to do: find out when the arraignment will be scheduled, file a motion to suppress, interview the witnesses, meet with the prosecutor and feel out the possibility of a plea.

I can see how that very quickly becomes a habit, so that after a while the human suffering involved doesn't even register."

"*You* get bogged down in the human suffering. You went around in a fog for three days after that baby-sitter mutilated that infant last year. And the mom of that one guy is still calling you."

"Only once in a while. I make a conscious effort to remind myself of the people involved. I don't want to get to the point where I forget entirely."

"Did Marie Corrigan forget entirely?"

"You never know what's in someone else's heart," Theresa said. "But my best guess is yes, she did."

"Because she switched your fibers?"

Theresa glanced over from the driver's seat. "I told you that story, did I?"

"Over and over for about a week."

"Sorry."

"And then the guy killed someone else. Maybe he killed this lawyer, too. Or maybe the husband of his last victim."

"His last victim didn't have a husband. Her own family barely noticed she was dead. And the alleged perpetrator has been sighted in Texas."

"The prosecutor?"

"If he'd been that upset about the trial, he'd have requested a new one. He's already in private practice. The only person still upset about that case is me."

"Do you have an alibi?" Rachael teased.

"Yes. You. We were home watching *NCIS* reruns all night."

"Yeah, but I'm your daughter. You can't believe anything I'd say." The girl twirled her hair for a few moments. "I still can't believe she stole your evidence and you let her get away with it."

Theresa said, "No, some unknown entity 'misplaced' it. And there was nothing I could do."

"What about justice?"

"Sometimes justice loses."

Another silence. *This is parenting,* Theresa thought. You feel guilty when you lie to your kids and sometimes guiltier when you tell them the truth. You want them to believe in the right things but to be prepared for the reality that others don't.

Rachael said, "So now you get to be her jury. And you've reached your verdict."

The words hit Theresa like an unexpected wave, one that knocks you off your board not because it's that violent but because you didn't see it coming. She had judged Marie Corrigan's life and character and found both wanting. She would search for her killer, but only because he seemed even more depraved than his victim, not because she felt that Marie Corrigan deserved the justice she'd worked so hard to ravage. And Theresa would say nothing, only maintain her mask of righteous objectivity.

But didn't every human do that? Each person judges the next every minute of every day—people's faces, their clothes, the way they pronounce a word or discipline their children.

But then again, why shouldn't they? Minds were trained from infancy to gather information and draw conclusions from it; ignoring that information would be foolish and a bit insulting. Why shouldn't a human being observe other people's character and actions and decide from that how to deal with them, what to think of them? What was so wrong with that?

Another parenting question: Stick to the party line and insist that every life is sacred? Or tell the truth, that some are more sacred than others and some, as a measure of their character, not at all?

They were silent for another two miles. Then Theresa used a lesson she'd learned from her mother and said, "Let's talk about something more pleasant. Tell me about William. He seems nice."

With a smile and a carefully casual voice, Rachael explained that he lived in Solon, played the drums, and was so kind to everyone. "He's always willing to help Shawna unpack the toiletries, and that's not even his job. He keeps Ray company on the loading dock—another charity case of his—while he has a smoke. Ray, not William." William also had a cat and attended Bowling Green, planning to study, believe it or not, law.

"No!" Theresa cried in mock horror. "Not another friggin' lawyer!"

"Criminal law, no less. At least he'll have a steady income, getting all those scumbags back out on the street."

"Heavy sigh," Theresa said, and gave one for emphasis. Then, more seriously, "I should have him talk to Sonia. She could fill him in on things the law-school recruiters wouldn't, maybe talk him into the civil side."

"Relax," Rachael said, gathering her belongings as they pulled in to the driveway. "Maybe he'll be a prosecutor."

Theresa was about to say that that might not be an improvement for his home life, but Rachael had already run off to let the dog out. Besides, Theresa had already introduced the two kids to Sonia, and the lawyer—oddly—hadn't had much to say.

So what about this William? Nice enough, but with . . . what? An edge? An intensity? Maybe just a depth out of proportion for such a young man?

To stick with the legal theme, when it came to William, the jury was still out.

Theresa went inside to make dinner and feed the dog.

CHAPTER 8

THURSDAY

Her boss began to sing the next morning, never a good start to any day.

" 'Ding, dong, the witch is dead,' " Leo DiCiccio rang out in what might pass for a baritone under certain conditions—the trace-evidence lab of the medical examiner's office not being one of them.

"That's harsh, dude," Theresa said.

"Yeah, I can see you're all broken up about it, too. So she finally smacked the wrong ass, did she?"

Theresa spread Marie Corrigan's clothing out on the table before her, getting a better look. The red satin blouse, turned inside out, had a collar and three-quarter-length sleeves, one missing button, and four amorphous bloodstains on the back and the right shoulder. She pressed adhesive tape to the surface, picking it up and putting it down until she had done so to the entire surface. Then she turned the blouse right side out and repeated the procedure, careful to label the tapings as being from the inside or outside, front or back. "Who knows? It's a hotel. There's a ton of people there for this convention—"

"All aggressive alpha males."

Neil Kelly, waiting around for the autopsy to begin, spoke up. "That's what my partner thinks. Power junkies."

Theresa patted a piece of tape onto a sheet of clear acetate, frowning at her supervisor. "What, are we profilers now? Sure, guys from out of town, looking for some adventures where their wives can't catch them. But there are guests who aren't at the convention. There's the Tower City Mall—so who's to say someone didn't take a stroll through the Ritz, then go to the basement and catch a rapid to the airport and be out of town before anyone even found Marie's body? Then there's the substantial staff, who, incidentally, should be the only ones capable of getting into the Presidential Suite in the first place."

"'Should be' being the operative phrase," Neil said. "The hotel insists that all of their key cards are accounted for and their staff members are vetted before hire. We were there until ten o'clock last night interviewing every last one of them, and so far nobody stands out. A cook with two DUIs is the shadiest character we've found so far."

"There's got to be a way to trace those key cards, see who swiped that one last."

"We've got the computer-crimes people working on it now. But I'm not holding my breath. They're trained to look for child porn in hard drives, and the Ritz is not jumping up to hand over all their codes. What are you thinking, about that shirt?"

Theresa had been folding and scrunching the blouse in various conformations. "I was trying to see if maybe someone wadded it up with one bloody hand, or even two. I wondered yesterday but don't think that someone dried his hands on it, at least not after washing them. The blood is undiluted. But if I had to make a guess, I'd say the killer hit her first and then removed this, so blood from a wound got on it as he pulled it off."

"So he beat her to death and then undressed her?" Neil suggested. "What? You're hesitating."

"Her skull had some deep lacerations. I can't prove it, but I would think there would be more blood on this if she'd had all those injuries when it was removed. I'm guessing she had only the first one or two. Otherwise the whole back of this thing would be solid bloodstain. And he didn't unbutton it first, either."

"Don't sound very sexy, does it? Hitting her on the head before she's even got her clothes off."

"Unless that's why he hit her on the head. Because she *wouldn't* take her clothes off."

"Bingo," Neil said thoughtfully. "So we're not looking for someone she wanted to have sex with. We're looking for someone she *didn't*."

Leo snorted. "If she didn't want to have sex with him, why was she there? She said she would and then changed her mind. Nothing more likely to enrage a red-blooded male."

The phone rang, and then the department secretary told them that the pathologist wanted to begin the autopsy. Neil Kelly pushed himself off the counter he'd been leaning against and asked Theresa if she would be attending.

"I'll be right there. Just want to package these tapings first."

The detective left with the slightest air of reluctance.

"I think he wants you to hold his hand," Leo said.

Theresa placed the sheet of acetate under the stereomicroscope. "I'm not catching him if he faints. I've got a nerve under my shoulder blade that still hurts from the last time I got in the way of a weak-kneed detective."

"He likes you."

"Not you, too."

Leo chuckled and shuffled away, now humming "If I Only Had a Brain."

Under her breath Theresa muttered, "If only."

Between the rows of overhead lights and the tiled walls and floors, washed down at the end of every day, the autopsy room was the brightest, cleanest room in the building. And, as the dieners could go home when the day's cutting had been completed, whether that was sooner or later, the most efficient. The assistants had no reason to lollygag and every reason not to. Plastic jars were labeled, flesh cut open, tables hosed down with the highest possible proficiency.

At the center of this pool of dispassionate science, Marie Corrigan lay on a steel table with gutters at its sides to drain away her blood, her vitality, her beauty, and her malice. And she had had plenty of all three. Even in the courtroom, constrained on all sides by laws and traditions and unwritten rules of conduct, Marie Corrigan had lit up the air like a fallen high-tension wire, throwing out sparks with unpredictable abandon. And you never knew when that wire might twist in your direction.

Only four weeks earlier, Marie had demanded to know why England and Germany and Australia and "every other civilized country on the planet" required a set number of points of minutiae—the spots in a fingerprint pattern where the ridges end and divide—and the United States did not. No one had seen her client shoot the store owner into a coma, the gun had never been found, and a mother couldn't recognize her only child from what passed as the surveillance video. Only an impression of the suspect's index finger on the store owner's glasses, which he had pulled off before delivering a 9-millimeter bullet to the man's chest, tied her client to the scene. Marie had to destroy that print.

Theresa had explained that other countries required points as a convenience, that was all. Reducing quality-control measures to a number made everyday life much simpler, but those numbers did not have any scientific significance. Ten points were not necessarily better than eight, or twelve better than both. "It's like being pregnant," Theresa had said. "You're not more pregnant at six months than you are at three. You might be more noticeable, but you're not more pregnant. You either are or you aren't." Marie Corrigan had glared at her from in front of the jury box, pacing up and back, distracting the jury from the testimony with her raven-black hair and her exquisite suit, wrapped around her impressive body as if it longed for her touch.

"Examiners in the United States use eight as a standard, though, even though they won't admit it. Don't they?"

"Traditionally it was a rule of thumb. But the number still doesn't confer any special significance on the match."

"And Great Britain uses thirty-six?" Marie went on, giving a look of surprised alarm to the jury and repeating the number for emphasis.

"Never," Theresa said. "They used to use sixteen, and they stopped that in 2001. Now they have no set number required for an identification, just like the United States."

An obscure factoid that the jury surely didn't care about. They seemed much more interested in the defense lawyer's style than in the equally obscure objection she'd invented. The men wanted to possess her, and the women wanted to be her. Most anyway. One portly middle-aged housewife in an ill-fitting cotton blazer peered at Marie through eyes narrowed to slits.

Marie, however, cared very much about this obscure factoid, both because it worked against her case and because she hadn't known it. In revenge she kept Theresa on the stand another fifteen minutes with a list of renowned experts who had written in protest of a single-fingerprint conviction. Unfortunately, none of her experts were fingerprint analysts and all were defense attorneys. As Theresa stepped down from the stand, Marie Corrigan stood back and gave her a long, ultimately pitying look, from Theresa's few graying strands down to her Payless shoe-store pumps.

Marie Corrigan had been a bitch, pure and simple. And she'd been bloody good at it—and therein lay the tiny hint of admiration Theresa could never help but feel for a woman with power. She might despise that woman but would always be too honest not to admit that to walk into a room and command the attention of everyone there, to risk their ire, to risk their challenge, to refuse to be the good girl, that took a certain type of courage. And Theresa always admired courage.

All the same, when she now gazed at the pale, still form on the steel gurney, she felt absolutely nothing. Certainly nothing like regret, or even pity.

"So girlfriend didn't have a good day yesterday, eh?" The pathologist interrupted her thoughts. Christine Johnson, tall and black and brilliant and blunt enough to take on Sonia Battle in a cage fight—now, *that* would be an interesting encounter, Theresa thought, and vowed to get the two together for lunch one day—raised one eyebrow at Theresa as if she might be at least partially responsible.

"She was dead when I got there," Theresa protested.

"Besides, I think it may have been the night before last. What do you think?"

Detective Kelly watched the body, his face stony, only the deep swallowing motion of his Adam's apple betraying his discomfort. Some people never got used to it. Theresa knew guys who had been Homicide detectives for twenty years and still turned green at the sight of a body. But they dealt, as Neil was dealing. At least he hadn't turned completely pale—yet. She'd meant what she said about not catching him.

Christine prodded the lividity, checked the intake sheet for the core temperature at reception, and poked around one eyeball. "I'd say you're probably right. Where's the ligature?"

Theresa held up the paper bag containing the cut pair of nylons. "SuperSheer, size B, so I'd say they were hers. Unless she likes to go the fashionable bare-legs approach."

"I doubt it, not with these veins. How does someone who looks like her have varicose problems?"

"Standing in front of a jury all day in three-inch heels," Theresa guessed. She took another look at Marie Corrigan. Like the detective, she'd trained herself to view another person's nakedness quickly and thoroughly, to think of it as just skin, epidermis, a double layer of lipid molecules, and a canvas on which the killer might have left his mark. The woman's breasts still perked upright, the surest sign that they were fake, but Marie had somehow resisted the tattoo craze. No other injuries or bruises had come to light, no defensive wounds on the small hands. Theresa saw nothing new, and the diener began to wash away anything that might have remained.

She asked Christine, "Did you ever have a case with her?"

"Did I. Once she wanted me to agree that the damage

to an eighteen-month-old's genitals could have been a birth defect. Another time she sneered at my med-school credentials and told the jury I'd graduated fourth-last in my class."

Theresa worded her response carefully. "Somehow I suspect that's not true."

The doctor nearly pinned her to the other steel table with one scalpel-sharp glance. "You *suspect*?"

Theresa thought fast. "How did she make such a mistake?"

"Two Christine Johnsons. Somehow she didn't notice the one on the list noted 'valedictorian.' The point is, she went and looked that up, because she had no other way to attack my testimony."

"Yeah." Neil Kelly spoke up. "That'd be her."

"So what's your story?" Theresa asked him.

"What? How did I get to be a cop or how did I draw the short straw to land this case? If the former, I'm a cop because my dad, my uncle, and my older brother were all cops, and I guess I lack the imagination to break away from the pack. If the latter, because my partner had the bad sense to pick up his phone when it rang."

Theresa laughed. "No, your Marie story. Anything more recent than her police-brutality complaint?"

The spark left his eyes faster than a cigarette tossed into the lake fizzled out. "No."

Things we won't admit, even to ourselves. Theresa let it go and instead watched Christine hover over the back of Marie Corrigan's ravaged skull, cleaning the wounds, having a photograph taken, then a photograph with a scale. Then she sketched, shaved the hair away, cleaned again, had it photographed again. The straight black locks that Marie Corrigan liked to swirl around her shoulders as she mesmerized those in the jury box were tossed into a large red-lined box to be burned in a biohazard incinerator.

Christine pressed the shaved areas with two firm fingers. This produced a creaking sound almost like crumpled cellophane. "We have at least four blows here that split the skin and cracked the bone underneath, and I think one or two that only bruised."

Christine's assistant took a stainless-steel scalpel, installed a fresh blade, and, without ceremony, cut Marie Corrigan open from her shoulders to her belly button. A smell of blood and offal filled the air; it was like being in a room full of raw meat—not horrible, but certainly not pleasant.

A second circuit of activity commenced in the other half of the room as a second team unloaded a car-accident victim with one mangled leg onto the next table.

Neil Kelly paled.

Theresa tried to distract him with a preliminary report of what she'd found on Marie Corrigan's clothing. "Some fibers, gray wool, black spandex, pink synthetic, tan stuff that probably matches the rug, and the ubiquitous white cotton. The hair caught in the knot of the nylons is brown and has something on it."

" 'Something'?"

"A light coating of some sort of hair product, like gel. There's also some globules sticking to the black spandex. I'm guessing wax. Then there's two cat hairs, one gray, one tan. Did she have a cat? Did you go to her apartment?"

"We were there most of the night." He sucked in only as many cautious, shallow breaths as necessary.

Christine pulled out the saline bags that had so enhanced the victim's figure and set them aside so a note could be made of the serial numbers.

"She didn't have so much as a goldfish. A lot of clothes, nothing in the fridge except vodka and diet pop, and a collection of DVDs."

"What kind of DVDs?"

"Chick flicks, believe it or not. I mean . . . uh," he stammered as both women glanced at him. "I mean, things like *Sleepless in Seattle* and *Nights in Rodanthe*."

Theresa said, "Don't tell me our girl Marie was a closet romantic."

"Apparently so. They seem to be the only things in her closet. We didn't find any bondage porn, no dominatrix outfits in the closet, no bullwhips next to her thong underwear. Not even a little black book."

"E-mail contacts?"

"Tons of people, but no way to distinguish acquaintances from family from very special friends. No salacious e-mails, no threats. Work, meetings, and fashion consultations with her sister in Wichita. If she had secrets, she didn't put them in writing."

"Cell-phone directory?"

"No phone. We found her purse, which was in her car, which was in the Tower City garage. Locked, apparently unmolested, and badly overdue for an oil change. The care she put into her appearance did not extend to her vehicle. No home phone."

Theresa pondered this as she watched Christine remove the liver and slice it into sections, using what looked like a bread knife.

"Lungs were good," the doctor reported. "Liver might have given her problems in another twenty years."

"Vodka," Neil said solemnly.

And little else in her apartment. "So maybe her boyfriend came up with the bondage idea. She didn't cooperate, he gets mad, hits her, then figures he might as well finish the job."

"You know what else we didn't find?" Neil went on. "Work. Files, briefs, affidavits. What kind of lawyer

doesn't have thirty pounds of paper with them everywhere they go?"

"She kept work and home separated?" Theresa suggested. "Lord knows I do. Not only because of Rachael,
but because I'm not allowed to take anything out of the
building. It's all confidential."

"According to everyone up to and including her land-
lady, she only cared about two things: trying cases and
screwing guys. And she doesn't bring any work home
with her? No, one of her colleagues got to her place
before we did and cleaned it out. Her desk had only
some scraps of paper, a lot of dust, and two speakers
that should have been plugged into a laptop. They took
it back to the illustrious firm of Goldman & Jackson,
Esquires, and when Powell and I showed up there this
morning, they wouldn't admit it and wouldn't let us in
to her office. Attorney-client privilege."

"You must have expected that."

"We did. But what do you do when someone's offed?
You round up the usual suspects, who they slept with,
who owed them money, who should have gotten their
promotion. That law firm was her life. How are we supposed to find those suspects when they've put her life in
a file drawer and locked it?"

Theresa sighed with him.

"Powell is still there. They said they'd let him in after
they removed all the open case files. I'm betting he'll find
two paper clips and a pad of blank Post-it notes."

Christine moved back to the body. "Nice teeth. Somebody used bleaching agents until she could signal the
Ninth Fleet." Then she left the diener to work on the
larynx while she took the stomach and opened it up on
the polyethylene cutting board. Empty, which did not
come as a surprise.

"She should have gone to Michael Symon's place,"

Theresa said. "She'd probably still be alive, or at least have had a great last meal. What? Christine, you're *hmm*-ing."

"Lesions in her esophagus. She must have had some stomach troubles—acid reflux or an ulcer. Defending a bunch of scumbags for a living would give *me* an ulcer."

Theresa remembered what Sonia had said. "Could it be bulimia?"

"Possibly. She's a little underweight."

"That would fit with the white teeth. Don't their teeth usually turn yellow from all the vomiting? She would have to bleach them."

"Possibly. Or she wanted to look like a toothpaste model in front of the jury. Who knows?" The pathologist removed the uterus, which always looked so much smaller than Theresa expected it to, a smooth, dense-looking little sac.

Neil Kelly frowned at it as if he were not quite sure what it was but sure as hell wasn't going to ask, and said, "Corrigan's assistant told us of a few threats she's received over the years. She got some juvenile off for killing a girl in his class, and the girl's mother left her nasty messages for months. She defended the guy who shot the pizza-delivery guy and got a pile of hate mail on that one, mostly from the victim's grandmother, even though the guy pled and got life without parole anyway. Then the black lobby filed an ethics complaint with the board when she got that redneck a reduced sentence after he beat that college football player into a coma. And supposedly the New Nazis put a price on her head for getting a homeboy off with time served after he held up their treasurer and helped himself to a year's dues. Go ahead and snicker. I did.

"But these are all a year or two old," he went on.

"That's why the assistant could discuss them—those cases are resolved. I said I need to know who's threatening her *today*. She said she couldn't help me. Privileged. I think she used the word 'privileged' fifteen times in three minutes."

"It's true," Theresa pointed out.

"It's also gonna keep us from wrapping this up."

"Uterus is normal," Christine announced to no one in particular.

"Can you tell if she was raped?" the detective asked.

"No—meaning no, I can't tell. There's no sign of injury."

"Was she pregnant?"

"No."

"She ever have a child?" he persisted.

"I'd say no."

Theresa turned to Neil Kelly. "Why do you ask?"

"I always ask."

When he said nothing more, she did. "Speaking of romance—"

"What's romantic about babies?" Christine interrupted. "Puking up formula, screaming all night. Romance? Hah."

Theresa said, "That's a bit . . . um, vociferous. Is there something you want to talk about?"

"I'm just saying. Nothing romantic about babies."

"Making them?" Neil suggested.

Theresa said, "I heard she was dating Dennis Britton."

Neil nodded. "Yeah, we heard that, too. Unfortunately, he's about the only one at that whole convention with something like an alibi. He, the convention organizers, and the keynote speaker—the upper tier of the group—"

Theresa nodded. She'd been to conventions and knew how it went. Throw together a large group of people

who'd never met and they would instantly sort themselves out into a decreasing gradient of prestige.

"They adjourned to the bar after the last session, then
adjourned to Morton's steak house. Don't ask me who
picked up the bill. I'm sure that's privileged, too. From
there they adjourned to the House of Blues, but the mu-
sic was too loud, and eventually they had to face the
fact that none of them are thirty and hip anymore, so
they adjourned once again, this time over to the Crazy
Horse, where for a fee the girls would pretend they *were*
thirty and hip. Three other guys dropped Britton off at
his house in Gates Mills, where I'm betting the missus
will vouch for the rest of the night."

"Maybe not, if she finds out about him and Marie."

Neil raised his voice to be heard over the bone saw
at the next table. "Married to a guy like Britton? She
knows. Or she's brain-dead, one or the other."

Christine and the diener flipped the body over so
he could slice open the scalp. Neil Kelly's color had
returned—after the first few organs are removed, it's
not so bad—but now he winced. Again Theresa tried to
help. "I forgot to tell you, I looked at the swabs I took
yesterday. No sperm."

He made a visible attempt to focus on her words and
not on the way the diener used a small scraper to peel the
flesh off the damaged cranium. "Yeah? None?"

"None on the oral, vaginal, anal swabs, or her panties. Nothing. Don will run the DNA, see if we get a mix-
ture of epithelial cells. That's all we can do."

"So he knocks her on the head and ties her up in order
to do what he wants, and then doesn't do it," Neil mused.

"Or never intended to. He only wanted to kill her and
staged the sex part to throw us off."

"But if sex isn't part of the equation, why'd she go
there with him in the first place?"

"The only other thing she cared about," Theresa reminded him. "A case."

Christine blotted the broken skull with a towel, then said, "Impressive. He did this with a chair? On a carpeted floor?"

"Nice thick carpet, too," Theresa told her.

"That was one angry dude." The doctor pointed out the individual blows and how two of them had crushed the bone into small pieces. Two more had caused hairline fractures and two a deep bruise. "You'd have the weight of the chair working for you but the cushion of the carpet working against you."

"Did the blow kill her?" Theresa asked, ignoring Neil Kelly's snort at this question. Often the secondary effects of a blow to the head—blood loss, internal bleeding that put pressure on the brain, damage to the cerebellum—were what actually snuffed out the last hope of life. "There could have been a lot more blood under the body. I think her heart didn't pump too long after the blows."

"Pieces of broken bone penetrated her brain, where they most likely cut off the nerve system that tells the heart to beat and lungs to breathe. Then she died," Christine said.

All three were silent for a moment, watching the photographer document the damage. She took a myriad of photos—of the skull, the macerated brain under the skull, the skull pieces themselves once removed to the plastic "gray board"—all with a small metric ruler next to the significant area. Theresa wondered if the killer had waited, checked Marie Corrigan's pulse to be sure she'd died, or if he'd stumbled away, frightened by his own violence.

It probably depended on whether he'd gone there to love her or kill her.

CHAPTER 9

Theresa found the toxicologist in open territory for a change. For the most part, Oliver seemed such a fixture in his corner of the tox lab that she found it hard to believe he even had a home to go to. She knew of no evidence to suggest he ever left the lab, save for court appearances, mandatory meetings, and lunch. Today proved no exception.

"Do you suppose this room has ever been cleaned?" he demanded of Theresa as he covered the cracked Formica of an ancient table with paper towels. "Since construction, I mean?"

The lunchroom's decor marched in step with that of the rest of the building. The walls were a dirtied cream color, and the linoleum had never been stylish even when new. Amenities consisted of two noisy machines that dispensed cans of pop only when in the proper mood, a microwave, and a set of largely empty cabinets grouped around a stained sink. Light on atmosphere, but functional.

"The floor is mopped regularly. Otherwise people are supposed to clean up after themselves," Theresa replied.

"And therein lies the rub. Such an expectation is naïve at best and, in a building crawling with diseases and carcinogens, fatal at worst."

"I've been here ten years," she said. "I haven't developed any loathsome disease yet."

"That you know of." He flicked his scrawny ponytail over one heavy shoulder and unwrapped a sandwich at least four inches thick, containing turkey and salami and tomatoes and who knew what else, keeping the plastic wrap around the bread and its contents. This wasn't lunch, of course, not at 10:00 A.M. Merely a midmorning snack. "What do you want?"

"I wanted to know if the vaginal swab I sent you showed any sort of lubricant or spermicide. You know, stuff that would be on a condom."

"No little swimmers for you to dissect?"

"None."

"Just as well." Oliver took a huge bite, then barely paused to chew before adding, "If you do catch the guy, the city will throw him a parade anyway."

"Be that as it may, I still want to dot my i's."

"Your little FTIR couldn't tell you?" Oliver felt his mass spectrometer to be the vastly superior instrument. "Oh, that's right, it can't do anything with organic compounds, can it?"

"I wouldn't say not *anything*. . . ." Theresa couldn't help protesting, but Oliver decided that he would rather give his sandwich his full attention than spar with her. She waited patiently through another two bites and resolved to send him the globules she'd found sticking to Marie's skirt fibers.

Then he seemed to notice her presence anew and said, "None."

"No such compounds found in her?" Theresa clarified. He snorted, which apparently caused a piece of turkey to skirt the epiglottis. A cough turned into a choke, and his face turned from its usual color of rising dough to a more alarming puce. Theresa thought she might have to attempt a Heimlich maneuver and sincerely hoped not, since that would place her too close to Oliver's less-than-hygienic flesh. But then he hacked, swallowed, and sucked in air, sparing them both an unwanted intimacy.

She waited until his breathing and hue returned to normal to ask after his condition, which he ignored and said, "Nothing man-made inside her womanly chamber. A temporary situation, I'm sure. She excelled in making the butterflies in every male's gonads twirl up a little hurricane."

"But not you, huh?"

"A stupid bimbo like that? I should think not."

"That's a rather strong statement." Oliver didn't usually *call* anyone stupid, only allowed his attitude and phrasing to make it clear he felt that to be the case.

"Do I make weak ones? I *liked* testifying in front of her. She at least put some effort into her job, despite the fact that the woman couldn't even pronounce 'dimethyloxybutarate.' And she thought she'd trip me up in that last DUI case? Ha."

"Ha indeed. And your admiration had nothing to do with the open-throated blouse and the tight skirt?"

"Nothing whatsoever. I am a *scientist*."

"Glad to hear it. Gotta go," Theresa added as her phone popped up with a text message: PC LL—the trace-lab secretary's code for "phone call, landline." Theresa hustled across the hall to pick up.

"Did you see the news last night?" a stressed-out voice nearly shouted in her ear.

"Sonia?"

"They announced to the world that Marie was found stripped and hog-tied. Tell me everyone in the city is not getting their rocks off on that image right now."

"Sonia, no, I didn't see the news, but you have to assume they're going to lead with the most salacious detail—wait, how did they know that?"

"All the lawyers knew, and I'm sure it went through the cops like wildfire. Most of whom are men."

"So are the lawyers!" Theresa pointed out.

"I'm sure it was the first thing out of your detectives' mouths when Channel 15 called."

"I'm sure it wasn't. It would have been a handy way to weed out any crackpot confessions from the real thing. You have to stop taking this so personally, Sonia. The inevitable gloating over Marie's death is not an attack on all defense attorneys. It's an attack on Marie. She was aggressive and abrasive—"

"So am I."

Theresa sat down, closed her eyes. "You are a hard worker and mount a vigorous defense. Marie chose to be a lying manipulator. People would not feel the same way about you if you were murdered."

"They would. Have you seen the forums?"

"The what?"

"The comments that people post at the end of the *Plain Dealer* story. Go to Cleveland.com."

"Oh, for the love of chocolate, Sonia, you're not reading *those*? They'll make you want to go home and lock your doors and avoid all human contact, even when the topic is as innocuous as flowers outside city hall or the proper way to install a mailbox. *Never* read forums." Theresa could only imagine the comments.

"The most understated one, with the fewest spelling errors, quotes Shakespeare's *Henry VI*."

"Let me guess: 'The first thing we do, let's kill all the lawyers.'"

"Yes—which was only suggested by the character so that their rebellion would succeed without anyone there to support the law."

"A rebellion against an oppressive, serfdom-supporting regime. I would think you'd be on the peasants' side in that fight."

Sonia pointedly ignored that aspect of the English king's reign and went on to read entries that curled Theresa's hair and surely violated several communications statutes. Several people had written in to say that the person who'd attacked them, stolen their money, even shot them still walked the streets because of one Marie Corrigan. Victims claimed that the woman had convinced juries that *they'd* been the ones at fault. Marie had been called every designation *except* attorney, including, by one particularly wordy participant, "a filthy, wretched creature driven by twisted, power-mad impulses, who ground the suffering of others beneath her heel in order to buy designer shoes."

Theresa stifled a snicker over that one in deference to her friend as she accessed the Internet.

"No one points out that she raised money for the United Way or that she mentored with the female law students' organization at Cleveland State every year since graduation. *I* don't even do that."

Good Lord, was all Theresa could think. She'd warped young minds—rather, trained more people to be like her? "Again, Sonia, you have to let this go. Marie would not have asked you to be her champion, and she's beyond all this vitriol anyway. Save your crusading for someone who needs it."

The attorney sighed, the long breath rushing through the phone receiver like an electronic tsunami. "All right,

I'll try. It's just so hard being surrounded by a bunch of Neanderthals who spent their time picturing Marie naked anyway. Now they have an excuse."

Theresa skimmed the forum posts. "Here's a nice one." She read a short note by a former client who said that Marie had saved him from jail on a "totally bogus" possession charge. This led to other commentators' opinions on the bigoted and oppressive nature of the police and from there into a flame war between the law-and-order types versus those in the mean streets. Theresa clicked on the X in the upper-right-hand corner.

The one note of confidence did little to cheer Sonia. "Must be some rich white boy. None of my clients would use such an embarrassingly outdated term as 'bogus.'"

"No 'bogus'? Denied!"

"Besides, most of Marie's current clients are rich. She wanted to be a lawyer to the stars, and I guess she made it."

Yeah, Theresa thought, by riding Dennis Britton's coattails and her own short skirts. But she kept that opinion to herself, having picked up the wistful tone in Sonia's words. Who *didn't* want to be beautiful, sexy, and outrageously successful? Provided, of course, that you didn't think about the cost.

Sonia grumbled on. "No one mentions how she'd go on her own time to talk to inner-city high-school classes about working hard and following your dreams. She didn't come from money, you know. Everything she achieved, she had to fight for. Look, I have to go. The first session is about to start."

Glad to steer Sonia's attention to any subject other than Marie Corrigan, Theresa said, "Yeah? What's it about?"

"Impeaching expert . . . um . . . witnesses."

"Wow. Learning how to circumvent pesky people like me, huh?"

"Yeah, well, not exactly." A pause. "I mean, I'm not *attending* the session. . . . I'm teaching it."

Another pause. Then Theresa said, "Okay, well, when I'm speaking to you again, there's something I want to talk to you about."

"Oh, relax. I don't talk about forensic experts— much. Mostly just psychologists."

Another pause. "Okay, well, when I'm speaking to you again, I want you to tell me why you got so quiet last night."

"I wasn't," she said, with such a lack of conviction that Theresa scented blood and pursued.

"What do you think of Rachael's friend William?"

Another pause, a longer one. "Nice kid, I'm sure. I have to go."

"Sonia! What is *up* with you?"

"Really, it's about to start, I'm heading for the podium now, and I have to get my PowerPoint loaded. Talk to you later."

Click.

Theresa stared at the receiver for a moment before replacing it in its cradle, then continued to stare, ignoring the blinding summer sun through the lab windows and the fact that Leo had approached with a stack of blue-covered case reports, no doubt marked up with his red pen so he could be seen to be doing his job, and now stood tapping one foot.

I don't like this. I don't like this at all.

She picked up the phone again and dialed her cousin. Leo dumped the stack on her desk and walked away.

Frank said, "Just so we're clear on this, you don't want Rachael to know?"

"She'd probably never speak to me again. One year of

college under her belt, but she's still in that teenage 'I'm an adult with a right to privacy, and you have to respect limits la-di-da' stage. And it's all a matter of public record, right? It's not like I'm spying on the kid."

"All right, I'm looking." She could hear him tapping keys. "William Rosedale. Got four of them. Dates of birth: '63."

"No."

"How about '58?"

"No."

"Or '93?"

"Maybe."

"Rachael's dating a black kid?"

"No, white. And she's not dating him, not yet."

"Then what's your problem?"

"I can tell when she's interested and when she's really interested. And when a public defender clams up around him and then won't even deny it, I get worried." Theresa had lived with Sonia for three years and knew her every mood. Whenever she was less than voluble, that meant uncertainty, fear, or worry. Which, in turn, worried Theresa.

"Last one's '99. Too young to interest Rachael. So no matches—that's good, right?"

Theresa drummed her fingers on the Sirchie catalog. "Maybe not. Sonia does mostly juvenile cases."

"What is *up* with that bitch anyway?"

"Don't call her that. Ever."

"Look, I can understand an us-versus-them mentality, but she goes way overboard."

"Sonia has her reasons."

"Yeah, you said there was some history with her brother. Is it reason enough to be completely unreasonable?"

Theresa fiddled with the plaque on her desk that

read NON ILLEGITIMI CARBORUNDUM—faux Latin for
"Don't let the bastards grind you down"—and debated
briefly with herself. Then she said, "When Sonia was in
high school, her dad split. Sonia's older brother, unsur-
prisingly, began to act out."

"Let me guess. He was a good kid, just fell in with
the wrong crowd." Every parent's stock answer. Theresa
and Frank had heard it so many times they could recite
it in their sleep. No parents ever wanted to face the fact
that their kid *was* the wrong crowd.

"More or less. He and some buddies stole beer and
cigarettes from a 7-Eleven, flashed a gun at the clerk,
and ran out the door, tripping over two patrolmen who
had stopped for coffee. There's a scuffle, and her brother
got a billy club in his left eye."

"He lose the eye?"

"Yep. Then he got a judge who wanted to teach these
boys a lesson and put them in adult lockup. Her brother
was a naïve eighteen-year-old with one eye and didn't
last long. He hung himself after three weeks."

"Tragic," Frank said, and she knew he meant it to a
certain extent. "So this is the fault of all cops?"

"She figures her brother got a death sentence for
stealing beer."

"It was armed robbery, not joyriding in Daddy's car.
What she sees as youthful high jinks looks to me like the
first act of a budding career criminal."

"I hear you. But according to her, she's seen the same
story a million times since. She spends most of her time
trying to get her clients into drug programs and halfway
houses and places that might actually help them become
more productive citizens, and she's stymied at every
point by cops, prosecutors, and judges who think these
kids are incorrigible and worthless. Yes, some are, but

she figures she has to try—for the sake of the few who aren't and for the sake of the taxpayers who have to pay for all these trials and jails."

"My heart bleeds. You want frustration? Try arresting the same guy for assaulting every girl he dates over and over because his charges get pled down to nothing. You want a sob story? The last woman that got mixed up with him lost her baby."

"I know, hon," she sympathized. "You're preachin' to the choir here, and I know the answer is that there is no easy answer. But it broke something inside Sonia that's never healed. She would still cry in her sleep sometimes, five, six, seven years later. But look, back to William Rosedale. Would juvenile records show up on your database?"

"No. I can't get into them without a reason. Have to protect those sweet children's rights."

"What kind of a reason do you have to have?"

"There's a variety, but my niece sorta kinda liking this boy at work is not one of them."

Theresa examined the sense of urgency she felt, trying to decide if she was a paranoid or a simply conscientious mother. Unfortunately, the paranoid explanation seemed to have more going for it. "Isn't there anything else you can do, without getting in trouble?"

"You make it sound like my boss will send me to the principal's office. I'm a cop. We *live* to get in trouble. Just get some more information out of your lawyer friend so I can figure out where to look."

"I'll try, but— Damn, my phone's ringing. Can you hang on a minute?"

"Only a minute."

Theresa flicked open her Nextel. "This is Kelly," the cop said without preamble, "and you're not going to believe this."

"Okay, I promise I won't believe it."

Her humor went unappreciated, or perhaps unregistered. The words tumbled from him as if personally painful. "We've got another one. Another freakin' dead lawyer."

CHAPTER 10

The lobby of the Ritz, true to the genteel, blue-blooded roots from whence Theresa imagined it sprang, had not changed much in the past twenty-four hours despite having had two murders in about that same period. Rachael continued to hand out room keys with only a shadow of tension behind her bright smile, the older lady in the pink sweater accepted another Bloody Mary from a waiter who didn't look old enough to serve it, and Sonia crossed the elegant carpet clearly ready to embody her last name.

"They're killing us, Theresa," she began, as if laying out her argument before this jury of one. "Someone's declared war on defense attorneys. Yesterday that would have sounded completely insane to me, but after seeing the response to Marie's death I believe it absolutely. The news, the paper, things I hear on the rapid transit—people don't hate al-Qaeda as much as they hate us. Surfer Girl even started leaving death threats on my answering machine again."

Theresa wanted to offer sympathy; she could see how upset Sonia felt in the way she obviously hadn't combed her hair since early that morning, hadn't noticed a large run on the inside of her left calf, and her blouse, never well tucked into her conservative skirt, hung in a lopsided pouf. But when Theresa opened her mouth, all she could think to say was, "Why do you call her Surfer Girl?"

This distracted Sonia, but only momentarily. "Because I happened to notice her surf-shop T-shirt in the split second before she punched me in the mouth. Why?"

Theresa shifted her grip on the equipment she carried in both hands. "Just wondering. How are you doing?"

"They're killing us off—how do you think I'm doing?" Sonia gave her a piercing glance that moved her right from the jury box to the witness stand. "You've heard about Bruce?"

"Is that the guy they just found?"

"Yeah. Your two cop buddies are up there now, I think dancing a jig over his body."

Enough. "That's unreasonable, Sonia. They were doing everything possible to investigate Marie's death—with, I might add, no cooperation at all from her office—and those cops are the ones who will be up most of the night again tonight to find this new guy's killer while you're in bed dreaming up ways to make them look like idiots on the stand."

Sonia had the grace to flush, a faint rose that spread to the roots of her lank blond hair.

"And who's Bruce?" Theresa demanded.

"Bruce Raffel. He's the one whose body they just found. He's from Atlanta, but—"

"Don't tell me you know him, too."

"Sort of."

"Theresa!" Neil Kelly appeared at her elbow. "Body's upstairs."

"Okay. Sonia—"

He added, "The hotel doesn't want us hanging in the lobby. They're worried we might scare the guests."

Theresa popped Sonia's cell phone from the plastic clip at her waist.

"Hey!"

"This is my number I'm putting in here, missy. I want you to call me before you go home for the day. I need to talk to you."

Neil looked at her in alarm. "You're not discussing the case with—"

"Who? The enemy?" Sonia snapped.

"Not the case," Theresa said over them, and then, with a glance at Rachael thirty feet away, "about William Rosedale."

The flush left Sonia Battle's face.

Theresa followed Neil Kelly to the elevator bank, shifting her crime-scene kit to her other hand. She would probably need more equipment out of her car before she finished, and she'd have to rouse the fresh-faced valet to bring it around for her for yet another fee. The county would not be happy with the expenses, but what could she do? The traffic cops wouldn't let her park it on Public Square. Neil jammed his finger into the "up" button with a violent snap; exhaustion had probably set in.

"Who's William Rosedale?" he asked as soon as the doors closed.

"Personal matter. Who's Bruce Raffel?"

Neil paused just a beat before responding, no doubt debating whether to push her to define "personal." Sometimes cops got a little too accustomed to interrogating witnesses and felt free to ask anyone about anything. Lord knows Frank did. But then part of that was due to their having grown up together, and an even larger part due to Frank being Frank.

Neil apparently—and wisely—decided to err on the side of caution, swallowing his curiosity with a heavy gulp. "Victim number two. Defense lawyer from the firm of Jones, Klein and Washington in Atlanta. Thirty-six, divorced, two children, checked in Tuesday. At least there's no mystery about how he got into the room."

The elevator car stopped on the fourteenth floor. "Why not?"

"It's his. Standard king, no smoking, single, paid for by a credit card issued to Jones, Klein and Washington. Can I carry something for you?"

She handed him her ALS and stopped asking questions, preferring to see the rest for herself. They emerged into the hallway. It stood empty except for the bland but tastefully framed artwork on the walls and, she could swear, the same two cops who'd stood guard outside Marie Corrigan's room. After they recorded her name on the contamination list, she donned two Tyvek booties and went through the door Neil held for her. She tried to observe everything around her as she went but really saw only the dead man's knees, protruding from the other side of the bed and pointing their empty faces at the TV set.

She drew closer, careful to check the carpeting beneath each step before placing her foot, until she reached the far corner of the bed.

In the space between the bed and the deeply burnished end table next to the window, a man lay facedown, his hands and feet tied together behind his back with what looked like a black dress sock. No other clothing interrupted the expanse of naked skin. His head had taken more than one blow, and dried blood seeped through the carpet underneath it.

"Wow," Theresa said.

"Not exactly my response, but I know what you mean," Neil said.

"Some sort of sex club gone wrong?" Theresa said aloud. "Or maybe Sonia's right."

"Right about what?"

"Someone's declared war."

The battered body of Bruce Raffel had been discovered by an already nervous maid at approximately nine-thirty that morning. She had knocked, announced herself, received no answer, and entered. After seeing the body, she'd screamed, caught her breath, screamed again, screamed a third time and maybe a fourth (she lost count), and run out. She assumed the door had shut behind her but couldn't be sure. She hit the button for the elevator, decided she didn't want to be stuck in one with a homicidal maniac in the event he got in on another floor and found an unarmed maid waiting to be murdered, so she ran to the stairwell. One look down fourteen flights of dingy, isolated concrete steps and she changed her mind about the elevator, returning to it just as the bell dinged and the doors opened. Inside were an elderly man and his equally elderly wife, in town from Phoenix to visit their daughter, and by the time the car reached the lobby they were as agitated as the maid by her hysterical and largely incoherent tale. Upon entering the lobby, she shrieked at the desk clerks until they summoned the unlucky day manager. The maid informed her of the situation and, almost in the same breath, of her intention to quit just as soon as they could cut her a check to include that morning's hours. From there she went directly to her locker. By the time the cops arrived, she had all her belongings stowed in a cardboard box that had once held frozen fries and had decided not to wait for the check.

Bruce Raffel's body was cold, Theresa observed, the

purplish lividity on his dorsal surface fixed. She guessed he'd been dead since the evening before. The bed appeared to have been slept in, covers rumpled and shoved completely to the opposite side; half of the heavy comforter rested on the floor. Theresa could see a few dark hairs—possibly the victim's—scattered on the snow-white sheets. Small blotches of dried blood, the castoff of several blows, traveled upward across the side of the bed. The weapon of choice, again, was the desk chair, a straight-backed wooden job with a seat cushioned in beige tapestry-look canvas. Perhaps Bruce Raffel had not been as hardheaded as Marie Corrigan, or maybe the killer grew weary—Theresa could see only three distinct gashes in the man's scalp. The black hair had already begun to thin; in another few years he would have worried about how to hide his bald spot from the jury. With his head turned slightly toward the window, Theresa could see that he had small brown eyes, fleshy cheeks, and did not go in for the five-o'clock shadow currently considered fashionable. He had shaved closely enough to nick his chin in two places.

His limbs had been bound by a pair of socks, she could now see—one had been knotted around his wrists and then the other looped through it to truss up the ankles. He wore no rings, only nails bitten to the quick and a few ink stains. Bruce Raffel had been taking notes in the past day or two, trying to get the most out of the conference.

Theresa straightened and looked around. Raffel had used the desk as a luggage rack, and clothes spilled out of the leather bag. One of the water glasses had been used and still had water in it—she would swab that for DNA. The plastic laundry bag sat on the floor next to the desk but seemed to hold only two pairs of socks and two pairs of cotton boxers, size XL, with the logo of some sports team Theresa didn't recognize. Not surprising, of course—there were only a few team logos she *would* recognize, all of them based in Cleveland.

Next to the bed, a man's watch and wallet and forty-two cents in change had been left on top of a *Cleveland* magazine, the watch carefully on its back, strap stretched out. Next to it sat a framed picture of two young boys, one behind the other on the back of a Jet Ski too big for them. One trail of cast-off blood had gone by the photo, and the blue water and sky were speckled with tiny red dots. Theresa's gaze lingered over the two small children who were never going to see their father again. She hoped their mother would invent some more palatable story to explain Bruce Raffel's death—a car accident, a heart attack—anything but hog-tied and bludgeoned in a cold hotel room in a strange city, anything but an S&M lark gone badly awry. Considering her line of work, Theresa did not have the horror of lies that perhaps she should. Sometimes the only humane option was to tell anything but the truth.

The picture on its nightstand, the suitcase—nothing showed any sign of a struggle. The desk chair with its one bloody appendage remained the only overturned item in the room. Bruce Raffel had died without the benefit of a pitched battle. A pair of pants, a striped dress shirt, and a pair of satin boxer shorts had been laid over the edge of the armchair next to the window, not left in a heap on the floor the way Marie Corrigan's were. Did that mean he had taken them off voluntarily?

The room had that same hermetic quality of the Presidential Suite but a more used smell of old cleaner, dusty carpet, and Bruce Raffel's aftershave.

Neil Kelly watched her in complete silence, either letting her draw her own conclusions or lost in his own thoughts. She asked him if they had any sort of timeline.

"Powell's working on it. The hotel's got nothing. This room was last cleaned around eleven o'clock yesterday, same maid, who swears she saw nothing unusual—no contraband, meaning drugs or cigarettes (they take the no-smoking policy *very* seriously here)—and none of what she called 'kinky stuff.' Aside from that, no room service, no requests for extra pillows, no phone messages, nothing."

Theresa had returned to the dead man's side. "They have a record of phone calls?"

"No, only messages. They can't have guests insisting a desk clerk didn't deliver a message. But phone calls from inside or outside the hotel, there's no record of that."

Theresa began to photograph, starting from the door and working through the room before reaching the body. The body, she could be certain, would remain unmolested; the separation of the crime scene—the body belonged to the M.E.'s office, everything else to the police department—had been ingrained over decades. But at any moment, Powell and other police officers could show up and begin a thorough search, and the scene would never again be as it had been when she first arrived. Though that had not been a problem with the first murder.

Now she noticed a piece of paper underneath the pants on the armchair. It belonged to a spiral-bound notebook, the kind every schoolkid in America uses, down to the chewed-up ballpoint pen jammed into the spiral. It had been left folded over to a blank sheet with "*M*" and a phone number scrawled at an angle.

Neil read over her shoulder, his breath tickling her ear. "Could be Marie."

"Yeah." It could also be Mark, or Mickey, or Marissa.

Without another word he took out his phone and dialed the digits. Even with the phone pressed to his ear, Theresa could overhear those three tones designed for maximum obnoxiousness, along with the message that the number could not be completed as dialed.

"Not this area code," Neil guessed.

"Probably Atlanta."

Theresa turned the book over. Half of the opposite page had been covered with notes, written in a meandering hand that seemed identical to the *M* notation. She paged back one more sheet and found where the conscientious defense attorney had labeled the top of the paper with the date and *"'Litigating Postconviction Innocence Cases Without DNA,' 3 pm."*

"So he was alive to attend this session yesterday afternoon at least. That fits with the condition of the body."

"Provided that's his notebook."

Theresa had a sudden vision of the killer setting it down before sweetly removing Bruce Raffel's clothing and then forgetting about the book afterward. She flipped to the front, her fingers stumbling on the pages, Neil Kelly hanging close enough to press his chest to her shoulder, both of them caught in a frenzy of *Could it really be that easy?*

Answer: no. Bruce Raffel, a good student to the last, had printed his name and phone number in Sharpie marker, right over the Mead logo. The exchange, she noticed, did not match the number next to the initial *M*. Theresa turned back to the page with the phone number and left the notebook on the chair. With nothing else to look at in the bedroom, she went into the bathroom. Neil Kelly called someone to request the Atlanta area codes.

She dusted the bathroom floor, again finding no shoe prints except ones identical to the sneakers under Raffel's suitcase. Setting down some empty paper bags to stand on—no sense tracking black powder onto the light-colored carpeting, even if it would have to be replaced—Theresa examined the contents of the room. Making the most of the available counter space, the attorney had spread deodorant, a bottle of Lectric Shave, toothbrush and paste, comb, Nexxus hair gel, a bottle of generic aspirin, brush-style hair dryer, and a bottle of Centrum vitamins, its label worn enough to make Theresa suspect that it had been pressed into use as a pill case and now contained something other than Centrum vitamins. A quick peek revealed a variety of pills, none of which appeared familiar to her. She would have to take that along, let Toxicology work on identification.

She touched a few areas of the sink and the toilet with Hemastix. No reaction. If the killer had gotten blood on his hands and cleaned up in the bathroom, he had rinsed away all evidence of same. Three of each kind of towel plus a bath mat remained present, all apparently clean except for a hand towel on the sink. Bruce Raffel had not done much in the room since the maid had cleaned the previous day.

Theresa reentered the bedroom just as Neil Kelly pulled a small brown bag, the size of a kid's lunch, from Raffel's suitcase.

"What's that?" she asked.

"He had it shoved under his boxers and next to his bottle of Airborne. I'm not sure I want to touch it."

She laughed. "You're wearing gloves."

"Sometimes gloves aren't enough." He set the bag down, reached in, and pulled out a thin black leather belt. It had a perpendicular strap containing a ring and further on a wider patch with some sort of embedded object.

"What is that?"

He got that goofy twelve-year-old-boy smirk that men got at any mention of sex. "You don't know?"

"I could probably figure it out, but I don't think I want to."

Powell appeared in the doorway. The lines in his face had deepened with lack of sleep, and the strands of his comb-over had gone astray. "I finished up at the esteemed firm of Goldman & Jackson. What's that?"

Neil held up the belt. "The Lawyers Gone Wild theory just caught some traction."

"You're telling me. Wait until you see what I found in that bitch's office."

CHAPTER 11

"I don't know," Theresa said once the two men finished giggling over their respective finds: Bruce had packed not only the belt getup but a small leather whip and a set of buckled leather cuffs with matching covered cords, apparently to attach the cuffs to bedposts or other furniture without scratching their finish. Marie had kept a bland-looking metal file box at the bottom of her desk drawer with an industrial-size box of condoms (half full) and four different kinds of lubricating gel.

"It's okay not to understand it." Powell held the whip with two fingers and said, with either kindness or sarcasm, "It probably means you're normal."

Theresa applied a strip of clear packaging tape to the carpeting next to Bruce Raffel's thigh, determined to find even the tiniest hair or fiber or flake of skin. In the absence of bodily fluids—and she didn't see any—they would have to grasp at any straw of physical evidence. She intended to use magnetic powder on his skin, on the off chance they might find a print. Theresa couldn't escape the sinking feeling that the killer had come, killed, and left without dropping any handy clues in his—or her—wake. "He's got three faint marks on his back that could be old whip scars, but no one's been using a whip on Marie's perfect skin. At least not recently."

"Of course not. She probably used it on others."

Theresa went on, ticking off her other objections. "If this guy died because some sex game got out of control, then why were his toys still in a bag at the bottom of his suitcase? Why did the killer use his socks when he had these leather cuffs handy—not to mention a couple of neckties?"

"Raffel didn't need to get out his toys because the killer brought his own?" Neil Kelly guessed.

"But used the victim's socks?"

"Couldn't leave his own stuff behind."

"Again, no fresh marks, no chafing on the wrists, and no one struck him with anything other than this chair. If this is all about sex, why are Bruce's toys out of reach and Marie's supplies are back in her office instead of the Presidential Suite?"

"Are you always on a first-name basis with your victims?" Neil asked her. He seemed to find this curious.

"I find it less confusing than 'Vic 1' and 'Vic 2.' And how would Bruce Raffel and Marie Corrigan know people in common? Unless there's some sort of nation-wide sex club and they get together at every convention or know how to contact the local members in any city—"

"Kind of like the Masons," Neil said.

"But the meetings are a lot more fun," Powell put in. "Besides, I've got an answer to that. I spoke with Bruce Raffel's office manager—he, Raffel, has only lived in Atlanta for the past year. Before that, he lived here."

"In Cleveland?" Neil asked. "Please tell me he worked for the illustrious firm of Goldman & Jackson."

"No such luck. Hernandez, O'Malley & Ferrari, five years. Started at the public defender's office but jumped ship as soon as he had enough time on his résumé. Well, I think they *all* start at the public defender's office—Corrigan, too. Only the die-hard bleeding hearts stay there."

"Like the prosecutor's office," Neil mused. "Only the power junkies and the true believers stay there. Anyone who wants to turn a decent buck goes into private practice."

"Did the two of them work at the PD at the same time?" Theresa asked. She finished with the back of the victim's body and now turned him, stiff with rigor, to one side. His face and chest were a mottled purple from the blood pooled there, his nose squashed into an unnatural shape from having been driven into the carpet and left there as the cells began to break down. His brown eyes stared, beginning to cloud, his mouth open in a silent scream.

Powell said, "I have Corrigan's résumé, but not his yet. See anything interesting?"

Theresa intended to discuss the state of rigor but surprised herself by saying, "I don't think he wanted to die." Then, at the odd looks from the two detectives, she added, "No injuries to the face. It's all to the back of the head. No defensive bruises or cuts on the hands. He didn't get into a fight. I'd say rigor is beginning to fade, so I'd guess time of death—and it's little more than a guess, you'll have to get a more accurate estimation from the pathologist—would be yesterday evening. After the conference ended for the day, but not into the wee hours."

Theresa studied the mashed face, tried to imagine the nose on a normal day. Now she remembered. She had testified in front of Bruce Raffel at least twice, both gunshot cases. But she'd been to the courthouse because of him many times. He liked to subpoena all the prosecution witnesses or potential witnesses or just the dispatcher who answered the 911 call, hoping that at least one of them would not show up, and he could then ask for a mistrial. He would have vague reasons for needing her testimony and even vaguer reasons for not using her once she'd spent a taxpayer-paid morning twiddling her thumbs while her work piled up, but that was the power of a legal subpoena. She could do nothing about it. It never worked, and even if it had, a mistrial did not delete the case—but apparently any delay was a good thing in the practice of law.

Blood had soaked into the carpet, spread even further than in Marie's case. Perhaps Raffel had lived a bit longer, but Theresa saw no signs that the man had moved after the blows to the head. The pool of blood was neatly circular, without any smears or swipes other than a slight break in its outer border. She tugged on the socks around the wrists, felt that some elasticity remained. He had not stretched them to their limit trying to escape. Even the dried rivulets down the sides of the dead man's skull remained in clear, distinct lines, not mussed or redirected. How do you get a man to lie quietly on the floor while you bash his head in?

Because he's not expecting to get his head bashed in? Or because he's already quiet, unconscious, dead to the world? Theresa glanced at the water glass again. She would not only swab the edge for DNA, she'd take the water inside to make sure it contained only molecules of oxygen and hydrogen.

She spread magnetic powder over Bruce Raffel's body, without discovering any usable prints, only vague smudges, marked and removed the sock, listening absently as Powell and Kelly discussed how to proceed. Questioning over three hundred defense attorneys about their last known contact with Marie Corrigan in order to get a timeline was one thing. Questioning them about their sex lives was quite another.

Theresa tried to look past the trees. Someone had entered this room and killed Bruce Raffel with a chair provided by the hotel and a pair of socks provided by the victim. How did he get in? With the same passkey that got them into the Presidential Suite to kill Marie Corrigan. Or Bruce had let him—or her—in, either because he knew the person, had invited him, or because whoever it was had provided some reasonable excuse for him to do so. Maintenance to check the heater. A maid, carrying towels. Room service, though no evidence of food or beverages remained. Too many possibilities.

Once the man was dead, how did the killer get out?

He walked out the door, after first using the peephole to be sure no one was in the hallway.

Theresa took her fingerprint kit and dusted the back of the door. A few smudges appeared, marks probably made by fingers but without the visible ridges necessary to use them for identification. She hit the interior doorknob, too, though it had already been handled by the hysterical maid, the hotel manager, and countless police officers. The door was difficult to open or prop, so even gloved they would have rubbed off any prints by now. But she tried anyway, because you never knew. Miracles could happen.

But not today. No prints. She tried the doorjamb, too. Nothing but smudges.

The body snatchers arrived. She helped them move Bruce Raffel into a white plastic body bag, watching to be sure no one stepped in the pooled blood under his head. It appeared to be dry, but such an amount soaking into a carpet would take a long time to dry completely and would squoosh up if stepped on. And she had an idea.

The pool of blood had that one abnormality to its

surface, on the edge away from the bed. The killer could have stepped in it, gotten a splotch on his toe. Or knelt in it or leaned a palm on it, who knew? What would be crystal clear on a tile floor was only a suggestion on the rough loops of the Berber carpet. But if it had been a foot, perhaps he'd left them a trail. She pulled out her small Maglite, her back protesting as she examined the floor anew.

Trying to find a smear of dark red on the burgundy-patterned carpet made needles and haystacks seem like a bar bet. Theresa trained her eyes on the lighter, cream-colored flecks in the pattern and found a darkened one. A bit farther on, she found another. She took another look at the bathroom—with the added light from the extra-bright flashlight, she searched for another smudge of blood. The stuff could be remarkably tough to get rid of—just ask Lady Macbeth.

Nothing. The killer didn't seem to have cleaned up in the bathroom, but he also wouldn't have risked wiping any bloodied hands on his clothing and walk out advertising his recent deeds.

Most likely the killer hadn't gotten any blood on himself, other than the one foot. The seat of the murder weapon could have blocked any spray, and the body hadn't been moved after the injuries were inflicted. The killer could have walked out of the room and immediately blended back into the ebb and flow of the hotel population, into a public area where he could leave entire handprints and it wouldn't prove a thing. Even if he didn't have a good reason to be on the fourteenth floor, there were plenty of so-so reasons to choose from. *I meant to get off on a different floor. I wanted to visit a buddy of mine but then forgot his room number. I had to make a delivery, and Dispatch sent me to the wrong place. I wanted to get some exercise and walk a bit, and*

I prefer quiet hotel hallways to the bustle of the mall downstairs. I was looking for the ice machine.

Reasons that wouldn't sound exactly right but couldn't be proved wrong.

Theresa looked up and down the hallway. *If I had just killed someone,* she thought, *I don't think I'd want to get into an elevator.* You never knew who you might run into, who might remember seeing you on that floor at just that time.

She found the stairwell door, gave it a thorough once-over. No blood that she could see. Maybe she should ask hotel management if she could turn out all the lights on the floor and spray the entire hallway with Bluestar. Yeah. They'd be crazy about *that* idea.

She brushed black powder onto the stairwell door's push bar and the outer edge of the door. This dark coating revealed nothing but dirt, smudges, and the swirl marks left by a maid with a spray bottle of disinfectant. The hotel wouldn't be crazy about *that* either.

She pushed the door open. The gray-painted concrete steps traveled upward and downward, framed by a matching curved-pipe banister. One could check in to the most expensive hotel in the world and the stairwell would still look as if it should be attached to a factory. Decor stopped at the fire door.

Up or down? Depended on whether the killer had a room at the hotel to return to or whether he simply wanted to get out of the place after committing a bloody murder. Theresa guessed down. She stripped off her blackened gloves and set her fingerprinting kit out of the way. Then, with the aid of a flashlight, she examined the landing, the banister, and each descending step. A door opened from one of the thirty-three floors that fed into the stairwell, but the echo made it difficult to tell if the sound came from above or below.

On the second step down, she found another pink fiber. Unfortunately, the stairwells were not cleaned anywhere near as often as the rooms, and on the same one step she also found enough hairs, fibers, dust, and lint to roll into a good-size bunny. She dutifully pulled it all into a manila envelope with a pair of plastic tweezers.

Footsteps tapped over their own echoes; the sounds sorted themselves out, and she realized that someone was coming up.

Theresa usually opted to take the stairs; they worked off more calories and, at least in the medical examiner's office building, were faster than the elevator. Other than that, she hated stairwells on principle, particularly ones in parking garages, the Justice Center, and hotels. Closed off behind heavy doors and often dimly lit, they were an invitation to crime.

On the third step, she found more hairs, more fibers, a scrap of thin cardboard with a perforated edge that had probably come from a box of cookies or crackers or some other snack, and a piece of crumpled cellophane. This all went into another manila envelope. She would have to go to her car and get some more of those if she intended to do the entire flight between fourteen and thirteen. Did they have a thirteenth floor? So many hotels had left it out for so many years. Ditto the thirteenth row on trains or airplanes. What about cruise ships?

"That's dedication."

She turned her head a bit too fast, annoyed that someone had snuck up on her, annoyed that she had allowed a five-foot-ten, two-hundred-pound-plus-plenty-of-spare-change man who now breathed with a slight wheeze to sneak up on her. Annoyed that it would be *this* man.

Her favorite defense attorney.

"Ms. MacLean," he said by way of greeting, eyebrows raised under slicked-back hair and his hand rest-

ing on the banister she hadn't fingerprinted yet. Last
seen asking her why she hadn't found gunshot residue on
his dead, disadvantaged, carjacking client if he had fired
upon the officers at the scene, then scoffing at the idea
that the driving rainstorm occurring at the same moment might have had any effect on the adhesion qualities
of tiny microscopic particles. The well-cut suit managed
to look good even on his ungainly body, and he carried
a leather briefcase, worn enough to be an unexpected
sign of humanity.

"Dennis." She used his first name on purpose, letting
familiarity imply contempt.

"Are you really going to examine every shed hair in
this entire hotel? I've never known you to show such ini-
tiative before."

She gritted her teeth and concentrated on picking up
another tuft of dust and fibers. No adequate response
came to mind, save for pushing him down the stairs.
She settled for, "I imagine there's quite a bit you don't
know."

"Such as?"

She straightened, deciding to stop at the fifth step
down, a completely unscientific and arbitrary decision that this man in particular would crucify her for
in court, should he notice. So she faced him and asked,
"Do you know who killed Marie Corrigan?"

This seemed to catch him off guard, if only for an
instant. He must have been expecting a snarky comment
about himself. "You have me there. No, I don't."

"Any ideas?" She enjoyed being able to ask the questions for once.

"Not a one. Marie was an excellent attorney, and her
death is a grave loss to the legal community." He rattled
this off with less attention than a kindergartner reciting
ABCs.

"You don't seem too broken up about it."

A quick, annoyed glance. Because he didn't relish being the witness for once, or because he'd really cared about Marie? "As an attorney I'm surrounded by stressed, emotional, volatile people. I've learned to keep my feelings to myself. I would think you would understand that."

She did not retreat. "Is this supposed to be some sort of bonding moment?"

His ability to flush had doubtless been lost long before, but he could still frown. "You shouldn't be surprised that I want Marie's killer caught, much more than you do. She was my friend. *You're* probably rooting for the guy to get away with it."

She reached out, languidly plucking a stray hair from his lapel. "What about Bruce Raffel? Was he your friend, too?"

He answered this more slowly. "I didn't really know him."

She took a shot in the dark, since Britton, Marie, and Bruce Raffel would all be within ten years of age of one another. "Not even when you were all at the public defender's office?"

His jaw stilled. "That was a long time and many, many cases ago."

Interesting.

"And maybe you should leave the interrogations to your cousin and concentrate on picking up your little pieces of whatever. Shouldn't you be wearing booties?"

Oooh, bitchy. Though she wondered for a moment if she *should* be wearing booties—and realized that it would be stupid. She'd taken them off as she left Bruce Raffel's room, and putting a fresh pair on would be pointless. This was a public area; cross-contamination between the hallway and the stairwell occurred all day

every day. Which, yes, meant that collecting items from
the stairwell had to be an exercise in futility. The most
compelling argument she could find to support her actions would be, *It can't hurt*.

But now she could enjoy *not* having to answer questions either. She smiled, turned, and made her way back
up to the fourteenth floor, where she stored the fiber
from his lapel in an envelope, its surreptitious nature
giving her a spiteful kick. Then she put Dennis Britton
out of her mind. For now.

Speaking of Bluestar . . . The spray reagent would
react with the iron content in blood, causing it to glow
with a blue-white luster. She doubted that the blood trail
would last long—it might not even leave the room, as
the carpet wiped the blood off the bottom of the killer's
shoe with every step—but might as well try. The hotel
probably wouldn't be crazy about the idea, but the clear
solution dried quickly and wouldn't stain or bleach. It
shouldn't anyway.

"Gentlemen," she told the two detectives, "we need
to make it dark in here."

"You need us to turn off the lights?" Neil asked.

"For starters."

They drew the curtains, overlapping the sides and using the uninvolved chair to hold them in place. The hair
dryer in the bathroom had a night-light built in, so that
had to be unplugged. Ditto the clock radio and the tele-
phone. The TV had a red "ready" light, but she could
live with that. With all the other lights out, the crack
under the door glowed like a Times Square billboard,
and Theresa shoved a towel into it, all the while shaking
the plastic spray bottle with her other hand to dissolve
the reagent. Then she made her way back to the far side
of the bed.

"Ow."

"You all right?" A voice from her left—Neil.

"Yeah, just hit the bed frame," she said, despite believing she might have broken one of two of her toes. Then she stepped into something large and soft.

"That's me," Powell growled. "Is this really necessary? We only closed the curtains before."

"We were looking for semen with an alternate light source and colored goggles. The Bluestar will make the blood fluoresce, but more or less depending on the amount of blood present, and colored filters won't intensify it. On top of that, the reaction begins to fade instantly." She moved gingerly, going around him, passing by the warmth of Neil's body in front of the dresser. "Despite what you see on TV, just turning out the lights isn't going to do it. The darker it is, the easier it will be to see any reaction."

Her eyes finally learned to use what little sunshine crept from the edges of the curtain, and she knelt next to the nightstand, in front of the armchair. She pulled a Sharpie from her pocket to mark any positive reactions. Tape wouldn't work, because the surface would be wet from the Bluestar, and she figured the carpet was a goner anyway. "Ready?"

She heard cloth moving, as if they were trying to nod before realizing how pointless it was. "Yes," Neil said.

She shook the bottle one last time and sprayed, starting with the bed. Nothing but a vague luminescence, probably from the cleaning products. Then the nightstand, where the cast-off patterns she'd seen before sprang into view as a tiny, glittering chain. Then she twisted to try the armchair. Nothing. She did not spray the murder weapon, the straight-backed desk chair. She already knew that had blood on it and didn't want to wash any fingerprints away with the Bluestar. The chair would be processed at the lab.

She turned to the carpet, avoiding the blood pool—it would only blind them. The first smear she'd seen, on the cream-colored fleck, showed up. She crawled in its direction, drew a circle around it with the Sharpie, and continued spraying. She heard the detectives back up, probably to avoid getting Bluestar on their shoes.

"Should we be breathing that stuff?" Powell asked. "With no ventilation in here?"

"It won't hurt you."

As if to mock him, the air conditioner chose that moment to switch on and gave a discreet hum.

Another smudge, near the middle of the foot of the bed. She marked and moved on. The detectives moved back again, more fumbling sounds. Powell swore. Theresa smiled, since no one could see. "It's not that bad. At the M.E.'s we get used to working with both pitch dark and dead bodies together."

"No way," Powell breathed. He sounded truly startled.

"Way. Trace-metal detection tests, where we spray the hands looking for a reaction from a gun or knife. It's so dark you can't see your hand in front of your face. If there's any chance the job is going to give you the creeps, that will be your litmus test."

"It doesn't bother you?" Neil asked.

"They don't come back to life." She sprayed. Another smudge, growing a bit fainter. "Then there's infrared photography and X-ray development. You get used to the dark pretty quick." She didn't tell them that the only thing she wouldn't have anything to do with when the light burned out was the freight elevator. We all had our limits. "We're up to the door, and there's still a faint trace. We're going to have to go into the hallway."

This was much easier said than done. A guest wandering out of his room or off the elevator into the pitch dark could trip and break something, for which the hotel would be held responsible. Worse, the guest might feel uncomfortable, and the Ritz-Carlton prided itself on the comfort of its guests. Having to find her way to her room by touch might convince a guest to make next month's reservation at the Renaissance.

So it took two maids, Karla the day manager, and head of security Marcus Dean himself to make sure that all the rooms on the floor were empty, then man the elevators and both stairwells for the safety of the guests. And that didn't even address the question of turning out the lights.

The lights in the hallways were designed to never, ever turn off. If some blackout or nuclear attack occurred, the emergency lights would turn on. These, too, had no on-off switch but would have to be dismounted and their batteries removed. The regular lights had no wall switch, not even behind a locked electrical panel. All lighting controls were down in the security office, and in addition the entire hotel was hardwired together. To get one hallway dark, all would have to go dark, and all the murders in the world couldn't convince the hotel to take on that kind of liability.

"How about this?" Theresa suggested to Dean. "Can we just unscrew the bulbs?"

He summoned two maintenance men, who disabled both the lights and the emergency backups. It was a lot of work just to make a hallway dark, but Theresa had become accustomed to it. Spraying a blood-detection fluid always turned into two hours of preparation for two minutes of glowing bluish stains.

Finally they were ready. One maintenance man stood on a ladder, his heavily gloved hand on the last lightbulb, far enough away, she hoped, that the trail would not lead past him. She didn't want to blunder into his ladder in the dark.

She took up her position on the floor at the door to Bruce Raffel's room and insisted that Powell and Neil flank her, ready to observe the brief reactions that could indicate a trail of blood.

"And this isn't going to stain the carpets?" Marcus Dean asked, for the third time.

"You'll never know we were here," Theresa assured him.

"Then why you got a Sharpie in your hand?"

"Good point," she conceded, and pulled out a supply of glow-in-the-dark stickers in the shape of hollow squares. "But no one can kick these things out of place once I put them down, understand? They're not going to stick to the carpet, because it will be wet."

"Wet?" the day manager asked with a note of panic.

What part of "spraying" hadn't she understood? "Just a little wet," Theresa soothed. "Watch your feet around these squares or we'll have to start over."

"Okay," the woman squeaked, as if already holding her breath. "You're Rachael's mother, aren't you?"

"Go ahead," Theresa said to the maintenance man. The hallway and all present were plunged into blackness.

She let her eyes adjust. It didn't take long. The draperies at each end of the hallway were meant to decorate, not block light, and though she had added her own tarps, the bright sunlight outside still leaked around the edges and from under the doors to the empty guest rooms. Not perfect, but as perfect as they could get. She shook the bottle in her hand and sprayed in a wide fan. She could hear the liquid squirt, but it had no odor to speak of.

The cops scuttled out of the way, as if still convinced that the liquid might somehow damage their shoes.

There. The small, amorphous stain that the killer's

shoe had picked up glowed at a spot to her right. She placed a sticker, reminding everyone again not to bump it and reminding herself most of all. She moved carefully to one side, already feeling the wetness in her knees, and sprayed another fan.

Another stain. It came as no surprise to her that the killer had not taken the elevator.

She sprayed again, used another glow-in-the-dark sticker. The intensity was holding up fairly well—the killer must have really soaked that one little piece of his shoe. She couldn't see any sort of consistent shape to it, no clues to the tread. Because of the looped carpet threads, it appeared slightly different at each incarnation.

More spray. A little harder to see, either because the blood had worn off the shoe or because the light from an emergency-exit sign interfered with her eyesight. Just as she'd thought: The killer had come out of Bruce Raffel's room and made a beeline for the exit.

Theresa stated the obvious. "He went into the stairwell."

Marcus Dean heaved a sigh that should have rattled the windows. "Oh, shit."

Despite this pronouncement, making the stairwell dark turned out to be both easier and more complicated than the hallway. There were no outside windows to leak light, but there were also thirty-two floors' worth of emergency-exit doors that had to be manned to keep guests from breaking their necks, legs, and other litigious parts. In the end they took the bulbs out of the lighting four floors up and four floors down and put staff members at the doors to those floors only. And Theresa had to promise to work fast.

She began at the hallway door, spraying to see several small glowing spots jump to life. Most took on the obvious shape of drips, spilled liquid, some sort of cleaner, or food that fluoresced. One had a sharp edge, however, almost a semicircle; that could be her partial footprint. The spot had seemed larger but less defined on the carpeting. The soft carpeting pressed up into every nook and cranny of the sole, but the rigid and not-perfectly-level concrete floor of the hallway did not.

Theresa moved inside the stairwell and made the two detectives stand against the wall so she could shut the hallway door, closing off that source of ambient light. The darkness got much darker.

She hadn't thought only four floors in either direction would make that much of a difference, that the remaining emergency lighting would seep from the middle of the stairwell and ruin her vision, but she'd been wrong. The tight turns and landings blotted it out as if she'd been struck blind. Her fingers clenched around the spray nozzle, sending out the glowing liquid just to make certain she could still see it.

She could. The tiny, sharp mark showed up again, along with the drips and drabs of countless guests and staff. Theresa crawled forward, feeling the layers of dust and grit, grateful she had latex gloves and vowing to undress in the utility room immediately upon entering her home. Cleaning the stairwells could not be a high priority. The staff didn't care, and the guests didn't use the creepy, unglamorous places.

Unless they'd just killed someone.

"Don't touch the railing," she warned the detectives behind her. They said nothing, though one gave an impatient *pfff*. Powell. He flanked her left, because she could smell Neil's aftershave on her right. She could feel their large, warm bodies in the darkness, close to her but not touching. This should have reassured her, but instead their forms felt circling and predatory. Waiting.

She followed the landing, moving away from the hallway door. Another spray, another kaleidoscope of blue-white glows came into view in a variety of shapes and intensities.

But no sharp, curved spot. Where had he gone?

She stopped near the center of the landing and pivoted her body, spraying to her right, toward the ascending flight of steps.

And found the mark again. And again, near the bottom step.

"Are you seeing anything?" Powell demanded. "Still finding that blood?"

She made some sort of affirming sound and placed a paper frame around her spot. It appeared again two steps up, though the rubber coating on the edge of the step made the outline less defined.

"He went *up*?" Neil said.

"He's a guest," Powell said. "One of these pervo lawyers, just like we thought."

"Or on the staff," Neil said.

Theresa let them theorize and concentrated on her trail, but it faded to nothing by the half landing. Then she had the lights turned back on and collected the blood.

Why go up instead of down?

She stored her blood samples and her fingerprint cards while Marcus Dean and his staff tightened the emergency lamps' bulbs and drifted back to their usual duties.

At this point Theresa gave the crime scene another once-over, but she'd done all she could think of to do—despite the always present, unsettling conviction that she had forgotten something, overlooked some vital piece of evidence, or failed to consider a scenario that would return later in the form of her boss, a cop, an attorney, or a judge biting her head off. Probably Dennis Britton, with her luck. But she could not see what else to collect or examine. On a microscopic level, a hotel room might be a churning soup of abandoned trace evidence like fibers or skin cells, but they were all pretty simple in a macroscopic sense. The occupant brought a few things with him. The rest of the place was generic, interchangeable.

Just outside Bruce Raffel's room, her phone rang. Frank.

"I'm coming over there," he said without preamble. "Meet me in the lobby."

"I'm wrapping up my exam of the crime scene. I'll just be another—"

"Now."

Her stomach began to knot from the bottom up. "Frank, what's wrong?"

"You have to get your daughter away from that guy."

CHAPTER 12

Theresa borrowed an empty maid's cart to secure the evidence and her equipment in the county station wagon, keeping only her camera and other rudimentary items. The cart reduced this chore to one trip, but it still took twenty precious minutes before she could ride the elevator to the lobby. Her heart began to pound. His own tendencies aside, her cousin usually tried to convince Theresa to be less protective of Rachael, not more. Something in William Rosedale's past must have changed his mind.

The lobby teemed with people, lawyers on break before the two-o'clock sessions began, and she did not see Frank among them. She didn't even know where he was coming from; if he'd called from his office, he would probably walk the two blocks instead of getting his car out of the police-headquarters garage and then having to find another space around Tower City. She moved through the crowd. Though most were dressed in casual clothes, she could tell by their glances that her scuffed sneakers and Target stretch khakis seemed to peg her as not belonging.

She passed by the front desk, where Rachael handed a key card to a tall man in African garb, and reached the lounge. Still no Frank, but she did see a familiar mop of dishwater-blond hair.

"Sonia!"

The attorney moved away from two young men with what sounded like a snarky comment, clutching an over-stuffed briefcase with one broken handle. She squeezed through another clique of lawyers to reach Theresa. "Hey, how's it going? Any clues? I know you can't tell me, but please say you're going to catch this psycho."

"Tell me about William Rosedale."

White spots appeared in the perpetual flush of Sonia's cheeks. "I . . . I can't."

"Can't or won't? It's because he's a client, isn't it?"

"He *was* a client, for about a half hour, and he was in shock at the time, poor kid, which is probably why he doesn't recognize me. But it's still privileged, Theresa—you know that. I'm sorry." And indeed she did look sorry, so sorry that Theresa gripped the woman's elbow with little consideration for comfort and dragged her across the lounge, dropping her into a chair next to the window. It gave them a skinny view of the Cuyahoga River before the federal courthouse next door got in the way.

Theresa sat across from her, a round marble table between their knees. "Talk."

"I can't tell you anything, Theresa. This isn't a witness stand, and I'm sorry, but you don't have the power to compel my testimony."

"This is *my* witness stand, and it's my daughter. I'm compelling."

Sonia's face settled into an expression of genuine empathy. Theresa wondered if her clients often saw this same look. "I very briefly represented William Rosedale, four years ago. It was a juvenile case and has been duly sealed. If you want to know more than that, you'll have to ask him."

Theresa considered this, considered how seriously Sonia took her job, and sat back against the cobalt upholstery. The lawyer seemed to breathe a sigh of relief.

Besides, Theresa thought, she'd find out from Frank soon enough. Theresa surveyed the now-thinning crowd. No cousin.

"I have to get to my next seminar," Sonia said. " 'Victory in Street-Crime Cases.' "

"Be careful, Sonia. Have you heard from Surfer Girl? You should take any threat seriously."

"Oh, please. She's frustrated and grieving. If I lost my fiancé to a drunk driver, I'd be frustrated and grieving, too—it hardly makes her a psycho sex slayer."

"Don't be too sure. That empathetic heart is going to get you in trouble someday."

"Has all my life. Why stop now? But what are you finding with Bruce? Is it the same person who killed Marie? It's got to be, right?"

" 'Bruce'? Did you know him? He was from Cleveland originally."

"Um . . . no, not really. He was at the PD when I started there, but only for another month or two. Then he went to private."

"Uh-huh. What else can you tell me about him?"

Sonia hesitated, no doubt wondering what part of an acquaintanceship could be considered privileged. "He wasn't a bad attorney. Sort of a steamroller, but he could come up with some pretty ingenious motions when he took the time to apply himself. He made one heck of a mens rea argument to get that ATM robber twenty years instead of life. You remember that one—the guy robbed a woman while she was making an ATM withdrawal and wound up shooting her."

"*Wound up* shooting her? He shot her dead for fifty bucks, with her two children in the backseat. And somehow that's not his fault?"

"Of course it's his *fault*. But he didn't have the desire or purpose in mind to murder, only to rob."

"I'm sorry, you take a gun to an ATM intending to rob somebody, then you can't just say 'I didn't mean to' after pulling the trigger."

"Legally, it makes a difference—at least it did to the jury. Anyway, that was Bruce." A waitress in black pants and a snow-white shirt came by for drink orders, but they waved her off.

"Why did he move to Atlanta?" Theresa asked. "Did he accumulate too many enemies here?"

Sonia laughed. "He moved because a firm there offered him a larger salary. He didn't care about power, only money. When it came to money, he was as driven as Marie. Maybe that's why they got along."

"They knew each other?"

Again that pause, as if deciding what she could share without abetting the enemy. "He and Marie dated for a short time. I mean, they hooked up for three or four months—I don't know if you'd call it dating. Marie never did anything as ordinary as *dating*. But they were tight for a while, both in and out of the courtroom."

"While you were all at the public defender's office?"

"After that, I think. They worked for different firms, but they'd still show up in court on each other's cases occasionally. They made a good team, in their way. Bruce came up with the out-of-the-box thinking—wild, hyper-aggressive tacks. Marie had the stage presence to make them work. They should have opened their own office. They could have gotten Vlad the Impaler off with time served."

"Why didn't they?"

"Egos, I think. Too big to be in the same room for long, much less the same office."

"How do you know all this if you were only acquainted with them?"

A faint blush. "I told you, Cleveland's a big small town in a lot of ways. Scuttlebutt said Marie was pregnant at one point."

"When was that?"

"After Bruce left the PD. But nothing came of it. I'll bet she actually ate dinner for a change and the bulge in her belly set someone's imagination running."

But then Bruce moved to another city. . . . "Did you ever hear gossip about their relationship getting . . . kinky?"

"You mean S&M, like how you found their bodies?"

"Yes."

She expected Sonia to scoff, to agree with her theory that the sexual aspects of the murders had been staged to heap further humiliation upon the victims. But the lawyer said nothing, pensively tracing an ebony line through the glossy marble of the tabletop.

"Sonia? Don't tell me there's something to it? That there's really some secret dominatrix ring of criminal defense attorneys?"

"What? No, of course not."

"Sonia, I'm not looking to smear their names. But if you want me to find out who killed them, you have to tell me what was going on in their lives. The killer left them trussed up for some reason. He wanted us to see them like that, and that fact could tell us who he is. Or she."

Sonia merely chuckled, though without much mirth. "I hate to disappoint your colleagues, but there is no secret or even not-so-secret sex club of kinky defense lawyers. Do we have the same amount of office relationships, affairs, and meaningless hookups as any other

profession? Yes, certainly. Probably even more so." Sonia abruptly leaned forward, both palms flat on the cool
stone. "You have to understand what it's like being an
attorney. We're adrenaline junkies, like Navy SEALs or
car salesmen. We love the stalking, the hunt, the triumph
of winning. We like to argue. *I* like to argue. Why do
you think I persist in this job where sometimes my own
clients hate me even more than the cops do, because I'm
white or because I'm female or because I got an education and they didn't? The victims think I'm a sellout to
my own gender, and the judges treat me like I'm a high-
school girl drawing bleeding hearts in her notebook."

"Why do you, then?"

The woman gave her a crooked smile. "Because I love
it. You probably think I'm nuts, but I love my job. I like
to make deals. These people need me, even when they
won't admit it. I love being able to get help for them, and
even when I can't, at least someone tried on their behalf. If I quit, what would I do? Write up real-estate con-
tracts? Manage a charity, spend my time begging rich
people for money? I'd wake up every morning knowing
that day would be a waste, and every day afterward."

"Okay," Theresa said.

"Anyway, it's like why cops date cops—because no one
else understands the lousy hours. So if Bruce balanced
being an asshole in court with letting someone beat on
him in the bedroom, it's really not that surprising."

Theresa blinked at her friend. "How did you know
that?"

"Oops. This is one of those Perry Mason moments,
isn't it? When the witness lets something slip? Because
once or twice I was the one doing the beating, okay?"

The skin tingled at the nape of Theresa's neck. "*What?*
You and Bruce . . . ? I'm sorry. Are you okay?"

"Please, Theresa, it's not like I'm upset. Not everyone is like you—true blue, in it for love. Bruce and I got together years ago, because it was mutually convenient. Love wasn't part of the deal. *Dinner* wasn't part of the deal."

"And leather accessories were?"

"Do you think I'd get a man into bed *without* wearing a mask?"

That was not the answer Theresa had expected. "Sonia, that's not fair, and it's not correct—"

"Don't even think about giving me the 'but you have a lovely personality' bit!" Sonia snapped, as passionately as in any closing argument. "We roomed together for three years. How many dates did I have?"

Theresa refused to answer but thought, *One*. Maybe two.

"So don't pretend you don't know what I'm talking about. Men hate my personality even more than they hate my looks—and I'm not interested in changing either. Besides, the masks, the accoutrements . . . it made it so different from the courtroom. I could pretend the sex happened in an alternate universe, that it wasn't really real." She slumped back. "Not to mention that I didn't mind a chance to hit back, let someone else's heart or whatever bleed for a change."

Theresa offered neither comfort nor censure, both of which would ring hollow. Like any woman, she didn't like certain aspects of her looks, but at least she'd never had to know how it felt to dislike every *single* aspect. "And that's all Bruce was to you?"

"Absolutely. He was a slightly more prudent choice than a complete stranger in a bar, who might be a disease-riddled psycho. That's all."

Sonia spoke with utter finality, but still Theresa wondered if there might be some things she wouldn't admit, even to herself—and if Bruce Raffel had been one of those things. "So Bruce had a kinky side. What about Marie?"

"Don't know for sure, but I would doubt it. Rumors regarding Marie Corrigan have run the gamut from blackmailing a judge to eating babies, but S&M? No. You want to know about Marie Corrigan's proclivities, you'll have to ask Dennis Britton. And while you're there, ask him how his first wife died."

"What? Sonia, I know you don't like him, but really—"

The attorney checked her watch, and Theresa glanced up to see Frank striding toward them.

"Her name was Ellie Baker," Sonia said. "I met her my first week on the job. She eventually specialized in white-collar crimes, the lowly bookkeepers who snap one day and run off to the Bahamas with the monthly payroll. She was smart and tough and kind of a health nut. There's only one thing she wasn't, and that's why she's dead."

Theresa raised an eyebrow.

"She wasn't rich."

Then Sonia bailed out, of both the conversation and the room.

Not rich, Theresa thought. Unlike Mrs. Britton number two . . . No, Sonia's imagination had run away with her. Dennis Britton had married her friend, and then she died. He had coerced her client, and then he died. The same overboardness that made Sonia accuse cops of planting evidence on her misunderstood clients made her see patterns that didn't exist. Better to concentrate on the murders, which did.

Frank reached Theresa, dropping into the abandoned chair. "You shouldn't have let her get away. She was his attorney, at least at first."

The fist of fire grasped her stomach again. "I've got that much. What did he need an attorney for?"

Frank leaned in toward her, his voice low and controlled and deadly. "Rape."

Theresa blinked, absorbing the word in all its horror. Then he added, "And murder."

PART II

JENNA

Theresa forced herself to stay in her chair. Rachael was right around the corner, checking guests in and out and fielding requests for more towels, just as she had been for the past month. *Your daughter is in no more danger than she was this morning or last week. Do not panic.*

Such a large chunk of parenthood consisted of telling oneself not to panic.

"Start from the beginning," Theresa said.

"You're not going to faint, are you? You don't look so good."

"What am I, some Victorian maiden? Spill."

Now that he was not the only upset person in the room, Frank's shoulders relaxed a tick. "Besides, it's not like she's engaged to the kid. It's just a workplace flirtation. Get her another job and all will be well. Okay, here goes: Four years ago, when William was sixteen, a classmate of his, Jenna Simone, also sixteen, was found raped—presumably raped, no DNA—and bludgeoned in his living room. His parents were out of town. Apparently young William got passed-out drunk, then woke up with a hangover and blood on his hands. He called the cops. They took one look around and arrested him. Jenna's car was parked out front. William said he'd gone to a school dance and had no idea how he got home with Jenna. They were acquainted, but not dating or in any sort of relationship. I'm getting this from a friend reading me the arrest report, which was all she could find. Everything else is locked up tight. The parents had everything sealed."

"That's all you can find out?"

"The *records* are sealed—but, happily, you can't seal people. The first officer on the scene is now working in Parma. Vice, on nights. I'll give him a call later.

"Wait, this wasn't that long ago. Why don't I remember it?"

"Dunno. It wasn't our case, it was Westlake's. I did try to call the two detectives who did the investigation— one retired last year and moved to Florida. Shook the dust of this place off his feet and never looked back, apparently doesn't stay in touch with nobody."

Theresa looked away, chewing one thumbnail, and at that precise moment William Rosedale crossed the lobby. He and the other boy, the roly-poly one from the tower group, waited for an elevator.

He caught sight of Theresa and nodded without smiling, doing nothing to endear himself to the mother of a girl interested in him. Maybe, she thought with sudden hope, he wasn't interested in Rachael. Then she remembered the way he had brushed her daughter's hair, watched her lips as she spoke. He was interested, all right. More than interested.

So maybe he just didn't care what Theresa thought.

Frank was continuing. "I called the other guy, but he's tied up with a search warrant on a fence at the moment. I've met him—good guy, he'll talk to me. He's back working Property instead of Persons, though. Maybe this case got to him, he decided he'd rather deal with thieves than murderers. Can't blame him there."

Theresa's heart pounded. *Surely the boy must see that I know, I must be staring at him as if he'd just turned a bright shade of fuchsia.* Maybe not, maybe there was enough space between them to put a silk screen over her widened eyes and gritted teeth.

She forced a smile that felt sick to her and lifted a hand. The elevator arrived, and William stepped into it with one long-legged stride. The other boy did not but turned to enter Muse. The restaurant sat on the other side of the lobby, featuring an always-burning fireplace.

"Frank," she asked, past a lump in her throat that felt like coal, thick and dusty, "why is that boy not in jail?"

"Two words," Frank said. "Marie Corrigan."

"I thought you said Sonia was his attorney."

"Yeah, for about a day and a half until Mummy and Daddy got back with their checkbook. Then Marie took over. I don't know how she did it, but she kept it in juvenile court and *then* got a not-guilty verdict." Frank jerked his tie loose and rested the back of his head against the top of the chair. "I couldn't stand the woman, but she was one hell of a lawyer. And you know juries are always ten times more cautious when sentencing a juvenile. No matter what they've done, it's tough to look at some kid and send him to jail for the rest of his life."

"How did Marie get the case?"

"I said I don't know. I got her name from the clerk of courts, but the transcripts are sealed, the depos are sealed, everything is sealed."

"Except people. The prosecutor—"

"Exactly. Brian Morgan. You better talk to him, though. He's not so crazy about me."

"Why?"

The waitress came by again. Theresa declined a drink order. She didn't feel bad about occupying a table without buying anything—they were the only people in the lounge. A hushed quiet had descended with the attorneys all in their sessions. She still itched to go check on Rachael but fought it. She had seen William leave the floor. Rachael worked right around the corner, in full view of others. Don't panic.

"He thinks I exaggerated probable cause to get an arrest warrant on that guy who killed the pizza-delivery man. Then the judge looked at him cross-eyed, and I guess it hurt his feelings. Don't know why he fussed— the judge gave us the warrant and the guy confessed, so it's all water under the Hope Memorial Bridge."

"You took a chance."

"Every day is a chance."

"Where is he today? Morgan?"

"I don't know. I could only do so much in a morning, cuz. I wanted to get over here as soon as I could to tell Rachael to clean out her locker."

"That's going to be easier said than done."

"No surprise there. She's as stubborn as you are. Look at it this way: As soon as I get his record unsealed, I'm sure the hotel will find a way to fire him. That will at least get him partially out of Rachael's life."

"They can't fire him if he wasn't convicted, can they?" Theresa asked.

"As I said, they'd find a way. Keeping someone with that record on staff would be too big a liability."

"And Rachael will believe that we ruined this kid's life over a charge that hasn't even been proved, and she'll never speak to me again. Plus, wouldn't you get in trouble for using your authority to examine sealed records?"

"If there hadn't been two murders in this hotel, yes.

But we're checking criminal histories on every employee as part of the investigation. So we can protest to Rachael, truthfully, that it's not our fault."

"As soon as the record is unsealed."

"Yes. Until then, okay—I can't really inform the hotel. If this kid or his family really protested, it would get sticky for me."

"Should we tell Neil and Powell?"

"Neil?" Frank asked. "If it were just Marie Corrigan, I would say yes. But this kid killed a teenage girl, probably for turning him down. He might have killed Marie Corrigan for the same reason, but Bruce Raffel? What possible connection could he have to Bruce Raffel? There's no reason for him to have a grudge against lawyers, when they're the ones who saved his ass. Again, let's get the records unsealed and then let Kelly and Powell draw their own conclusions."

"So in the meantime I need to warn my daughter off a boy I think she really likes." Theresa resumed chewing one of her thumbnails. "This is going to take some finesse."

"Oh, yeah. And that's your middle name."

She got to her feet, feeling considerably older than she had a half hour previously. "Thanks for the vote of confidence. And thanks, Frank—thanks a lot."

He rose as well, acknowledging what she'd said with only a bobbing nod. He would do anything for Rachael, she knew, especially since Theresa had split from her husband. But if anyone had less finesse than she did, it was Frank. She had to keep him from trying to order his niece around, or the girl would only become more intractable.

And somehow she expected that "intractable" would be putting it mildly. Rachael had battled Theresa's overprotectiveness for years. This wouldn't be only one more skirmish—more like all-out warfare.

CHAPTER 14

Frank went back to work, promising to get in touch with the detective who'd investigated the death of Jenna Simone. Perhaps, he pointed out as they waited by the elevator bank, there was a valid reason the kid got off. Maybe he really didn't do it.

"Sure," Theresa said with controlled despair, "maybe there's a perfectly rational explanation for why he was found next to her body with her blood on his hands."

"Yeah." Frank pressed the "down" button. "Maybe."

She left him there and proceeded to the front desk, each step taking longer than it should. The thirty or so feet to the marble counter seemed to have tripled. She did not see Rachael. *Please,* she begged the angels, *please don't let her be waiting for William on the tower observation deck, fifty-two floors above the earth.*

Behind the desk stood the skinny black girl she'd met the day before—Lorraine.

Upon request, however, Lorraine produced Rachael with a speed that had Theresa melting in gratitude. She'd merely been in the ladies' room. Since the front-desk area seemed well populated, Theresa asked only that Rachael remain there until Theresa could collect her at the end of her shift. No delivering things to rooms, no leaving the lobby for any reason.

"Whatever. I hardly ever do anyway, unless someone drops off flowers or something. I think I'm safe, Mom. I'm not a lawyer."

"No one's safe at the moment. Just promise me, okay—"

A firm hand grasped her elbow, and a harried-looking Neil Kelly asked if she wanted to come back to the crime scene. The body snatchers had arrived for the corpse.

She went with him, giving only a backward glance to her daughter. Rachael watched them, suspicious. Children knew when their parents were holding back, and Rachael could sometimes read Theresa as easily as if she were a fast-food menu.

"You all right?" Neil Kelly asked once the elevator doors had closed.

"Yeah," she said. "Just tired."

"I knew it," Powell said as Theresa helped the two body snatchers, one as tall and muscular as the other was short and undernourished, bundle Bruce Raffel into a white plastic body bag. "I figured these shysters would be into something kinky."

"Only Bruce." Theresa taped the carpeting underneath where the body had lain. "There's no reason to think Marie had any unusual habits."

"But she dated him, so it follows. It's a power thing, I'm telling you. Dominating in the courtroom, dominating in the bedroom. She wouldn't give up any details about how Raffel liked it?"

"I didn't ask."

"We'll get subpoenas—for her, the partners of both victims, assistants, paralegals."

The idea pained Theresa. Bad enough she'd told them about Sonia and Bruce, though Sonia would expect that. She stopped taping the carpeting that had been underneath Bruce Raffel's body to ask, "Do you have to?"

Neil Kelly looked at her with a touch of pity. "Two bodies piled up, and this woman knew both of them. She may be able to connect the dots for us. How much should we worry about people's feelings? Especially since they're the same people who are going to say we didn't solve these murders because we don't like them?"

"You're going to subpoena her to compel testimony about a casual hookup that occurred two or three years before the crime. I'm glad I don't have your job." Theresa could imagine few things more depressing than listening to endless rationalizations of how these strangers were perfectly okay with such an empty emotional life that mindless pairings became an acceptable substitute. Poor Sonia. But then Neil Kelly had probably heard much more depressing stories than that, and there were worse factors than mindless. After discussing it further, he and Powell decided, with obvious disappointment, that they'd never get a judge to sign off.

Surely cops were no strangers to the lifestyle themselves, when out with cop groupies and other hangers-on. Lots of late nights, unpredictable locations . . . She thought of her cousin. Would Frank . . . ?

Hell, Frank would probably lead by example. Her cousin needed something real in his life. Theresa had been half hoping that something romantic would develop between him and his smart, attractive partner ever since they'd been assigned to work together, but nothing had—so far. Maybe Frank knew better than to get involved with a co-worker. More likely Angela knew better than to get involved with Frank.

What about Neil Kelly? Theresa watched him surreptitiously, wondering what his fantasies might entail.

Neil startled her from this dangerous reverie by asking, "She tell you anything else?"

"Yeah—she said I should ask Dennis Britton how his first wife died."

"You got me," Neil said. "I didn't know there *was* a first Mrs. Britton."

"Car accident," Powell said, much more seriously than Theresa would have expected, so that both Neil and Theresa stared at the man. "Before your time, pard. His wife missed the end of a parking lot and drove down a hill, stopped short. Nothing mysterious."

Still, Theresa sensed a touch of hesitation. "Are you sure?"

"We *made* sure. Nothing would have delighted my unit more than arresting Dennis Britton for the murder of his wife. We looked at everything—the autopsy results, the parking-lot video, the guy's alibi, the position of the driver's seat. Everything. It would have to be the perfect murder, and he's not *that* smart. Your gal pal really got a hard-on for Dennis Britton, doesn't she?"

Neil said, "He *was* the victim's boyfriend, and Marie and Brucie here had been serious at one point. Maybe the two of them used this conference to get together for old times' sake and Britton didn't like it."

"So he kills her in a fit of pique but then comes back to finish the job with Raffel, after having a day to cool down?"

Neil elaborated his theory. "Or Raffel killed Marie and Britton got revenge. Or Raffel knew that Britton should be the number-one suspect and why, so Britton needed to shut him up. I've been here long enough to testify in a couple of Britton's cases, and I've figured out one thing: The guy doesn't like to lose."

Powell nodded. "I know. He was trying to get some guy off on self-defense one time, insisting that his client had grabbed the gun out of this cheesy gun locker because he felt threatened, when the locker was all the way at the back of the house. The day of a jury visit, we walk into the house, jury in tow, and lo and behold suddenly the locker is in the front hallway. Britton insisted it had been there the night of the murder and his client had moved it later. So they only moved it back. But somehow this detail had slipped his mind until just before the jury visit. Every attorney bends the truth, but he just drops it in the can and flushes."

Theresa pushed herself off the wall she'd been leaning on and rubbed her lower back. The scent of dried blood, sharp and dusty, filled her nose. She'd had enough of these cut-off, too-quiet rooms, the pervasive insulation sucking out not only noise but thought, and feeling, and life. "You said Britton had an alibi for Marie's murder."

"For *most* of the evening. But unless you can be sure she died sometime before eleven o'clock or so, when he finally sent his entourage away and returned to the humble abode his wife paid over two million for, then we can't really be sure, can we? He could have swung upstairs to meet Corrigan for a quick one before heading home."

"And Marie waited all that time?"

"No, she would have been up to her own devices. But she'd have waited because she needed his coattails to climb. He could always get another piece on the side. The balance of power favored him." Powell added, in ponderous tones, "It's all about power. Who has it, who wants it."

"Sounds to me like it's all about sex," Neil said.

"Sex *is* power."

"I'm suspecting your divorce wasn't quite as unfair as you led me to believe, partner."

Theresa said, "I'll talk to Christine. Maybe she can narrow it down. Did you ever find Marie's cell phone? If they did meet up, there might be calls or texts."

On cue, her phone buzzed at her waist.

"She had locked her purse in her trunk," Neil told her. "I guess she didn't want to carry it. Still no phone, though. We're going to subpoena the cell company for the call history."

A text, from Rachael: TAKING BUS. LNG NUFF DAY!

Damn it, the girl had left without her. But if she were on public transportation, surrounded by people . . . assuming she'd made it to the bus, assuming William hadn't offered to walk her to the station. *I'm getting off now, too,* he might have said. *I'll walk you.*

"So the killer took her phone," Powell was saying. "Why? Because he'd called her to hook up. Maybe even texted like our scientist here."

Theresa barely heard him. Through a series of frantic and misspelled texts—afterward she wondered why she didn't just call—she learned that Rachael had indeed boarded the bus and would get together with her grandmother to coordinate dinner. Theresa breathed out, texted back how pleased it made her to have a daughter who liked to cook, hung up, and tried to recall what the detectives had been talking about. "How long will it take to get that information from the cell company?"

"That depends on them. Days, if we're lucky. Otherwise weeks."

Theresa gathered her tapings, stowed them in an envelope. "I'm done here."

Neil thanked her, then walked her to the elevator. "Heading home?"

"No, back to the lab."

"Going to get right to work on dead lawyer number two?"

"Sort of."

CHAPTER 15

Frank never wanted to see another lawyer as long as he lived. He thought so most of the time anyway, but today it felt particularly apt. Yesterday the conference attendees had been shocked by Marie Corrigan's death but assumed it to be the result of random violence or some bad situation of Marie's own choosing. Interestingly, out-of-town strangers favored the first theory, while those who had actually known Marie tended toward the second.

With Bruce Raffel's death, however, the events became anything but random, and each of the gathered attorneys was torn between fear of becoming a suspect and fear of becoming the next victim. It made them conflicted, which in turn made them more flippin' annoying than ever before in Frank's experience. The ones from out of town weren't quite as bad. They would almost certainly never be seen in this town again and were therefore free to simply answer the questions asked. When did they last see Bruce Raffel? Did they speak with him, did he express any fear or anger toward anyone, did he mention any plans for the evening or the rest of the convention? The Cleveland lawyers, though, could not let even fear of brutal murder sway them from their smarmy "I'm smarter than you" stance and did their best to ask more questions than they answered, and they answered only after examining each question from every angle. An attorney Frank had encountered at an armed-robbery trial said he'd talked with Bruce during a coffee break but wouldn't say what they'd discussed because it involved an open case.

"He seem worried about anything?" Frank asked, a standard question.

"Hell no. He kept saying how great it was to be back in Cleveland. You ask me, the guy was lonely. He thought he'd dumped us losers for the sunny South, but they didn't roll out the red carpet for him. That southern-hospitality thing is a crock, he said. At least for him." The guy shook his head. "Kinda pathetic."

Another had seen Bruce and Marie in the hallway between the first and second sessions on Tuesday but would not characterize their conversation as friendly, neutral, or antagonistic. He told Frank, "That's your job, to know what everybody's thinking just from looking at them. I don't claim to be clairvoyant, like our fine officers of the law who consider 'knowing' that a guy has drugs in his trunk to be sufficient probable cause." He did admit that the two were not shouting, frowning, or kissing. An attorney Frank remembered from a drunk-driving case during his rookie days tried to make a Hannibal Lecter–like tit-for-tat trade and would tell whether he'd ever spoken to either victim if Frank gave him a complete description of Marie's body, including any attendant hardware.

Frank got through the list, sent the last lawyer away— a surprisingly sweet girl whose vacant stare made him think her brain was powered by a gerbil running in a plastic wheel—and glanced over at his partner. Angela Sanchez sat with one hand propping her chin, listening with apparent dismay to the convoluted *CSI*-induced theory of a lawyer from, if Frank correctly placed the accent, Jersey. She gave Frank a "kill me now" glance, sat up, and focused anew on her interviewee. Frank checked out the other table, where Detective Powell spoke to a teased blond attorney, trying without success to keep his eyes from wandering to her low-cut blouse. Frank decided that he needed a drink. Himself, not Powell, though the older cop probably did, too.

He got up and went down to the lounge.

Of course he couldn't drink, being on duty, so coffee would have to do. He took a seat at the short black-granite bar, empty except for a discarded straw wrapper, and waited a good five minutes for a 'tender to show up. It was two in the afternoon, not a big time for meals or drinks, so staff appeared in the lounge area only sporadically. She took his order and went to fetch it, leaving the straw wrapper. The same girl returned five minutes later, plunked down a lukewarm cup, and disappeared again, still ignoring the discarded wrapper. Wasn't this supposed to be a super-fancy, too-perfect, expensive hotel? "God is in the details," Frank muttered, and shot the paper ball off the granite with a flick of his finger. It flew across the space behind the bar and lodged between a square container of Jack Daniel's and a squat bottle of Crown Royal.

With a sigh, Frank wished he and Angela could have caught this case, been the lead detectives. He hated assisting. It wasn't that he begrudged other detectives their cases and their collars, even high-profile ones like this. It was just so *boring*. All drudge work, asking the standard people the standard questions, establishing a timeline, dotting the *i*'s and crossing the *t*'s, knowing that even if the guy is caught, it won't be you who gets to slap on the cuffs. Boring.

But for all his inner whining, he had to admit that they'd learned most of what they needed to know. Last time he compared notes with the other detectives, they could establish that the final sighting of Bruce Raffel had been at approximately five-fifteen. After the luncheon he had attended a workshop entitled "Offensive Defenses"—Frank wondered if they'd really thought that title through—from two to three and then something called "Litigating Postconviction Innocence Cases Without DNA" until the conference wrapped up at 5:00 P.M. Long day, Frank had to admit. From there, Bruce had stopped in the lounge and glad-handed a few people but couldn't get near the bar for the line and didn't see, or wasn't invited into, any groups. "Seemed to me," another Atlanta attorney had confided to Frank, "he wasn't one of the Cleveland gang anymore. Not shut out, but not welcomed in. Sort of at loose ends."

"And not in the Atlanta gang yet?"

The man had shrugged. "It's a pretty big gang, and he's only been there a year. I don't really know him, but what I do know I don't like. He breezed down there thinking we'd all be a bunch of hillbillies. The guy had no clue how many Ivy League grads we have in my office alone. I think he got his license by mail order."

Bruce had sidled out of the bar by ten after five or so and gone to the elevator. No one saw him after that. Correction: No one *admitted* seeing him after that. No one, male or female, admitted to having sex with him on that evening or any prior evening, and no one admitted to killing him.

With no signs of forced entry or even a struggle, Frank assumed that Bruce Raffel had let his killer into his room. But that would be easy—a man in a fancy hotel would open the door to anyone who knocked. Why not? All the other person had to do was mumble something about a delivery, or the convention, or room maintenance, and he would open the door. The killer could work without neighbors peering through the living-room curtains, without leaving a strange car parked at the curb. A convenient peephole to make sure the coast was clear before leaving. A hotel, Frank had begun to realize, is a very handy place to kill someone.

The killer had gotten into the Presidential Suite the day before—the killer or Marie, that is, and either way the killer would still have the key card used—so perhaps the killer had been waiting in Bruce's room.

Frank had given up on that and turned back to the question of motive, pondering who would want to kill lawyers (answer: everyone), when Marcus Dean walked into the lounge. At least six foot five, his scalp shaved down to peach fuzz, military posture. He nodded at Frank and surveyed the room—not much to survey, the only other occupants being a frail lady in a pastel sweater and a sullen teenager listening to his iPod. So the head of security settled into one of the high stools at the granite bar. Dean had been very helpful during this investigation, but not particularly friendly. Uncomfortable, yet Frank thought he could understand why. Marcus had gone from a Vice detective, poised to move into SWAT if he wanted it, to a hotel gumshoe. It was a good, honest, and, given the Ritz-Carlton's budget, probably quite lucrative job, but it had to be the emotional equivalent of being a teenage boy and having your friend catch you washing dishes with your mom. Nothing wrong with it, exactly. But not cool.

"How's it going?" Marcus asked, his voice rolling out of him, a slow but deadly tsunami.

"No breaks yet. The guy went back to his room and someone killed him, that's about all we got so far."

"What about the bitch?"

Frank didn't ask who Dean meant. He referred to Marie by the same term himself. "Nothing there either. Autopsy says she was negative for semen, so that screws us. We could be chasing our tails trying to connect it to this convention when we've just got a run-of-the-mill psycho on our hands."

"I was up most of the night thinking about that," Marcus said. "If they'd been killed in their own rooms, then maybe some predator decided to make my hotel his hunting ground. Half of my rooms are rented to lawyers this week, so he can knock on any door and have a fifty-fifty chance that it will be opened by a lawyer—and anyone will open the door. Wear something that looks like a uniform, say something that sounds like a valid reason, and they'll open it. People feel too much at home in hotels, like they've stepped into a very tastefully designed playpen where they can't be hurt."

"I had the same thought. Problem is, our two victims knew each other, dated each other. Kind of takes 'random' off the table. The killer meant to kill these two in particular. Which brings us back to the beginning: How could either Marie Corrigan or her killer get into that suite without the key card?"

The big man's shoulders slid downward. "That's the other thing I lay awake most of last night wondering."

"Get an answer?"

"Just this: Nobody could. Unless he was some kind of genius superhacker."

"But it's just a magnetic strip—"

"Yeah, I know, and kids out on Quincy who never made it past the eighth grade have those zippers to copy credit cards. But he would still have to get a card in the first place, and even then it would take some serious geek skills to copy."

"So he rents the room—"

"The room code is changed after every checkout."

"So how did he do it?"

Marcus shrugged, an elegant gesture of resignation. "The old-fashioned way. Stole or bribed a key from someone who works here. Bribed, it would have to be, because all the pass cards are accounted for. Except that I spoke to every single person who has one—eighteen people, including me. Every one of them could produce his or her card, and they all swore up and down they didn't give it to anyone else, not even another worker. So who's lying?" He shrugged again. "I don't know. Even on the job, I never got that human-lie-detector ability down."

Frank sipped his now-cold coffee. "On the other hand, maybe we just narrowed the suspect pool to eighteen—seventeen—people."

Marcus snorted a laugh. "Thanks for the vote of confidence, man, but I'm the only one of the eighteen who even knew Marie Corrigan. The rest of them got nothing to do with lawyers. Half are kids, and the other half have been working here so long that I really don't think it's likely they just decided to up and start killing people."

"Could somebody have stolen one off a maid's cart, then put it back before she noticed?"

"Maids don't keep their key cards anywhere but in their pockets. Leaving it on the cart is grounds for instant termination."

"How many masters are there?"

"Three. Me, Karla, and the owner."

"What about him?"

Marcus just laughed. "Lives in Miami. Therefore doesn't even need his card, but he likes that feeling of privilege."

Frank pondered that for a moment and then, at the risk of implicating his own niece asked, "Can't staff make a new key at the front desk?"

"Yeah, but they didn't. When a card is written, it's recorded in the computer, including when the key was made and when it's scheduled to shut off."

"Could someone hack the computer instead of the door lock?"

Another snort. "Unlikely. I keep the passwords to the computer system."

"What if you get hit by a bus?"

"Then Karla takes a bolt cutter to my cabinet. Besides, even if someone had my password, he'd still need to be one hell of a hacker. Anyone who could pull that off would have better things to do than murder lawyers. I would be noticing supplies going missing and customer complaints of lost items going up. Nobody who works here is that computer-savvy. Including me."

Because he could no longer help it, Frank asked, "What's it like? Working here?" Meaning, *What's it like to be something other than a cop, and does it suck as much as I think it would?*

The question did not seem to offend Marcus. He stared into the liquor bottles, their labels and colored liquids reflected in his eyes, which were nearly as dark as the granite bar. Then the wrinkles in his forehead cleared as if he had surprised himself with the answer: "Not bad. At first I was like, shit, what have I *done?*"

Frank nodded, imagining feeling the same way.

"But it's not bad. The hours are so much better. In Vice, man, it seemed like every friggin' search warrant we served had to be done in the middle of the night, like it was a rule or something: Search warrants couldn't be done during hours when people might actually be awake. Of course, no overtime hours means no overtime pay, but

I'm divorced now, so I don't need so much extra cash. The job ain't bad, though. It's not as boring as I thought it would be. Being a cop was all about reacting. Somebody's selling drugs, so we take him down. A dude beats another dude, so we take him down. But this is all about trying to figure out what *could* happen and then preventing it. I have to step back and think, if I wanted to rob these rooms, what would I do? Pop in while the maid is cleaning, pretend it's my room? Tag along behind a maintenance man, catch the door before it closes? If I wanted to appropriate a few cases of booze from the storeroom, how would I do it? How do I move them, how do I try to keep them from being missed? It's all logistics." He tapped his temple. "I like the head part of it."

Frank watched the waitress bring the old lady another coffee, then flounce off before he could catch her eye for a refill.

"It's a different story every minute," Marcus Dean continued. "People do weird stuff, man, just weird. I had a guy check in, dressed nice, platinum credit card, quiet and respectable. In twenty minutes we've got all sorts of traffic to his floor—non-guests, people coming and going. A call to my old co-workers and they pull the guy out of the room with a stock of coke, Ecstasy, and meth. And that's not the funny part. The funny part, the cops don't hold the undeclared guest in the room, so his buddy asks if he could keep the room since it's paid for, and the arrested guy says okay. He goes off to jail, and his buddy calls room service every hour, ordering an eight-dollar can of pop or a fifteen-dollar bowl of soup, charges it to the room. Which was on the first guy's credit card. The first guy finally thinks better of this and calls the card company from jail to shut off the card. Then we could finally toss out guy number two.

"And the kids, man. Rich people do an even worse job

of looking after their kids than poor people. That's what made me craziest about working in the projects, seeing these toddlers in filthy clothes, more or less fending for themselves, but here I've found kindergarten-age kids wandering to the gift shop. Their clothes are cleaner, that's the only difference. Last month we had a sports team, one of those exclusive schools, younger kids. The boys were fine, really. Their *parents* turned the hallways into their personal lounge, getting drunker and louder with each case of beer. Night manager kept talking to them, but no one on three floors got any sleep that night. It's always something. Just like being a cop," he said, eyebrows lifting with this sudden revelation, "except no one gets shot."

"Usually," Frank joked.

"Usually."

"Why'd you leave the department?" Frank asked. Maybe too personal, but surely Marcus had been asked that question before. And Frank really wanted to know how someone could walk away from the job. It sounded impossible to him.

Marcus studied the bottles lined against the glass wall, maybe deciding on an answer. In the end he only shrugged and said, "Got tired of the BS. The whole freakin' war on drugs—let me tell you something about our fine pharmaceutical representatives. They know what they're doing. They structure their work so there's no paper trail, all verbal cues and quick handoffs. No evidence. We'd work months to get a conviction on a guy, and by the time the lawyers got done with it, he'd get the minimum sentence. His assistants would take over until their time was up, and the whole trade goes on without a hiccup. Working Narco is not quite like anything else. At least when you got a guy for murder, either he goes away or he sure ain't likely to do it again real soon. But drugs, it don't even pause."

Nothing Frank hadn't heard before, but something he knew to be gospel true and therefore deserving respect. "Frustrating."

"You got it." Marcus frowned at the bottles now, apparently focusing on the Crown Royal.

Frank hastily pressed on. Technically, Marcus was a suspect, and not only because of the key cards. "I heard you beat a guy half to death."

Marcus glanced over at him, and Frank couldn't help the tiny frisson of fear that comes with seriously ticking off a behemoth. But the anger in the other man's face quickly faded into melancholy. "That's marking the truth up about two hundred percent—as usual. I hit a guy, yeah. Arrested him in the park with a bag of pills and two underage girls, and he got smart with me. I shouldn't have done it, sure, but half to death? More like a bruise and one loose tooth."

"That was it?"

"We're cops," Marcus said, slipping into the inaccurate tense. "That's *never* it. So I could have gone before the board, given up my gun, get loaned to the front desk or the property room for a few months, but I—" He stared at his own reflection long enough for Frank to run through eleven or twelve different endings for that sentence, then said, "I didn't feel like it."

He got up and walked around the bar, plucking the paper ball from between the two bottles and dropping it into a trash can. "I just didn't feel like it."

Forearms folded over the granite, he stared Frank down as if daring him to dispute the story.

Which Frank had no intention of doing. "You have this same convention here last year?"

"No, it rotates. Sure wish they could have picked Moline or something this time."

"Any of these attorneys frequent this place even before the convention?"

"Not that I noticed. I know some of 'em, and I don't remember seeing them here before. Why, you thinking about the sex-club idea?"

"You heard about that?"

Marcus laughed and straightened. "Everybody's heard about it, man. But these rooms don't rent by the hour. This is the *Ritz*. People come here for one of three reasons: because it's a real special event, because they want to impress somebody, or because they've got so much money they don't care what the rate is. Lawyers make a good buck, but not *that* good. If their little club had regular meetings in this place, no one could afford to be a member. Except maybe for Britton."

"That was my thinking, too. What about Marie Corrigan?"

"What about her?"

"Ever see her around here?"

"Nope. Doesn't mean she wasn't. I don't see most of the guests, unless they raise some kind of ruckus."

"See her anywhere else?"

This time the momentary irritation didn't melt into melancholy. "What do you mean?"

"I heard you asked Marie Corrigan out. More than once."

A pause ensued. Frank had encountered that pause in every interview he'd ever conducted. Every one, every time. Sometimes more than once during the conversation, but always at least once. It ensued as the person being questioned debated about whether or not to lie to him. People calculated the damage if they didn't and the risk if they did and, most important, the odds that Frank would find out anyway. And then they usually—

"Yes."

—realized that those odds were really, really good.

"Where'd you hear that?" Marcus asked.

"Around." Actually, it came from nothing more than a vague rumor passed to Angela from a friend of hers in Records whose brother-in-law's stepdaughter clerked in the PD's office. Something like that.

"But it was a couple of years ago," Marcus went on. "I'd just gotten divorced, and— You ever get divorced?"

Frank shook his head. "Never married."

"Not that I was happy about splitting up—I wasn't— but still, when you've had that ring around your finger for a lot of years and suddenly you don't, you're like a kid getting out of school for the summer. I can ask out anyone I want! I can take anything in a skirt back to my apartment, and there ain't nothin' nobody can say to me about it!" He laughed, and it seemed genuine. "Eventually I figured out that hot young things don't *want* to go back to some broken-down cop's crappy apartment, but for a while there I was like a stupid dog, the kind that barks at anything that moves. And say what you like about that vicious bitch, but she was hot."

"What happened?"

"She wasn't interested in a broken-down cop's crappy apartment either. Or a cop. Or a black cop. Or a guy who didn't drive a Beemer, I don't know."

"Harsh."

"She was good at harsh. Once she mocked out the spelling errors in my partner's report. So okay, cops aren't hired for their literary abilities, but she kept on it until she convinced the jury that he didn't know a blood-stain from a glass of orange juice."

"She did that to me, too," Frank admitted. "At least

mine was only a deposition. Made me paranoid about *i* before *e* for a while."

"Yeah. So I hope you wrap this up here—or just get all these lawyers out of my hotel, that would be fine, too—so my job can go back to telling unruly guests when to quiet down. But if you do find who killed Marie Corrigan, give me a minute with him before you slap on the cuffs."

"Yeah?"

"Yeah. I want to shake his hand."

CHAPTER 16

While the records of live juveniles—such as fingerprints, affidavits, and court proceedings—are kept strictly separate from the adult files, the records of *deceased* juveniles are not segregated in any way. Privacy has become useless to them, and since all autopsy reports and attendant information are considered confidential, there's no reason to consider the medical examiner's records on children any *more* confidential. So, as a frequent visitor to the records department, Theresa could find the file on Jenna Simone's homicide as easily as she could the record of a fifty-two-year-old heart-attack victim.

She set it on the small reading table crammed to one side of the records office, under the watchful eye of two secretaries. Both women had worked there long enough to settle into firmly defined and complementary personality profiles. One was a jumbled mass of curly hair and sweetness, always with at least fifteen disjointed files and a bowl of candy on her desk, who knew all the people in the building, their children, and their pets and would ask after the welfare of each one upon every visit. The other sat sternly, impassively, her desk bare except for one file at a time and a framed photo of her daughter, who, on the lone occasion Theresa dared to glance at it, appeared as stern as her mother. Attempts at small talk were met with a stony silence. Theresa often wondered what each would be like if she had a different office mate, if each woman hadn't been assigned such an extreme to play off. Would the stern one relax a bit? Would the grandmotherly type allow herself to get snappish once in a while?

Theresa opened the file. She acted only out of idle curiosity, she told herself; no crisis or even worry existed. Rachael did not date this boy, merely worked with him. It could all be a mistake; Sonia had briefly met him at a younger age, and surely William Rosedale could not be that uncommon a name. Frankly, Theresa should be working on the evidence gathered from around Marie Corrigan and Bruce Raffel as the taxpayers of Cuyahoga County paid her to do, instead of indulging her own overprotective tendencies. But her gaze fell on an eight-by-ten glossy photo of Jenna Simone, naked, dead, her hair soaked in a dried red liquid, her face blotted out under this coating of her own blood. And Theresa forgot all about the taxpayers of Cuyahoga County.

The girl lay on the floor of a stylish living room, furnished with gray Berber carpeting and charcoal leather couches. Pale gray sheers covered the window next to the edge of a fireplace. The girl's body rested in between a coffee table, its picture books still spread out in a real-estate agent's vignette, and an overstuffed sofa. Facedown, head turned slightly to the right, legs spread, her left hand disappearing under the couch and her right flung out, fingernails digging into the thick carpet as if trying to gain traction, to crawl out from under the force that had battered her skull. Something in bright turquoise had been tossed under the coffee table, probably her shirt, and a dark blob near her feet appeared to be her pants.

The blood had formed a pool underneath her head, soaking into the carpet and spreading out, with a series of dots and blobs around it—on the carpet, the sofa, and even the coffee-table books. Just like Marie Corrigan. Just like Bruce Raffel.

Why don't I remember this? Theresa wondered again. She checked the date—June 27, three years prior.

Oh.

She had been home from work on June 27, three years prior. She had been home from work for most of that July, too, because her fiancé had just been killed during the investigation of a bank robbery at the Federal Reserve.

At least that explained why she had no memory of such a brutal murder. She had no memory of the rest of that summer.

Theresa shrugged and went back to the file. The autopsy report came next.

It was not lengthy; it didn't need to be. Jenna Simone had been a perfectly healthy sixteen-year-old until some-one took a blunt object to her skull. She had not been a virgin prior to the attack. Small tears indicated rape, but no sperm was found and no DNA obtained. She'd been struck three times on the back of the skull with something thin, straight, and hard. No weapon had been submitted for comparison, the doctor noted—not as a comment on the investigation but because it might be years before the case came to trial and the pathologist would need an answer when the defense attorney asked why the wounds had not been compared to a weapon. By then it would be hard to remember any theories about what could have caused the wounds when time and many more autopsies came in between. So the doctor had also noted that the fireplace poker had disappeared and that a rod of such size and strength could have been used to cause the defects in the girl's cranium. Theresa instantly saw the prosecutor's problem: The suspect was present, but without the weapon. If he'd gotten rid of the poker, why not get rid of the body? If the body would be too difficult to dispose of, why not keep the poker and invent a story about a bushy-haired stranger who'd invaded his home in a botched robbery, found William passing out, and a vulnerable Jenna? A story that wouldn't fool a five-year-old but couldn't exactly be *dis*proved either. Men had beaten a murder charge with less. Perhaps William really had been in a drunken haze, unable to summon up even a slightly good plan to cover up his guilt—and yet able to make the weapon disappear.

There were no other wounds on her body, no bruises, nothing but one chipped fingernail. Jenna had not been drunk. Normally the toxicology results would be in a separate report, but since the case had gone to trial and the results had become part of a public record, they remained in the file. Jenna Simone had had a small amount of alcohol in her system, equivalent to perhaps one beer, and no other narcotics or stimulants.

Next came only a single page of laboratory notes, written in Don's neat handwriting. He had examined the victim's clothing—the DNA analyst had picked up Theresa's slack while she'd been lost in a funk. Westlake PD had submitted four items: a turquoise shirt with thin straps and a built-in shelf bra; a pair of blue denim jeans, Tommy Hilfiger size four boot-cut; a pair of silky purple panties, no tag; and a pair of high-heeled leather sandals with black-and-white leopard-print uppers. These were worn but clean, with no bloodstains. The panties were free of blood and negative for semen. The jeans—how did teenagers stay so preternaturally thin? Theresa wondered; in her youth no one under the age of eight would have fit into a size four—were also unstained. The turquoise top had smears of blood, but no evidence of semen. All items had been taped for hairs and fibers and submitted to the hair/fiber analyst—Theresa, in other words. So she did not feel surprised when she turned to the next report to see her own handwriting, somewhat less tidy than Don's.

She had included a micrograph of matching carpet fibers and finally felt a glimmer of recognition at the gray, trilobal threads. Of the hairs found on the body, one was consistent with William, one with his mother, and one, short and black, matched no one. No conclusions could be drawn from this, as the body lay in the suspect's own house and not in an isolated location—meaning that Theresa assumed the Rosedales had as many guests and visitors in their home as any other family. A wealthy family, probably quite social . . . How much had that changed? Had their friends stood by them, or did the incident cause a bit of coolness in the country club's locker room?

That concluded the reports. Two thick packets of photographs had been left in the file, most likely printed up for the prosecution's review or at the pathologist's request. Since the M.E.'s office had gone to digital instead of 35-millimeter, photos were stored and accessed through the computer network to save the cost of actually printing them. But some doctors still preferred to work with prints instead of their computer monitor, or the prosecutors tried to save money by asking the M.E.'s office to print the photos.

Theresa skimmed through the autopsy photos with determined professionalism, making no connection between the raw flesh on the steel table and her own daughter. Not even a glimmer. Not even when she viewed the bare white bone of Jenna Simone's skull, pieced back together for the photographer like a jigsaw puzzle.

The other packet, much thinner, contained photographs of the clothing, each item front and back. No surprises. The bloodstains stood out in sharp relief against the bright blue, a large blotch at the hemline and then a series of three and a half lines under the right armpit. Something like Marie Corrigan—blood on the shirt only. As if the bludgeoning had been inflicted before the clothing had been removed. But if both females and their killer hadn't been in the process of removing clothing, then what had provoked such a fatal argument? Because the women wouldn't even consider removing it? Or because both killers didn't even try to persuade them?

A surprisingly brief newspaper clipping gave her only a few additional facts: Jenna had had no current boyfriend and had met up with her girlfriends at the dance. A friend of William's had confirmed that they'd arrived at the dance together but then he'd lost track of William. William's car was found in the school parking lot.

And there the file of Jenna Simone's death ended.

Theresa moved to the cabinet and placed the folder back in numerical order.

The case could not be more open and shut. And yet William Rosedale had walked out of the courtroom a free man. How?

One person might have some insight. And, happily for her, he worked right upstairs.

She pushed the file drawer to close it, then grabbed it again as a name caught her eye. It closed on her right thumb, not enough to bruise but enough to hurt like the dickens. She pulled out the new file with her left hand and read the name on the tab.

Cases were filed by number, not name. Only one and a half months after Jenna Simone's murder, Ellie Baker Britton had died. The first wife of her lawyer nemesis.

CHAPTER 17

Frank slammed the door of the Crown Vic just a little too hard, and the sound rattled his eardrums. He'd developed a headache after the day spent inside the hotel, the air a little too stuffy, the witnesses a little too reticent. He needed to go home, where a shot of Jack Daniel's and some satellite TV cured most ills. Maybe two shots.

The house in front of him had high windows, an impeccable paint job, and columns. Actual freakin' columns, white and tall.

Maybe three shots.

"We're in the wrong line of work," his partner, Angela, observed from the other side of the car.

"You took the words right out of my mouth."

"Meat Loaf."

He blinked at her for a moment before making the association. They had fallen into a habit of throwing out snatches of song lyrics as a challenge for the other to identify. It gave them something to do in the slow moments, when other detective teams might talk about sports, politics, or their personal problems. Angela didn't follow sports, Frank ignored any politics that didn't immediately affect him, and Angela kept most of her personal life to herself. Frank thought he did, too, but sometimes suspected that he simply didn't *have* a personal life to keep.

Dennis Britton, on the other hand, probably did. He certainly had the house for it.

His sweeping three-story mansion in Gates Mills backed up to the Chagrin River, surrounded by oak trees, a five-car garage, and a smaller home that may once have belonged to servants and probably still did. Frank couldn't picture Britton spending the weekend trimming the bushes or washing the windows. Frank couldn't picture Britton without a suit and tie.

An older BMW sat on the pristine driveway, next to a current-model Corvette. Hers and his, Frank guessed. Old money and new. Or maybe just old. No need to spend your own salary on your toys when your wife comes from one of the richest families in the country.

Angela sighed.

"Stop it," he told her. She gave him a quizzical look, and he expounded, "Neither of us is looking forward to this, and we should be. Here's our chance to put this asshole on the hot seat instead of him doing it to us. We should be breathing fire, not all depressed and intimidated. The man's at the top of our list for two brutal murders, and we're not leaving here without answers. Right?"

She smiled. "Right. Should we give some sort of tribal yell, or say 'hike' or something?"

Frank looked up at the high windows. "We'll skip that part for now."

He walked briskly to the massive front door and knocked confidently, mainly confident that all the pep talks in the world weren't going to help. He had nothing on Dennis Britton, nothing to implicate him in any real way, and Dennis Britton would know that as well as he would know the definition of "habeas corpus." But the police shooting case was on temporary hiatus after the judge developed a case of food poisoning from a bad breakfast, leaving Britton an unexpectedly free afternoon. Frank wanted to make sure the lawyer didn't enjoy it.

The door swung open, revealing the expected towering foyer and sweeping staircase, marble tile, and a boy of about thirteen. He had the baggy pants and oversize T-shirt of his age group with twice the required sullenness. "Yeah?"

"We're here to see Dennis Britton." Frank had expected either a maid complete with French outfit or the lord or lady him- or herself, and this kid threw him off. Britton and the current lady hadn't been married long enough to have one this age, so he must be from a previous marriage or some kind of houseguest. Frank searched the kid's face for any sign that Britton had procreated, but nothing seemed familiar except the faint sneer. That was dead-on.

"I think he's in the garage," the kid said, and shut the door.

The smooth white surface now two inches from his nose, Frank said, "I guess we'll try the garage. Wonder why Junior isn't in school."

"He probably has private tutors," Angela snapped out as they descended the front steps. Maybe the kid reminded her of her own, but Frank didn't ask. Let people start talking about their kids and you'd wind up hearing about every scraped knee or school-yard bully or teacher who "just doesn't get him" until you wanted to cover your ears and hum the theme from *Barney*. He never asked about Angela's kids.

Frank had been in garages with numbered slots for tools, garages impassable with stored junk, garages made of gaping planks that would fall over in the first strong wind, but he had never before been in a garage that required both a key card and a numeric code to enter. It appeared to be the emergency bunker to the main house's headquarters. Frank tried the knob. It didn't budge, leaving him no choice but to push the little metal button next to the little metal speaker plate. He refused to say anything, figuring the button would buzz and the two security cameras pointed at him would show Britton who they were.

He should have known better.

"*Yes?*"

Frank repeated his objective.

"*What for?*" the voice said.

"What do you think?" He wasn't going to get into a pissing contest with a disembodied voice no matter how much it would amuse the attorney. Problem was, he didn't know what to do if Britton didn't let them in. He had no warrant, and if he put his foot in *this* door, he'd have to go to the hospital.

"*I already talked to you,*" Britton said, his voice calm and smarmy even after passing through several electronic components.

"It's okay, Britton," Frank said. "We can wait."

Then he turned around, faced the meticulously landscaped area, and leaned his back against the building as if he had all the time in the world, not so much as glancing at the cameras. He lit a cigarette as a final show of nonchalance, making sure to scatter the ashes. Angela wandered over to the flower beds and appeared to examine the various flora.

It took ten minutes and Frank grinding his menthol butt into the sparkling buff concrete before Britton apparently felt he had scored some sort of point and let them in. And lo and behold, he wore a plain T-shirt tucked into straining jeans. No suit or tie.

Calling the space a garage seemed vastly inadequate. The ceiling rose at least thirty feet above them, and the walls sat in an enormous square, with space for five cars both front to back and side to side, so that with a little organization at least twenty-five could be parked inside. All of it had been painted a nearly blinding white. In the southwest corner stood a large metal lift, so that Britton could hoist his babies into the air instead of having to crawl under them like any average joe. Frank had never seen one in a private home before.

Despite the space there were only three automobiles present: a brown Jaguar, a purplish thing that looked like it hailed from the early days of Motown and mini-skirts, and a metallic blue Corvette with large pipes running along each side. It had suffered some sort of indignity to its right front fender, and a raw fiberglass hole gaped just behind the headlights. Britton trimmed pieces of it with a pair of gleaming side cutters. "Have you found out who killed Marie yet?"

Just as well to skip the small talk. Pretending this was a friendly chat would be as pointless as Britton's pretending that one of his depositions was a friendly chat. "You're still our best suspect."

That didn't even get a raised eyebrow. "Because we were friends?"

"Is that what they're calling it these days?" Angela asked.

"No, they call it something that's not repeatable in polite company."

"Didn't think polite was your style." She continued to observe the car instead of him.

He seemed genuinely offended. "I'm always polite."

Frank said, "Then let me ask you, politely, to tell us about your relationship with Marie."

Britton picked up a vinyl block with sandpaper attached to the bottom of it. "We slept together."

"That's it? Just slept together? You weren't star-crossed lovers or anything?"

This had the unintended effect of making Britton laugh. "Neither Marie nor I believed in stars. We enjoyed each other's company and understood each other's work. That's it."

Maybe, Frank thought, *that's as good as it gets for him.* Letting anyone closer than that would be dangerous—when you're king of the hill, everyone's looking to knock you off. *And I thought my social life sucked.*

"I'm surprised you're not using this break for some last-minute cramming, what with your client facing the death penalty and all."

"Helps me think."

Which meant he knew his client was doomed no matter what, or that he had a team of underlings to do all the work for him? Or he meant that working on cars helped him think. Frank returned to Marie Corrigan. "She have any enemies? I mean serious enemies, anyone she felt might physically harm her?"

"'To earn the enmity of some men is a compliment,'" Britton said, rubbing the sandpaper over the edges of the hole. "I forget who said that."

"I'm more interested in what Marie said."

"You won't believe me, but I've thought of nothing else for two days. If she felt a threat from someone, she never told me about it. But she might not have. Marie didn't show fear, ever. Not even to me."

"Maybe she didn't express it as fear, exactly," Angela qualified. "Were there any cases she talked about, maybe more than usual?"

"No. We didn't talk much about work, again believe it or not. Our time together was limited."

"Right, because of your wife."

"No." He frowned, either at Angela or at the tough fiberglass. "Because of our schedules."

Frank said, "So fitting in sex with you could be tough. Is that why she went back to Bruce Raffel the second he got back into town?"

"Raffel? Don't make me laugh."

"It's funny when your girlfriend's old boyfriend comes sniffing around?"

Britton sanded some more. "He was more of an unofficial co-counsel than a boyfriend, in my humble opinion. They thought alike, especially when it came to *U.S. v. Booker* issues. Anyway, Marie has lots of old boyfriends. Most still live here."

"How many of them got her pregnant?"

Again the unintended effect. Britton snickered. "You've been listening to rumors. Marie was never pregnant, not by Bruce, not by anybody. Some frumpy secretary made that one up."

"Did you see Bruce Raffel at the convention?"

"Yeah, he came to my seminar on the first day. I don't think I ran into him after that. We didn't speak."

"You didn't hold any sort of grudge against Bruce Raffel?"

Britton set down the sanding block, picked up a plastic jar of something or other. "Nope."

"He and Marie, they got along. Really well, more than one person told us—you just said so yourself. And things weren't going so great for Raffel in the big city. Maybe he planned to come back home, pick up your girlfriend, start stealing your cases again?"

If the idea bothered Britton, he hid it masterfully. "Let him try."

"So you weren't angry at Marie, maybe for hooking up with him, maybe for hooking up with someone else at the convention?"

A snort. "I wouldn't be angry if Marie had hooked up with the Ohio Supreme Court. I'd be impressed. Besides, you know I couldn't have killed her."

"Because you loved her too much?" Angela suggested.

Again the quick frown. "No, because I was with other people the entire evening."

"About that," Frank said. "Turns out your alibi isn't quite as solid as it seemed at first."

CHAPTER 18

He waited until Britton looked up, then made a show of pulling out his palm-size notebook and flipping a few pages. "There were five of you who went to the hotel bar after attending the last session of the day—which was, I believe, 'Strategies for Invoking the Fifth Amendment.' From the bar you all went to Morton's steak house, where you paid a big bill and a small tip, and then to House of Blues. They must make good drinks at the House of Blues, because that's where people's memories get a little fuzzy. Your alibi men are equally split—two say you went to the Crazy Horse with them, and two say you showed up later."

Britton set down the jar and returned to trimming his car's gaping hole. "I'll bet I can guess which two. The assistant registrar of the convention and our illustrious keynote speaker tried to outdo each other with blue martinis. They probably aren't sure *they* were there, much less me."

"No, the two with bad hangovers insist you were with them every minute. It's your more sober compatriots who think you did a disappearing act." *Slightly* more sober. "And, you see, the cabdriver doesn't remember you either."

Britton barely paused. "Because you can't fit five guys into a cab. I grabbed another one."

"All by yourself?"

"With the effort it took for my colleagues to get into the vehicle in the first place, I wasn't going to ask them to get back out. I just slammed the door and hailed the next one."

Frank hesitated. The cab company hadn't said anything about a single fare immediately following the first, but then he hadn't asked. And there were several major cab companies in the city, as well as minor ones. He considered bluffing Britton—considered it very briefly.

Besides, he had more. "Then there's your destination. The Crazy Horse remembers your four friends—not that they're the only ones in history to walk in drunker than they walked out, but still memorable—and remember only four. No fifth."

"As I just explained, I arrived a few minutes later."

"Got lost in traffic?" As if traffic would be a problem, downtown after dark with no ball games scheduled.

"It took me a few minutes to find a cab."

Again Frank considered bluffing, then abandoned the idea. No one in the dim lighting and cacophony of the Crazy Horse would remember a single man in a business suit, not unless he tipped with hundred-dollar bills, and Frank suspected that Britton would not. "Just letting you know that your alibi has some potential holes. You're sure you didn't walk two blocks back to the Ritz for a quickie with Marie?"

"Positive." Britton was watching Angela, but not in a flirtatious way, more like a disapproving mother watching a child as she slowly circled the purplish car, as tense as if he had a body stuffed in the trunk. It said "Stutz" on the radiator and "Bearcat" on the grille. Frank hoped his partner would make the mistake of touching the immaculately painted body, so that just once he could see Britton discombobulated.

"You sure about that?" Frank pressed.

"Asked and answered."

"Because I'm kind of wondering who left the sperm in Marie, if it wasn't you."

This got Britton's gaze back from Angela, if only momentarily. An odd expression crossed his face—a flash of anger that immediately turned pensive, then to something Frank would not have believed possible from this man. Sadness.

"Was she raped?" Britton asked, without the trademark smirk. "They're saying she was."

Frank let him stew for a bit before answering. "There's no sign of it."

Relief. "Oh. Well, I don't know who the sperm belongs to. I haven't—hadn't—seen Marie for at least a week. I mean other than at the convention, where we were both too busy to shed our clothing."

"Would you give us a DNA sample?" Angela asked, her hip perilously close to the Stutz's right fender.

"Not on your life."

"Just for elimination purposes?"

"And trust you to throw out my profile when the case is over, that it won't be 'accidentally' retained for eternity? As if."

"Okay. Then help us figure out who it might belong to, and maybe he'll give us a sample."

Frank took it up. "What about Marie's other 'friends'? What about the club?"

Britton snickered. "The defense attorneys' S&M sex club? That's the focus of the police department? Maybe you should leave investigating to that bright little cousin of yours."

Frank curled his toes and focused, mightily, to keep his voice level. "People are usually murdered for one of two reasons: sex and money. No one stood to gain monetarily from Marie's death. Therefore we look at sex partners. Including you. So tell us about her. Did she enjoy sadomasochism?" Frank really didn't want to ask, didn't want a reason to have to picture Britton naked with Marie Corrigan. The idea made him distinctly nauseous.

"Marie thought that life comes with enough pain. Why add more?" Britton watched Angela, and not just because she'd finally moved away from his precious Stutz. "At least not with me."

"And with others?" she asked, cool and unruffled. Britton could leer at her all he wanted, Frank realized with an odd sense of pride. Angela Sanchez would never blink.

"I wouldn't know, would I? Marie was a chameleon that way, able to be different things to different people. Look." Britton suddenly straightened up, leaning both hands on the car's fender under its protective cloth, but he didn't seem angry. Perhaps he felt cheered by his work on the fender. "We all need a rest period from the shark tank once in a while. But nothing leaves the four walls once you pay the motel clerk. Besides, we're still not nearly as incestuous as *your* little clan. You cops marry, divorce, and remarry one another so quickly that I can't keep up. Tell me you two aren't sleeping together."

It became Angela's turn to burst out laughing, saving Frank the necessity of a reply.

Though she didn't need to laugh *that* hard. "You said *supposed* to stay within the four walls. Did Marie leave the past in the motel room?"

This caused Britton to fiddle with his tools, picking them up and carrying them to a box the size of a refrigerator. It was one of three in the garage. "I don't know. She would tell me things she probably shouldn't have, that So-and-So wore a girdle for his potbelly and that this guy messed up by blowing off a depo, and this guy is screwing a judge. But she probably only told me these things, not anyone else."

"Because you were special," Angela said, in a tone of patent disbelief.

"That's right."

"Why?"

"Because I own the most lucrative law firm in town, and Marie would have told me anything to come in as a partner." He said this briskly, oh so sophisticated, but the low tones in his voice told the truth: The sexiest woman in town hadn't hopped into bed with him because of his looks or personality. "And I think we're done here."

Angela pressed. "Let's assume Marie didn't shoot off her mouth with you but with other . . . friends as well. Who might have taken offense?"

"Enough to kill her? I can't believe that. We're lawyers. We're used to getting stabbed in the back."

"Who had she spoken of recently?"

"Lovely grammar," he commented, "but there's no way I'm going to tattle on my fellow colleagues with once-removed hearsay. And I've told you all I can. You can see yourselves out."

"Marie is dead," she reminded him.

"And there's nothing I can do about that. And don't pretend you're motivated by compassion or justice or anything other than an opportunity to dig into the people you can't stand. You couldn't care less who killed Marie. You're only glad she's dead."

Frank was getting used to hearing that. "So you think we'll let her killer slide?"

"I don't think you're going to look too hard."

"Meaning that when one of your clients goes to jail, it's because *you* didn't care enough?"

Frank turned on the ball of his foot, making his escape while still able to celebrate the victory of having had the last word with Dennis Britton.

But before he made it to the outside world, the door opened and a woman entered. She wore an all-white pantsuit that swished gently as she walked, and she had the firmest belly and blondest hair that money could buy. The lady of the manor. She glanced at the detectives without surprise or interest and spoke to her husband. "Time to go."

The amused sneer had returned to Britton's face. "These detectives probably want to ask you what time I got home on Tuesday night, Taylor."

Without any change of expression, due to either surgical procedures or utter disinterest, Britton's wife said, "About one A.M."

Frank said, "Thank you. And what about last night?" Raffel's ex-wife had told them that the man had spent Tuesday evening with his sons, staying well into the evening and leaving only when she'd insisted that they go to bed, school night and all, but without a concrete time of death on Marie a window still existed. The idea that Bruce Raffel had killed Marie and Britton had taken revenge seemed far-fetched to Frank, but stranger things had happened. Besides, he liked watching this woman's magnificent cheekbones as she spoke.

Husband and wife looked at each other before answering, but then married people often confer in silence. She said, "Dennis brought some of his convention people back to the house for dinner and drinks. They were here from—what, six P.M. to about midnight?"

He nodded.

"And then you drove them home?" Frank asked Britton.

"No," Taylor Britton answered. "They had their own cars. After they left, we went to bed—and yes, together."

Frank wondered what this icily beautiful woman felt, if anything. Did she care enough about the Marie Corrigans in her husband's life to resort to murder? Perhaps he should ask where *she'd* been on Thursday night. But that wouldn't explain Bruce Raffel, and no doubt both deaths would have been contracted out anyway. She didn't do her own dishes, laundry, or nail filing—why would she commit her own murder?

"Go ahead, Detective," Britton said.

"What?"

"You're dying to ask my wife if she knew about me and Marie Corrigan. So go ahead."

The City's Greatest Defense Attorney, reading people like a hastily written brief. Frank turned to Mrs. Britton.

Apparently Botox hadn't completely robbed the woman of the ability to show emotion, because right now she looked pissed as hell. Having an open marriage was one thing. Flaunting it to the hired help, quite another.

But damned if she would let that show. "Yes, I had been aware of her existence—and of her complete unimportance as well. Good day, Officers." To Britton she repeated, "Time to go," and accompanied it with a look that spoke volumes. Most pages of which would have read, *"Upon pain of death."*

Britton appeared pleased with himself, having once

again completed his trademark move of ticking off everyone in the room. "Satisfied?"

"No," Frank said.

"Not remotely," Angela said, and they left.

The two detectives did not speak until they had cleared the sweeping driveway and found their way back to I-271. Then Angela asked for his thoughts.

"I really want it to be him, because I hate the guy," Frank admitted, certainly not telling her anything she didn't already know. "And because it would seem like justice to me, two sharks fighting each other to the death. He who lives by the sword dies by the sword, that kind of thing."

"You want to believe that karma really works."

"Yeah."

"But you don't like him for it."

"Why kill her? Maybe she got a little too loose-lipped about their relationship, maybe she got something on him and pressed for that partnership. Maybe she even wanted him to leave his wife. But then why tell us about her tendency to gossip? He's had plenty of secret meetings with Marie Corrigan—why not kill her in some no-tell motel or in a dark corner of the Metroparks? Why wait until they're in the Ritz-Carlton?"

Angela said, "Hotels have that anonymity that dinner at 1890 doesn't. And the convention provides a handy group of suspects."

"If you want to hide an enemy, hide it in a forest of enemies."

"You're awfully philosophical this evening, but yes. Anyone can walk into a hotel. It would be an easy place for an enemy to get to her, easier than her law firm or her apartment at least."

"Then how did this enemy get a key to the Presidential Suite?"

His partner sighed. "I don't know. I'm just throwing out the idea that if Marie died on an average day in Cleveland, he would be the big fish in our suspect pool. But the convention muddies that water. The problem is, nothing says 'premeditated' to me. It still looks like someone broke into the Presidential Suite for a little nookie with Marie, and they had a fight. A crime of passion, pure and simple."

"She inspired a lot of passion, and not always the nookie type."

"But that still takes me back to Britton, who had a history of quickies with the victim, who—despite his openness just now—needed to keep them discreet or his wife might lock him out of his garage. But this convention begins and he and Marie are surrounded by hotel rooms. Wouldn't the temptation—"

Frank said, "But why wouldn't Marie just rent a room? Why break into the Presidential Suite?"

"Because she's cheap? Because she'd have a line of suitors–slash–potential witnesses outside her own door? For the same reason anyone uses that suite—to impress people? Who knows?" Angela slumped her head against the headrest as she drove. "But I'm with you. I'd really like it to be him."

Frank chuckled. "Why?"

"Because karma *should* count for something. Do you know what kind of car that was?"

"The Stutz or the Corvette?"

"The Corvette. It's a '63 split-window coupe with a 327 four-speed."

Frank stared at her as they passed the Chagrin Road exit. "You a closet pistonhead, Sanchez?"

"Don't know a cylinder from a valve stem. What I do know is that ever since I got satellite TV, my son spends most of his viewing hours watching Mecum's auto auction. Point is, Britton was doing his own bodywork on a car that is easily worth a hundred thousand dollars. More if it's all original, which I doubt. Not in that color."

"If I paid that much for a car, it had better do my laundry and make me pancakes."

"If you paid that much for a car, would you fiddle with it if you didn't know what you were doing?"

"Britton is the type of guy who always thinks he knows what he's doing." Frank reached for a cigarette, remembered they were inside a city-owned vehicle, and put the pack back into his pocket. "But yes."

"Yes?"

"Yes, I have not forgotten how Dennis Britton's first wife died."

CHAPTER 19

Theresa found Don in his usual lair, the small DNA-analysis room at the back of the building. A tall man with brown skin, half of which came from his black father and half from his Hispanic mother, he stood settling microtubes into their niches in the Perkin-Elmer Profiler Plus. It would analyze the short tandem repeats in each DNA sample and report them on a chart. Unlike how it goes on TV, the computer monitor would not light up with a large banner that said *"Match!"* but Don managed to enjoy his job even without such dramatics. And Theresa enjoyed everything about Don but, again, wouldn't admit it, even to herself.

"You," he said to Theresa.

"It's not my fault."

"Fourteen samples? Fourteen?"

"They're hotel rooms. You know what they're like."

"I didn't want to. I really wanted to be able to have some plausible deniability in my mind, but now I'll never stay in another one again. If I don't have a relative in town that I can flop with, I'm not going. Besides, that's nearly all my sample kits for the week. We'll have a pile of cases backed up by next Friday waiting for a shipment. So everyone else's murder and suicide and death and rape will be put on hold for friggin' Marie Corrigan."

"I take it you were no more a fan than anyone else."

"Of her—body, sure. Of her personality, no. Not since she asked me if I could have switched the DNA samples here in the lab."

"On the stand?"

"Yeah, in front of the jury. Not saying I did, of course, merely asking if it would be possible. I said sure, I'd risk my career to frame your poor innocent client, whom I don't know and have never met, in order to avenge the murder of some other person I didn't know and had never met."

"Wow. What happened?"

"The judge sent the jury out and yelled at all of us. Me more than her. I guess he didn't care for the 'poor innocent client' comment. Thought it was prejudicial, with all that sarcasm dripping from my voice. But it was okay for her to practically accuse me of a felony for no reason whatsoever."

"And you're normally so easygoing," she teased. "You weren't at the Ritz-Carlton on Tuesday night, were you?"

"No, but I'd have been happy to hand that guy the two-by-four or whatever he used on her head."

"A chair. Would you really?"

Don leaned against the counter and rubbed some of the shine off his forehead. "No, not really. Just don't expect me to shed a lot of tears over *that* grave. So what can I do for you? And it had better not be more DNA samples."

"No, though it does involve Marie Corrigan. I need you to cast your mind back about three years. Sixteen-year-old white girl in Westlake, found bludgeoned in a schoolmate's house, a boy, same age." She didn't bother with the names or the exact date or address or anything like that, because details like that tended to slip out of the mind almost as quickly as they enter. Only the story remains.

"Yeah . . . yeah, I remember. Little girl, head beat in. I didn't really do much with that one—had no DNA. Either she wasn't raped at all or the guy must have had a vasectomy."

"A teenage boy would hardly have a vasectomy."

Don snorted. "Some should. But it didn't do much for the prosecution's case, as I recall."

"Where were the parents?"

"Whose, the boy's? Out of town, I think—no, out of the country. Someplace hoity-toity, like Paris or something. I had the impression they had money."

"Who called the cops?"

No reaction. Don checked the colored lights on the Thermocycler and straightened a stack of printouts, then said, "No idea. I can't remember another single thing about the case. Just sitting on the stand while Marie Corrigan asked if DNA had been obtained from the possible semen. She phrased the question a little differently each time, but emphasized the word 'possible' quite consistently. She was right, of course, with a weak acid phosphatase reaction and no sperm, it could have been heavy vaginal secretions and not semen at all. After about five times, the judge finally said, 'I think the witness has testified there was no foreign DNA found.'"

"Were you surprised at the verdict?"

"Verdict?"

"Not guilty."

"Oh, yeah, I remember that now. You talk to the prosecutor?"

"Yeah, but he didn't tell me anything I didn't already

know. He couldn't explain the verdict but didn't complain about it either. Usually they're a little bit bitter when they think someone got away with murder."

"Especially that prosecutor."

A spark of hope glimmered in Theresa's soul. She knew the guy, and no way would he have been swayed by Marie Corrigan's breasts. So if his heart *still* wasn't in it, maybe he thought William really was innocent.

Don went on. "She said he was drugged, not drunk. The defendant. I guess they found no alcohol and one tiny Rohypnol metabolite in his system."

"In *his* blood? Not hers?"

"Yeah, but because Mommy and Daddy lawyered up so fast the sample wasn't drawn for nearly forty hours, so any alcohol and almost certainly any other metabolites would have cleared his system by then. But she made a big deal about it, got an expert to say that his symptoms—which we had only his word for—were consistent with a date-rape drug. He got off. With double jeopardy attached."

"So he could never be tried again. How did the defendant look?"

Another blank expression. A witness's time on the stand is dominated by the prosecutor, the defense attorney, and sometimes the judge. In between those interactions, eye contact needed to be made with the members of the jury. Theresa often left a courtroom with no recollection of the defendant whatsoever.

Don said, "I don't remember. I'm afraid I was too distracted by Miss Corrigan's tight little skirt."

"*Don.*"

He held up his hands to fend off her irritation. "Say what you like about her as a person—but she *was* hot."

"So's pepper spray," Theresa snapped, and went back to work.

CHAPTER 20

Frank and Angela returned to the police station, sans any incriminating evidence against Dennis Britton, not that they'd really expected the city's best defense attorney to have a bloodstained passkey to the Ritz hanging out of his toolbox. But that didn't make Frank feel any better.

He had begun to write up his report when Angela appeared at her desk, which faced his, with Neil Kelly in tow. Kelly carried two file boxes, one stacked atop the other, both heavy, judging from the thump they made when he deposited them on the corner of Frank's desk.

"He followed me back," Angela stated, apparently in her own defense.

"From the ladies' room?"

"Need some help, mate," Neil said. "This is Bruce Raffel's career in Cleveland. His law firm courteously slaughtered a few forests to make us copies of at least the public-record stuff. We could get it ourselves from the clerk of courts, but they had an intern who needed something to do. I got the feeling they don't like that intern much. Or us. I think my hernia came back just moving this stuff from the car."

Even with desperate effort, Frank couldn't think of a good excuse. "What are we looking for?"

"That's the fun part." Neil stole a chair from behind the desk of some detective lucky enough to have gone home for the day. "We have no flippin' idea."

"Terrific."

They read in silence for a while, tales of murder and robbery and assault, each one banal and yet unique at the same time.

"This guy might have a reason to kill Raffel," Angela said, her nose in a crisp manila file. "He got fifteen years for armed robbery—nah, he's still in the can. Kind of makes me think Bruce wasn't quite up to Marie's level of ability."

Neil said, "I had to testify in front of him a few times. The personality of a pit bull with none of Marie's flash. But he could pull stuff out of his ass that you wouldn't see coming."

"He got this chick a hung jury," Frank said.

"What'd she do?"

"Shot her husband, then tried to make it look like a burglary gone bad while she collected the insurance money." He read on. "Hell, she's one of the Ashworths."

"The mob?" Angela asked.

"The closest thing Cleveland has to a mob, yeah."

"I remember that case," Neil said, massaging his jaw. "About two years ago. She had married this street thug who couldn't handle the rigors of the family business. To make it worse, he had a roving eye, so either she got tired of that or her brothers got tired of losing money through some lousy in-law, and no one was too upset when the guy bled to death in his living room. The defendant had family and money, and the victim had neither, so the not-guilty verdict came as no surprise."

Frank closed the file. "Then no one would be looking to avenge that particular murder."

Neil leaned back to stretch, groaning loudly enough to rattle the grimy windows as he worked out a crick in his spine. "The trial was nothing. All the drama happened before the trial began. The defendant—Marissa—was a newly widowed babe with a lot of money. Every defense lawyer in town begged to take her case. Instead she ignores big brother's advice to use the family attorney and entrusts her future to up-and-comer Dennis Britton."

"But—" Frank checked the name on the manila folder.

"Yes, but. She retained Britton, and all the other disappointed suitors went away. All but one. Two months later she fired Britton and opened her arms—and everything else—to Raffel."

"I'll bet Britton didn't care for that."

"Furious. Fur-i-ous. Not 'fire off an e-mail' furious, but 'get into a shouting match at the Barristers Club' furious."

"And you just thought of this now?"

"It was two years ago. Water under the bridge in lawyer time. Raffel got her off—harped on the missing murder weapon until the jury got dizzy—and I guess Britton let the humiliation spur him on to new heights. Now he's top of the heap, and Raffel left town. He who laughs last has no motive to murder."

"I wouldn't be too sure," Frank said. "Britton had the hottest case, and Raffel stole it. Now he has the hottest babe. If he saw Raffel trying to steal that—"

"Maybe," Angela said. "But we have no real reason to think Bruce and Marie reconnected at the conference. We checked her cell-phone records—no calls between them. You said no one at her office has heard her mention his name since he left town. It's kind of a stretch that Britton, who has a booming practice and a wealthy marriage to protect, would risk all that to get revenge for a professional slight."

"There's nothing professional about one's . . . um, manhood," Neil said. "He swallowed his pride once and moved on, but if he saw history repeating itself . . . He wouldn't be the first guy to throw away everything just to prove he's got the biggest . . . um . . ."

"Manhood," Angela finished. "It's a possibility. It's also possible that he killed Marie during an argument but went back and killed Bruce for more practical reasons. Bruce would suspect him immediately in the murder, for one thing."

"So did we," Frank pointed out.

"Or maybe Marie told Bruce something. Something she knew about Britton that she would only share with an old lover."

"So Raffel tries to put the squeeze on Britton. Raffel is lower on the totem pole now, not doing so great, and Britton has married well."

"Maybe." Now Angela stretched, but without the groan and leaning forward instead of back. "All we've got is maybes."

Frank put the file aside. They all resumed reading.

"So," Neil said to him. "Your cousin."

"Mmm?"

"She seeing anyone?"

Frank got this question a lot. He usually lied and said yes. But Neil Kelly had spent some time with Theresa in the past two days and might already know the answer, so he hedged. "I think so."

"Really? A cop?"

"No." This wasn't technically a lie. Theresa saw her

co-workers at the lab every day, and some were men who weren't cops. And no matter what she said, she'd be on Don Delgado like frosting on cake if it weren't for the eleven-year age difference. Women got all hung up on age.

"Who?" Neil persisted.

"None of your damn business."

Across from him Angela gave a little shake as if suppressing a chuckle.

Frank tried to change the subject. "Didn't you find a phone number with an initial in his room?"

Neil nodded. "Our mysterious *M* is a client outside Atlanta who wanted a return phone call. DUI case. What, you don't let her date cops?"

"The last cop she dated wound up dead."

"Did you shoot the guy?"

The guy had been Frank's former partner, and he would not banter about the man's death with a goofball like Neil Kelly. "Besides, cops' track records? How many times you been divorced?"

Neil declined to answer, which meant it had to be at least twice. Of course Frank didn't want his cousin to date cops—why the hell would he? Britton had been right on the mark with his "incestuous" comment. Frank reached for another file.

"I just think she's nice," Neil said, with the patent innocence of a six-year-old asking about the contents of a gum machine instead of flat-out requesting a quarter. "But you're right. I should speak to her."

"You should leave her alone," Frank said. "Here's that robbery-murder at the ATM."

Angela said, "I remember that one. Disgusting."

"That the guy only got ten years?"

"That murder in the commission of a robbery is somehow not murder."

Frank skimmed the file. "Raffel moved to Atlanta

only three months after the trial ended. Maybe he felt guilty."

Angela snorted.

"But this is the interesting part. The guy had a partner, who gave him the gun and waited on the street corner to keep an eye out for cops and witnesses. The partner pled to conspiracy, got a slap on the wrist because, of course, they'd only intended to *rob* a young mother and her children at gunpoint—the whole *killing* thing was just an oops. Said partner's counsel was none other than our Miss Corrigan."

"Get out!" Neil exclaimed.

"It's right here on the docket. Wonder why they didn't sever the trials."

"Because Marie and Brucie got along so well?"

"Isn't that a conflict of interest?" Angela asked.

Frank said, "I don't think so. There's nothing that says counsels can't be friends—very good friends. And both defendants did pretty well, so *they've* got nothing to complain about."

"But the victim does," his partner pointed out. "Did she have a husband? Family?"

"Don't know."

"Look at the penalty phase," she suggested. "The prosecution would have called them."

Frank scanned a few more pages. Witnesses called for the trial phase had to have something specific and relevant to say about the crime. During the sentencing phase, witnesses could be called merely to tug at heartstrings. "Here. I— Uh . . ." This was one of those cats that, once out of the bag, would never go back in without severe scratching and blood loss. "Penalty-phase witness list for the prosecution. Third from the top."

"Yeah?"

"Marcus Dean. Brother of the victim."

A silence ensued, until Neil Kelly leaped into it. "No, no, no," he said. "Don't even think it."

"You knew," Frank said. Another reason not to let his cousin date this guy.

"Of course. Didn't you?" If Neil wasn't genuinely surprised at Frank's ignorance of this fact, then he deserved an Academy Award.

"I remember the victim's brother being a cop," Angela said. "I didn't realize it was him."

Frank mentally nodded. He had never met Dean then, so the name hadn't stuck. But surely his ex-partner would have followed the case more closely, known who the lawyers were. "It didn't occur to you that the two lawyers in your ex-partner's sister's murder case dying on two consecutive days might not be coincidence?"

"I didn't attend the trial, so I didn't know about Corrigan."

"And when Raffel turns up dead on Dean's own job site, that didn't strike you as, oh, suspicious?"

"He's a *cop*," Neil hissed.

"Cops can kill. I don't like the idea any more than you do, but—"

Neil leaned over the table, gaze furious but voice tight and controlled. "I said he's a *cop,* meaning that if he was going to come back on someone, he'd have the guy shanked in jail, not bash in the head of the guy's attorney. And even if he *would* do that, it's been over a year. He waits all that time and then kills them in the one spot in the city immediately connected to him? Come on. He'd have to be a raging lunatic."

Frank did not move. "It might not be the most sensible plan, but people aren't always sensible. I can't believe you knew of a connection between both victims and the friggin' head of Ritz-Carlton security."

"I can't believe you *didn't*," Neil shot back.

CHAPTER 21

Theresa spent the afternoon engaging in the somewhat-less-than-boisterous process of putting two glass slides on the side-by-side stages of the comparison microscope to check the colors, sizes, cross-sectional shapes, pigmentation, and other characteristics of the hairs and fibers found on and around the two victims. This process always wound up taking longer than expected and, in this situation, still could not positively establish that the two lawyers had been killed by the same person.

Marie had one foreign hair found with her body, caught in the knot binding her wrists: a four-inch-long auburn strand with no root and a coating of product. Analysis of this product with the FTIR gave her a myriad of strange peaks corresponding to the inorganic chemistry of the product, the only recognizable ones being ethoxydiglycol and hydrogen peroxide. A touch of ethanolamine made her think of hair coloring, something like the shampoo-in hair color marketed to men to cover gray. This particular hair had not been gray, but perhaps too many surrounding ones had.

Bruce also had two foreign hairs, one about the

same length as the auburn hair and a similar color, but minus the dying product. Visually it appeared slightly different, with more pigmentation and a less distinct medulla, so that it might be a different hair from the same head or a different hair from a different person entirely. The other was short, with an undulating shaft and heavily pigmented with dark brown color—a black hair. There were only two colors of hair pigmentation, brown and yellow, plus the form of yellow that produced red.

Microscopy alone could not tell her more than that. She turned the hairs from Bruce Raffel's body over to Don for DNA analysis. He could do nothing with the auburn one from Marie's knot, since it had no root and therefore no adhering follicular skin cells, which would contain DNA. The shaft of a hair is composed of proteins called keratins, essentially dead cells. If Theresa wanted any further information from this section of hair, she'd have to ship it to the FBI with a detailed and articulate request for mitochondrial-DNA analysis.

One of these hairs could belong to the killer or none of them could, artifacts left over from other guests, other lives. She considered the fibers.

Most of the fibers had come from the carpet each victim had lain upon, no surprise there. A pink acrylic fiber had been found on Marie's body, a brown acetate one on Bruce's. Blue cotton on Marie, a pink cotton on Bruce similar in hue to the pink acrylic. The microscopic globules attached to the fine spandex thread found on Marie's skirt turned out to be a number of esters, or fatty acids, and some fatty alcohols. In short, wax, probably used on cars, shoes, or furniture. Either the spandex had the wax or Marie had leaned against her car, picking up the wax on her skirt, which in turn gave the spandex fiber something to cling to. Theresa shut down the

FTIR, wondering what Marie Corrigan would drive—a restored Jaguar or an Escalade? A black Viper might be appropriate. She found no wax or spandex on Bruce.

The two victims had only one item in common: cat hair. Someone had a gray-colored Persian mix, but was it the killer, or the maid, or some other staff member? Or even a guest whose room had been vacuumed by the same machine used in the victim's rooms? Hotel murders were murder, no pun intended.

The stray hair from Dennis Britton's lapel came from a cat, but not a gray Persian.

Maybe Marie had a cat, or Bruce. They might have encountered each other, given a hug for old times' sake. Maybe more than a hug. Maybe they only sat next to each other at one of the seminars, transferring the cat hair. Maybe anything. And why had Marie Corrigan's shirt been removed after she'd been struck and was bleeding, but Bruce Raffel's clothing had been neatly put aside? Who would Bruce Raffel have taken off his clothes for? Besides Marie Corrigan? It was maddening.

Neither attorney had been under the influence of drugs or alcohol. The pills in Bruce Raffel's bottle were simply vitamins and the water in his glass simply water.

Theresa then needed to process the chair—an ungainly piece of evidence if ever there was one. It wouldn't fit in the superglue chamber designed for guns and tools, so she constructed one out of two cardboard boxes in which paper towels had been delivered to the laboratory. Packaging tape connected them and sealed up the edges, and she used a box cutter to slice a small flap in one bottom corner. With the chair enclosed inside, she slid in an electric mug warmer and then placed a foil tray carrying a dime-size puddle of superglue on top of it. Careful not to spill it, she trailed the cord out of the flap and then closed and sealed that opening. She stood back to survey this disposable structure. Not high-tech, but sometimes high-tech wasn't needed.

She left it on the floor of the amphitheater after writing *"Don't touch"* in Sharpie marker on its sides. Provided no one stumbled into it, upset the superglue, or somehow moved the mug warmer against the cardboard to start a fire and incinerate her evidence, all would be well. She grabbed a much-needed cup of coffee and checked her e-mail before returning to find the box apparently unmolested.

Holding her breath to keep from breathing in the fumes, she opened the box.

The dark wooden chair now had various swirls and marks permanently marring its finish. The two pieces of wood supporting the backrest, which the killer must have gripped in order to swing the object with enough force to shatter a skull, had a heavy concentration of marks and smudges but not a single usable ridge. Several—in the straight, wide pattern of fingers—had a roughened, almost bubbly appearance. Latex gloves. Who wore latex gloves? Doctors. Cops. Paramedics, maids, food-service workers—anyone about to commit a crime who had a single brain cell in his or her head; they were sold by the box at Home Depot.

The DNA analyst appeared at her elbow. "Something you need to see."

Don led the way to the back room of the trace-evidence lab, briskly enough to worry her. As the DNA-analysis equipment hummed around them, he said, "The auburn hair from Raffel had a smooth, complete bulb."

"It had finished growing." Theresa nodded.

"And so it didn't have enough skin cells clinging to the root to give us sufficient DNA—mitochondrial is the only hope there, so we'll have to send it out if and when a suspect is available. But the black hair found on

Raffel's body, that had plenty, so I ran it through the database without doing the quantification step."

"But—"

"Yeah, it's not proper, but I had plenty of sample and I'll be rerunning it with all the proper steps, so as long as I call it a preliminary test instead of a conclusive one, we're good."

"And you got a match?"

"No."

Theresa rubbed one eyebrow. "That was what you wanted to show me?"

"No. This is." He held up a printout showing two STR profiles, one from the unknown hair, one from a sample already in the database. "I got somebody pretty close. Twelve out of fifteen alleles."

She studied the printout. The biochemical phenomenon behind each colored peak meant little to her, but even Theresa could see how many of those peaks lined up between the two samples. "Could that be coincidence?"

"Possibly. But what's more likely is that the depositor of the unknown hair is a close relative of this person in the database. But here the plot thickens. The person in the database is a victim, not a suspect. Her name was Tamika Johnson. Any idea who that is—or was?"

"Sounds vaguely familiar," Theresa said. "I'll look it up."

CHAPTER 22

Children, Frank thought, were nature's great explorers. Nothing pleased them more than something new—new shoes, a new cereal, most of all a new space to run around in. He watched a well-coiffed woman check in with her brood. She wore a running suit that probably cost more than half his closet and carted along two girls and a boy without actually looking at any of them at any time. The children proved his point. In the five minutes since arriving, all three had crisscrossed every inch of the lobby, discovered where every door and hallway led (much to the displeasure of an unseen voice inside the manager's office), and touched every piece of expensive-looking artwork around, including the paintings, though they had to stand on the cushioned settee to reach two of them. As they did this, they relayed each discovery to one another by a series of very sharp screeches, unrecognizable as speech except perhaps to dogs and birds. Frank avoided children as a rule, but for once this display of overindulged, expensive youth did not irritate him. Instead he tried to recall when something as simple as an unexplored twenty-by-twenty area of real estate could make him so happy.

He could not.

Maybe hotels were as magical as fairylands or Disney World to children, a fabulous way station that had all the comforts of home without Mommy and Daddy's vested interest in same. But to adults they became necessary evils, a foreign territory entered only with a qualified gratitude. An adult could just pretend that the marble floors and the artworks and the turndown service distracted him from laying his head on a pillow slept upon by hundreds of strangers, with nothing more than a thin and presumably well-washed piece of cotton in between one's face and the germs, bugs, and dead skin cells left by those hundreds. They could only pretend to enjoy the abandon that came so naturally to children. An adult's unsettled concern hovered until he returned home to bask in his own—benign—germs and bugs and dead cells.

Then Marcus Dean came by, and Frank stood up to ask, "Got a minute?"

The former cop studied him for a moment. Frank must have looked grim, for Marcus seemed to sense that this was a less-than-friendly visit, that Frank wouldn't have come in person only to ask if he'd found out how the Presidential Suite had been breached. "Step into my office."

Frank followed the man to a functional, cream-colored square in the maze behind the front desk. He had expected it to look like a cop's desk or a manager's office, crammed with papers and files and a manual here or there, all of them balanced in precarious piles on top of boxes, CDs, and old coffee cups. But apparently Dean liked organization; three matching file cabinets along one wall were neat and closed, the desk clear except for a phone, an in-box, and the minimum computer equipment now necessary to everyday life. Wall art consisted of a large framed photograph of a beach, possibly Caribbean, the water so turquoise it looked fake. Frank sat in a well-upholstered chair opposite the desk.

"How's it going?" Dean asked, but with a wary manner.

"Nothing is really panning out. Angela's talking to your GM again about a few former employees. Any idea yet how the guy got into the Presidential Suite?"

"Nope. No keys made for it, no passkeys missing."

"You said they couldn't copy a room key because the code is changed after each checkout. What about copying a passkey?"

Dean rubbed the bridge of his nose. "Yeah, that would work. Except that the three of us who have them never let them out of our sight upon pain of death. And none have been lost. And on top of that, we change the pass code every month anyway."

"Oh," Frank said, losing interest. In his experience there were always ways in and out of places for people who worked there. Maintenance men could open many doors, some electronic devices could be overcome with strong magnets or a jolt of power, or the space where the bolt entered could be stuffed with paper so the lock couldn't close in the first place. "We finished checking out all your people. No red flags. Your head maintenance guy had two DUIs in another state but seems to have straightened out since then. Everyone else is just speeding tickets and divorce cases. No burglary, theft, or violent crimes."

"I'm pretty careful about that."

"I can imagine."

Dean nodded, and his shoulders relaxed by about a millimeter. "Sometimes I feel more like a lawyer than a cop in this job. My first thought in any situation isn't about catching the bad guy or even preventing future crimes, but 'Is the hotel liable?'"

"You've got high-dollar customers here. I'm sure they can afford high-dollar lawyers when something goes wrong."

"The kicker is this: When something *does* go wrong, it's usually their own fault because they're so damn careless. They're too used to having people to watch their belongings and their safety and their kids. You find anything else about my staff?"

"Two flags came up for juvenile records. We're still trying to get a peek at those." The juvenile-court judge had dragged his feet, and the records remained sealed, so Frank did not inform Dean of William Rosedale's past. They had a more pertinent suspect to discuss at the moment. "Something else came up, though."

"What?"

"Tamika Johnson."

Dean gave no sign of surprise or even worry, only the thoughtful gravity he'd carried in his face since Frank met him the day before. "I thought it might."

"The young mother shot to death at the ATM for the fifty dollars she'd just withdrawn, while her kids screamed in the backseat. Bruce Raffel represented the defendant. A lot of people in Cleveland thought the guy should have gotten the death penalty, but he didn't. Thanks to Raffel."

Dean cut the recap short. "She was my sister."

"Tamika Johnson."

"Half sister, actually. Three and a half years younger than me. My dad— My mother had disappeared somewhere into junkie heaven, and my dad took up with Tamika's mother. I guess we were typical birth-order kids, I worked hard in school, tried to be sensible, listened to all my dad's stories about keeping away from the drugs, a man's got to provide for his family, how you've got no real life if you can't be proud of what you see in the mirror every morning. Tamika, she was the bouncy one, the one who made other kids laugh, the one who avoided her textbooks like the plague and passed all her classes anyhow."

Frank let the man tell it his way. The insulation in the offices equaled that in the guest rooms, and only a low hum of noise from the lobby crept in.

"My dad—better at giving advice than taking it—was a good guy, but with real questionable taste in women. Tamika's mom didn't turn out a whole lot better than my own, not for a long while at any rate. For too many years there, we had no one to rely on but each other."

"And you were her big brother."

A snort, then a melancholy smile. "Lord knows I tried, but Tamika didn't need much protecting. She proved no better at picking out a spouse than our dad had, but otherwise she did okay. Worked hard. Had cute and completely uncontrollable children just like herself."

When he didn't continue, Frank said, "Until she was murdered."

"Yeah. I was working Vice at the time, on nights, so I'd been at work about an hour when I got the call. I went lights and sirens to the hospital, but it was . . ."

Too late. "What happened at the trial?"

He snorted the melancholy away. "No one expected Raffel to do much. We had ballistics, a witness, and DNA. The best he could hope for would be to keep the guy out of the electric chair. But he came up with this mens rea thing and somehow talked the jury into manslaughter. *Manslaughter,* for murder in the commission of a felony. Now Tamika's mom is making an effort to be a better mother to her grandchildren than she was to Tamika. I see them three or four times a week, trying to be some sort of dad, but it's not enough. Her mom and me together, we're still not enough. And her killer will be out in another ten if he behaves."

"Unbelievable."

"Britton I would have expected it from. But Raffel? That's like you hopping on a boat to Paris with your trusty ten-speed and winning the Tour de France. I mean—"

"When I haven't been on a bike since I was twelve. Yeah, I know what you mean. So . . . uh, you weren't a big fan of Bruce Raffel."

Marcus Dean stared over the top of his pristine desk until Frank felt like sinking into his chair, worn down by that laser-beam gaze. He knew the moment he saw Dean's name on that witness list that he'd have to come here, have to ask these questions, and have to face his fellow officers after treating a former fellow officer like a suspect. Neil Kelly had been especially vehement. He'd known Marcus Dean, had worked with him in Vice. Only the rankest fool would think the ex-cop had suddenly transformed into an S&M-oriented psycho killer.

However, facts remained. Access to the passkey cards gave Dean the most opportunity of anyone who had motive. He had the most motive of anyone who had opportunity. And it didn't take a lot of method to hit someone over the head with a chair.

"I've got to check it out," Frank said now to Dean. "You know that."

The man nodded, still more sad than angry. "I didn't kill him. I didn't even know he was here until we found his body. If I was going to kill someone, I would wait another ten years and kill the guy who pulled the trigger and blew my sister's brains all over her kids' winter coats. I'm not saying I might not still do that."

"I believe you," Frank said truthfully, thinking, *But then I want to.*

"Sure. What do you need, an alibi or something? I don't really have one. I'd already had one murder on my watch, so instead of going home last night I walked the halls, reviewed the lobby cameras—again—and hunted up everyone on duty to make sure they were where they were supposed to be. I went home to catch a few z's at about two, came back at five. The rest of the time I was here, there, and everywhere, so no, I don't have any sort of alibi."

"I get that. But I have to ask about Marie."

Dean had taken inquiries about Raffel in stride, but bringing up the other lawyer seemed to throw him. "What?"

"The partner of your sister's killer. Marie Corrigan represented him."

"Oh, yeah." Said in a tone of faint surprise, as if he had genuinely forgotten.

"So—no offense—if you had motive to get some revenge on Raffel, the same goes for Marie."

Dean shook his head. "No, the other dude, the partner—he was just some hopped-up kid. He didn't have a weapon and didn't know that the other guy did. Marie convinced him to roll on the shooter, and that helped get what bit of a conviction we got. I didn't resent Marie for that."

Frank pursued, just as he would with any other suspect. "Not for that? But for something else? For turning you down when you asked her out?"

This threw him, too.

"If I followed that policy, the streets would be littered with corpses," the man said, though the idea of women turning him down on a regular basis seemed overly modest. "No, I . . . that's where I met her, you know. At the trial for my sister's murder. Watching her strut around that courtroom, her blouse tailored so that it looked like her chest would bust out of it at any moment, trying to set free a guy who participated in the murder of the best friend I'll ever have. And I wanted her. From the moment they started jury selection, the minute she flicked that long hair over the shoulder of that little body, I wanted her." He shook his head again, this time at himself. "That's messed up, that is."

"So you asked her out," Frank prodded, with no wish to prolong this conversation. "And she turned you down. I imagine she could be pretty humiliating."

Dean didn't react immediately to that. He traced the edge of his desk blotter with one finger, avoiding Frank's gaze. "She didn't, actually, turn me down. Not at first."

"Oh, no, no." Frank rubbed the bridge of his nose. "No. Don't tell me you slept with her."

Now the man glanced up, then away. "Yep."

"Aw, hell." This hadn't looked good to begin with, and it had just gotten much worse. Incidences of violence in conjunction with stalking behavior increased greatly when there had previously been an intimate relationship, and everybody knew it.

"Just once," Dean added. "I don't know why, maybe she wanted to try something new, maybe she figured it would mess with my mind, her being all tied up with my sister's murder trial like that. Maybe no one else offered that particular evening, I don't know. Just once. After *that*, she rejected me. In no uncertain terms."

"And this was during the trial, two years ago?"

"Yep."

"You could have filed an ethics complaint. She could get disbarred for sleeping with a witness."

"I wasn't a witness. Character witness, maybe. I know I could have screwed with her right back, but—I didn't."

"She was representing the guy who helped kill your sister."

"Plus, she booted my ass, yes. But . . ."

Frank sighed, decided to pursue it. "But what?"

"That one night," Dean began, staring at the blotter, the in-box, anywhere but at Frank, "she woke up sobbing. And it wasn't because she found herself in a black man's bed. It was some kind of nightmare."

"What about?"

Dean shrugged. "She wouldn't say. But everybody comes from somewhere. And something in that somewhere wasn't good for her."

"So you let it slide."

"She was wrong, but I was more wrong. You know what they say at the academy: The scumbags we arrest aren't all bad, the people we protect aren't all good. I'm just saying the woman had depths. They might have been murky and mean, but she had depths."

Frank considered this. He also considered that Dean was simply trying to balance his horror of his sister's murder with his attraction to her killer's partner's lawyer. "So sex with her, it was—"

"Normal!" Dean said immediately. Typical, for a man to react more strongly to a suspicion of perversion than a suspicion of murder. "Not to mention fantastic. But completely normal."

"When did the relationship end?"

"Once is not a relationship. I called, pursued. She'd cut my balls off—verbally—but it took a week or two before I got the hint. It took three or four months before I had the guts to pursue anyone else, but maybe that was just as well. My sister's killer went to jail, I had my little snafu on the job and decided on a career change, and I never saw Marie Corrigan again until this convention started."

"Did you talk to her?"

"Nope. Saw her flitting around in her world, but I

stayed in mine. I don't know if she noticed me, or would even recognize me if she did. I didn't kill her, and I didn't kill Bruce Raffel."

"I believe you," Frank said again, though he didn't, not really.

CHAPTER 23

The sun hovered on the horizon and colored the sky with layers of pink and purple when Theresa stopped by the police station to see if Frank had uncovered anything more about William Rosedale. It wasn't a conversation she wished to have over the phone. She needed a face-to-face with her cousin, needed a reason to believe that she was overreacting and that everything would be fine. Which was silly to ask of Frank. Her cousin was many things, with even-keeled not necessarily one of them.

She didn't quite make it to Frank's desk before meeting Neil Kelly in the stark hallway, toting a plastic milk crate full of manila folders. "He's not here—your cousin. He and Angela went to interview a manager the hotel fired two months ago."

"Oh." She stifled her disappointment. "So you think this manager is killing defense attorneys just to make his former employees look bad?"

"Not really, but it's one possible explanation for how the killer got a key to the Presidential Suite. The computer records whenever a new card is programmed, but we only looked at the past week. If it's further back than that, we might never stumble on it."

"I thought they changed the codes every time someone checks out."

"I thought so, too, but that's not the passkey code. Though that's changed as well—I can't quite picture how it all works anyway, all those little magnetized electrons zipping around, so I'm left checking out the remaining court cases of the dearly departed for possible suspects. Do you have a minute?"

"Um . . . sure."

"Got comfortable shoes? I have another crate like this one—could you help me carry them two city blocks? Then I'll walk you back to your car. You parked on the street?"

Theresa answered in the affirmative all the way around and accepted the blue plastic crate, waiting while he retrieved the second from the conference room, a little energized to find herself alone with Neil Kelly. But she still needed her cousin. She needed somebody. But she never liked to disturb Frank when he could be in the middle of an interview. He might have worked on someone for an hour to get the guy to a point where he was ready to spill some incredibly useful fact, only to have that intimate, confessional spell broken by the digitally rendered theme from *Psycho*.

So she lifted the crate with energy born of nerves and followed the detective down the elevator and through the vast lobby, exiting onto Lakeside Avenue. Neil turned left, and she followed. He made a few attempts at small talk, but she wasn't in the mood for that, instead recapping her hair and fiber analyses from the two murders. She also gave him the heads-up, as lead detective, about the DNA analysis of the black hair. She'd looked up the

Tamika Johnson case, finding Marcus Dean's name in the reports. He had identified his sister's body.

Neil Kelly stopped walking, his face darkening, and for one moment she thought he was going to shout at her. Then it passed, replaced by weariness and a deep worry. "Damn. Damn. Damn."

"Yes," she agreed.

"He didn't do it, I'm telling you. I know the guy."

"I don't want to believe it, either—"

"No. There's no 'want to' about it. He didn't do it. There's got to be some mistake. You said the results were preliminary."

"Yes—"

"Don't talk to anyone about this, then. No one. If the press gets ahold of it . . . If we arrest him, all cops are monsters. If we don't arrest him, then cops covered up for their brother cop. Either way we suck."

"I would never talk about an open investigation, not to the media or anyone else."

He calmed, started walking again. "Of course. Sorry."

"But Bruce Raffel *was* the attorney in the case. What about other people in Tamika's family?"

"Yeah, we just went over that one. But her oldest child would still only be about ten now, and her mother's pushing seventy. Baby daddy took a hike years ago."

"It would have to be a blood relative anyway."

"Oh, yeah. If she had anyone else, they didn't show up in court."

She shifted her crate to the other hip. "Maybe he'll give us a DNA sample."

"Maybe. Your cousin was going to have a quick chat with him about it before he blew out of town. I'll see what he and Angela think of the conversation before we go asking a cop to hand over a mouth swab. Thanks for giving me the heads-up. And thanks for the help with these boxes—this way I don't have to make a second trip, and I've seen enough of the homicide unit for a few hours. We may have a psycho killer slaughtering defense attorneys at the Ritz-Carlton, but most of us pulled an all-nighter last night, and I can't do two of those in a row anymore. It's kind of hard to believe," he added.

"That all-nighters get exponentially harder after you pass forty?" They turned right on West Third Street.

"That we're all working so hard to find out who killed these two, when killing them was more or less a public service."

"Neil—"

"Yeah, I know, I'm not supposed to say that out loud. But we're all thinking it, right? Even you." He glanced over at her.

She got a better grip on the crate as they crossed above a set of train tracks. "Where are we going?"

"My place, at the end of this street. I promised you two city blocks, and I keep my promises. Truthfully, tell me you've shed any tears for Marie Corrigan." He stopped again, turning to her. "I saw your face when you looked at her. Admit it."

There are things we won't admit, even to ourselves.

She couldn't confess to feeling hatred, something her mother had trained her to believe unacceptable. She couldn't admit that some human lives were better ended sooner rather than later, something religion and most political theory had trained her to believe unacceptable.

So she punted, once again shifting the weight of the box she held. "I'm lucky that the relative personal worth of Marie Corrigan is not my problem. I'm not in the habit of attaching emotion to our victims. If I did, I'd have to get into another line of work."

He simply leaned closer, until their plastic crates bumped and joined, holding her gaze with an intensity to which she'd grown completely unaccustomed. "Tell me the truth."

She gulped. Felt ridiculous for doing so. "No, I'm not shedding any tears. But I'm still trying to find her killer. So are you."

He straightened. "Guess that makes us a bit schizophrenic, then."

"No. It makes us professional."

They passed the Cleveland Browns Stadium, empty and quiet, the breeze from the lake in front of them fresh and clean against her face. "There aren't any places at the end of the street."

"Think I'm leading you astray, do ya?"

"Do you slip into that hint of a brogue for comic effect, or were you actually born overseas?"

"I was born on the wild moors of Elgin, Illinois. I guess I just picked it up from my Irish grandpa. That's your line of work making you suspicious of everyone. I come by any accent honestly, and there *are* places at the end of this street—see?"

She saw only the lake, a warehouse, a small collection of boats.

"Second from the end, with the blue flag at the top of the mast."

"You live on a *boat*?"

"I do. Don't look like that, it's not as if I'm homeless. Similar, perhaps." She followed him down a set of wooden steps to a concrete dock. It couldn't be called a marina, even, only a loose assortment of bobbing watercraft. Two had company names stenciled on their sides, one appeared to be an emergency towing vehicle, and then a houseboat that seemed to be held together by duct tape and chewing gum. Neil's sailboat appeared, in the diminishing light, to be in good repair if one overlooked the scuffs on the bow and a bait bucket that smelled as if it hadn't been emptied in a while. But the deck was clear, and a sturdy door secured the cabin below. It rocked gently from side to side as he stepped over the gunwale, then turned to take her crate from her. "I intended this to be temporary, only a rent-saving idea to tide me over during the divorce, but I got used to it. It's close to work, and I always hated cutting grass anyway."

She took the hand he offered and stepped down to the deck, realizing too late that she had no real reason to stay. "Doesn't it get cold in the winter?"

"Extremely. I need someone to keep me warm."

She tried to look stern and not smile.

"So I'm thinking of getting a collie. Or a retriever, shorter hair. Want a drink?"

Now she did grin. "I'd love one, but I have to drive home. My daughter's going to wonder where I am." She felt her smile disappear at the thought. "And I need to know where she is."

"She seemed like a sensible girl to me," he said, in what sounded like a very subtle reproach.

"The problem isn't her. Need some help carrying them below?"

"Yes. No, truthfully. I didn't really need help to get them here. I just wanted an excuse to show you my cool bachelor pad."

"And it's *very* cool," she said with a laugh, relieved at his honesty. Moving into even closer quarters with him would be dangerous, and she had enough danger in her life at present. She should leave now. *Right* now.

Instead she turned and walked to the outer side of the deck, feeling the cool evening breeze caress her face. She didn't want to leave. She wanted to spend a lot more time with Neil Kelly, who moved behind her and stood close enough to make her painfully aware of that fact.

"So what's the problem, then?"

"I . . . um—I sort of take a long time to get used to people," she began, wondering how to phrase this. Even though she found him attractive, she almost certainly wouldn't act on it, because she didn't let people close, not ever. Other people, through no fault of their own, were never what you thought you wanted. Best to avoid the whole circus.

No matter how tempted—

"I meant with your daughter," he said.

"Oh, that." Relief with disappointment. "Well, that's a long story."

He turned her to face him, very gently, arms fully extended to keep her at arms' length. He didn't draw her close, didn't touch her face. He only said, "Tell me."

So she did.

I might need his help, she justified, as well as a little perspective. Frank was too close to the situation, too close to her and Rachael. She could talk to Angela, of course, but Angela didn't have those ropes of muscle underneath the skin on her forearms and eyes that Theresa could get lost in.

She told him about Rachael's new friend, about Jenna Simone's murder, about the trial and his representation by Marie Corrigan.

Whatever Neil Kelly had been expecting her to relate, the tale of William Rosedale could not have been it. He appeared by turns surprised, bewildered, and then very, very concerned. By the end of her brief summation, he had slumped to the gunwale, pensive. "Tell her to quit, go home, and never see the guy again. Though I don't see how he could have killed Marie Corrigan. The restaurant chef said they were insanely busy Tuesday night and none of his staff took even a smoke break from five o'clock until ten-thirty or so, which is about our entire window."

"It wouldn't have taken long. And time of death can't be fixed that accurately."

"True, but he would never have had access to the Presidential Suite."

"Unless—" She forced herself to choke it out. "Someone at the front desk made him a key."

Rachael worked at the front desk. But Rachael would have made the connection as soon as Marie Corrigan turned up dead. It was unthinkable.

Wasn't it?

"But no one did. That would have been recorded in the mainframe, and it wasn't. No one made a key. And why on earth would he kill Bruce Raffel?"

Theresa could breathe again. "Good points. Truly, I don't think William murdered either of the lawyers. All I know is I *do* think he killed Jenna Simone."

"Rachael's got to get away from him."

"I know. Problem is, that ain't gonna fly with her. My daughter can't be rerouted when she feels she's right."

"You mean like her mother, who blacked out an entire hotel?" He gave her a gentle smile. "So you think she'll side with him?"

She let her knees sway with the boat as a wave pushed at the stern. "Yes. I know her, despite what she thinks, despite what I sometimes think myself. I know when she's serious about something. She's serious about this boy."

He stood up, closing the short distance between them once again. He didn't try to talk her down. Like the majority of people in law enforcement, he knew that the most obvious suspect was almost always the right one. "First of all, you have to stop calling him a boy. He's a monster in boy's clothing, and you have to make her see that. Show her the crime-scene photos, take her to the girl's grave."

"I can't do that."

"You'll do whatever you have to do to keep her safe. Won't you?"

Even if Rachael never spoke to her again, even if she dropped out of school and withheld all future grandchildren. "Yes."

Now he did touch her face, letting his fingers rest on the edge of her jaw. "Good. Since that's settled, I think there's something else we should discuss."

"Yes."

The lake breeze did nothing to cool her skin as his thumb traced the very edge of her lower lip.

"Or not," he said.

Nothing shocks the system like the first kiss of someone new, that electric brush of the unknown, and Theresa's knees threatened to buckle at the pleasure of it. He touched her only with his mouth and one hand, lips that tasted slightly of coffee stroking and prodding until she broke down and put her hands on his chest, sliding them around to his back. Then an incredible sensation of his fingers on her stomach, her hips, the small of her back, until they were pressed together from shoulder to groin and the breath went out of her, and in a few minutes her brain felt obligated to mention that she was grinding against him in full view of the city of Cleveland.

When his lips trailed down her neck, she asked herself what the hell she thought she was doing. She barely knew the man, and he was a cop. They were generally trustworthy in every area *except* this one.

"Come belowdecks with me," he murmured.

"No!" The idea rattled her system so that she stepped back, one foot stumbling over the bait bucket, and Neil had to grab her quickly to keep her from falling into the lake. Fortunately, he seemed to take this discombobulation as a compliment.

"Okay, okay. I only planned to make coffee, since it's getting chilly up here. I didn't mean it as an assumption of your virtue or ease of same."

Words poured out with a giggle. "I'm sorry, but I really have to go. . . . My daughter . . . I like . . . I like your boat—"

He gave her nose one very light tap. "Okay. That will do for a start, anyway."

And so she grinned wickedly as they climbed back onto the dock, strolled past the stadium, and most of the way up West Third Street. She grinned even harder when he would slide an arm around her shoulders for ten or twelve paces. Amazing how one could walk the planet for forty-odd years and still feel like a schoolgirl. The breeze carried the scent of freedom, and the city glittered like Oz.

At her car he trapped her in the acute angle of the open door. "Thank you for a very interesting, if too brief, evening, Ms. MacLean. I believe we'll have to do this again, leaving out the 'brief' part."

"Absolutely. As soon as we find out who's killing lawyers and get my daughter away from her new friend."

He frowned at that. "Can't guarantee I'm willing to wait."

She protested when he bent to kiss her, gesturing up at the many lit windows of the Justice Center. "Someone might see us. Bad enough for me, but you have to work here."

"And your cousin will kick my ass, I know. I don't care." He kissed her anyway, letting his mouth explore hers until she leaned on the car roof for support, and breaking away proved difficult and prolonged. "I don't hide who I am, Theresa."

Then he went and stood on the curb until she started up the car and pulled away. When she turned the corner onto Ontario, she caught sight of him in the rearview mirror and for several minutes could form no coherent thoughts at all.

CHAPTER 24

Theresa patted the dog and scratched the cat before dumping her purse on the counter. Rachael's work shoes were by the door, and no messages blinked from the digital recorder.

No sound from upstairs. Rachael had probably gone next door to hit up her grandmother for some dinner, always a more reliable source than her I-hate-to-cook mother. So Theresa changed clothes, washed her face, and walked up the grassy knoll to the house in which she'd grown up.

Her mother stood at the stove over a pan of yellow-colored liquid with the consistency of gravy. "What is that?" Theresa asked.

"It's an experiment." Sixty-seven years on the planet had not begun to dull Agnes's appetite for learning. Theresa, on the other hand, sometimes felt she had absorbed all the information possible and her brain had locked its doors and turned off the porch light. But perhaps it had more to do with the nature of the information.

"I'm trying a mint-infused custard puff," her mother

said. "How was your day? Rachael said you found an-other dead lawyer. You have some sort of serial killer?"

The experimental nature of the dish didn't put Theresa off. A true foodie, Agnes often devised new dishes for the diner where she worked, and even her failures were edible, while her successes were something to celebrate.

"Apparently. Either these two were involved in some-thing that ticked off the wrong person or someone really doesn't like lawyers. I keep trying to think of a serial killer who targeted people of a certain profession, and I can't think of any. Except for prostitutes and real-estate agents, professions that make it easy to get the victims alone and isolated. That's a choice of convenience. But I don't know of any cases where someone targeted law-yers or doctors or used-car salesmen."

Agnes stirred, the glossy, buff-colored stuff churning and changing with each pass of the wooden spoon. "It happens on TV every other week."

"Of course it does. But in real life, not so much." The-resa's finger crept toward the shining, perfect surface of the custard.

"Hot," her mother warned. "Maybe the guy is killing hotel guests and they both just happened to be lawyers."

"That's one theory. Hotels are tailor-made for crime—nothing but strangers coming and going, mul-tiple exits, good soundproofing. If the killer had started up next week—or checked in to the hotel next week—the odds might be equally good that he would kill two video-game designers, or aluminum salesmen, or mem-bers of a visiting football team."

"But you don't think so."

"Too many people really *wanted* to kill Marie Cor-rigan. It would be ironic for her to be murdered by some random psychopath with no personal grudge. And this feels personal."

Agnes took the pan off the burner and, in one of those masterpieces of timing that Theresa had never been able to pull off, removed a tray of lightly browned, puffed-up pastries from the oven. "Do you have any suspects?"

"I've got a favorite." Theresa snatched up one of the puffs.

"Hot," her mother warned again. Theresa passed it from hand to hand as she described Sonia's—and now her own—suspicion of Dennis Britton. "That's all it is, though, suspicion. Nothing approaching proof. But then he's defended enough murderers to be good about proof. Maybe good enough to get away with killing his wife."

"His wife's dead?"

Theresa had been unable to resist a look after stumbling onto Elizabeth (Ellie) Britton's file. It hadn't taken long.

The healthy brunette had been thirty-two years old, five-five, and 130 pounds. She had been driving a three-year-old Honda Accord that went over the embankment behind a business on Canal Road, near I-480 in Garfield Heights. Why she would have arrived well after closing time (passing a security camera over the side door) or why she somehow missed the end of the parking lot behind their building remained unknown. She apparently drove off the asphalt, through some trees, and down a short but steep hill to the Cuyahoga River. A rotting tree stump stopped the car from submerging, leaving it stranded on the bank.

Ellie had died only a month and a half after Jenna Simone. Again, this explained why Theresa had no recollection of the case—she'd still been in a funk over her fiancé's death. Plus, it had been reported as a car accident, and Theresa hadn't been as familiar with attorney Dennis Britton then as she now had the misfortune to be. She didn't mention any of this to her mother, only summarized the autopsy report: The victim had received a blow straight across the forehead, consistent with having hit the steering wheel upon impact. Decomposition had advanced slightly faster than usual as the corpse lay in an open car in mid-July, next to the river's humid environment. Even without the stump, it would have been unlikely for the car to wash away in the shallow river, but the hood of the car had entered the water and a pool had formed at the victim's feet. Police found the victim in the driver's seat, wearing a seat belt. After the impact her head came to lodge between the headrest and the open window. Either the blow to the head or the loss of blood had caused a lack of brain functioning until the involuntary muscles failed and her heart stopped. Keys were in the ignition, her purse and wallet found intact. The toxicology results showed no traces of alcohol, sedatives, or any illegal drug use.

As in Jenna Simone's file, a few of the scene photographs had been printed. Dr. Phil Banachek had done the autopsy; perhaps the aging pathologist preferred to work from the photos rather than make his way down a sloping forest hillside with his aching knees.

They showed what Theresa had already imagined: a damaged Honda, its nose stuck in the flowing Cuyahoga; a bloated, maggot-infested corpse, with wisps of brown hair escaping through the open window and hanging down the side of the driver's door alongside narrow streaks of blood; a smear of blood on the steering wheel and one on the passenger door; the view from the passenger side—the body slumped, another streak of blood visible against the light gray interior of the driver's door . . . not much blood for someone who bled out, even partially, but there could be more behind the body itself or poured down into the window well; an oversize Gucci purse on the edge of the passenger seat with a briefcase on the floor, its papers scattered; more blood on the passenger door, its window rolled down as well; and the view from the parking lot, deep ruts in moist ground at the edge of the lot, the Honda visible in the distance. The car had traveled in a straight line. There were no concrete barriers to stop it or even alert the driver that the asphalt ended, which seemed like a lawsuit waiting to happen. But the victim's aggressive lawyer husband had not filed one.

Scary to think that a life could be lost so easily, by simply driving four feet too far in a dark parking lot.

Between bites of the pastry, Theresa told her mother that a vehicle-inspection sheet reported the Honda to be in working condition, with all relevant parts functioning as expected. This meant that the seat belt and the brake and gas pedals were working properly. The headlights, however, had not been turned on at the time of impact.

There were no police reports in the file—not any reason for there to be, unless the pathologist requested them and tossed them into the file when done. But a second newspaper clipping told her more. The parking lot and the building belonged to Rule and Sons, a manufacturing plant and home of the main witness against Ellie's client in a case of high-dollar employee theft. The owner and two managers had been dodging her calls, and she may have gone there to see them before resorting to subpoena, a common technique for her. The parking lot had no fence and not much lighting. They had never felt the need, the owner said, as they functioned solely during business hours. The security camera had only been installed because of the aforementioned theft case.

Her husband, Dennis Britton, had last seen Ellie that morning before they left for work. They lived only a mile away, off Brecksville Road on the other side of the river.

She did not come home after work so far as he could tell. He had arrived at about 7:00 P.M., unsurprised to find the house empty—they both worked long days, even on Fridays. But when she hadn't returned by bedtime and calls to her cell phone went unanswered, he became concerned. He did not call the police at first, knowing that they wouldn't be too interested in an able-bodied adult who'd stayed out late, but called his wife's friends and co-workers. The co-workers reported that she had left the law office—a small group specializing in drunk-driving cases, not where her husband worked—at around 6:00 P.M. on Friday. No one had heard from Ellie since. As soon as he could, he filed a missing-persons report with the Garfield Heights police department. Dennis Britton made a point of saying that the police officers had been polite and helpful—Theresa found this sudden admiration of the boys in blue suspicious, to say the least, but the rest of his behavior had been pitch-perfect.

The article even snuck in the small fact that the police had dusted the trunk of the car for palm prints, to see if someone had pushed it into the ravine. Nothing.

A couple of kids playing on the other side of the river had seen the car on Saturday morning but didn't mention it to their parents until after the news broke. An employee arriving for work at Rule and Sons bright and early on Monday morning, who made a habit of parking in the shade at the back of the lot, noticed the tire tracks leading into the brush. This, along with the security camera, which showed the Honda Accord passing the entrance at 8:40 P.M., fixed the time of death at Friday night.

Ellie Britton, while alive, had been a pretty woman with straight dark hair and a prominent nose. The article did not include a photo of the grieving husband.

"Sounds like she took a wrong turn in the dark," Theresa's mother said as she filled the puffs with custard. "She'd hardly be the first person in history to do that. Why does your friend think her husband killed her?"

"That's what I'm trying to figure out. There are a few things I don't like, such as why wouldn't she have hit the brakes when she felt the terrain dip? And if she *had* hit the brakes, wouldn't the seat belt lock up to prevent her from slamming into the steering wheel? I guess she could have slipped out of the shoulder strap. But why douse her lights in a dark parking lot? How could the final impact be harsh enough to crack her skull but not hard enough to throw her purse forward onto the floor? How did a smear of blood get on the other side of the vehicle, onto the passenger-side door?"

"Good Lord," her mother said. "The details you notice."

"Not really. There are always the unexplainables. Items fly around, peculiar coincidences occur, homeowners actually forgot to lock a door they insist they *always* lock. Maybe the blow didn't kill Ellie Britton outright but was enough to cause a slowing of the motor functions, maybe a touch of positional asphyxia. The blood on the passenger door could have squirted there; usually the initial blow doesn't bleed a lot, but head wounds bleed especially well. I've seen way more bizarre examples of blood flight characteristics. Maybe she had a habit of turning off her lights before parking to minimize the chances of forgetting about them entirely and returning to a car with a dead battery. I've done that."

"Or maybe the guy killed her."

"Or maybe," Theresa agreed, snitching another one of the now-sufficiently-cooled puffs and popping it into her mouth, only to realize that it had *not* sufficiently cooled.

Perhaps Dennis Britton had killed his wife, put her in the passenger seat of her own car, then driven to the parking lot of a business involved in one of her cases, a business he lived only a mile from and whose terrain he might be familiar with. He moved her to the driver's seat, turned out the lights to lessen the chance of discovery, pushed it over the edge, and hoped it would float away down the river, decomposing the body until no clues remained. Then he simply walked home. Not a perfect murder, perhaps, but near enough as made no difference.

Or perhaps Theresa simply wanted to believe that.

"So what did you do with this file?" her mother asked.

"I put it back in the cabinet. Powell's right—if there was any way to prove that Dennis Britton killed his wife, the cops would have. Everybody hates lawyers, as Sonia keeps reminding me."

"Especially you."

"Do not." Theresa frowned. What had she just told Neil Kelly about mothers and daughters?

Mothers and daughters . . .

"Where *is* Rachael anyway?"

"She went on a date." Agnes took a spatula to finish up the pan.

Theresa felt a prickling along her scalp, like the first tiny tremors that herald an earthquake to come. "What?"

"She came over, said she didn't need dinner because that boy from work was picking her up."

"William."

"Yes, William. He must have pulled into your drive, because I didn't see him. She looked cute, though, wearing that purple top you gave her at Christmas. I asked where they were going, but I don't think she heard me, she rushed off so fast— What's the matter?"

Don't panic, Theresa told herself. *Don't scream. And don't worry your mother.* "Nothing, I just remembered something I have to do for work."

Her mother nodded but had too many working instincts to be entirely convinced. Mothers and daughters . . . "I think she really likes this one."

"So do I."

PART III

RACHAEL

Frank had visited the Office of the Public Defender perhaps three times in his fifteen-year career as a police officer. Depositions—where attorneys could question witnesses on the record but without the damper of a judge or jury—were taken in the neutral territory of the court reporters' offices, and there would be no other reason for Frank to hang out around defense lawyers. It wasn't like they were friends. Though with one or two exceptions, he felt the same way about prosecutors. Lawyers lived in a specific, contained universe, where nothing mattered except their own strategies. Frank preferred to leave them to it.

In fact, the last time he'd set foot inside PD, they'd still been in the threadbare building on Prospect. He had to use Google to find the new place, a scant four hundred feet from the police department. It looked about the same, a weary collection of hallways without any particular decor. Newer paint, that was all.

Frank and Angela had already spoken with the Ritz-Carlton's disgruntled former employee, a general manager who, though he wouldn't admit it, had been let go for following the maids around too closely and too consistently for it to be considered a quality-control effort. He now worked at a convenience store and did not feel any more gruntled toward the Ritz-Carlton but had, they learned, been in Chicago for a grandmother's birthday on the night Marie Corrigan was killed.

So now the two cops perched in surprisingly comfortable chairs across from Maryann Mercer, who'd been Bruce Raffel's supervisor during that attorney's time at the PD. Maryann had been working the system longer than Frank had been with the police department, yet she still managed to have a sense of humor. She had her graying hair pulled back in a thick ponytail and wore sandals with socks under her tailored slacks. As with most law grads, she had applied to both the prosecutor's office and the PD and gone with whichever one offered a job first. But most newly minted lawyers used the PD as a way station, a stepping-stone to a private firm; the ones who didn't were either very ambitious, very unambitious, or true believers (or, as in Frank's parlance, crazy). Maryann fell into the third category.

"Did you keep in touch?" Angela now asked her. "With Bruce? Or Marie?"

"Saw them around, said hi while passing through the corridors of power. I wouldn't call it keeping in touch. They shook the dust of this place off their feet as soon as they had an offer and never looked back."

"They got along when they worked here?"

"Like a house afire. Symbiotic. They thought alike," she added, then pondered her own words for a moment. "No, not alike, kind of complementary. You probably weren't fond of Bruce"—she looked at them for confirmation, received uniform nods—"but he was smart. A lot smarter than he seemed. Innovative. And Marie— she was plenty smart, don't get me wrong, but she had the charm, the personal connection. She had that mischievous quality, that ability—I mean aside from being gorgeous—to make you like her even when she was slicing your heart out. Put them together and they were unstoppable. They would pretty much only work with each other after a while. Formed a sort of unofficial partnership, pooled their cases."

"Was that a problem? Office-wise?" Angela asked.

"Are you kidding? They cleared cases right and left. I should complain about that?"

"But their relationship was personal as well?"

Maryann Mercer laughed. "Did they screw each other? Like rabbits. On their respective desks, even, to hear the cleaning staff tell it. Might as well. You're only young once."

"Any bondage involved?"

"Wouldn't know, wouldn't have asked."

"The rest of your staff didn't mind the drama?"

Maryann laughed again, the amusement utterly genuine. "What is this, grade school? Two APDs getting it on is not drama. I have a hearing tomorrow over whether a mentally ill ten-year-old who stabbed his mom to death is going to prison or Northwood Regional. I'd almost rather it be prison. At least he'd have a scheduled release date. So a little sex among the children is not considered drama. No one cared. Well, except for Bruce's wife. Poor thing."

"What happened to her?"

"Waddled in here nine months pregnant, and I had to stall her with a glass of water so Bruce and Marie could get their clothes back on. Figured she'd dump him right then and there, but no, had the baby. I heard she had another one after that before she finally gave up on him. One thing you have to say about Bruce, he was crazy about those boys. No angle there. One hundred percent gaga. About the mother, not so much. Of course, men are all like that. They think loving their children makes up for everything else they do. Loving a kid is easy. Raising them, that's a whole 'nother stretch of badly maintained road."

"Who left the office first?" Frank asked, ignoring the social commentary. They had already checked Bruce's ex-wife, now happily remarried and working as a paralegal for a tax firm. The woman had motive to kill both Bruce and Marie, but between her job, her husband, two boys and now a girl, soccer practice, and a vet appointment, she seemed to be fairly well spoken for during the time periods in question.

Maryann rubbed the back of her neck. "Bruce, I'm pretty sure."

"Why?"

"Job offer. More money."

"Was Marie angry?"

"She wasn't happy, but it had to happen. They were too young and poor to open their own office, and it'd be hard to find a firm to take both of them at once. Don't think it bothered them much. They were just starting out, world's their oyster. Plenty of time to move and settle and move again. Didn't realize how rare it is to find someone you can really work with."

"What about Dennis Britton?" Angela asked.

Maryann slowed down, but not by much. "Huh. Dennis. Yeah, he was in the mix here, too."

"He mix with Marie?"

"Dunno. Maybe. Like I said, only young once."

"Any conflicts between him and Bruce?"

"Not that I recall. Both alpha males with a capital A, so after they circle awhile, they're either going to hunt as a pack or leave blood on the snow."

"Which was it?"

"Stains on the industrial-grade carpeting. Remember when that guy robbed that guy of yours at the Shell station on Ontario?"

Frank nodded. Barely out of his teens but armed with a Desert Eagle, a young man had made a very questionable choice of victim. Not only did his target have six inches and nearly a hundred pounds on him, he also happened to be an off-duty detective. The young robber panicked upon hearing this and pulled the trigger, winging the cop and shattering the windshield of his own getaway vehicle. From there, matters did not improve, at least not for him.

"Guy was screwed six ways from Sunday, and I didn't know what to do for him. Most of our clients are a bit challenged in the education department, but this guy didn't have the brains to shuck a peanut before eating it."

"Exactly the sort of citizen we want running around town robbing people with a loaded .44."

"Yeah, yeah," Maryann said. "Bruce had already done a police who-shot-first thing, so he let me know he would be a good one to handle it. But I gave it to Dennis, figuring he needed the experience. Guy got twenty years. Bruce harped on Dennis right after the sentencing, and the two of them turned into Tasmanian devils. Me and another APD had to tear them apart, and Dennis had to redecorate his office. I didn't do that again."

"Get in the middle of a fight?"

"Assign cases based on the attorney's needs instead of the client's. Every case is different and unpredictable, yes, but the guy would be out by now if I'd assigned his case to Bruce. I'm pretty sure of that."

"And that would be so much better for all concerned," Frank said. "Britton got plenty of experience in the long run anyway. He's got a police shooting trial going right now."

"I know. *Now* I wouldn't have any qualms. He's going to make you work for it," she warned.

"Not worried," Frank assured her, then realized he had fallen into the attorney's staccato style of talking. "Is there anything else you can tell us about Bruce, Marie, and Dennis Britton?"

Maryann's face stilled. "Only that they were strong, smart people. Whoever killed Marie and Bruce has killed the people who would have helped him when he gets caught."

"Thanks for assuming that's going to happen."

A smile more like a grimace. "That's what we try to tell our clients here. Crime doesn't pay. Everyone, eventually, gets caught."

"Do they listen?" Angela asked.

"If they did," Maryann said, "we'd both be out of a job."

CHAPTER 26

Don't panic.

Theresa repeated these words to herself as she paced in circles around her kitchen floor. *Don't panic. Just because your daughter is missing, last seen with an almost-convicted rapist and murderer.*

I should have told her. I should have told her immediately, given her notice to Karla, taken her home, and hired an armed guard. Instead I had to give him the benefit of the doubt, try to wait out her interest. Rachael is halfway through a horrible death because I tried to be PC.

If she's not already dead.

Unwanted images flashed quickly, but not quickly enough. A sweet necking session grows too insistent. Rachael hesitates, begins to protest, maybe not even that seriously but enough to set off the rage. First a slap, then a punch, marring her precious child's face—

Enough.

She pulled out the white pages. There were only two Rosedales listed. One didn't answer—who would *not* have an answering machine in this day and age?—and the other connected to a teenage boy who didn't know a William. Theresa persisted until the poor kid rattled off the names of everyone in his family: Denise, Alex, Shane, Misty, and himself, Michael. Trying to help, he came up with a cousin named William, but that boy's last name wasn't Rosedale and he lived in New Mexico. He seemed about to move on to ancestors in the old country before Theresa regained enough presence of mind to thank him and hang up. Besides, anyone who'd been through what the Rosedales had been through would almost certainly have an unlisted phone number. Hell, *Theresa* had an unlisted phone number.

Not that they deserved any sympathy for what they'd been through. Their own fault for raising such a monster.

Political correctness had obviously been shown the door.

She tried Rachael's cell and got only that intensely annoying *"The party you are trying to reach"* message, because, of course, her battery had died and she hadn't taken the time to recharge it before rushing off with the means of her own destruction. Cell phones came with GPS these days, but it didn't work if the phone was off, and Rachael's phone probably didn't have that feature, because it was a cheap little prepaid number that they'd decided on after a few months of astronomical bills.

Theresa had feared for her daughter nearly every day of the child's life—every parent did—but this had to be the first time she felt positive, absolutely positive, of Rachael's death. And what a death—this was a million times worse than a car accident or meningitis or a dorm fire or any of the worst of the worst fates she had imagined befalling her daughter in years past. And while most of those theoretical fates were at least partly Theresa's fault, this one really was.

She would call Frank. Frank would panic, scream at

Theresa, and hold it against her for the rest of her life no matter how much he would deny it, but he could also put out a BOLO on the two kids and any vehicle registered to a William Rosedale. Provided William hadn't borrowed a friend's. Who was that dorky pal of his at the Ritz—Ray? He might know William's favorite hangouts.

But Frank first.

She had dialed three numbers when the door to the garage opened and Rachael walked in.

Her daughter didn't merely walk; she floated.

William did not follow, and Theresa heard the faint screech of tires as he left rubber marks on her driveway.

Don't scream, she told herself. *Your daughter has the beatific smile of a saint in a painting. Her limbs move as if in a dream, because she's in the throes of a budding love. Rachael's entire world is momentarily perfect, with no buts or if-onlys.* Theresa recognized the state because she'd been there herself, many years ago. These moments were so brief and so precious that to curtail one seemed a crime. *So don't scream.*

"WHERE THE HELL HAVE YOU BEEN?" she screamed.

Rachael thumped back to earth. The serene look turned to shock, anger, and betrayal.

"I'm sorry," Theresa said instantly, knowing that her heart felt more broken than Rachael's right now. "I'm sorry, honey. I didn't want to shout, but I was so, so scared. I really thought you were dead."

It took Rachael another few seconds to produce any sound from her moving lips. *"What?"*

"I'm so sorry, but I'm going to have to— Did you have a nice time with William?"

Rachael stepped back, still holding on to her purse, as if she might have to make a run for it from this lunatic who'd taken over her mother's body. "Yes-s."

"I'm so sorry, honey, but that's what we have to talk about. I have to tell you something." Theresa took a deep breath. "And it's going to hurt."

CHAPTER 27

Maryann Mercer had a phone call, so she didn't walk them out, leaving the two detectives free to roam the hallways. It was now 9:00 P.M., and Angela had that antsy bounce to her step that meant she needed to go home and make sure her kids went to bed on time. Frank said he wanted to look up the battle-ax and suggested Angela walk back to the station without him. His partner didn't question why he wanted to talk to Sonia Battle or why he preferred to do so without her.

There were lights on in some of the other offices, and he strolled, light-footed, feeling like a soldier who had parachuted behind enemy lines. All he needed was camo face paint and a flak jacket. He had no idea if Sonia would still be in her office but would have bet half his paycheck on it. She'd been at the convention all day and had no life outside her job. Of course she'd be in her office at 9:00 P.M. on a Thursday, catching up on paperwork, convinced that without her skills her poor downtrodden clients would be chewed up by the unfeeling machine that was the American criminal-justice system. And that's exactly where he found her.

She had a corner office, which meant nothing in this instance. No more than ten feet square and still only one window, bland carpeting, and fake-wood furniture. It looked, in short, exactly like the prosecutors' offices. Add a few desks and it could be the homicide unit.

Being female, she had a few items that could be called decor: a frame on her desk, a poster of Paris, and a Legolas action figure, which stood precarious guard atop a stack of manila folders held closed with neon-colored rubber bands.

"Have you been to France?" he asked.

She didn't look up. "Of course not. What do you want?"

"Why 'of course'?"

"Because I'm a frustrated middle-aged spinster, which means no traveling companion, not to mention that I live on a government salary that barely covers my rent and a parking space." Now she did look up, pen still poised over a yellow legal pad. "I'm a bleeding-heart liberal with more compassion than sense, so my co-workers who actually have lives dump their unfinished work, dead-end cases, and on-call holidays on me because they know I don't. Dinner every night is fast food eaten over my kitchen sink, and my only consistent sexual relationship involves double-A batteries. Is there a stereotype I've missed?"

"Are you wearing Birkenstocks?"

She stuck her foot out from behind the desk, showing him one sensible black pump, but he thought he saw the hint of a smile tug at her lips. He took that as an invitation and slipped into one of the chairs opposite her desk.

"Still in heels at eight-thirty P.M. Forget the moral dilemma of putting dangerous people back on the street—is the money really worth having to stuff yourself into suits and ties and heels all day, every day?"

She said nothing, so he went on. "Dress codes in every other area of life have relaxed. Seems as if a courtroom is the only place left that still has rules. No pun intended. Maybe that's why you lawyers like them."

"I got into law entirely for the fashion, yes. What do you want?"

"To talk to you about William Rosedale."

"I can't tell you anything. It's all still privileged."

"He's working with my niece. Two more people just turned up dead on his watch."

She swallowed but did not look away. "I was his attorney, even though just briefly. You know I can't say a thing."

"Theresa's daughter," he pressed, figuring she hadn't been kidding about that "more compassion than sense" crack.

She frowned, flushed. "Actually, I *can* tell you everything I know without violating privilege. I was assigned to William only for the few hours between his family's tax lawyer running away like a little girl and the moment I got Marie on board. Normally the state would let those few hours hang, but they're really strict about juveniles not taking one breath without legal representation. Maryann gave me the basics—dead girl, his house, blood all over. I handle mostly drug charges, not homicides, so my only actions on his behalf were to advise his shell-shocked parents to hire Marie and to ask Marie to talk to the parents. I was off his case before I even learned the victim's name. I billed about an hour and a half and spent maybe ninety seconds of it face-to-face with my client, which is probably why he doesn't even remember me."

"Why Marie?"

"I wanted him tried as a juvenile, and that's not my area. Not that she did a lot of juvenile work, but she had co-chaired on that seventeen-year-old who divided his girlfriend into seven parts and wrapped each one in a garbage bag. She'd kept him in juvenile court, and I hoped she could do the same for William—which she did. If I'd held on to his case, he'd already be halfway through his postconviction motions with an injection date scheduled. I *begged* Marie to take the case."

"She didn't want to?"

Sonia picked up a coffee mug with a tag dangling near the handle, sipped, frowned, and set it back down. "Bloody murder among pretty children in the suburbs? Of course she did. Marie just liked to be begged."

"You knew her well." He wondered just *how* well, and she flashed him a wicked grin to let him know she knew he was wondering. A warm little flush came to life in his stomach, startling him—probably just hunger. The building around them stood silent, as if they were the only two people left in it.

"It would be difficult not to. Marie was pretty up front about her desires. Vulnerabilities, much less so."

"Could one or the other have gotten her killed?"

Sonia sighed. "If I knew, I'd tell you."

"Really?"

"As long as it wasn't one of my clients, yes. My recitation of stereotypes aside, I'm not the knee-jerk reactionary you think I am. I'm not so stupid that I can't see that when two people who knew each other—and well—are killed in the same time and place, then that's probably because of something between those two people. But I don't know what that is. I might know some of Marie's dirty little secrets—like sometimes she'd puke up her lunch—and I might know some of Bruce's dirty little secrets—like he loved a good lash to the coccyx—but I don't know any of Bruce *and* Marie's dirty little secrets."

Frank involuntarily began to picture Sonia naked and

holding a whip, and it gave him that puzzling flush again so that he recrossed his legs and coughed. "Did they ever screw over a client? Or have a client *think* they screwed him over? Have a victim swear revenge?"

"When they worked together here, we were all just starting out. They did smaller cases—theft, burglary, possession. Routine. Half the time the victims didn't even come to court, and it would have been years ago."

"Maybe our guy's been inside all this time."

She shook her head, the fine blond locks escaping from behind her ears. "Sorry. I got nothing. The fireworks during their tenure here burst from between Bruce and Marie, not among their clients or opposing parties."

"What about more recently? They kept in touch, at least until Bruce moved, right?"

She agreed but still couldn't offer any insights. She spoke with Marie occasionally but couldn't think of any recent dramas in that attorney's life. Frank watched carefully for some spark of envy or anger when she spoke of Bruce and Marie's on-and-off relationship, and he saw none. Sonia showed much more emotion over talk of Dennis Britton than over either of the two victims. She hated the man, that was clear. But even she doubted that he would have killed either Bruce or Marie, and certainly not out of sexual jealousy.

"I'll be seeing him tomorrow," Frank admitted without knowing why. "The officer-involved shooting."

"Wear brass undershorts," she advised.

"What about Bruce? Anything haunting his past? He got a little out there with his sex life—maybe he ran into someone a little *too* dominant? She wants to reconnect when he's in town but finds him with Marie, someone equally dominant in her own way?"

Sonia shook her head again, and he tried again. "Maybe it's his wife. She's finally realized that she played the fool for years, and all she's got to show for it are some lousy child-support checks."

"I'll bet they're not too lousy. And I doubt she would have waited until now to kill him."

"So who would have?" he said at last.

She didn't respond immediately, and his radar perked up. "You're thinking about someone."

"No, not someone. It's just— You said haunting his past, and I just thought . . . The only case I've ever heard Bruce talk about as if he had a few regrets, it would be the Corwin case. His client tried to rob a lady at her ATM, and the gun went off—"

"Tamika Johnson. Shot in front of her three children."

"Yeah," Sonia agreed. "Bruce worked his usual magic, got a really reduced sentence, much more than he expected, because he didn't know that one of the witnesses would go on a bender and completely discredit himself on the stand. Bruce and I were . . . um, seeing each other then. Usually after a trial he'd celebrate, drink himself silly, and then forget all about it by the middle of the following week. This one, three, four, six weeks later, he was still saying things like how his little boys would still be in grade school when this guy got out. For some reason that seemed to bother him."

"Can't imagine why," Frank said.

Now Sonia flushed, and it had nothing to do with sexual tension. "Whatever. That's the only thing I can think of."

Frank tried to step back. "His kids would have been only a little younger than the victim's. Maybe that bugged him."

She picked up her mug again, swirled it, then put it down with the same expression of disgust as before.

"People tend to get wiggy when kids in cases remind

them of their own," Frank added. In his opinion, people were wiggy about kids, period. This must have showed in his voice and seemed to mollify the also-childless Sonia, because she accepted his business card and agreed to call him if she thought of anything else.

He didn't find the idea entirely repulsive, which had to mean he'd been working too hard. Standing, he felt his gaze fall on the framed photo on her desk. Three kittens in a basket, one reaching out a tentative paw to make first contact with that green stuff called grass. "You have cats?"

Her face, which had relaxed into something remotely like friendliness, closed up again. "Of course. Fulfilling my role as the crazy cat lady for my apartment complex is a vital component of the frustrated-spinster stereotype. Let me show you out."

CHAPTER 28

FRIDAY

Theresa stared out her car window, wondering what in the hell she thought she was doing.

Rachael hadn't believed her, of course. Maybe if Theresa had led into the topic without such an explosive beginning, she'd have had a better chance of convincing the girl. But once Rachael saw her as unbalanced, nothing Theresa said after that could adjust her opinion.

"You've known him for ten minutes, Mom. I've been working with him every day for over a month now. He's nice, he's helpful—he's so stable. I never see him get upset about anything no matter how many directions he's jerked in. He's so kind to Ray—that dweeby guy, you remember. Ray told me himself that they've been friends since grade school and that William has always looked out for him, even got him the job."

"I'm not saying he's a raging ogre every minute of the day, Rachael. Ted Bundy was a very reliable employee, too."

"William is not Ted Bundy!"

"Honey. He was found next to the body with her blood all over him. In his own *home*. They were seen leaving the school dance together. I know you don't want to hear this, but how much more evidence could you possibly need?"

"Then why is he not in jail? Your own justice system agrees with me, but that's irrelevant to you. In your opinion I have the judgment of a ten-year-old!" Rachael said, and from there the conversation deteriorated into the familiar treatise on Theresa's refusal to see that Rachael had grown up, which forced Theresa to point out that if Rachael couldn't accept documented facts, then she *hadn't* really grown up. After that, things got really rocky.

Rachael even refused to say where they'd been, which in her daughter's conversational shorthand meant that they hadn't been anywhere, instead parked in a dimly lit spot getting much closer than Theresa cared to think about. No wonder Rachael wasn't in a mood to be sensible. Theresa hadn't been too sensible earlier in the evening with a man *she* barely knew.

Theresa even suggested a trip to the medical examiner's office to see the crime-scene photographs of the murdered Jenna Simone. Rachael—reasonably—failed to see how that would help, since she didn't dispute that the teen had been murdered, only that William had done it. Rachael eventually agreed to turn down any future private outings until this question could be resolved to Theresa's satisfaction, provided that didn't take longer than a week—yes, her daughter was smart enough to include a completion date. Maybe she *should* consider law school.

Rachael also agreed not to mention the murder to William, not because it might send him into a homicidal rage but to protect him from gossip at work.

But Rachael flatly refused to quit her job, and they

both stalked off to bed, to fume and wonder and do anything but sleep. Theresa was comforted by the thought that at least Rachael wasn't scheduled to work today but William was, so her daughter should be safe at home for the next twelve hours or so.

What a strange, strange situation. Rachael working side by side with a rapist and murderer, and Theresa couldn't do a thing about it. She had made an offer (though impossible for her to fulfill) to make up Rachael's salary for the rest of the summer, but Rachael refused. Jobs were scarce in today's economy, she liked this one, and she couldn't quit every time a co-worker had a stain on his record.

Theresa couldn't call the cops, who'd taken their best shot at the kid already. She *could* tell the hotel, but firing him would risk a lawsuit, since he hadn't been convicted of anything—and Rachael would never trust her again. She couldn't locate the Rosedales, and Rachael wouldn't admit knowing their first names or location. The boy didn't have a parole officer or any legal restrictions on his movements. Which meant that unless she wanted to lock her daughter in her room until college started up again—an idea that had its merits—Theresa was powerless.

It must be true what they said about desperate times and commensurate measures, because instead of being at work, Theresa now sat in her car at the curb in front of the house where Jenna Simone had lived.

She'd already taken a look at the crime scene, a handsome two-story Colonial on a corner lot with a neatly manicured lawn and a Little Tikes play set in the backyard, the American dream softened by the early-morning mist. Theresa wondered if real-estate agents had disclosed the history of their living room to the young parents who now lived here. Maybe the price had been too good to pass up, or maybe they didn't believe in ghosts. Either way she wasn't going to get out and ask them.

From there she drove about two miles to Jenna Simone's address, passing the high school. The homes on this street weren't as large or as new, but just as tidily maintained and just as uninformative to stare at. The crime hadn't occurred here, and the bland façade wouldn't give any clue even if it had.

Jenna and William had been classmates, but that was all the reports and the newspaper articles would say. Were they friends? Had they dated? Jenna had apparently given William a ride home of her own free will. There'd been no signs of struggle inside the vehicle, parked courteously in the turnaround of William's driveway. The neighbors had not seen or heard anything amiss. Had Jenna entered William's home voluntarily? Why? Because she wanted to be there? Or simply because she thought she had nothing to fear?

While Theresa stared at Jenna's former home as if it might be able to tell her, the door opened and an older woman exited. Thin, wearing clean sweatpants and a jersey cardigan buttoned all the way to her neck, she shuffled down the driveway in bedroom slippers, heading for the paper box on a post at the curb. Something about her seemed familiar.

She caught sight of Theresa, and her pace slowed. She ducked her head to get a better look at the car's occupant and apparently decided that the forensic scientist appeared harmless enough. She continued to the curb, ignored the newspaper, and came up to the open passenger-side window.

Theresa decided that driving away would seem even creepier, so she smiled. "Hi. Sorry to be parked at your curb."

She had no idea what to say after that but needn't have worried.

"Are you a reporter?" the woman asked.

"What? No."

"Because you've missed the anniversary by a few weeks."

"Anni—"

"Of my daughter's murder."

CHAPTER 29

"I'm not a reporter," Theresa said, "but would you mind talking to me for a few minutes about your daughter's death? I have no right to ask, and I don't want to upset you—"

"The only thing that upsets me is people *not* asking about Jenna's murder. I *want* them to ask me, ask the cops, ask the courts, all day and all night. Why don't you come inside? I have coffee brewing."

"I would really appreciate that," Theresa said, with no idea how to explain *why* she would appreciate hearing about a mother's worst nightmare from another mother, why she wanted to take a sunny morning on which this woman had been about to enjoy a peaceful breakfast with her paper and instead make her relive what no human being should have to withstand.

Maybe because she was desperate. Maybe because she didn't know what else to do. She locked her car and followed the woman through the strengthening daylight, right up to the neat little door in the neat little house.

The neat little door had barely closed behind them when the woman asked, "So who are you? My name's

Coral, by the way. The kitchen's straight ahead. Have a seat."

Theresa couldn't give her credentials, imagining news articles about the M.E. office staff harassing the families of murder victims. She bought time by commenting on the coziness of the room. Yellow patterned wallpaper and white curtains and fixtures, ceramic tile, a baseball trophy on the windowsill over the sink. Next to it sat a prescription pill bottle. Theresa decided to rinse her hands at the faucet later, get a peek at the label.

Mrs. Simone reasonably persisted. "But who are you, if you're not a reporter?"

"I believe that my daughter has made the acquaintance of the boy accused of killing your daughter. I'm here because I just don't know what to do. I can't call the cops, and I can't lock my daughter in her room. I need to convince her that this boy is dangerous, but I don't know how."

That brought Mrs. Simone up short, and Theresa felt inexplicably guilty at the outpouring of sympathy that followed. "You poor dear! How terrible! How did she meet him? Where is he?" She clapped a mug of steaming liquid onto the table in front of Theresa, spilling some of it, and wiry fingers clasped Theresa's arm. "Where is he?" she demanded again, in a puff of Folgers-scented breath.

"I don't know where he lives. She met him at work."

"Where does she work?"

"I . . . probably shouldn't say."

Her host did not take that well, and her eyes narrowed. Then she slumped into the chair across from Theresa and said, "I've been looking all over for him."

Theresa didn't want to ask any of these questions, but she was here and Mrs. Simone wanted to talk. "Why?"

"*Why?* He murdered my *child*. He raped and murdered my Jenna, and he's walking around free and the authorities are protecting *his* privacy like he's some kind of victim! Of course I try to . . . monitor him. Someone's got to. For the sake of girls like your daughter."

"When was the last time you saw him?"

"The day they let him go. The day that group of brain-dead morons trooped back into that box they were kept in and said 'Not guilty.'" Despite this woman's vehement words, Theresa decided that she was not crazy, drug-addled, or even unbalanced. She was merely a sensible but grieving mother. It made Theresa feel guiltier still, as if she were there under false pretenses even though she wasn't—the danger to Rachael felt very real indeed.

"Did Jenna know this William from school?"

"Yes. Her friends said so at the trial, but I don't remember her mentioning him to me. She could have. She probably talked about a hundred different kids just during those two years of high school."

"I know what you mean—teenage girls. What did her friends say about him?"

"That he was in Jenna's chemistry class, but they didn't know of any relationship beyond that. 'They knew each other to say hi' was how they put it. They were friendly, but he had never asked her out or vice versa."

Theresa sipped at the hot, bitter liquid. She helped herself to sugar from a shaker on the table; she wanted cream, but it seemed callous to ask her hostess for both her most painful memories *and* access to her dairy products. "Were these friends at the dance, too?"

The woman nodded, her hands wrapped around the warm coffee mug. If other people lived in the house, they either had not stirred yet or had already left for the day. Not so much as a creak sounded upstairs. "Yes, but they were off chasing boys, of course. One saw Jenna leave with him but didn't speak to her."

"Were they surprised that Jenna left the party with him?"

"Not really. Everyone figured it the same way: William was drunk, and Jenna gave him a ride home."

"Leaving his car at the school. Where did this alcohol come from, at a school party?"

"Alcohol shows up at every school party, according to the kids. Not even a murder trial could make them 'fess up to who brought it. He probably brought it himself, since no one else got that drunk and his parents have a well-stocked liquor cabinet. There was testimony about that at the trial, too."

But had he been drunk? Or drugged, as Marie had said? "So Jenna probably intended to drop him off, then come back and get her friends. Was that like her, to leave a dance to give a ride to someone she didn't know that well?"

Coral Simone pressed a tissue to her nose, to stifle not a tear but a small sneeze, and nodded. "Jenna was very softhearted—to everyone but her mother, like most teenage girls."

"Tell me about it."

"She never wanted to see anyone get in trouble. Once, when she was about ten, one of her brothers—Teddy, my middle one—left his bike behind my husband's car, who crumpled it leaving for work that morning. We had to harp on Teddy constantly about responsibility—he was just that kind of a kid. He's twenty-two now and still loses his cell phone every other week. So Jenna said she had borrowed it and left it in the driveway. Didn't fool her father or me for a second, since she could hardly reach the pedals, but she tried."

Theresa hoped she would never have to tell Rachael's

childhood stories this way—as if the pain ran so deep that the words were squeezed up from below. "Where are your boys now?" She had no reason to ask, other than to get the woman's mind away from Jenna for a second.

"My oldest is working with his father in Chicago, and the other has one more year at Caltech."

It occurred to Theresa that Coral Simone might only have a few years on her but looked a good two decades older. Her flesh seemed to stretch over the bone with nothing in between, as if grief had eaten up everything that was soft in her body. Was this what losing a child did to you? "So your husband—"

"Already had one foot out the door but stuck around for another year after Jenna was murdered. More for the boys than for me, but I'm grateful to him for that. Once they headed for college, though, that was all she wrote. He packed his bags and never came back, and honestly, I'm grateful to him for that, too. If I had to hear one more word about acceptance, about moving on, I think I'd have— My daughter died seventy years too soon, died bewildered and screaming. How am I supposed to *accept* that?"

"I'm so sorry," Theresa said, acutely aware of the inadequacy of those words.

"So where does your daughter work?" Coral Simone repeated. Then she sneezed again and saved Theresa from answering. "I'm sorry. Do you have a cat?"

"Um . . . yes."

Coral Simone wiped her nose. "I'm allergic. Did you follow the trial at all?"

"What happened at the trial? Why was he found not guilty?"

"How did he get off, you mean?" Coral stood and refilled their cups, as if this might be a long tale. "Two things. The murder weapon and that bitch lawyer of his."

"Marie Corrigan."

"Yes. The one who was just killed at that hotel downtown. Don't ask me to shed any tears for *her*." The woman smiled in a way that made the hair on Theresa's arms stand up, though in Coral's shoes she would have felt exactly the same way—and that *really* gave her the creeps.

"She got murdered, too," the woman went on. "The coincidence of that just blew me away, but then I thought, she surrounds herself with murderers, so it's really not so surprising, is it? Anyway, first she got him tried as a juvenile and not an adult. Then she went on and on about the murder weapon, how he'd passed out so he couldn't have gotten rid of it, and if he could have, then he also could have cleaned up the scene or called his parents for help—the same parents who spent every penny they had either bribing or suing the papers, the TV, the national channels, even the school to keep their son's name out of the public eye."

Theresa interrupted this rant to ask, "What do you think happened to the weapon?"

Coral Simone sneezed again and wiped her eyes. "The cops did look for it. Have you seen the house? It's on a corner lot, and there's a little bit of woods behind it, running up the street. They searched the entire area with a metal detector and even dogs. She harped on that, too, that if the police looked so thoroughly and couldn't find it, it was well and truly gone, and he couldn't have done it because he was passed out. And if he wasn't passed out and hid the murder weapon, why not hide Jenna's body? Maybe he had an accomplice," Coral went on. "The cops questioned all his friends, and I questioned all Jenna's friends about his friends until their parents told me to stop calling. Women I'd known for years, and they hung up on me. They still have *their* daughters. . . . Anyway, they never found any accomplice. I thought he could have buried it along a pipe or by an electrical cable, someplace where a metal detector would already go off and be disregarded. He could have wedged it inside his car frame somehow. I don't really know. Or, I thought, maybe he never used a fireplace poker at all. Maybe he used something that looked like it, then cleaned it and hid it in plain sight around the house. There's an endless list of places to hide something in a house, believe me. My oldest smoked for a while, and I'm still finding packs of cigarettes he forgot about. Would you like to see her room?"

"Um . . . yes."

Coral stood up, and Theresa used the opportunity to take her cup to the sink, acting the polite and helpful guest while she checked out the windowsill. Next to Coral's trophy sat a good-size bottle of alprazolam with her name on it. Not too surprising. *If someone had murdered my daughter,* Theresa thought, *I'd need some Xanax to sleep, too.*

Theresa followed Coral upstairs into a TV version of a teenage girl's room. White-and-pastel quilt on the bed, pale blue walls, white furniture with photos tucked into the corners of the mirror and necklaces strung on the bedposts. A small shelf held more sports trophies and medals. Schoolbooks still sat on the end table, and a video-game controller snaked out from a little television on the bookshelf. An aluminum bat stood in the corner, handle end up, a pair of batting gloves propped over them. The wooden furniture gleamed as if it had just been polished that morning.

Coral folded herself into a white wicker armchair as Theresa slowly circled the room, coming to a stop in front of the vanity table. She studied the photos. Jenna had been slender, with straight blond hair past her shoulders. Every teenage boy's dream.

"You keep this room so clean," Theresa said, meaning, *You've turned it not only into a shrine, but an obsessively well-kept shrine.*

"Dust bothers me," Coral Simone said simply. "And my evenings are free."

"Where do you work?"

"Parry Engineering. I'm a data programmer, mostly low coercivity. It's decent pay, flexible hours. Which is why I have this morning off."

In most of the photos Jenna appeared with other girls, but here and there a boy cropped up. There were none of William. "Was Jenna dating anyone when she died?"

"Not steadily. She had broken up with a boy about a month before that, but they hadn't dated very long. That seems to be different about this generation. When I was young, I felt like a complete loser if I didn't have a steady boyfriend. Girls now don't seem to care so much about that. I guess it's an improvement."

Theresa picked up a heart-shaped piece of wood about the size and thickness of her palm. It had Jenna's name burned into it, along with a few other decorative curlicues, and held down a shopping list Jenna had scribbled on a Hello Kitty notepad: *"tampons, underwear, mascara (coupon!),"* and something that looked like *"paint."*

"Her chem-lab partner made her that," Coral said. "I should clarify about dating—she always had boys asking her *out.* But she didn't go unless she really felt interested. She wouldn't let a boy spend time or money on her just for her to have something to do. My boys . . . well, they have their father's attitude toward fairness, but to Jenna, justice meant something."

Theresa looked at her, sensing a not-too-subtle point in the making.

"And then it failed her so badly," Coral finished.

Theresa glanced over the bookcase—romance novels, crime dramas, two shelves of movies from Disney to horror, and more framed photographs, most with younger versions of Jenna and her brothers, her parents, her team. "Was it just the missing murder weapon that caused the jury to acquit?"

"Him." Coral still refrained from speaking the boy's name, only that venomous pronoun. "That woman put him on the stand, and the prosecution couldn't shake him. He answered every question with 'I don't remember,' pretending to look sad, on and on until the jury began to feel sorry for him. My daughter is *dead*, but she's away and out of sight and he's *there*, see? They brought in every girl in their class, all these sweet young girls who said he was such a nice cub and would never hurt anyone. Even Jenna's *friends* didn't believe he could have done it—another reason they stopped talking to me."

"He didn't give any sort of explanation at all?"

"*She* did." Apparently Marie Corrigan could not be named within the Simone household either. "She took just what I was talking about—how Jenna didn't have a steady boyfriend but boys would ask her out all the time. She tracked down every boy Jenna had dated since grade school and called them to the stand. Nice boys who were only trying to *help*, who said how much they liked Jenna. When she ran out of them, she called in boys who had *wanted* to go out with Jenna."

"Why?"

"To turn my daughter into some sort of fatal attraction. She stood there with that fake sad expression, as if commiserating with their loss, but then twisted their words, reminding the jury how 'popular' Jenna was—by which she meant 'loose,' anyone could see that—as if Jenna toyed with every boy in three counties and tossed them aside like candy wrappers."

"Phantom suspects."

"Exactly. She invented this jealous beau who followed Jenna to that house, killed her, and left."

"The bushy-haired stranger."

Coral paused. "What?"

"An industry term, named after Sam Sheppard's phantom assailant. It's a standard defense strategy: Some other dude did it."

Another boy, pursuing Jenna, sees her leave with William and follows. Two intoxicated teenagers probably didn't lock the front door behind them, so he goes in, and— It sounded ridiculous, but within the realm of possibility. Teenage hormones ran pretty strong, and it would explain the missing murder weapon. "There were no injuries to William?"

"Not a scratch."

"Was he really that drunk? Or . . . incapacitated?"

Coral gave her a grim smile. "Impossible to tell. The estate lawyer arrived about the same time as the police did. He didn't give a statement or any body samples for over forty-eight hours."

Theresa nodded. "By which time everything could have metabolized. And they never came up with this mysterious jealous suitor."

Coral snorted, which turned into a sneeze. "Of course not. He didn't exist. No, he fooled everyone. He fooled Jenna. He will fool your daughter." She fixed Theresa with a stare. "You have to get her away from him. *Now.* This instant."

"I couldn't agree more."

"Where does she work? Where is he?"

"What would you do if I told you?" Theresa asked, as gently as possible, mincing her way across this minefield.

An unholy smirk lifted a corner of the woman's mouth, but it looked more like a snarl. "What do you think I'm going to do, sneak up behind him and blow his head off? Believe me, I dream of that every night. Unfortunately, I don't own a gun, and if I did, I would have done it as he walked out of that courthouse. No, I just want to monitor him, as I said."

Theresa leaned against the bedpost. "I'm so sorry, Coral. But if you go to my daughter's workplace and tell them about William, she'll never forgive me. Give me some time to fix this—at least let me get her out of the way first. If he's pushed, I don't know what he'll do, and I don't want her to be in the middle of it when he does."

"You need to tell me where he is."

"I will. As soon as I convince my daughter to get away from him—and stay away. Then I'll tell you."

Coral's gaze never wavered. "You promise?"

It took a few seconds, but Theresa said, "I promise."

Coral was a fellow mother, a grieving mother, a woman who'd had more tragedy in the past few years than most people had in a few lifetimes. So why did Theresa feel as if she'd just made a pact with the devil?

Coral gave a casual and unconvincing shrug. "I can't do anything anyway. I can't even inform his employer of his criminal record, legally, since it was a juvenile case and sealed. I just want to tell him that someone's paying attention to what he's doing. I want him to know I'm going to dog him until the end of my days."

"You don't think that might be dangerous?"

"The concept of danger only applies to people who have something to lose," Coral said.

The doorbell rang, startling them both.

Her host exclaimed, "Oh, my gosh. They're here already."

"Who is?"

But Coral Simone rushed into the hallway and flew down the stairs with swift, sure feet. "And I'm not even dressed yet."

Theresa followed, to watch from a careful distance at the bottom of the stairs as the door was flung open to reveal three other ladies: a younger woman of about thirty with an athlete's body and a HANG TEN SURF SHOP T-shirt; a birdlike, gray-haired one in a yellow turtleneck; and a tall, African-American matron whose face and body were all jutting angles underneath a widow's peak. She carried a plate of muffins that smelled delectable, and she wore a brooch made out of magnetic poetry squares. They were, as Theresa learned from the flurry of conversation and explanations, there for a support-group meeting, but they had plenty of time, dear, don't worry. Each one seemed sweet and caring.

"This is Theresa," Coral said with one foot on the steps, unbuttoning her jersey cardigan to reveal a pink T-shirt.

"Is she joining the group?" the younger one asked, showing no enthusiasm for the idea of a new member.

"Not yet," Coral said.

Theresa asked, "Group?"

"Families of Murder Victims," Coral explained.

Not *yet*?

Theresa returned to her car, late for work, sucking in the fresh spring air and thanking God that her own daughter was home asleep and temporarily safe, praying that she would never have need of a support group. Any kind of support group, but especially that one.

However.

Coral's pink T-shirt had triggered a memory. The

woman *had* looked familiar, and at first Theresa thought that she might have seen Coral's picture in the newspaper articles, but now she recalled that the articles didn't have any photos of the family. She had seen Coral, though, and in pink.

She'd been wearing a pink twinset, having tea in the lobby of the Ritz-Carlton on the day Marie Corrigan was found dead.

CHAPTER 30

"I figured I'd find you here," Don said, flicking on the lights.

"I needed to think."

"And what better place?" He dropped his lanky frame into the seat beside her and stuck his too-large feet far out in front of him, deceptively casual. "The old teaching amphitheater. A table we made out of an autopsy table, a chalkboard, windows blacked out for video presentations, tile that's had so much spilled blood seep into its pores that it couldn't possibly hold any more, the smells wafting in from the autopsy suite next door. Perfect."

"I would prefer the meditation garden," she admitted. "Except we don't have one."

"What's the matter, kiddo?"

"My daughter's dating a rapist and murderer."

"Oh, okay. I thought it was something serious."

"This kid is let go, starts over, tries to leave his past behind him. No arrests, gets a job. But then his ex-lawyer is murdered and possibly raped. Why would he want to kill the woman who set him free?"

"She kept him out of jail. That doesn't mean she gave him everything he wanted."

Theresa turned to look at him. "You think he was physically attracted to her and she rejected him?"

"Super-hot older chick whose temporary mission in life is to take care of him? Clients fall in love with their therapist, their doctor, their priest. Why not their lawyer?"

"Only people who can't distinguish between professional and personal interest."

"Or, in the case of a horny teenager, don't care."

Theresa slumped further, until the rigid wooden back of the theater seat dug into her back. "That's just what I've been thinking. He falls for her, but when the case is over, she's on to other things. Then the convention comes to his hotel and he sees her again. Who better to filch a passkey to the Presidential Suite, and who needs the extra clout of a laid-out hotel room than an insecure teen? But Marie's surrounded by her peers and has bigger fish to fillet than some gawky ex-client. She rejects him, just as Jenna did, and winds up the same way."

"And this would possibly be known as justice."

"No . . . if the world were just, he'd be in jail where he belongs and my daughter would never have met him."

Don put an arm around her shoulders, which comforted her a little more than it should have. The things we won't admit.

"There's only one problem," Theresa continued.

"Bruce Raffel."

"There's no connection between him and William Rosedale. He and Marie did not work at the same firm when Jenna was murdered. Maybe it's the same motive we thought of with Dennis Britton—that Bruce and Marie were reconnecting, only it was William who got jeal-

ous. But how would he even know that? And why kill
Bruce a day later?"

"He blames Bruce Raffel for causing him to kill Marie. 'She wanted you instead of me, angering me, so I
killed her. So that's really your fault, of course, because
I'm a sociopath and nothing is ever *my* fault.' Has your
cousin checked his alibi?"

"I'm sure it's going to be tough when the kid works
there and our time of death is 'sometime during the evening.' I don't know if anyone has even asked him for an
alibi. There's no official reason to consider him a suspect. They questioned all the staff, but not in a stringent
way."

"Sans rubber hose?"

"It's a hotel. There are multiple entrances, windows,
staff in and out twenty-four hours a day. A bunch of kids
use the observation deck as a smoking lounge, and no
one seems to care."

"Okay." Don sighed in sympathy. "What does the
evidence say?"

"That the victims didn't see it coming. That somebody had a key to the Presidential Suite and isn't saying.
After that, all I've got is two human hairs, two cat hairs,
three fibers, and a smear of wax."

"And no other suspects?"

"They're lawyers. Everybody hates them."

"Harsh."

She'd met a new suspect only that morning. Surely
Coral Simone had more motive to kill Marie Corrigan
than William Rosedale had, and Theresa felt fairly sure
she'd seen Coral on the premises.

Except that Coral apparently didn't know that William worked there, would have no access to the Presidential Suite, and would need a dose of Benadryl if she
found herself in the same room with a gray Persian.

Coral had no connection to Bruce Raffel, and Marie Corrigan would be unlikely to turn her back on her.

"Any one of these masses stand out?" Don asked.

"One." Theresa sighed. "Unfortunately, he's a cop."

"Double harsh."

CHAPTER 31

"DNA," Marcus Dean said with a face of stone. "You want my DNA."

"Yes," Theresa said.

Neil Kelly sat beside her in Dean's office. He swallowed hard and said, "This is the best way. Your DNA clears you, and any brief, shadowy suspicion is over. If we ignore it, it'll become the elephant in the room."

"It will stand there forever if I'm immortalized in an evidence inventory. Even if you catch the real guy, his defense attorney will jump on that: 'The cops thought one of their own did it—that's how little they know.' You'll be screwing your own case."

"Not if we collect it as an elimination sample," Theresa said. "It's not officially evidence and doesn't need to be entered as such, and it won't be added to any database. As long as it doesn't match, it's discarded and your privacy is protected like any other citizen's. It's the best course for you."

"Yeah," Dean scoffed.

"Yes," she insisted. *As long as you didn't do it.*

Neil said nothing. He had not wanted to do this; she'd

had to talk him into it, using the same argument. Cops tread very, very lightly when it came to suspecting other cops. That kind of situation never turned out well for anyone. Theresa didn't care too much about the weight of her footsteps at the moment, though.

But then Dean sighed, slumped back. "Tell you what, let me talk this over with my old partner here."

"Of course," she said. "No hurry."

The two men stood and left the room. He probably wanted to ask Neil how serious the suspicion of him had gotten, maybe what kind of protection he could expect from the Fraternal Order of Police union. None, she would guess, assuming that the free legal representation ended when the job did.

Restless, she paced a bit, then stopped to study three framed photographs on top of a filing cabinet. They seemed to be the only personal items in the room. In one, a small boy and girl grinned from a pile of Christmas wrapping paper, a lit tree in the background. Judging by the aging of the photo's color, it might date to Marcus's childhood. Another one showed two young men on a basketball court; one was definitely Marcus, before he'd decided to shave his head. The third was of a young woman with two small children, leaning against a car. This one had less dust on it than the other two. The woman had long black hair with a widow's peak, huge almond-shaped eyes, and a wide smile. A piece of paper beneath this photo served as a doily. In italic font a poem described the sharp and twisting pain of grief. *"With lovely light to cleare my cloudy grief. / Till then I wander carefull, comfortlesse, / In secret sorrow, and sad pensivenesse." Spenser.*

"Hey!"

Theresa nearly dropped the picture. Rachael's boss, Karla, stood in the doorway.

"I'm sorry—" Theresa began.

"I wanted to tell you I really appreciate Rachael coming in today. Almost half my staff is out with mysterious illnesses—which means they're afraid of the bogeyman. Some of them can barely write their names, but they're highly attuned to their own emotional state. I swear none of them have any concept of what it means to work for a living."

Theresa stammered, "Rachael's . . . she's here?"

"I had to call her in, I was desperate. The lawyers have given up pretending to have a conference and are checking out in droves, tails firmly tucked between their legs. I guess they're only tough when inside a courtroom. I swear they whine more than the kids I got working for me."

"Rachael's *here*?"

Karla nodded, the expression on her face turning odd as Theresa repeated herself. "On the front desk. What are you doing in here, by the way? Are you waiting for Marcus?"

Theresa rushed past her, down the hallway and around the corner. She didn't see Neil or Marcus Dean anywhere, and the blond girl at the desk was not her daughter.

Nor did the blond know exactly where her daughter had gone. "She's on break. She'll be back in about ten minutes."

"Where would she have gone?"

The young woman paused in trying to explain to a portly attorney from Des Moines that the pay-per-view charges to his bill could not be removed simply because he had passed out from the Jack Daniel's before he got past the opening credits. "I dunno, the ladies' room? Why don't you just wait here for her? She'll be back in ten. Rachael's real good about that."

Theresa checked the ladies' room, beautifully appointed in gleaming white, and the other offices around the lobby. No Rachael. She returned to the front desk, where the man began to point out that he had only *been* drinking to cope with the loss of two of his colleagues, swallowed up by the hotel's murderer.

"And the triple X movie?" the girl asked. "Was that to help you cope, too?"

"What's your name? I want to speak to your manager."

"Where else would she have gone?" Theresa demanded.

"Kristin, and you can talk to my manager all you want. She won't take the charges off either," the girl was telling the man, then added to Theresa while waving toward the elevator bank, "I don't know. She headed that way, I think."

Theresa thanked her and walked to the elevator, looking through the throng of people for Rachael without finding her. Karla had not exaggerated, and the lobby teemed with attorneys. Theresa hated to be harsh and think of the phrase "rats leaving a sinking ship," but she couldn't help it. Besides, why *shouldn't* rats leave a sinking ship? Wouldn't that be the logical thing to do?

William worked in the kitchen—perhaps Rachael had not been able to resist the temptation for a fresh look at the boy she now knew so much more about. That would be just like her. Theresa walked the fifteen feet to the Muse's doors, but they were locked, too early for the lunch service. She gave up and went to the elevator, flipping open her cell phone. Rachael had probably gone either down to the mall or up to the tower; Theresa would simply call her. She wondered if it were legal to have a GPS chip implanted in one's offspring.

But the phone rang before she could dial, and she answered as the doors closed behind her.

"Mom?"

It was her daughter.

And she sounded terrified.

The elevator began to move, interfering with the precious reception bars, and the call dissolved into static. " . . . observation de—William . . ."

Silence. "Rachael? *Rachael!*"

One last sputter. "Help m—"

Then nothing.

Theresa retained enough presence of mind to press the button for the forty-second floor.

CHAPTER 32

The doors opened, and she plunged into the all-black, crumbling room under renovation, nearly tripping over a five-gallon bucket of topping compound, and headed for the opening door to the observation rooms. A dark figure loomed up, filling the archway.

William Rosedale.

"I guess you know."

She threw on the brakes to leave some distance between them, the knowledge of what must have happened to her daughter solidifying in a nauseating ball of crushing density, imploding somewhere in the middle of her torso. "Where is she?"

Light from a window in the room behind him cast his face into shadows, and she could see only the silhouette of a somber expression, eerily calm. "I understand how you must feel."

"William. Where is my daughter?"

"I just want you to know, I would never hurt Rachael. I've never hurt anybody."

His mind had broken from reality. Either that or there was hope. "Where is she?"

"This way." He turned and disappeared.

She followed him through the doorway, every inch of her skin tingling as her body fought conflicting impulses—the drive to fling herself headlong into hell itself if her daughter were there and the fear that all its demons waited around each corner for her.

But then she heard the scrape of shoes on metal and realized that William was not in either observation room but was climbing the stairs to the upper, outside deck. She slipped inside the interior well, in time to see his feet turn on the first landing. She had no choice but to follow, and at least he didn't seem to be trying to corner her. Perhaps he really had snapped.

A single outline of brilliant light edged the door to the outside. William pulled it open and waited there for her.

Sunlight flooded in around him, and once again she followed him without hesitation. He had probably already killed her daughter, and he seemed sturdy enough to throw her over the side and send her plummeting seven hundred feet to the streets below. But Theresa would be sure to take him with her.

The wind off the lake hit her in the face as soon as she stepped into the open air. It never stopped, not at that height, only varied in intensity, and now it was strong enough to instantly tangle her hair and chap her skin. William had turned to the north and disappeared around the horizon of the deck's circle, and she followed. Then she saw Rachael.

Alive.

Relief weakened her only for a moment. Rachael's cheeks were red, and her face held an all-too-adult expression of terror and distress. *"Mom!"*

William stood between them. Was this an exhibition, an attempt to show Theresa that she was wrong about him? Or did he plan to murder her daughter in front of her, to punish Theresa for knowing his secret?

But then he did nothing as Rachael brushed by him, put her arms around her mother, and said, "I'm sorry."

Sorry? For what? Not believing her?

And Theresa held her daughter tightly, feeling the strong beat of the girl's heart, the pinned-on name tag biting into her breast, and smelled the ridiculously expensive shampoo that Rachael insisted on buying. Once again relief made her weak, but not weak enough to take her eyes off William.

He merely watched them, though, his expression tense and angry.

Then a shadow in the curve of the building deck moved. The pudgy, dark-haired friend of William's—Ray? Roy?—was also present, and he looked as upset as Rachael. The shade of his skin approached beet red, and his eyes shed unabashed tears. What the hell was going on?

"I'm sorry," Rachael said again.

"I should think so! You scared the crap out of me. All I heard was 'observation,' and then the phone went dead."

"Oh." Rachael stepped back, one arm still on her mother's shoulder, her body hiding Theresa's movements as she slipped her cell phone out of her pocket. "I tried to call back, but you didn't pick up. Were you in the elevator? Look, I—"

"You told him," Theresa asked, her gaze still on William, keeping her voice low and hoping the wind would carry it away from him.

"I know you told me not to, but I had to know—that's why we came up here, so that no one would overhear us. You can't keep a secret in this place. Mom, I believe him, he totally didn't— Anyway, that's when we found . . . it." She gave Theresa another half hug, putting her head briefly on her mother's shoulder. "Mom, I'm really sorry."

Theresa's mind, which had been charging along in one direction, had to stop and regroup. She glanced at William and then Ray; neither had moved or changed expression. Then she looked at her daughter as the girl released her and straightened up, wind-tossed, relatively calm, and somber in a very grown-up way.

"Rachael," she said. "What are you talking about?"

Her daughter tugged her gently at the sleeve, and they moved another fifteen degrees around the observation circle, until Theresa could see something resting in its white hollow. A person, or what used to be a person, sprawled at the foot of the scaffold.

At first it appeared to be only a ball of white, heavy flesh, but after a few shocked moments the various areas sorted themselves out into arms and legs, tied together by an understated navy blue tie. What had been blobs of muted colors here and there were articles of clothing, discarded and left to the elements, a corner of the white blouse giving a halfhearted flap as a finger of wind caught it. A face, turned to the side, the left cheek mashed against the curved shingle floor. Blood covered this face, running and pooling over the uneven surface, a distinct red against the white. It had dried in the brisk wind, matting the dishwater-blond hair.

Sonia Battle.

Rachael grasped her mother's shoulder, and suddenly all her words made sense.

PART IV

SONIA

CHAPTER 33

Not *Sonia*. Marie Corrigan and Bruce Raffel yes—people who had lived by the sword, decimating the lives of victims and those who tried to help them without concern, they could die by it—but not Sonia. Sonia was not some soulless, avaricious vulture who thrived on conflict and domination. Sonia *cared*.

Theresa wept as she called Neil Kelly. That and the wind made conversation difficult, but he said he would respond and not to move. She warned him that Rachael, William, and Ray were also present, without letting Rachael know that she had told another person William's secret.

"So let me get this straight." Theresa leaned against the outer wall. She had not moved, did not go any closer to Sonia's corpse. There would be plenty of time for that. "You came up here to talk."

"I had my morning break. I hadn't left the desk since I started at nine—I really was trying to do what you wanted." Rachael spoke without defense or rebellion in her voice. Stumbling on a dead body and seeing her mother cry—both extremely rare events—had that effect on her, to the point where she actually tried to use the cuff of her sleeve to dry Theresa's cheeks. Neither one of them ever carried tissues.

"And you came up here."

"I went to the kitchen to see William. It's what I do every day. I thought it would look odd if I didn't."

"The restaurant's closed."

The wind whipped around them like a live thing, a constant, annoying third party who wanted in on the conversation, keeping Rachael's hair in motion and stinging Theresa's eyes. "We use the back halls. And when I saw him . . . well, I hadn't believed it before, but I *really* didn't believe it. He's so *nice* to everyone, Mom. He was helping Ray unload the dishwasher when that's not even his job—"

"Ok*ay*."

"So I said I needed to talk to him, and we came up here, and I told him I heard about this Jenna girl, and he didn't get mad or anything, just said he knows he didn't do it but doesn't know who did. Then Ray came up to join us—he does that sometimes—so I didn't say anything else, but William said he'd understand if I didn't want to see him anymore and started walking away, and I followed, and then we saw . . . her."

"Then what did you do?"

"Screamed, I think. Then I called you. Then I told William to go down and meet you at the elevator."

"Not you?" *Do you know how many deaths I died, following him up those stairs?*

"I figured you'd be mad if I left him guarding the crime scene, even with Ray here, too," Rachael said. "Given his circumstances."

Theresa could only stare at her, deeply proud but deeply ashamed. "Honey, it's not your job to worry about the integrity of the crime scene. Don't ever put that above your personal safety."

"But I *was* safe. The killer was long gone."

"And how do you know that? You can only see a small portion of this ring at one time. How could you know he wasn't out of sight around the curve of the deck?" With only one means of egress, and Rachael standing in front of it.

"Because the blood had dried," Rachael said, as if that were obvious, prompting another feeling of pride mixed with *What have I done?* to course through Theresa. "And the way the clothes are sort of scattered around the edges, it kind of looked to me like they'd been left in a pile, but then the wind blew them around a little bit."

"Oh. Good point. Rachael, I want you to think carefully. Whose idea was it to come up here? Yours or William's?"

Her daughter frowned, almost a scowl, making her thoughts plain. All her hard work to protect and observe the crime scene, and her mother only wanted to pin the whole thing on her new boyfriend. "He didn't do it, Mom. Come on!"

"It's just a question, and one that I'm sure Neil Kelly is going to ask you in another few minutes."

Rachael sulked for a moment but then said, "Neither of us—really. We always come here on our breaks, so I guess we just automatically did. You have to admit, Mom, if he wanted to kill me, he could have already."

"I do admit that he's had ample opportunity. I want to believe him, honey, I want to believe your judgment, but I can't help the facts, and all the facts say that he killed Jenna Simone. So maybe you both gravitated here because it's your usual break spot, or maybe he wanted to show you his handiwork."

"Mom!"

"I can't ignore the possibility—but look, because it's only one of many possibilities, will you both go down and guide Detective Kelly up here?" With her mother upstairs and a police detective about to spill out of the elevator, the girl ought to be perfectly safe, and this tiny show of faith seemed to cheer Rachael up. It might give Neil a start, though.

Theresa called Frank, who remained silent at this news a little longer than she would have expected. But he was currently waiting in a dingy hallway at the Justice Center to testify in the officer-involved shooting trial and couldn't leave.

The other boy, Ray, had watched his friends walk away. "Can I go now?" he asked as she hung up. "I think I'd really like to go home."

"I'm afraid the officers will need a statement from you. It will be simple—you'll just tell them what happened."

This seemed to distress him further. He put one hand to his eyes and moaned.

"Are you all right?" Theresa asked, as gently as she could.

"This is just so awful. And they'll suspect him—I heard what they were talking about and what you just said to Rachael. Will didn't kill Jenna, and he sure didn't kill this lady here."

Theresa blinked in the strong wind. "You know about Jenna Simone?"

Duh. Of course he did. "We all went to the same school. Will and I have been friends since the seventh grade. I mean, he's always been a cool kid. He could be the coolest if he wanted to, but he's friends with a supergeek like me. Will is a really, really nice guy. He would never have hurt Jenna." Thinking about the incident apparently upset him all over again. "And now maybe they'll think he did this. It's not fair! I should never have gone to that dance. We should never have come up here today."

Should she warn him not to mention Jenna Simone to the officers? The juvenile records were sealed, so the odds were much better than Ray supposed that the officers might never make the connection between William the witness and William the suspect three years ago. Keep William's secret under wraps so it didn't muddy the investigative waters or risk Rachael's ire?

Risk, Theresa decided. It was not her job to protect William Rosedale from his past. Besides, Neil Kelly already knew. He could take it from there, or not, as he saw fit. "Do you remember William's trial?"

"Yeah," Ray sniffled. "I cut school to go, until my mother found out and said she'd ground me for life."

"Do you remember William's lawyer?"

"The hot chick?" A haze of goggle-eyed puppy love came over his face, drying his tears. "She was terrific! She totally cracked every witness they put on."

Theresa tried not to frown at this. "Did you know she was murdered on Thursday?"

Ray nodded, hard and rapidly. "Yeah, that was too bad. *Really* too bad. She *smoked*. That guy she was with was totally out of her range."

Theresa tried to sort out this statement. "What guy?"

"That other lawyer dude who was murdered. I saw his picture on the news. He looked . . . well, kinda like me. Totally out of range."

"Bruce Raffel?"

"Yeah, that was the name. The one who just got offed yesterday, right?"

"You saw them together?"

"Yeah," he said, as if that should be common knowledge.

"Here at the hotel?"

The tears had dried up. Now he looked at Theresa, apparently perplexed that she was apparently perplexed. "No, at William's trial. He was like her, whatever, co-chair? He'd come in and sit with her and William at their table sometimes. Not all the time, just sometimes."

"He assisted her at William's trial?"

"Yeah." Ray's face turned a shade of worry. "Why? It's . . . it's got nothing to do with William, you know, the dude turning up dead here. Will was with me all night—last night . . . I mean, the night before. I mean, we worked—"

"No, no, of course not," she soothed. "Did you see Marie and Bruce Raffel together this week? Here at the hotel?"

"No." He still seemed skittish; he'd said something wrong, and he knew it. He wanted to keep his friend out of trouble and instead had thrown him right into a thicket of it.

Theresa gestured toward Sonia's body. "What about this attorney? Did you see her and Bruce or Marie together this week? Any week?"

"Nope." He seemed more certain of that.

"Do you know her?"

The boy—young man, really—studiously avoided looking at the corpse. "No, man, I don't think so. I don't know any lawyers, and . . . I didn't get a good look at her. And I'm not going to."

Noises behind them spared him any further questions. Neil Kelly, Angela Sanchez, Rachael and William, and a uniformed patrol officer spilled out of the stairwell door.

Neil glanced at Ray, gave Theresa a more searching look, and asked if she was all right. But he barely waited for a reply before approaching the body. Just as well. She could hardly fold herself into his arms—even when it was the only thing she wanted to do at the moment—in front of Rachael and a bunch of cops.

"Stay here," Theresa instructed her daughter, and joined him.

Stop looking at Sonia as a friend, she told herself, *and look at her as a vitally important piece of evidence. Without this evidence the guy will stay free to kill again.*

Sonia Battle's wrists and ankles had been bent behind her and secured with a necktie. Her knees showed a few scrape marks, fresh but only slightly bloodied. Her hands were clean except for a light smudging of dirt on her right index and middle fingers. Theresa could count at least two deep lacerations to the skull. A bloodied two-by-four, about two feet in length, lay on the other side of her—most likely debris from the renovation of the inside observation deck. The killer had probably picked it up there, just as he'd picked up a chair in the hotel rooms. Why did this killer use weapons of opportunity? So he couldn't be caught with the incriminating item or because the crimes were truly unplanned, spur-of-the-moment's-passion attacks? But how could someone that impulsive avoid detection this long?

Why had Sonia come up here? She hadn't been afraid of the height but had hardly seemed entranced by it. Theresa prodded a fleshy thigh, startled at its pliability. Sonia hadn't been dead very long, probably not more than four hours. She certainly hadn't been there all night and so had not come here for a romantic starlight stroll.

Theresa didn't disturb the clothing since she hadn't photographed it, but it seemed to be Sonia's typical work uniform of black skirt, white blouse, nylons poking out from the bottom of the pile, and a pair of sensible, square-heeled shoes in patent leather. Their smooth surface, Theresa thought, might be able to hold a decent set of fingerprints.

Sonia had come to the deck early that morning, while Theresa had been brooding in the amphitheater next to Don, and Rachael had possibly been handing the killer his bill and telling him to have a good flight home. Why? To watch the sun rise? Or because, like Rachael, she needed to talk to someone and didn't want to be overheard. Someone who'd brought a two-by-four along to the meeting.

Sonia lay almost straight across the walkway, facing the scaffold with the top of her head touching the outer wall, pointing north toward the lake. It would have been incredibly uncomfortable, if not impossible, to sexually assault someone in that position. Theresa had no faith that they would find semen and its attendant DNA. The nudity, the hog-tying were all for show, a final indignity heaped upon a hated enemy.

And this *wind*. The killer could have dropped more hairs, more fibers, his driver's license, and Social Security card, and it all might be across the Cuyahoga, sailing over the old steel mill.

"Has anyone cleared the other side of this deck?" Angela asked, with good reason. The killer could be waiting there, out of sight around the bend of the ring, trapped. She and Theresa argued briefly, as Theresa wanted her to put protective booties over her shoes before traveling any further into what was now their crime scene, and none of them had any. Finally Angela agreed to go down to Marcus Dean's office and retrieve Theresa's crime-scene kit, full of booties and gloves and other items, while the armed patrol officer would stand guard at the door in case the killer decided to flee from the unseen curves of the deck. Angela would also escort Rachael back to the front desk, with strict instructions to remain there until Theresa returned for her. The strictest of instructions, Theresa emphasized, watching her daughter lean against

William's chest, his arms around her. The girl closed her eyes, obviously finding great comfort in this gentle support. He rubbed her back with one hand, then patted her hair and held it steady against the wind. Basically, he did to her daughter exactly what only a few moments before Theresa had been wishing Neil Kelly would do to her. Maybe, she thought suddenly, her daughter was right. William *was* a truly nice kid and someone else had killed Jenna Simone.

Maybe.

She turned to Neil, but he had not stopped staring at Sonia Battle's blood-soaked face.

"One more down," he said, without looking at her. "This keeps up, this planet might actually become livable again."

Theresa blinked in the strong wind. "What?"

Now he did glance at her, with an odd smile as if they were sharing a joke, as if this were just another day on the job and they hadn't been dry-humping each other on the deck of his boat the night before. "Another scumbag defense attorney knocked off her filthy little perch. I'm really starting to like this guy."

A gust of wind struck Theresa, and she felt as if it sucked all the oxygen away in its path, leaving her gasping to say, "Don't talk like that about her. She was my *friend*!"

"Then I'm sorry for your loss," he said, without sounding sorry at all. "But it's not a loss to anyone else, and I can't pretend it is. She put bad people back on the street. That was *all* she did, and she'd tear us down to do it."

Theresa extended a hand to steady herself on the outer wall's edge but stopped herself in time. Fingerprints. "No, she wouldn't. She did what she could for her client, but she never pulled any dirty tricks."

"Maybe not on you. I can tell you from personal experience that she wasn't so delicate with the rest of us." His voice faded toward the end, as if his brain had engaged; he immediately backpedaled. "Look, I'm sorry. I forgot you actually liked her. But you have to admit, Theresa, you were doing the Electric Slide on Marie Corrigan's grave along with the rest of us. Don't go getting on a high horse now."

She said nothing, because of course he spoke the complete truth, and it made her want to push him over the side. She had convinced herself that Marie Corrigan and Bruce Raffel didn't deserve the slightest consideration, didn't deserve even a *fare-thee-well* on their trip to the afterlife. But was that really true? And did she react so strongly to losing Sonia because she cared for the woman, or did she simply feel guilty?

She forced herself to put all this aside for the moment. The only thing she knew was that Sonia's death made her want to scream with grief and frustration, and she would find out who had caused it no matter how long it took.

She could throttle Neil Kelly later.

He'd grown tired of waiting for a response and went to step over the body. She put out a hand to stop him, splaying her fingers across that same chest she had so eagerly felt up the night before. "Don't."

"I just wanted to check out the rest of—"

"No. The path from the door to here is already shot with everyone walking on it, but the rest of it hasn't been touched. With all this glossy paint on everything, I'm going to check for fibers, shoe prints, fingerprints—everything I can think of. And," she added with a determination that startled her in its violence, "you're going to help me."

Two hours later she remained nauseous and had to fight the urge to call Rachael every four minutes to make sure she still toiled at the front desk, in full view of witnesses, and hadn't snuck off for another tête-à-tête with William. She and Neil Kelly had barely said five words to each other, not when she used his foot as a sandbag to steady her camera tripod in the strong wind, not when he held the snaking orange extension cord above Sonia's body so that Theresa could mince along as close to the wall as possible and vacuum the curving, bowl-like observation deck and its small scaffold (the unupholstered surface did not lend itself to taping), not when she spent forty minutes constructing a miniature greenhouse of stakes and clear plastic to form a superglue chamber over the dead woman. As the cyanoacrylate esters in the superglue permeated the nearly airtight space, they would bond to the amino acids left by the killer's fingers and, with luck, leave her a plasticized impression of his prints.

In theory anyway. It rarely worked.

First she had photographed and then cut off the tie holding Sonia's wrists and ankles—a charcoal gray polyester thing with understated pinstriping. Not a designer job in imported silk, but cheap and generic and therefore much more difficult to trace. Oh, for the days when people all sent their laundry out and detectives could find something called laundry marks on clothing. The killer wouldn't have used his own tie; most likely he bought one for the occasion. It could also belong to Sonia herself. It would go along with the black skirt, not to mention Sonia's personal style.

Either way it could still hold skin cells sloughed off the killer's hands when he pulled it tight around his victim's limbs. Theresa stowed the tie in a paper bag, clearing the way for the supergluing process.

"Wow."

Don Delgado appeared, having been summoned from the lab to bring extra equipment and a friendlier extra hand. She allowed him to step, very carefully, over the body to hold the tent structure steady.

"This is extreme," he observed.

"The circumstances are good for it. The . . . body . . . is fresh, the killer had to touch her bare skin to get her positioned, and we're outside so we don't have to worry about asphyxiating ourselves with cyanoacrylate fumes," she said, answering a question no one had asked—why they hadn't tried supergluing either of the other two victims' bodies.

"If we get one, photographing it's going to be a bitch," he warned. Usually light was their friend, the more the better, but not when it came to taking a picture that required good contrast to see the pattern.

Theresa ignored him, frustrated by the stubborn HotShot superglue container. The canisters were the size of tomato-paste cans, and since she used them only once in a blue moon, they tended to dry up sitting in the back of her car. If this one had, she'd have to send

Don back to the lab for a mug warmer and some foil tubs to hold the liquid superglue over a heat source, the same thing that these canisters did in one handy package. But she got it open and placed it under the tent, laying a wooden stake along the bottom of the hanging plastic sheet to seal it (as much as possible) to the uneven flooring, once again using Neil Kelly's foot as a weight to hold it down.

"How long is this going to take?" he asked.

"About forty-five minutes. First we fume. Then I take the superglue out but leave the chamber closed up so it can polymerize."

"You want me to stand here for forty-five minutes. Correct that, *another* forty-five minutes?"

"It's necessary," she said, now trapped between the body and the scaffold.

"It's not so bad," Don said, almost certainly having noticed the tension and trying to help. "Great view."

Neil said, "I've been staring at it for the past two hours. I'm kind of over the view. And I think I'm getting windburned."

Angela appeared. She had pulled her raven hair back into a hasty braid and clutched a sheaf of papers against her chest to keep them together. "Her car is in the garage, locked, no signs of disturbance, though it's hard to tell for sure. It's a rolling office, all scattered files and old coffee cups. A porter saw her in the lobby at about eight-fifteen this morning talking to two men. She seemed to be trying to talk them out of leaving, or berating them for leaving. The men weren't having any of it and got into the elevator, wheeling their suitcases behind them. Then the porter went on break, and no one else admits seeing her after that."

"Until Rachael finds her a little after ten-thirty," Theresa said.

"Why did she come up here?" Angela asked. "She didn't smoke, and you said she didn't seem crazy about heights."

Maybe it wasn't heights, Theresa thought. Maybe she wasn't crazy about seeing William Rosedale when we visited this deck the first time, but I'm not going to bring that up just yet, even though Sonia's former client had been all but convicted of a very similar murder years before. Keeping this information to herself might be construed by some as obstruction of justice, and it could turn out that if Theresa had revealed William's history earlier in the investigation, Sonia might still be alive. If that were true, then Theresa had sentenced Sonia to death merely in order to stay on her daughter's good side.

This hit her in the face more strongly than any gust of wind.

But she couldn't let remorse paralyze her, and besides, Neil Kelly knew William's story, and it was his investigation. He could figure out what to do about it. She would have to tell him about Bruce Raffel's connection to William's trial. But why would William murder the three people who'd set him free? That made no sense at all. Unless it was some sort of guilt-induced legal suicide— he had decided that his own acquittal was a travesty of justice—and if he were really that unbalanced, then he deserved a Motion Picture Academy lifetime achievement award.

"She was disturbed about the conference falling apart, came up here to be alone," Neil Kelly guessed, looking at Angela, but Theresa got the feeling he wanted to include her. Maybe he wanted to apologize for his boorish behavior. Maybe he wanted to let her know he forgave her for *her* boorish behavior. Maybe he thought there was still a chance of getting in her pants, and—this was the real hell of it—there was.

"Or," he went on, "she came here to meet somebody."

"Or she came with somebody," Theresa said. "There's no bruising to her face or her arms, no hunks of hair torn out. She came willingly, with someone she trusted."

"Maybe he put a gun in her back," Neil said. "Just because he didn't use it to kill her doesn't mean he didn't have one."

"So they come up here. Then what?" Angela asked Theresa.

"Then Sonia either didn't notice that he picked up a murder weapon when they passed through the inside observation deck below or she couldn't do much about it by that point. She turns away, to check out the view—or to run—and he brings the two-by-four down on the back of her head." Theresa pointed out a spray of blood on the chest-high outer wall. The elliptical drops downward, toward the floor of the deck. "She falls, he strikes her again, giving us this impact pattern halfway along this wall, two feet to the west of the first. She's trying to get away. She lands here, where we find her. I think, from the relatively small amount of blood on her blouse, that he undressed her then, trussed her up. Then he hit her again at least once, most likely twice, spattering blood along the platform here and up her bound arms to the tie around her wrists."

"She's already incapacitated, and still he caves her head in?" Angela asked.

"He wants to make sure she's dead," Theresa stated. "This isn't sick, out-of-control impulses. He came here to kill her, and he wanted to make sure he finished the job."

With the body enclosed in the superglue chamber, Theresa pulled on a set of coveralls and got out the black fingerprint powder. She began just past the body, hoping the preserved area might have kept some clues about Sonia's murderer. She balanced on the balls of her feet, hovering so close to Don's legs that she brushed his calves.

"You're not going to get fresh down there, are you?" he asked.

"No."

"Darn." The lab tech didn't move but continued to hold the upper edge of the superglue tent to keep it from either collapsing or blowing away. They had worked in close quarters before.

Sonia had a horizontal gash to the back of her skull, and given the artistic spray of blood along the floor of the deck at the same location, Theresa figured the blow had come when Sonia was already down. It would make more sense to have the attacker standing behind Sonia, between her and the stairwell, but this gash would be more easily administered from a position between her and the scaffold. The two-by-four had been dropped between Sonia and the scaffold, though the killer could easily have tossed it from the other side. It wasn't positive proof, but it was safe to assume that once Sonia was trussed up with her feet and wrists in the air, she fairly effectively blocked access. The killer might have turned and gone the other way, over the scaffold. Unless it was someone who was really afraid of heights, and this killer must like them. Otherwise he would have killed Sonia in the lower observation rooms, where the windows would have obscured the view from surrounding offices. No, either this killer didn't know that the staff used the deck as a smoking lounge and figured that no one would find the body for weeks or he wanted to maximize his visuals. He was all about the drama.

The scene cut Theresa a break on this one point: The glossy white paint created about the most ideal surface she'd ever found in an outdoor scene. Unfortunately, that wasn't saying much. It had already been coated with the residue of the city, hoisted aloft by the winds. Aside from the normal dust, dirt, and grime, there was overspray from the roiling lake, factory emissions, and the exhaust of twice-daily rush hour. As she brushed the fine black powder onto the two walls, the floor, and the scaffold of the U-shaped trench, all that came into view seemed to be smudges, layers of dirt, ancient bird droppings, and streaks of rain.

The floor of the deck and the scaffold platform did give up some shoe prints, partial and sometimes indistinct patches of various soles. No sign of the smooth triangle of Sonia's pumps, but pieces of rubber-soled shoes like boots or athletic trainers. She found traces of her own Reeboks, trailing along the inner edge where she'd carried the vacuum. She also found a smallish-looking Nike and the simple straight-line tread of a cheap canvas sneaker.

Each decently distinct pattern was then covered with three-inch-wide tape, which Theresa pressed and massaged until it was well and truly stuck and then removed to a glossy five-by-seven card, which she labeled and stored before inching forward to the next section of deck. A slow process, to put it mildly, and producing pieces of evidence that could be of extremely limited use. Who knew how many people in the building might have found their way to the observation deck at some point? Their shoe prints did not necessarily implicate them in murder. The killer had managed to avoid stepping in the victim's blood, and without that obvious timeline a shoe print could be explained away. But still she toiled.

Behind her the two men facing each other over the weak construction of wood strips and plastic were silent except when Angela returned on occasion to report some new development: The search warrant for Sonia's home had been written and now waited on a judge's reading and signature. One had been made up for her car as well. The murder weapon had almost definitely come from the enclosed observation rooms below; specks of white paint across the wood were similar to specks left across others. Co-workers at the public defender's office had expressed shock and grief but got predictably less voluble when asked about the victim's current casework, reporting that they either did not know anything about her present clients or were not aware of any extreme behavior among them. The more forthcoming attorneys insisted that Sonia hadn't complained of any threats and hadn't seemed to fear any one of her clients. But then, they invariably added, she wouldn't.

Angela intended to speak with the convention organizers and to find out if Sonia had had any particular plans for the day's schedule before the convention wound up unexpectedly canceled. Frank, she said, was still at the courthouse, a slave to Dennis Britton's whims.

Theresa continued to process for latent prints, beyond both the body and the platform now. A set of two fingerprints showed up on the outside wall, just under the upper edge and facing eastward and slightly downward, as if someone had been moving toward the body and put his left hand on the wall to steady himself. She set the edge of the tape down on one side of the prints, smoothed it over the black marks, and only then tore the other edge off the roll. That kept the wind from catching the tape and flapping its ends.

The sun pricked sweat from her glands, buried beneath a layer of clothes plus the heavy cotton overalls. The overalls had become covered with the powder, since she had to crawl through the already processed area to reach the next unprocessed area, but the overalls were designed for this purpose and washable, and the point here was not to stay clean. Using powder in the wind became a much bigger concern. The stuff was so fine as to be nearly invisible in the air, and she had no doubt that she would look like a Navy SEAL trying to breach some foreign shore by the time she had finished. The black powder would coat her face and her wrists, get caught in her hair, and turn up for the next day or two in her eyes, nose, and ears. It couldn't be wiped off; wiping would simply make it smear even more. The only solution would be a full-scale scrub-down in a sink with plenty of soap and water, removing all her makeup along with the powder. She didn't even want to think about the insides of her lungs.

Another print materialized, more shoe prints. At forty-five minutes she had completed nearly half the circular deck area and returned to the tent to remove the HotShot from underneath the plastic sheeting.

"Are we done?" Neil asked.

"No." She sealed the small canister into a Ziploc bag, just to keep the fumes from bothering the men until she could discard it. "Another half hour."

Don, bless his little heart, continued his attempt to make pleasant conversation. "How high are we?"

Neil said, "I think it's about seven hundred feet. No witnesses up here except a pigeon or two."

"What about the BP Building? Isn't it taller?"

"Nope."

"I thought they argued that this could still be the tallest building west of Ontario and it wouldn't really be going against the Van Sweringens' wishes to let something *east* of Ontario be taller."

"I wouldn't know," Neil said. "Before my time."

Theresa rechecked the weights along the edges of her makeshift tent. "They did argue. They lost, and the BP Building is shorter by about fifty feet."

"Key Bank is taller, though."

"Yeah, by over two hundred feet. Commerce finally triumphed over tradition."

"So maybe some early-rising executive looked out his window this morning."

Neil said, "Both buildings are at least five hundred feet away. That's a good distance to be able to see a person on a rooftop."

Theresa sneezed, then rubbed her nose with the back of her right hand. Since she'd removed her gloves, this made it the only clean spot on her body, but it didn't matter. She could tell from Don's expression that the powder that had settled on her face was now smeared into a thick black swipe. "Not only that, but after the first blow or two she would have gone down. The rest of their activity—removing the clothes, the bludgeoning—would have been hidden by the wall to anything except a plane." She paused, looked Neil in the face. "But you'll canvass anyway, won't you? All the upper floors of those two buildings?"

"No stone unturned," he promised. "Theresa?"

"What?"

"I'm sorry."

She wasn't ready to respond, and didn't, instead went back to processing the outside deck of the observation level, leaving out the quarter section of it where the kids and now the cops milled.

A half hour later, she finally put the powder and brush aside and secured her lifted latent prints in a manila envelope. Then she released the two men, wishing she'd had a reason to send them away before and pulling up the plastic tent. Uncovering Sonia's naked body felt as if she were exposing her friend to a new round of indignity. At least the wave of superglue fumes released from underneath the plastic reared up and made them turn away for a few seconds. Then the lake breeze cleared the air, and they stood and stared anew at the pasty flesh and bloodied skull.

Theresa had only superglued a body twice before, both times without positive results, but those victims hadn't been as fresh as Sonia. Don held the stiffening limbs for her while she brushed powder, ever so lightly, over the dead woman's skin. She paid special attention to the wrists and ankles, where the killer would have had to grasp and pull the limbs in order to wrap them up with the tie. Prints appeared, although as a mishmash of smears, overlapping and sliding. Theresa examined them with a magnifying glass but couldn't find a usable pattern in the lot.

Then, in the middle of Sonia's back, Theresa found the impression of three distinct fingers. They looked to be from a right hand placed on the left side of Sonia's back, angled downward. The killer had held Sonia's body in place while he pulled off her blouse; they seemed too thin to be Sonia's, assuming she could wrap her own hand around herself to that extent. This also made them too thin to be William's, Theresa thought with a distinct relief, picturing the tall boy's large hands. Perhaps Rachael was right about William. Perhaps Theresa had not been directly responsible for Sonia's death.

Theresa photographed, then lifted them as best she could, noting that most of the patterns were smudged. This did not surprise her. Finding a print on human skin could be considered a miracle as it was. Recovering one of comparable quality would give her the basis for an article in the *Journal of Forensic Sciences*.

Then she took a closer look. The prints weren't merely smudged, they had no discernible ridges at all. Instead they had an irregular, bubbly look to them—as if someone had been wearing latex gloves.

Terrific.

It made sense. No one who had ever watched Discovery would set out to commit a crime without wearing gloves.

Theresa said nothing to the two men who had just spent over an hour holding a tent in place so she could find fingerprints on the corpse. Besides, after latex gloves are worn for a while, they begin to conform to the fingers. A faint pattern might still be visible once she got the lifted prints under a magnifier. And thought happy thoughts. And prayed hard.

The killer, she reminded herself, had wanted to make sure Sonia was dead. A miracle recovery would greatly endanger him. Theresa examined her friend's neck. Sure enough, there were two heavy blotches right over the carotid artery. He had felt for a pulse. These, too, were nothing but a deep smudge.

The killer had thought to bring gloves, but not a murder weapon? Unlikely. He must already have noticed the pile of two-by-fours in the observation rooms. He had checked out the scene beforehand, made sure the observation deck would be relatively unobservable.

Or he simply walked around with latex gloves in his pocket, waiting for an opportunity to present itself. This was not as crazy as it sounded. According to the Boston Strangler, he never had a plan in mind. Until a potential victim opened her door, he never knew what he was going to say to her to get her to let him into the apartment. Then inspiration would strike, and so would he.

And eventually Theresa could not think of another single thing she could possibly collect from this area, but, as always, she hesitated. She could never walk away from even the simplest crime scene without worrying that she had missed something, forgotten something, trampled something.

But it had to be done. She and Don helped the body

snatchers load Sonia Battle into a vinyl body bag with carrying handles, since the regular gurney would be impossible to maneuver along the curving outer deck and down the narrow steps to the inside rooms. They gathered up the paper bags and manila envelopes holding the murder weapon, Sonia's clothing, and the various vacuumings and lifted prints. They would secure this evidence in their vehicles first, then come back for the equipment.

Neil Kelly waited off to the side, pacing a bit, looking as if he needed a cigarette, even though she'd never seen him smoke. He said nothing as they left, but when they returned, he had just clicked off his phone.

"I called Powell," he told them, looking at Theresa. "He's in Atlanta going through Raffel's apartment and office. His co-workers are a lot more cooperative than Marie's. They figure a murder in Cleveland won't have anything to do with them or their clients, so they opened their doors. He said to tell you that Raffel had a cat. Gray. Came as a surprise to his landlord."

"Persian?"

"Don't know. Is it important? I can call him back."

"If he could get some of its fur—just pet the thing and then brush his hand into an envelope, yes, that might be helpful. Thank you," Theresa forced herself to add, unsure of whether she meant it.

His behavior wasn't okay. But neither was hers.

She took one last look at the spot where her friend Sonia had lost her life, then turned to disappear into the gloom of the observation deck's stairwell. She said nothing more to Neil Kelly.

Theresa found Rachael at the front desk, obediently remaining in the public eye and looking more pale and exhausted than Theresa had seen her since finals week. "Hi, Mom. How's it going?"

"I'm finished up there. Look, I need to head back to

the lab and go through this boatload of stuff I just collected. I'd like you to come with me. I can work a lot better if I know you're right there—don't shake your head—"

"I want to finish out the day," Rachael said with a calm finality. "I owe Karla that much. After that, I'm done. I quit. I already told her. So did William."

"Good." Theresa sighed. "I can't tell you how happy I am to hear that."

"You don't have to. I can see it. So go work. I promise I won't go anywhere alone, I'll text you every five minutes, and I'll take the bus home. Go work your magical microscopes and catch this guy."

"But—"

"He isn't going to kill me, Mom. He's killing lawyers—and only lawyers."

This was true. Rachael was perfectly safe, provided William Rosedale was not their killer.

Provided.

CHAPTER 35

Theresa returned to the lab and called in favors, something she did only on the rarest of occasions. Unapologetically sweeping her current work out of the way, she sat down with the collected hairs and fibers and picked through each one, quickly but thoroughly. She talked Christine into doing the autopsy but did not attend. She doubted there could be much it would tell her beyond the obvious: that Sonia had been bludgeoned to death. She turned the clothing over to Don for taping, examination, and photography, and after that he could test the swabs Christine sent up for sperm, which Theresa doubted he'd find—not as a reflection on Sonia's personal life but because they hadn't found any fresh fluids on the other two victims. This could still all come back to sex, but if so, someone suffered from a failure to launch. She also gave him the buccal swabs of Marcus Dean, who had allowed her to collect them without further argument. She didn't know how Neil had reassured him enough to give up the samples, and she hadn't asked.

Theresa skipped lunch, consisting of cups of strong coffee that Leo brewed up. He stayed out of her way, did not protest the undemocratic use of her time, and sprayed the two-by-four with ninhydrin in an unsuccessful attempt to develop fingerprints. Leo could exhibit a shred of compassion in rare moments. Or maybe he just knew not to kick a dog when it was down. It might turn on you.

By late afternoon she had established several things.

Three fibers had been found on Sonia's body: a gray acrylic fiber, consistent with the tie used to bind her, a piece of fluffy pink cotton, and a yellow nylon fiber. Another tuft of similar pink cotton had been found on the murder weapon, but neither matched the pink fibers found on Marie Corrigan's body. Theresa didn't know what to make of the yellow.

A few hairs had been found. They all appeared to belong to Sonia except for one, short and blond. Its root looked elongated, stretched out of shape, which meant it had been from its scalp untimely ripped. It also meant it had a nice amount of skin cells attached to it. She turned the hair over to Don for DNA testing.

The prints she had collected from the walls were entered into the database and were now doing their cyberspace crawl through possible matches. The print on Sonia's back refused to give up even one discernible ridge. All Theresa could surmise from the superglue experiment was that the killer had worn latex or rubber gloves and apparently had slender fingers—unless they were large fingers that touched the skin lightly and so left only part of their surface impression behind . . . though Sonia had not been tiny. It would take some force to shift her body.

Fibers from these gloves had also been caught in the wood of the two-by-four. The chairs used in the first two murders had been smooth and varnished, but the rough fibers of the wood plank had ripped at the material, retaining tufts of polyester, spandex, and one tiny shred of leather.

The vacuumings gave her, along with a great amount of dirt, more hairs and fibers than she knew what to do with. None stood out as particularly significant in a cursory exam, and none seemed to match any prior findings of hers. She needed the killer's wardrobe to compare them to. Ditto the shoe prints.

After Don had examined, taped, and photographed Sonia's clothing, he could not report anything that she didn't already know. No fingerprints on the patent-leather pumps. The blouse had been torn open and removed promptly after the attack, or else the quickly pooling blood under Sonia's head would have seeped into the cloth. This tearing could indicate a struggle, or it might have been the fastest way for the killer to remove the clothing from the portly Sonia. The skirt had been unzipped and pulled off and the nylons turned inside out, then dumped into a pile with her sensible pumps. A few stray blood droplets had landed on the back of the blouse and skirt, indicating, again, that Sonia had fallen onto her chest after the first or second blow and remained there to be finished off.

The tapings gave up a few more gray acrylic fibers, more pink cotton, hair that apparently belonged to Sonia, brown cat hair in various hues. Theresa compared them to the cat hairs found on Marie Corrigan. Different animal entirely. Did Sonia have a cat? *I might have to be adopting more orphaned animals soon,* Theresa thought absently, and wondered how Harry and Nefertiti would react. . . . Harry would be fine. Nefertiti would first have to be coaxed off the ceiling and would never, ever forgive the usurpation of her territory. Adapting to Harry's presence had been bad enough, but after all he was of a lesser species and easily overlooked. The dog was a hangnail, but another cat would be a bullet to the brain.

A few odd, light-colored, ramrod-straight fibers caught her eye. Glass. She moved her lenses to the highest magnification, but that only gave her a better view: fiberglass with some sort of coating adhering to its surface. She mounted it on her FTIR's gold plate. The FTIR couldn't tell her anything about the glass itself, which fell outside the parameters of the instrument, but it might be able to determine the adherent. She moved the stage slowly, trying not to breathe on the minuscule piece of evidence, started up the computer program, lined up the transmission beam—and all the while her heart sank further, because this would almost certainly prove to be a waste of time. The observation deck was a construction zone. The fiberglass could have come from anywhere. The coating of the deck itself might be made out of fiberglass—light, durable, and extremely weather-resistant. She could spend the rest of the month locked in her lab and never get one step closer to finding Sonia's killer.

But such was the nature of the job. She let the machine hum, waited for the spectrum to pop up as a jagged line against an X-Y graph, a taller and more erratic version of an EKG. It showed several familiar peaks—carbon, epoxide groups—and something new. A little research proved it to be triethylenetetramine. Not so helpful. She couldn't even pronounce it, much less identify its uses. She printed the spectrum, labeled the peaks, and went across the hall to the toxicology department.

Oliver sat at his bench, closed off into its own little corner by a row of compressed-gas tanks and the large mass spectrometer. "I found some fiberglass on the body, with this adherent—probably epoxy, with something called triethylenetetramine," she told him. "What would that be?"

"Anything."

"Oliver, I need help." Sometimes that worked.

"I don't care." Sometimes it didn't.

"A good friend of mine has been brutally murdered."

"A lawyer," Oliver pointed out, and turned a page. "Excuse me if I don't break out the hankies. Besides, my answer is accurate. Anything. Triethylenetetramine is just a hardener for the epoxy, and the epoxy is there to hold the fiberglass together so it can form boats, cars, insulation, sports equipment, surfboards, sound-absorption panels. Where was she found again?"

"In the middle of a construction zone."

He shrugged, the heavy shoulders quaking as the muscles within rolled. "There you go."

She couldn't think of anything else to ask. Her brain already threatened to buckle under the weight of facts that refused to line up into anything resembling a pattern. "Thanks, Oliver."

"Just doing my underpaid and ultimately hopeless best for the betterment of humanity and the integrity of the criminal-justice system, not necessarily in that order. Now, go away and leave me alone. I mean it."

"Your dedication does you proud," she told him. "As does your compassion."

Don came around the corner, past the compressed-gas tanks, a grim cast to his face. "I have some results."

"Okay. Wait. Oliver—cars?"

"That's what I just said."

"What kind of cars?"

"Sporty little things driven by sporty little people who think they're immortal and therefore not concerned that the frame will shatter like an eggshell should it come into contact with a larger object, like a tractor-trailer or a wall."

"Cars like a 1963 split-window Corvette coupe that sells for over a hundred K?"

Don raised one brow. The toxicologist's eyes glazed a bit. Cars were not his thing, and he professed great disdain for those shallow enough to make them theirs.

"I have two suspects who have a connection to all three attorneys. The first is Coral Simone."

"Who?" Oliver asked.

"All three worked on her daughter's murder case. But Sonia's involvement was so brief that I don't know how Coral would even know about it, and I can't see any of our three attorneys turning their backs on her long enough for her to cave their heads in. Why would Marie meet with her in an empty hotel suite? Why would Bruce let her into his room? But they wouldn't have had any qualms about opening the door to Dennis Britton."

"*Britton?*" Oliver asked. He didn't have to ask who that was; he had tangled with Britton over the years as well. "*He's* your suspect number two? Why? Aside from the fact that he's a flaming asshole."

"Because he likes expensive sports cars, enough to do his own repairs. We've got fiberglass on both Marie's and Sonia's bodies and wax on Marie—car wax."

"*I* said wax," Oliver clarified. "*You* said car wax."

"True, but let's go with it for the sake of argument. The detectives said she barely kept gas in her SUV, so it wasn't from her own car. Britton has a cat—I plucked a cat hair off his jacket myself. Not the same gray Persian I found on Marie and Bruce, but people who have one cat often have two. He would know to distract us with the S&M sex angle. He couldn't stand to see a jerk like Bruce Raffel steal something from him again. With So-

nia gone, the ethics complaint she filed against him will
go away. And I think he killed his wife."

Don frowned. "Killed his *wife*? I remember the case,
but—"

"I know it was investigated out the wazoo, but I still
can't see how she could have struck the steering wheel
hard enough to crack her skull and not do more damage
to the car. Dr. Banachek might have thought of that,
but I don't think he ever looked at the car himself. I suspect they argued, Britton hit her in the head with a fireplace poker or one of his golf clubs—something thin and
straight—then staged the accident. In his early days, he
specialized in DUI accident-with-injury cases, so he not
only knows all about cars, he knows all about car acci-
dents. He'd know just what we would look for—the position of the driver's seat, lights on or off. Everything."

"Can you prove that?" Oliver asked.

"About his wife? Not a word."

"How's that going to work for you, then?"

"I think I can prove he killed Sonia and the others,
though. I'll need samples from his household pets, his
car. I've got spandex and leather on the two-by-four that
killed Sonia, glove prints on her skin. Spandex is more
often found in gloves made for sports, not warmth, and
you can bet a man with such fancy cars probably has a
pair of fancy driving gloves."

"You might want to put off asking for search warrants," Don said, holding up a sheet of paper. "Because
you don't have two suspects. You have three."

CHAPTER 36

Twenty minutes later she stepped off the Ritz-Carlton's plush elevator, to the immensely comforting sight of Rachael wearily checking in a family of five dressed from head to toe in designer-initialed clothing. Rachael had decided that she would simply stay at the front desk until Theresa was ready to go home, not willing to deal with a bus, rapid transit, or any other form of transportation save for her mother's battered Tempo, which fell right in line with Theresa's way of thinking. Of course, it only illustrated how badly the teen had been shaken in the past week. *If this child makes it to adulthood without having to spend her college tuition on therapy sessions,* Theresa thought, *it will be no thanks to me.*

It had been a long couple of days. She would deliver her news to Neil Kelly and leave him to deal with it. That part of the job was not hers. Then she would take her child and go home.

Theresa started to cross the floor, but a clawlike grip closed around her arm. "Where is he?"

She turned to see Coral Simone, in her trusty pink twinset and pressed slacks, looking like a PTA president except for the irritated blood vessels in her eyes and the deep furrow between her brows. She must have come straight from work; an ID key card hung around her neck.

"I'm sorry, what?" Theresa asked.

"You said your daughter met him at work. The paper said your daughter worked here, and it said who you were."

Don't look at Rachael. Don't look at Rachael. "Coral, I'm sorry I didn't tell you—"

"I don't care about that. None of the staff here will say anything to anyone, of course—they can't have more bad publicity, and she won't tell me either. I've sat here all morning when I should be at my chemo treatment and haven't seen him. Get your daughter to tell me where he is."

"You talked to Rachael?" This is not good. Not, not, not good.

The grip on her arm turned into a pat. "It said 'Rachael' on her name tag. I asked if he worked here. She said she couldn't tell me, that's all. It's okay. I don't want to scare her—or let her warn him. But you can find out where he is, right now. I know he's here—I saw that fat little friend of his. The molly one."

Theresa tried to keep up, to figure out how to handle this. "You know Ray?"

"Yeah. He was in my daughter's classes, too. Came to her funeral, cried like a baby. If that kid is here, then *he's* here also. Ray followed him like a puppy then, and I'm sure nothing's changed."

"William probably went home. The hotel probably sent him home. Rachael's only still here because she's waiting for me."

"Then can you get his home address for me? That might be even better." Again the amicable pat, a show of comfort between friends. She gazed at Theresa as if they were alone in the busy lobby, intense and sincere, both to a frightening degree. "I can solve both our problems."

Theresa couldn't help it; she pulled back. The fact that Coral Simone was a grieving suburban housewife did not reassure her in the least. The woman meant everything she said and had the brains to back it up. Theresa could not school the horror out of her expression, and Coral Simone's eyes narrowed.

"Isn't that what you want? To keep your daughter safe?" Coral said, keeping her voice down, her eyes full of madness but also pain, and bewildered grief. Her touch felt electric, as if it might crack open an alternate future, giving Theresa a glimpse of any parent's worst nightmare become reality. "Haven't you been through enough this week to get the tiniest, slightest inkling of what I've felt? Can't you guess now what it would feel like to lose her?"

"Yes," Theresa confessed. "Yes. Coral, I understand. I *really* do, because you're right—I'm a mother, too, and I know exactly what that means. I have some more information for you. There are some things I've figured out about your daughter's murder." That ought to grab her attention. "But I'm in the middle of the investigation about the lawyers, and there's something I have to take care of right now."

The woman did not seem convinced. Rather the opposite. She stood back herself, appraising Theresa in a new and skeptical light.

Neil Kelly appeared, leaving the lounge, and Theresa saw an out. "A Homicide detective is heading our way. Let me take care of him, and then we'll talk, okay? You're going to want to hear this, especially before you . . . do anything." Like attack William Rosedale in the lobby of the Ritz-Carlton.

Coral, obviously dubious but curious as well, nodded,

then either promised or threatened, "I won't be going anywhere."

She disappeared into the restaurant, where Theresa hoped William would stay in the kitchen until she had time to tell Neil about the sweet-looking, possibly unbalanced time bomb haunting the place.

"How are you doing?" Neil asked her.

"Tired. Come with me." She led the way, peeking into Marcus Dean's office. The security chief was not there, however, only an empty chair and a desk scattered with invoices: Wilson Electronics, Wowway cable, Parry Engineering. Theresa did not sit but faced Neil. "We have a major problem. The hair found on Bruce Raffel's body belongs to Marcus Dean."

The blood drained from Neil Kelly's face. For a moment she thought he would burst into tears, so much so that she forgot all her prior irritation and put her arms around him.

"It can't be. That can't be," he said.

"I'm sorry, honey. It's still very, very preliminary—Don cut all sorts of corners to get it done so fast, but it's probably correct. He'll do the full workup over the next day or two."

"I don't believe he did it."

She let go of him, stepped back. "I don't either."

"But you just said—"

"Dean has worked here for years. There's a possibility—slim, but definite—that his hair could be found in several rooms in this hotel. It's a *hotel*—that's what I've been complaining of from the start. It suffers from an incredible amount of traffic. Dean is up and down the hallways of this building every day. The maids are up and down, in and out of the rooms every day, using the same vacuums all over. It's just possible that the hair was on that carpeting before Bruce Raffel's body fell on it.

At least that's what a defense attorney will say. It's not a slam dunk."

"Besides, why would he even kill Raffel? Marie *maybe*, but Raffel? Or—"

"Sonia. Even if he were somehow jealous enough over a one-night stand to murder, where on earth would Sonia come in? Why would he kill her?"

It seemed as if Neil could breathe again. "Yeah. Why?"

"The hair is damning, but I still don't think he did it."

"Then who else is there?" Neil slumped into a chair. "We haven't found any other connection between the three attorneys. And we've looked, believe me we've looked."

"Not hard enough," Theresa said gently. "I think our more likely suspect is waiting in the lobby for me." She told him what Ray had said, that Bruce had assisted Marie at William's trial. "Sonia said as much to me, and the PD director told Frank that Bruce and Marie continued to work as unofficial partners even when they worked for different law firms. Plus, Coral's been here, I saw her here the day Marie's body was found. She's here now."

"That frail-looking lady you were just talking to in the lobby? You think *she* bludgeoned three attorneys to death?"

"She's skinny, but she's wiry. And that trophy over her kitchen sink had her name on it, not Jenna's. If she can swing a softball bat, I'm willing to bet she can swing a chair or a two-by-four just as effectively. The things that put me on to Dennis Britton—the fiberglass, the sports gloves—can apply to her as well."

"Britton?"

She explained the few clues that could possibly implicate Dennis Britton. "But the fiberglass could be from a bat instead of a car and the spandex and leather from a batting glove instead of a driving glove. I have to have samples from their homes to get any further—and the wax. Coral waxes the furniture in Jenna's room obsessively. The cat hair I can't explain—it could just be another hotel artifact. And then there's this." She held up one of the invoices from Marcus's desk.

"What is that?"

"Parry Engineering is billing Marcus for . . . let's see, four thousand blank key cards and a program update. Coral works for them. I just remembered when I saw the lanyard around her neck," Theresa explained, jangling the keys around her own neck for emphasis. "Coral *programs* things for them. How much do you want to bet that their program would have a master code, so that they could always write a card to open any door in the hotel? They'd have to, in case the hotel's computer crashed. How did Marie and/or the killer get into the Presidential Suite? There's only one way: You have to have a key."

"That's a leap. That's a jump wider than the Snake River Canyon."

"But, unlike practically everything else about this case, easily verified."

Neil hesitated, then said, "Dean has a key, too," as if he had to physically drag the words from his throat.

"I know."

Theresa's phone rang.

For the second time that day, her daughter's panicked voice came out of the tiny device. *"Why are you doing this?"*

She ran from the room.

CHAPTER 37

Barely controlled chaos ruled the lobby. Dinnertime on Friday. Weekend guests were checking in, with travel fatigue, hunger pangs, and too much net worth to be willing to wait in line. So lots of generalized snarkiness but no scenes of bloody murder. Also no William, no Rachael, no Coral Simone.

Theresa kept the phone pressed to one ear, holding the other ear closed with her left hand. She had said Rachael's name a few times, but the girl did not respond. Someone with Rachael spoke, but too softly for Theresa to identify the speaker or even the gender. Another murmur—the same person or maybe someone else. Theresa scanned the rest of the lobby, the lounge area, the elevator banks.

Rachael said, "Why are we going to the observation deck?"

Not again, Theresa pleaded silently, pushing the "up" button before she'd even completed the thought.

Murmuring again. Rachael must have her phone on, open, maybe hidden in a pocket or held behind her back. Theresa covered the tiny mike in her own phone so her breath or the lobby noise would not give this away.

Then she heard William say, "Let her go."

Definitely his voice, but who was "her"? Rachael? Or someone else?

"No! Leave her alone!"

No more sounds. Theresa moved the phone from her ear, glanced at the screen. CALL DISCONNECTED.

This couldn't be happening to her. Not again.

An elevator finally arrived. She pushed past the exiting guests, jabbed a button. Neil Kelly slid in just as the doors closed. "What the hell's going on?"

Theresa explained about the phone call. "Someone is taking my daughter to the top of the tower, and I think it's Coral Simone. Call somebody. Call Dean—he's got to be on the premises."

"He's got no authority once off hotel property." Neil's hand went to the butt of his gun as they circled the empty thirty-third floor to the tower elevator. "That Rosedale kid. He probably figures we're so busy with the dead lawyers that he can make his move now—"

"This may sound crazy, but I think William's the one in real danger."

"Listen to me," Neil said as if he hadn't heard her. He turned to face her, grasped both arms just below the shoulders, and looked into her eyes. "We'll get Rachael. Nothing will happen to her, okay? I promise."

They both knew he couldn't guarantee anything of the kind, but that didn't matter. Theresa was exhausted, bewildered, and terrified, and it was what she needed to hear at the moment. She allowed herself to slump into his arms and wrap herself against his sturdy frame. *Let him be able to deliver on that pledge,* she prayed, clutching him so tight that the keys on her lanyard pressed into her sternum.

"It will be all right," he breathed into her ear, grasping her hair with one hand. "We'll stop him."

"Not him," Theresa corrected. "Her."

They reached the fifty-second floor.

He insisted on leading the way, right hand on his gun, his left splayed outward to keep her behind him. But he moved quickly enough to keep her from going insane, advancing into the smaller, south-facing observation room, through the narrow hallway, into the larger, north-facing room with its wide windows and bare floors. They were empty and silent.

Neil continued into the very dim stairwell, moving up the two flights. Theresa followed him closely enough to feel the heat from his body as they climbed the creaking metal steps. Coral was someone to be empathized with, not arrested, right? They could hope. But Coral had not sought out William to have a cathartic chat, and Rachael would never have left the lobby at a simple verbal request. Coral, Theresa felt sure, would be armed. A gun or a knife. By this point Theresa wouldn't be surprised if the slender woman had dynamite strapped to her chest.

The top of the tower hadn't been designed for either efficiency or convenience, and certainly not for ease of apprehending a murderously grieving mom. There were no lights and no windows. Dark corners abounded. The door to the outside could be located only by the rim of fading light around its edge. Neil Kelly pulled it open, gently, and it moved inward as quietly as eighty-three-year-old, well-painted-over metal could—with a deafening metallic squeak.

Now Theresa heard voices.

They stepped over the high threshold into the curving bowl of the outer observation deck. The sun had begun to set, streaking the air over the lake with pink and purple, and the wind whipped up the water as the temperature faded. It would have been beautiful had she time to look at it.

Neil Kelly moved toward the north, Theresa immediately behind him, grateful that he did not waste even a split second trying to convince her to hang back, perhaps figuring they had little to fear from a single distraught mother. But she noticed he kept his hand on the butt of his gun and had unsnapped his holster. They moved quickly around to the point where Sonia's body had lain, the paint still streaked with her blood.

Coral stood on the workers' scaffold, a gun in her right hand and Rachael's elbow in the other, herself against the wall, Rachael at the edge of the platform. Theresa stopped. It was bad enough to see the barrel of a Glock pointed at her only child. Even worse was that nothing but a railing of thin cables that barely reached Rachael's thigh separated her from seven hundred feet of empty air.

William Rosedale stood in the niche between the steps and the outer wall, his back to Theresa, as Coral was saying to him, " . . . what you did in five minutes of drunken stupor destroyed every iota of the beautiful family I had, blasted it into dust."

Rachael's voice pierced the breeze. "What are you going to do, kill him? Everyone will know you did it, even if—"

Even if you kill me, too.

"I don't want to kill him! I want him to confess. To me, to you, to the entire city! *I just want to hear him admit it!*"

Calm. It was really important to stay calm here.

"Coral!" Neil raised his voice to be heard above the growing wind, but not shouting. "Drop the gun."

William's head swiveled toward them, and Rachael

jerked as if she wanted to run to her mother—turned into a little girl all over again—but Coral pulled her back. William looked about as terrified as a buff nineteen-year-old could look.

Coral did not seem the least dissuaded by the presence of two witnesses. She barely spared them a glance.

Theresa forced herself to breathe. "I told you I had some new information you'd want to hear."

"You let her stay here," Coral said, the depth of her voice belying her slight frame. "You know what he is, and you let her see him. Are you *nuts*?"

Theresa refrained from saying, *I'm not the one on top of the Terminal Tower waving a gun at two kids,* and instead said, "That's what I wanted to talk to you about."

"I didn't kill Jenna," William said to Theresa. The stoicism she'd seen this week had been decimated, wiped out by this relentless pursuit. His voice hovered on the edge of tears. "I would never have hurt Jenna. And I would never—"

"Shut up!" Coral screamed. "Stop saying that!"

Theresa said, "He's right. He didn't kill Jenna."

They both stared at her.

"His friend Ray did."

CHAPTER 38

"What?"

"*What?*"

Theresa squeezed past Neil Kelly, gently, slowly, never taking her eyes off the woman on the platform. He didn't stop her, probably waiting to see if she could talk Coral Simone into putting down the gun.

Theresa tried to take her eyes off her daughter, with nothing to hang on to except the woman who was threatening to kill her in order to force a confession from her boyfriend. If Coral pushed, she might grab the cables— Would they even hold . . . ? Theresa made herself stop. Concentrate. Then she started to talk.

"The bloody streaks on Jenna's shirt—three and a half lines. They're finger marks. Ray is missing half of his index finger." She asked William, "When did he lose that?"

The boy choked, coughed, then pulled himself together with visible effort. "Grade school. He was helping his dad mow the lawn—"

"Ray was with you that night, wasn't he? He was

at the dance with you, because you did everything together. Ray has been riding your coattails since grade school. He told me so himself."

"Ray wouldn't—"

"He also told me, 'I should never have gone to that dance.' Not 'William shouldn't have gone,' but 'I shouldn't.' What do you remember about that dance, William?"

"I . . . I remember going. But Ray couldn't kill somebody—"

"Speak!" Coral Simone demanded, surprising Theresa. But this didn't mean she subscribed to Theresa's theory. She merely wanted to wring every detail out of her daughter's last day on this earth. "What happened at the dance?"

"Ray was there, right?" Theresa pressed.

"Yeah . . . I picked him up. Jenna was there, other kids. I think we talked to her . . . then, I don't know." His body gave a jerk from time to time, first in one direction and then another as if both wanting to run and wanting to protect Rachael, neither possible under the threat of Coral Simone's .40-caliber.

"You were drugged, William. Traces of Rohypnol were found in your blood—*your* blood, not Jenna's."

"His lawyer made that up," Coral interrupted.

"The prosecutor would have tested the samples again if he thought that. William, do you remember taking any drugs that evening?"

"No, I wouldn't—I never took stuff like that. Why would I?"

"Exactly. Why would a randy teenage boy drug *himself*? But Ray could have slipped it to you. You appeared drunk, Ray asks her to help him get you home. She'd have done something like that, wouldn't she?" Theresa asked Coral Simone. "You said she never wanted to see another kid get in trouble."

The mother nodded. Slowly. But she didn't put the gun down, nor did she relax her hold on Rachael's arm.

Neil Kelly hovered behind Theresa, a warm mass at her elbow, waiting to see if she could talk Coral's finger off that trigger.

Scheherazade, only spinning tales to save a daughter's life this time. But they weren't just tales. . . . The more she talked, the more she convinced herself. "So there's Ray and Jenna, feeling like Good Samaritans. You're passed out. Your parents aren't home. This is Ray's plan, his big chance. He makes his pass. Now, Jenna is a sweet girl, but let's face it—she can have her pick of any boy in the class. She isn't about to suck face with a loser like Ray, is she?"

"This isn't true!" William said. "You don't know what you're talking about!"

"Ray has Klinefelter's syndrome, doesn't he?" she asked him, receiving a blank look in reply. "It's when a male has an extra X chromosome. Instead of XY, he's XXY. It's characterized by abnormal body proportions, which makes him look sort of droopy though he's of normal height, and enlarged breasts though he's not really overweight. Most commonly it causes infertility, which is why no sperm was found on Jenna. DNA can also be found in seminal fluid, but sexual problems are common with Klinefelter's, too, so likely he couldn't even produce that. This would have caused him a great deal of frustration, especially liking Jenna as much as he did. And he did, didn't he?"

She was guessing, but the look on William's face told her that she was guessing right on every point.

"He always talked to her," Coral admitted. "Jenna

mentioned him now and then. He'd ask her out, ask for her help with his homework, linger at her locker. She laughed about it—not to be mean, she just didn't think anything of it. All the boys acted like that with her."

Theresa went on. "You said he came to her funeral, cried harder than anybody. He cried again this morning—the sight of Sonia's body completely unnerved him, because it brought back bad memories of Jenna's death—because he was there."

William tried one last protest. "But then how did he get home? I drove us to the school."

"He walked. He said you and he had been friends since you walked to school together in grade school. He doesn't live far from you," she guessed, and William didn't disagree. "It's a perfect solution for him. Your car is at the school, Jenna's car is in your driveway, he can drop the murder weapon in the woods or maybe bury it on the way home. No one at the school will remember that you arrived at the dance together, because no one ever pays any attention to Ray, right?"

"He would never have done that to me!" Anger had finally erupted. The boy turned red, and his fists balled. He seemed to have completely forgotten about Coral's gun, about Coral. "He's the only one who stuck by me, the only one who didn't drop me like last year's Black-Berry model. He would never have let me go to jail for something he did. Never!"

"I'm sure it tore him up," Theresa agreed gently. "He said he went to your trial every day until his mother made him stop. He spoke of Marie Corrigan as if she were a saint, because she saved your life. When you were acquitted, no one was happier than Ray was, right? Not your parents, not even you."

She was proving William innocent, relieving him from a lifetime of infamy *and* Coral Simone's justice, and the kid only appeared younger and more vulnerable than she'd ever seen him. Knowledge of Ray's betrayal had decimated him, shredded the one last piece of comfort he'd been able to salvage from the previous three years.

"So you see, Coral—you would have executed the wrong boy."

At last the too-thin woman lowered the gun a few inches. "That's a lot of theorizing."

"Yes, it is. But I don't think it will be hard to prove. All we have to do is ask Ray. He's been carrying the weight of his guilt for three years, and he'll be only too relieved to shed it."

Coral appeared to ponder this, the pallor in her face brightened only slightly by the rosy cast of the setting sun. Theresa didn't dare look at her own daughter, or she might not be able to keep herself from rushing the platform and the crazed woman on it.

"You really think so?" Coral asked, barely audible over the evening breeze and still not ready to accept this new view of life. She had spent three years planning William Rosedale's destruction, and now it had all been for nothing.

"Yes." Theresa breathed out. This would work. Coral was coming down, both literally and figuratively.

Then, reversal. Coral took a new grip on the gun, pulled Rachael an inch closer to her, and said, "Let's find out. Call him."

William stared at her, uncomprehending. "*What?*"

"Your little friend Ray. Get out your phone and call him. Tell him to come here."

"No."

"He murdered my child."

William's mouth worked without sound for a moment, and then he said, "He's not here anyway."

"He'll come back. He'd crawl across broken glass jus
to hover in your orbit. Call him."

"He went home," the teen insisted. "His mothe
picked him up. She won't let him drive, and the bu
makes him nervous."

Another reason for Rachael to date this boy: He
couldn't lie worth—

"He left her naked and bloody for strangers to poke
and prod so that all the other kids could talk about it
on their MySpace pages. And then," Coral added with
a quick and fatal slice, "he let you take the blame for it.
Bring him here, and you and this girl can walk away."

For a moment the boy seemed to think about it, either wondering if cooperation would buy them time to
think of something else or realizing that his life had been
turned inside out and left a pale imitation of what it had
been, all due to someone who professed to be his closest
friend. Did he owe that person protection?

Neil Kelly finally spoke up. "Coral, put the gun down.
It's over."

"It is nowhere *near* over, Neil. How can you even say
that?"

Neil?

Neil?

Theresa turned to him, but even as her lips formed
the question—*How does she know your name?*—she
saw it. And wondered how she could have missed it all
this time.

"I'm sorry, Theresa," he said.

CHAPTER 39

The words hung in the air, like a familiar song sung in a different language, making it difficult to understand why the lyrics seem unintelligible to you. Theresa stared at him, waiting for comprehension, waiting for the pieces to fall into place just as they had with Ray's guilt in Jenna Simone's murder.

None of this explained where Neil Kelly came in.

"Who are—" she began. Then, "Ah."

"Isn't he the cop?" William asked in the silence.

"Mom?" Rachael asked. She had calmed in her mother's presence, enough to take calculating glances at her assailant that made Theresa's skin crawl, as if Rachael were sizing Coral up for an overthrow. Rachael was strong, athletic, and might underestimate the skinny woman holding the gun. But that strength faded again in light of the cavalry's apparent defection.

Theresa said to him, "You're a transplant. You've only been here three years, which means you moved to Cleveland right around the time Jenna died."

He nodded. "She was my niece."

Theresa looked from him to Coral. A minor resem-

blance, in the snub nose and dimpled cheeks, easily
missed on Coral's whipcord frame. Theresa couldn'
blame herself for not seeing it. She did blame hersel
for not seeing a host of other things. His utter, out-of-
proportion shock when she first told him of Rachael and
William. His vehement certainty that Marie Corrigan
deserved to die. His equally vehement certainty that
Marcus Dean was innocent. Just as with Ray and William, it tortured him to think his friend might suffer for
his own crime, even of omission. . . . Had he kissed her
on his houseboat only to distract her from the DNA results that pointed to Dean?

The great relief when she'd shifted her suspicions to
Dennis Britton.

How when she'd told him that Coral Simone had Rachael in the tower, he should have asked, "Who's Coral
Simone?"

Even Coral, who had slipped in the occasional Irish
slang, learned from their grandfather. "Cub" for boy,
"molly" for wimpy.

The simple fact that Neil should have told the entire
investigation team that a hotel employee had been tried
for an earlier, similar crime. Frank and Theresa had
been trying to protect Rachael. Neil shouldn't have been
similarly circumspect. But he couldn't have his fellow officers looking into the Simone murder, revealing his own
connection to the dead Marie Corrigan. "That's why
you were so vehement that I should get Rachael away
from William," Theresa said.

"Yes! I really did care. I didn't want you to suffer the
way my sister did. The way *I* did."

"And I thought you just wanted to get into my pants."

He smiled at her, sickly and worried and with a gun
held loosely in his hand, but he smiled. He had to be
looking for a way out of this. Quietly, she said to him,

"Don't do this, Neil. You can still step away. Coral's a grieving mother—they'll take that into consideration."

Wrong thing to say. Walking away from revenge for his niece's death was not an option but a sentence in itself, and he grasped the gun a little more tightly and pointed it a little more in her direction. "No matter what else happens, my career is over, we both know that. My life has ended here today. I might as well take that little bastard with me."

"Neil—"

"I'm sorry you and your daughter have to see this, I am. But it's too late now."

Coral and Neil had two guns and three murders between them. Theresa had no weapons, a daughter, and someone else's son to look out for. The only available way out involved a seven-hundred-foot drop. The sun was sinking fast, sucking the light from the air as it fell. Frank was a prisoner in the Justice Center, and she had no police radio with an "alert" button, only a cell phone she'd never have a chance to get at to call for the backup Neil had refused to summon. She was out of options.

She said to Coral—she could no longer make herself look at Neil—"So what are you going to do? Kill me *and* two kids, somehow convince yourself this is justice? Destroy three people who never did a thing to you?"

"Of course not," Neil said. "Nothing's going to happen to you, Theresa."

Both women ignored him.

Coral gestured to Rachael with the gun's barrel. "You want to make a deal to get your daughter out of here. Well, this is the deal. You say this kid didn't do it, fine. Get me the one who did and you can have these two back without a scratch. You would do the same thing if it had been *her* lying on his living-room floor, with her clothes ripped off and her head bashed in."

"Coral—"

"Look me in the eye and tell me that's not true."

"You can't ask him—"

"*Look at me!*"

Theresa swallowed. "I would want exactly what you want. But I wouldn't expect anyone else to help me."

Then William straightened; it could only have been an inch but seemed much more. He rested both hands on the platform and told Coral, "Even if he did what you say, I'm not leading him here like a deer to a blind. That might be him, but it's not me."

"You don't think so?" Coral got a fresh grip on her gun, still pointed—alarmingly—at Rachael's midsection. "Then she dies."

"Then I take you with me," Rachael said, and wrapped one hand around Coral's wrist. She gazed into the woman's eyes and added, "It's a long way down."

"Let her go, Coral," Theresa said, moving closer as quickly as she dared. Neil Kelly did nothing to stop her, so she put one foot on the bottom step. "If you want Ray, we'll get him. We'll get him into a court of law where he'll have to make a full confession, tell the world everything he did. But let Rachael go."

"I don't want to wait!" Coral shouted, her voice climbing to a shriek. She'd been in too much pain for too long, and rationality had slipped out the back door. "I've waited for three years! What did the courts do for me? Where's *my* justice?" She looked at Rachael as if seeing her for the first time, then back to Theresa. Then she got to the real heart of the matter: "Why do you get to have a daughter if I don't?"

Rachael grabbed the gun.

Coral tried to wrestle it back, shoving at her with a sharp thrust of one shoulder.

Rachael pulled, lost her balance.

Theresa took the last two steps without thinking, reaching toward them, feeling the tiniest flick of Rachael's hair before it brushed against the loose cable railing, the sensation still on her fingertips as she watched both Coral Simone and her only child disappear over the edge.

CHAPTER 40

Theresa rushed the edge of the platform. Her body absently grabbed the cable to keep herself from following, though her mind no longer cared. She heard William's cry of agony as if it were part of the wind and looked down just in time to see Coral Simone's body strike the edge of a lower roof, rebound, tumble outward in one slow movement, and keep going.

Then she realized that the falling bundle of denim and blond hair that was Rachael had been stopped. William had cried out not in loss but in pain as his right arm caught the girl's falling weight, and now she dangled from the deck's outer wall.

Theresa realized later that she had literally catapulted off the platform, heedless of the gusting wind, to leap over both the side railing and William to land on the narrow walkway. But in the instant it took her to straighten up and rush to the outer wall, Neil Kelly had beat her to it, slamming into William and reaching over to grab Rachael's fashionable leather belt. Together they hauled the girl to safety. The entire moment lasted perhaps two seconds, but Theresa couldn't even calculate how many eternities passed before she wrapped her arms around her child, both of them too terrified to scream, cry, or even breathe.

Finally William's groans distracted her. Only then did she notice the odd angle of his right arm. She and Rachael helped the boy to a seated position, and Rachael's feverish *Thankyouthankyouthankyou*s helped to distract him from the pain.

Neil Kelly had climbed the platform and stood gazing downward, leaning precariously outward to get a glimpse of his sister's body.

"Neil," Theresa said.

He leaned farther.

"Neil," she said again, much more sharply, and this time he looked.

He thought about it. She could see him debating the option.

She held out one hand. "Come down."

After another moment he did.

Then, holstering his weapon in favor of his radio, he calmly reported their location to the dispatcher and that there had been a death. He requested an ambulance as well as other officers.

He turned to Theresa.

She should be grateful, she knew. But all she could say was "About damn time."

CHAPTER 41

Angela arrived with plenty of help. Paramedics arrived with a nylon sling and eased William's arm into it.

Neil Kelly handed Theresa his gun, requested the police union attorney to which he was entitled, and then leaned against the deck's inner wall and waited quietly while his colleagues secured the scene and set up some lighting. Theresa watched Angela struggle with herself over whether or not to cuff him, then decide against it. She left a uniform at his side instead.

All this activity made for close working quarters, and Theresa found herself next to him while the EMTs bound up William's shoulder, Rachael holding his other hand.

She shouldn't say anything to Neil, she thought. She should just let him enjoy the view of the city lights and the coursing water beyond them. It might be his last glimpse for a very long time. And she shouldn't say anything, period.

But of course she couldn't stop herself. "Whose idea was it? Yours or hers?"

He stared at her. "You think I *knew*?"

"Stop playing me, Neil."

"I'm not—shit, if I *had* known, I would have stopped her!"

Theresa gazed at him, searching his face for any sign of untruth, but she didn't know him that well and had never been able to read people like a book. That was why she stuck with inanimate things, like microscopes and dead cells.

"I didn't even know about this convention. Coral comes here for lunch with her group every so often. She must have seen an advertisement or heard about it from the staff."

Theresa nodded. And when Coral realized or found out that her company provided the keycards for the hotel, it must have seemed like destiny. A plan began to form.

"I didn't know defense attorneys even *had* conventions until we got the call for Marie Corrigan's death. I knew she'd been his lawyer, of course—I'd come here to support Coral, attended the trial—but I figured at least two percentage points of this city's population hated that bitch, so I didn't think. . . . I went over Coral's to tell her. She acted surprised. We had a drink to celebrate." His expression grew pensive, now that he had a moment to think back and connect dots. "She wanted to hear all about it. The hotel room, what Marie's body looked like. Yeah, I shouldn't have been discussing an open case, but she's my *sister*. I swear, Theresa, she never gave me the slightest idea that she already knew all the answers."

Theresa rested her head against the cold brick, watching the lights at Browns Stadium. Wrong season for football—probably a high-school graduation. She kept six inches of space between their bodies, but it wasn't enough. She could still feel the electric pull of his flesh, the smell of his aftershave. "What about Bruce Raffel?"

"I didn't recognize him at the scene, but when I saw his photo in a suit and tie, he looked familiar. I'd attended a few days of the trial, and I must have seen him. At that point I began to wonder, yes, but—you couldn't even call it suspicion, only this little gnawing worry in the pit of my stomach. And there seemed to be other connections between Raffel and Corrigan—sex, past cases, Dennis Britton. I didn't ask Coral about it. I didn't want to know."

"If you had, Sonia Battle might still be alive."

"Do you think I don't know that?" The words couldn't come out fast enough; he seemed to choke on each one. "Coral attended every second of William's trial. She'd arrive an hour early, wouldn't leave until the attorneys did. Sat there through every recess, every sidebar. I was with her the day Sonia came in during a break and thanked Marie for taking the case. Once the jury's gone, attorneys don't really pay much attention to who's around them. Sonia laughed and said William would wind up on death row if she had tried it. She *laughed*. Coral went to the ladies' room and threw up."

Theresa found herself wanting to take his hand, to say something comforting. She didn't.

He swallowed hard and went on. "That's why I was so . . . harsh about her death, because that's when I knew. And I couldn't see a way out. I couldn't figure out how to save Coral. Or myself."

Family was family, she got that. You protect them as best you can. Except when it allowed someone else to die.

She watched Rachael, standing by as the paramedics helped the injured teenager to his feet. They had immobilized his shoulders with a wide Velcroed strap, like a cummerbund worn ten inches too high.

"On top of that, I had to run the investigation. I

couldn't break away to confront her. I had to keep pretending that everything was normal—at least normal for a cop investigating a triple homicide. I never thought Coral would come back here. I never told her Rachael worked here." The portable halogen lights were harsh and unforgiving, the beams picking up and emphasizing every line in his face. "I swear, Theresa, I never told her a thing about you."

"No. I did. Then she read about Rachael in the paper."

Neil, too, watched the two teens. "That kid's got nine lives. Coral lunched here all the time. It's a habit she got into when her husband was still around, and it's some principle or other of the support groups to reconnect each member with the things they enjoyed in life."

"William works in the kitchen, not out by the tables." If he had, maybe William would be dead and three lawyers would still be alive. "You would have let her shoot him, wouldn't you? That's why you didn't step in—"

"No," he insisted, not very convincingly. "Yes. I don't know. We hated him so much. . . . I just didn't want to walk away again. I wanted it to be over."

She looked at him, seeing real regret in his face. He would have killed William, taken his revenge for the death of his niece or removed a dangerous animal from society, however he chose to look at it. He would not, she thought, have killed Marie Corrigan or the other attorneys but got sucked into the process anyway. He might not go to jail, almost certainly would not go to jail, but he would never again be a cop.

"I should have faced the facts sooner, I should have owned up to my connection to Marie Corrigan, I should have immediately gotten up on that platform and taken that gun away from her," he said. "Now I've lost my sister and everything else as well."

"Like your job?"

"No. You." He looked her in the eyes. "I really liked you."

She pushed herself off the brick wall. "I really liked you, too. Until you pulled out a loaded gun ten feet from my daughter."

"Mom?" Rachael asked, trailing the paramedics off the deck. "Are you coming?"

She walked toward her daughter without another word.

"Theresa."

She didn't want to look back. She wanted a clean cut, to slice Neil Kelly out of her life as if he'd never been there.

Not possible, of course. There would be statements and hearings and maybe a trial. She turned.

"You'd have done the same thing, if it had been Rachael."

She didn't answer.

They followed the ambulance to the hospital, leaving the crime scene in Don's capable hands. Theresa wondered if, like cops, forensic scientists were forbidden to investigate crimes in which they'd been involved; if so, that was fine by her. She had no desire to see that observation deck again. She had no desire to photograph Coral Simone's ruined body, which had landed on the roof of the Ontario Street entrance. She had no desire to go over, for the fourth time, where she'd been standing when Coral confessed to the murders of three attorneys or when Neil Kelly pointed a gun at her. She had no desire to think, period.

"Mom?"

"What, honey?"

"Is that true? If someone murdered me, would you kill them?"

There are times when you should lie to your children. This might have been one of those times, but Theresa couldn't tell and didn't have the strength left to think it through. This was something she was willing to admit. "Without hesitation."

Rachael absorbed, accepted, nodded. "Good."

CHAPTER 42

Theresa waited with Frank outside courtroom B on the twenty-third floor, gazing down on the city and the lake. Her dislike for the setup that restricted this view from the common folk had not changed, but she needed some calming. Testifying in Neil Kelly's preliminary hearing wouldn't be pleasant.

"Coral told me when we first met that she programmed something called low coercivity," Theresa told her cousin. "I had no idea what she was talking about. Turns out that magnetic strip on plastic key cards is low coercivity for items that store little, usually temporary information, like bus passes and hotel keys. High coercivity would be used for credit cards, bank cards, things that retain a lot more information."

"Fascinating," her cousin said without inflection. "What was up with all the cat hair?"

"Americans love their pets. And their fur gets everywhere—I'm living proof." Theresa picked one of Nefertiti's strands off her skirt. "People spread around trace from their own homes with their clothes, their luggage, their shoes. Bruce ran into Marie, probably gave her a hug for old times' sake, transferred some of his pet dander to her. Sonia's hairs belonged to her own brood. The unidentified ones belong, I'm sure, to previous hotel guests."

Frank grunted, still unhappy at having been stuck in this building while the lives of his cousin and her child had been threatened high atop the Terminal Tower. He said he hated missing out on the action—it left him without much to say in the locker room—but she suspected he worried about her getting into scrapes when he wasn't around to get her out of them. "How's Rachael doing?"

"She got a job at Kohl's. Decent hours, and she gets a discount on clothes."

"And still dating this William?"

"He dislocated his shoulder and ripped two tendons and still wouldn't let go of her." Theresa shrugged. "I am therefore obligated to cut the kid some slack."

"It really was Ray who killed Jenna?"

"He confessed the moment they asked him. And get this—he refused the lawyer his parents hired and agreed to a plea before the assigned public defender could talk him out of it."

"That worked?"

"He's over eighteen now, legally an adult. He can do what he wants. You know the weird thing, though? What he kept apologizing for, over and over again? Not killing Jenna Simone. For letting William take the blame."

"What exactly did he think was going to happen when he left a dead girl next to his unconscious buddy? Speaking of which, why didn't he just roofie Jenna if he wanted into her pants?"

"He tried—thinking she'd start to pass out, he'd pop up like Sir Galahad and drive her home. William would want to stay at the party, would let Ray borrow his car—Ray didn't have a car, his parents didn't let him drive—but somehow the glasses got mixed up and William drank the dose instead. He figures okay, he'll still have her all to himself, and now she'll be impressed with what a good friend he is, but of course it didn't work out that way. She refused a kiss, and he snapped. Then he couldn't move her body by himself and he couldn't wake William up to help him. So he just went home and began to die. His words."

Frank shook his head. "He probably figures you can always get another girl but a true friend comes along only once or twice in a lifetime."

"Who's *your* true friend?" she asked, not knowing where the question came from, other than the sudden realization that she didn't know. Frank seemed to rely on partners, but one recent partner had been killed and now his partner was a woman, so that a few large and impenetrable barriers had to be maintained.

"The one I'd move a body for?"

"Yeah."

He snorted, smiled, and, being Frank, evaded the question. "You," he said, and kissed her cheek. Then he paced a few steps, turned, paced back. "Hard to believe our serial killer was a soccer mom."

"Softball. And what they say about mama bears goes for all the species. You know, I see how she got into the Presidential Suite, but how did she get Marie Corrigan to show up there?"

Frank said, "Same way you meet with any lawyer. You make an appointment."

"What do you mean?"

"From her credit-card bills, she lunched at the Ritz often enough that she could have learned of this convention about a month and a half in advance, giving her plenty of time to plan. That's about when Marie's paralegal said she started getting phone calls from a 'Mrs.

Jones' with a vague story about needing to get her son out of trouble, how it had to be kept quiet because they didn't want their family name in the papers, et cetera. Never any details, at least none that Marie shared with the paralegal. She must have given a very old-money type of sound to it, which would have gotten Marie's attention. So she could have—and this is all theory, mind you—strung Marie along, then suggested a meeting at the Ritz. She had to call at the last minute to tell Marie which room, because of course she couldn't be sure the Presidential Suite would be empty. Coral even used a prepaid, disposable cell phone. Probably learned that from her brother's tales of the street."

"Did Bruce get any mysterious calls?" Theresa asked.

"None that we've heard of. He was staying there, though, so that made him easier. All she had to do was follow him to his room and then knock on the door with some excuse. Once he opens it, she's got a gun to guarantee her entry."

"Then why not shoot him?" Theresa asked, answering herself before he had a chance. "The noise."

"And the satisfaction of caving his head in with her own two hands. She'd waited a long time to make someone pay for her daughter's death."

Theresa shuddered.

Frank didn't bring up Sonia, but Theresa figured it for a similar scenario. All Coral had to do was ask Sonia for a word. The attorney probably wouldn't have recognized her and, even if she had, would be too kind to blow the woman off. She'd have accompanied Coral to the observation deck even without a gun.

Her cousin put an arm around her, brought her back to the nuts and bolts of the case, the inanimate, objective parts. "You've dotted all your *i*'s?"

"Most. The spandex fiber with the wax globules

came from her batting glove. Coral still played soft-ball every Saturday night, and she polished her furni-ture about every other day, because that's what you do when you have nothing to occupy your evenings except bad memories."

"She's not you."

"But I could be her," Theresa said. "If it had been Rachael."

"It wasn't," Frank said. "I'm sorry about Sonia. And, of course, poor little Marie."

"Yeah."

He peered at her. "You're still happy she's dead, aren't you?"

Theresa thought a moment before answering. "I'm sorry she died the way she did. She didn't deserve that, I guess."

A door to one of the judges' chambers opened, and a man emerged, but not from courtroom B and they ig-nored him.

"You *guess*?"

"I can't know. Did she manipulate the system to keep dangerous people on the street because she honestly felt that was her job? Did she do it because she wanted to be exciting and rich? Or did she enjoy manipulating, get a rush from releasing evil into the fold, thrill at doing what everyone else told her was the wrong thing? I can't know what's in someone else's heart."

"I know what was in Marie Corrigan's heart." Frank removed his arm and sat on the air conditioner. "Spiders and pus."

"What about Marie Corrigan?" The man who had left the judge's chambers stopped in front of them. Den-nis Britton. "Thanks for finding out who killed her, by the way. I know she would appreciate it."

Neither Theresa nor, she suspected, her cousin could

think of a thing to say that wouldn't be insulting at best and toxic at worst, so they remained silent.

"My profession lost some good ones last month," he went on. "I'll have to carry on for them, Marie and Bruce."

"And Sonia," Theresa said.

Britton snorted. "Sonia Battle. Overweight, overzealous, and overdue for a good— Anyway. She thought I killed my wife, you know."

Theresa straightened. Wearing heels put her exactly at the same eye level, and she let him have her full attention, waited for his.

"So do I," she said. "And I also intend to carry on."

NOTES AND ACKNOWLEDGMENTS

Anyone familiar with the beautiful Cleveland Ritz-Carlton will notice that I seriously fudged reality for this novel. It is not truly located immediately below the Terminal Tower and their orderliness and security are too top-notch to allow the difficulties these characters encounter, but as I am such a fan of the chain I could not bring myself to choose the tower as a setting and then make up a fictitious hotel. Speaking of the Terminal Tower, the observation deck actually reopened to the public in 2010.

Likewise, though Corrigan is a common name in Cleveland, the characters in this book are not designed to resemble actual persons in any way, shape, or form. I have no idea what the new public defender's offices look like and their lack of decor in this book is my own invention based on years of visits to county attorneys' offices.

For once I have no texts to list in a bibliography, but I would like to reference the Crazy Hotel Workers forum and of course my great good friend Google.

I'd like to thank my siblings and our mother, Florence, who accompanied me on a fact-finding trip to check out the Ritz-Carlton's lobby, its coffee service, and of course the ladies' restroom (the truest measure of any facility's quality and refinement). Also my husband, Russ, for his technical expertise; our friend Clint Williams, who got me into secret places; Cleveland attorney Kim Hammond for the legal terminology; and congratulations to Bouchercon character-naming-rights winner Maryann Mercer.

I'd also like to thank my incredible editor, David Highfill, and everyone else at William Morrow. And, of course, Stephanie Lehmann and my agent, the late Elaine Koster, who gave me a chance when no one else would. I am, and will remain, eternally grateful.

AWARD-WINNING THRILLERS FEATURING EMMA CALDRIDGE BY

JAMIE FREVELETTI

Running From the Devil

978-0-06-168423-4

A biochemist and an ultramarathon runner, Emma Caldridge is en route from Miami to Bogota when her plane goes down in the mountains near the Venezuelan border. Thrown unhurt from the wreckage, she watches in horror as guerillas drag the other passengers into the jungle. Emma has no choice but to follow—and stumbles across an injured government agent who was left behind to die.

Running Dark

978-0-06-168425-8

Emma Caldridge is halfway through South Africa's Comrades ultramarathon when a roadside bomb explodes. When she wakes up, dazed and disoriented, a stranger is injecting her with an unknown substance that leaves her stronger than before. Then the man vanishes. Emma wants answers and she turns to Edward Banner of the security company Darkview.

The Ninth Day

978-0-06-202531-9

Hiking in Arizona, Emma Caldridge suddenly finds herself a prisoner of Mexico's most feared drug cartel. Across the border she makes a shocking discovery in the marijuana fields outside Ciudad Juarez: plants rotting with a flesh-eating toxin that causes a horrible death within nine days of exposure. Emma herself has been infected and there is no antidote. Time is running out for Emma to find a cure.

FRE 1011

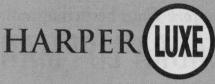